"This book has everything I love: Clean, crisp worldbuilding. Characters that live and breathe. A story that teases and surprises me. I like *Master Assassins* so much I wish I'd written it, but deep down, I know I couldn't have written it this well."

—*New York Times* bestselling author Patrick Rothfuss

"The prose is spectacularly good. Your adrenaline will flow. Your emotions will be toyed with. You will find yourself drawn in, turning the pages and worrying that fewer and fewer remain. I read a lot of good books. Quite a few very good books. This is one of the rare 6-star series openers I've encountered."

—Mark Lawrence, author of *Prince of Thorns* and *Red Sister*

"Robert Redick really nailed this one. What a great story! Fascinating plot and characters, and all of the author's formidable skills at play. I cannot wait to read the next one."

—*New York Times* bestselling author Terry Brooks

"An exquisitely written mix of heart-stopping action, masterful storytelling, and enchantment. Redick is a gifted wordsmith with a ferocious imagination. *Master Assassins* will produce many sleepless nights. I guarantee it."

—*New York Times* bestselling author Mira Bartók

"A blazingly smart thrill-ride of an adventure. The world of *Master Assassins* is deep, mysterious, terrifying, and utterly real, and I'll follow Redick's heroes, the mismatched brothers Kandri and Mektu, wherever they go in it. I can't recommend this book highly enough."

—Daryl Gregory, author of *Spoonbenders*

"With spare, sharp-edged prose, Redick balances his rollicking adventure story against a tale of love and uneasy brotherhood, offering a thrilling glimpse into a world both haunting and haunted. His finest work to date."

—Jedediah Berry, author of *The Manual of Detection*

MASTER ASSASSINS

ALSO BY ROBERT V.S. REDICK

THE CHATHRAND VOYAGE QUARTET
The Red Wolf Conspiracy
The Rats and the Ruling Sea
The River of Shadows
The Night of the Swarm

BOOK ONE OF THE FIRE SACRAMENTS

MASTER ASSASSINS

ROBERT V.S. REDICK

Talos Press
New York

Talos Press books may be purchased in bulk at special discounts for sales promotion, corporate gifts, fund-raising, or educational purposes. Special editions can also be created to specifications. For details, contact the Special Sales Department, Talos Press, 307 West 36th Street, 11th Floor, New York, NY 10018 or info@skyhorsepublishing.com.

Talos Press® is a registered trademark of Skyhorse Publishing, Inc.®, a Delaware corporation.

Visit our website at www.talospress.com.

10 9 8 7 6 5 4 3 2 1

Library of Congress Cataloging-in-Publication Data

Names: Redick, Robert V. S., author.
Title: Master assassins / Robert V.S. Redick.
Description: New York : Talos Press, [2018] | Series: The Fire Sacraments ; book 1
Identifiers: LCCN 2017031355 (print) | LCCN 2017037004 (ebook) | ISBN 9781945863202 (Ebook) | ISBN 9781945863370 (hardcover : alk. paper)
Subjects: | GSAFD: Fantasy fiction.
Classification: LCC PS3618.E4336 (ebook) | LCC PS3618.E4336 M37 2018 (print) | DDC 813/.6--dc23
LC record available at https://lccn.loc.gov/2017031355

Cover artwork by Lauren Saint-Onge
Cover design by Shawn T. King
Map illustration by Thomas Rey

Printed in the United States of America

For Bogor City, and the kids who teased me there.

AUTHOR'S NOTE

Even a cursory reading of this book should make clear that the religions of Urrath are fictions with no Terran equivalents. Given the extent of prejudice and misinformation about Islam, however, I wish to state unequivocally that the Prophet of *The Fire Sacraments* is neither inspired by nor derived in any way from the Prophet Muhammad.

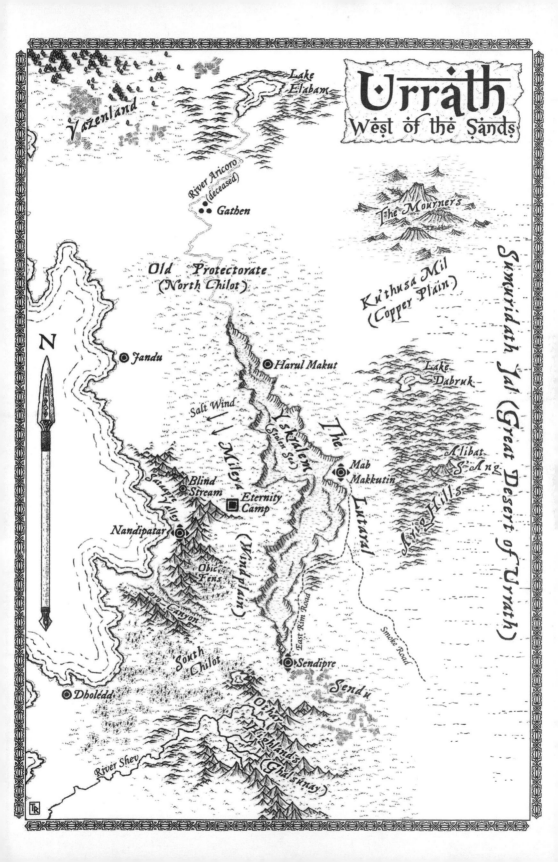

Down the fanatic, down the clown;
Down, down, hammer them down
YEATS

I. ETERNITY CAMP

Here is the door you have been seeking,
Behind it the promised flood.
KASRAJI INCANTATION

By the third day the rumor can no longer be contained. It is whispered in the black tents, shared like smokes among the men on patrol, murmured in the drill yard before the bellowed morning prayer. It is weird and horrific and yet a curse no one can fail to understand. Someone's mind has been stolen, and the thief still walks the camp.

The signs are innumerable. The Master of Horses finds two stallions lamed overnight. An armory clerk displays a broadsword twisted into a spiral like a blade of grass. A cook discovers worms thick as men's fingers writhing in the belly of a well-roasted boar. And the Prophet's eldest son has a toothache.

These calamities, and others shared over dawn biscuits or evening rubbish-fires or blazing midday marches, point to a single conclusion. The camp is under attack, and the assailant can only be a *yatra*, a spirit-thief, which as everyone knows can work dark magic from within its victim's pilfered soul.

Kandri Hinjuman, Distinguished Corporal, smiles at this talk of possession, but the frowns of his fellow soldiers bring him quickly to his senses. The Prophet's Firstborn! Nothing touching that family is a matter for mirth. The son's toothache, moreover, has struck just hours after he announced the date of the spring offensive. And isn't the boar his gift to the soldiers, in honor of the victories ahead?

Kandri tries to drop the matter—sorcery isn't high on his list of preoccupations; they're at war—but to his surprise, the hostile looks only multiply, as though he has crossed some threshold of recklessness. Finally, one evening after final prayers, a sergeant beckons him near.

"It's not you," he whispers. "It's that half-brother of yours."

"Mektu, sir?" Kandri jumps, startling the man. "What the hell has he done now?"

"Talk, that's what," says the sergeant. "He won't shut up about the yatra, and he's got the men scared to death. It's the way he tells the stories. It's the look on his face."

Kandri understands the sergeant all too well, and that night he barely sleeps. In the morning, anxious and miserable, he prowls the camp until he locates his brother.

"You jackass," he says. "You'll get us killed, talking like that."

They are behind a recreation tent on the camp's southern perimeter; the air reeks of cane liquor and unwashed men. An impenetrable wall of fish-hook-tree branches cuts off the view of the drylands beyond. It is very early: Kandri hears the flat, tireless tolling of goat bells as a herd flows around a corner of the thorn wall, and a child's laugh, and the rising chord of the fiddler trees, aerial roots rasping one on another, singing home the little brown bats that roost in their arms.

"Us?" says Mektu.

"Of course us," Kandri snaps. "The Prophet knows who our father is. She knows everything about the Old Man."

Mektu raises an eyebrow, as if to say, *Not everything.*

Kandri shakes his head. "What a pig you are," he says. "I hope they send you off to fight ghouls in the marshes. I'd do a dance, I swear."

Mektu shakes his head. "You'd miss me. Everyone needs someone they can trust."

Kandri can't quite keep the smile off his face. Mektu laughs aloud, throws an arm over his shoulder, kisses his forehead. Kandri is laughing too, but perhaps he tenses at his brother's touch, for Mektu abruptly releases him and steps back.

"You don't believe me."

He is a lean soldier with a spine that is never quite straight. His laugh has something of a horse's whinny; his eyes meander like gnats. Kandri is shorter but more sound. He has bested Mektu often at wrestling and battle-dance, which are juried sports in the Army of Revelation. But he has also seen his half-brother drunk and brawling, and hopes never to fight him in earnest.

"How do you know it's a yatra?" Kandri demands. "Bad things happen all the time."

"That's the proof," says Mektu. "Each day's worse than the one before. Betali thinks it was called out of the desert by a witch."

"Betali's a fool. And high before breakfast. Last week he said he was engaged to a goat."

Mektu's face darkens. "It's here, brother," he says.

"Then whose mind has it taken? No one knows. No one *ever* knows."

"What if I told you I did?"

Kandri turns him a wry smile, but the look fades quickly into one of alarm. "You don't really," he murmurs. "Do you?"

Among the worst powers ascribed to a yatra is the ability to sense when it has been detected. To look out through stolen eyes, read the faces around it, and know who has guessed the truth. Such persons are doomed; the yatra will not rest until it kills them.

Mektu snaps a branch from the fishhook-tree fence. He draws his thumb over a long, savage thorn.

"You've never faced one," he says.

Kandri bites his lips. He's heard the stories, from the time before he came to live with Mektu and the rest of the family. Absurd stories, conflicting, intractable as weeds. How a yatra assaulted their little brother, the youngest, who still sleeps with a knife in his hand. Or was the target that spinster aunt, who set the orphanage on fire? Or their father, who rises, dresses, unlocks gates, walks for miles in his sleep? Or Mektu himself?

"There's never any proof," Kandri hears himself say. "I don't believe the damned things exist."

"Four cases last year."

Kandri chuckles. Four rumored yatras in the world's greatest army. All of them elsewhere, naturally: in some mountain division or wilderness fort, never here in Eternity Camp where the question might be settled. But perhaps this time it will be settled. The eldest son has a toothache, after all.

5

Then he sees the flash of red on Mektu's finger, bright in the morning sun. "Never laugh at them," says his half-brother. "They can't stand it when you laugh."

ଚ

Many nights thereafter, in the wastes and hovels and palaces of Urrath, Kandri will lie brooding on the power of shame. What did he unleash, by laughing at Mektu then? If he had summoned more patience, if he had listened to his half-brother's ravings a bit more generously, if he had simply kept his silence, everything might have been different. Even the murders, even that catastrophic night. His feet might have carried him elsewhere; he might never have glimpsed the crooked shack or heard the cries from within. He and Mektu might still be as they once were: unnoticed, invisible, far less than a footnote to this war.

Imagine that, he will think. To be ordinary, to be something the world overlooks. No one's obsession, no one's idea of evil incarnate, blood traitors, spears hurled with cold precision at the Gods.

ଚ

That evening the brothers meet again. Kandri is in their unit's dinner line, which snakes out of the mess tent and into the yard. The area is crowded with fighting men seated on stumps and makeshift benches, eating from tin plates and calabashes, waving away flies. Boys from the village hover about the edges of the yard, laughing and horsing around, waiting for the peels and bones and gristle their mothers will transform into soup.

Mektu steps from the tent and approaches him, wearing an odd little smile. "Bugger off," he says.

Kandri scowls. "What the hell is your problem? *You* walked up to *me*."

Mektu shakes his head. "They're going to throw us at the Ghalsúnay again. Just us, the Eighth Legion, against the same pricks who cut us to ribbons two years ago. I meant *Crol kira.* Bug over, bugger out. You're with me, aren't you?"

His brother is still smiling. Kandri feels his blood run cold. He turns away, furiously composed, and walks straight out of the yard. Mektu is speaking of desertion, of *bugging out.* He has garbled the phrase in Kasraji, the world's dying common tongue, but then helpfully repeated himself in the language of their clan, which nearly everyone in the army speaks. It is the act of a lunatic. *Only your love, children, can light the way to Heaven's Path*, the Prophet teaches. *Without that flame we are lost, all of us, and the world shall wither like a seedling in a cave.* Love is compulsory. Even a dispirited sigh can mean punishment. Desertion means death by torture, live coals in the eye sockets, shards of glass down the throat.

Kandri smokes for an hour behind his legion's stables, hiding from Mektu, squatting low on his heels. Dinner is over; he won't get a crumb before breakfast. And tonight he will have to avoid the drinking areas. His brother will appear in one of them to play his allotted role in the camp, somewhere between daring eccentric and despised clown. It has always been the same with Mektu: the amusing stories, the elaborate jokes. The poetry committed to memory, lofty or obscene. The brilliant vocal impressions. Kandri's brother can draw an audience just by opening his mouth.

But only a fool seeks attention in Eternity Camp. Before the yatra panic began, there was talk of a new and horrific loyalty test, conceived by the Prophet's seers in the bowels of the Palace of Radiance, a means of distinguishing between the faithful and the false. Does such a test truly exist? And if it does, how would each of them fare?

I might pass, Kandri thinks. *I might get that lucky. He would not.*

For Mektu has a gift for saying the wrong thing. You can take him to a birthday party and count the minutes until he makes a child cry. At weddings, he is apt to mention the last woman the groom has slept with ("You're a lucky girl, Chelli. Just ask Sukina.") Kandri once dragged him to the hospital to visit their dying grandmother; Mektu lectured her about the dangers of sunstroke, and propositioned the nurse.

You could only shake your head. And find a way to protect yourself, of course. To help your brother without wearing him like a chain.

They are not close, Kandri reminds himself. They call each other "brother," dropping the *half-*, and burn sage for their ancestors, and swap shirts on New Year's morning like all brothers in the Chiloto clan. Yet what do such courtesies change? Blood means nothing, finally, and a man who pokes tigers with a stick will one day be mauled. You can take the stick away, but he'll find another. Last week the Prophet's youngest son, a boy barely into his teens, stabbed the village tailor and set fire to his shop. The old man had mended his vest with the wrong color thread. Sticks are everywhere. You have to walk about with closed fists or they will jump into your hands.

૪૦

But can it possibly be true? Another assault on the Ghalsúnay? Kandri nurses his cheroot down to a lip-scorching bud. He thinks: Chindilan, that's a question for Chindilan. The Master Smith knows more about what is going on in the sprawling camp than anyone. He is no gossip; it is merely that the officers confide in him while he repairs their sabers, their bejeweled daggers and *qamas* and *mattoglins*, all those distinguishing blades. They like him, those officers. He asks no favors, drops no hints about the lightness of his purse. He simply works, and listens to their chatter, and no one ever learns what he overhears—no one save the brothers, that is.

Kandri leaves his hiding place, wades back into the evening throng. Great rows of tents and barracks, some a mile long or more, channel the men into surging lines. In the twilight, cheers and laughter, empty bottles, ribald songs. Priests in plum-colored robes move among the soldiers, lofting shepherds' sticks. From each stick dangles a paper lamp, and within each of these fragile spheres dances an uncanny flame, some mixture of oils that shimmer from green to blue to yellow, and moan like the wind in a cave. Ghost lamps, calling to the ancestral dead, seeking their aid against the yatra.

Kandri squeezes north through the crowd, in the direction of the weapons shop. Eternity Camp is a ramshackle city, a glued-together mass of shabby wards pertaining to the many branches of the Army of Revelation. At its center squats the Palace of Radiance, a hulking complex built on the spot where the last Važek governor was hanged, ending six centuries of occupation and massacres for the Chiloto people.

Around the palace walls, thirty thousand soldiers make their homes under canvas or tin. Another forty thousand are dispersed among the various fronts. Recently the most savage fighting has been in the north. The Prophet has taken land from the Važeks there; she will take everything from the Važeks, one day.

The brothers made the march into Važenland during their second deployment. Perhaps because they had some slight medical training—or perhaps because Chindilan had called in a favor—they were sent into the front-line carnage less often than many. Long weeks of guilt and nausea lard Kandri's memories of that campaign: prayers for the men he dragged back from the lines, prying their hands from arrows before they ripped them out and bled to death, stuffing viscera back into bellies, trying to distinguish burned clothes from skin.

They were resented: in that medical rear guard, survival was more likely than not. A year later, when they fought the Ghalsúnay, there was no rear guard, and no true front for that matter. Only doomed incursions into dry wooded hills, blundering and panic, slaughter from every side.

He shakes his head. There are memories and memories, the Prophet teaches. One sort is a chalice of fire and a sacrament, the other a cup of poison, drawn from black swamps of despair. He will not drink from the swamp. After all, it is a night of comforts: the first of three comprising the Feast of the Boar. The holiday is a great favorite, the army's only bacchanal. It ends on the solemn Day of Revelation, which marks the Prophet's first encounter with the Gods and the start of her journey on Heaven's Path.

The mob thins swiftly, north of the Palace. Kandri shivers: the day's warmth is gone. The sun has set behind the Coastal Range; in the east, stars blaze already, untwinkling as always over the desert, the fierce, famished spider-eyes of heaven.

He thinks: *My brother's deluded. The Prophet won't make us fight the Ghalsúnay alone. We're her children, she says so. Why would she send us to our deaths?"*

Men with torches by the East Gate, surrounding a pair of wrestlers, cheering them on. Outside, on the village road, a few early prostitutes in skintight wraps.

"Touch me. Touch me! Use those soft little hands."

A low voice, slippery as oil soap. Kandri frowns: he knows the voice; it belongs to Skem, the Waxman. There they are in the shadow of the hospital: the pusher and his unlucky whore. Kandri almost shouts an insult. He loathes Skem; quite a few men do. He has seen the effects of wax, a drug applied warm to the skin, a drug that holds off hunger and fear but makes animals of addicts, a drug that corrodes the soul. But why confront Skem? What good can it do? The camp has a dozen wax dealers and they thrive on abuse. Kandri walks on, suddenly breathless. Muffled cries from behind him. Tang of antiseptic on the breeze.

He stops.

Bemused, he looks down at his feet. Damned if he should be stopping. No good will come of it. Don't look back there. Just don't.

He looks back. There are three people, not two, by the hospital wall. The one he took for the prostitute is in fact a man, standing beside Skem and helping him restrain a much smaller figure. A child. Kandri spits out a curse and starts toward them, noisily, making his intentions plain.

The men turn. Kandri catches a whiff of the clove oil Skem combs into his beard. He does not know the second man, a pale, enormously muscled soldier with a bottle tucked under his arm. But the man knows him, apparently. "It's crazy Mektu's brother," he says.

"No insults," says Skem. "We're all brothers here. You need a fix, Hinju-man? Normally you'd have to tell me by third rotation, but you're in luck, I have plenty. Wait around the corner 'til we're finished."

"I'm not a waxer," says Kandri.

"Then fuck off?" suggests the larger man.

They are holding a village boy. Gag in his mouth, pants around his ankles. The boy's white eyes turn to Kandri, pleading. Skem's fingers are tight around his neck.

"You can have a turn when we're finished," he says. "But I'll need a few *ghams* from you, Kandri. Only fair."

Kandri feels his throat constrict. He is not a brawler, either; in fact he hates to fight. The very prospect afflicts him with a clammy sorrow like the onset of disease. He unbuckles his machete. It hangs there, loose on his belt. He looks the big soldier in the eye.

"You just step away," he says.

With a lazy motion, Skem pulls the boy against his side. Fitted over his knuckles is a thrusting dagger, five or six inches long. He rests the flat of the blade on the boy's cheek. Then he glances at Kandri, and his look is oddly coy.

"Do you know what I think?" he says. "I think you're a bit sentimental, Hinjuman. Maybe you had a sheltered childhood. Or a baby brother you were fond of. That's all right. In fact, it's sort of endearing."

"In a bitch," says the pale soldier.

"But little Faru here," Skem continues, "is nothing to any of us. A gnat. Or in the words of our Prophet, *one leaf in a forest aflame.* What's more, you don't fuck with me. Everyone knows that. Because if you do, if you fuck with the Waxman, someone calls on you in the night."

Kandri stands very still. This rumor too has reached his ears: that Skem employs some kind of enforcer. An assassin, that is. A man who waits in darkness, cuts throats from behind, vanishes without bloodying his hands.

The big man drains his bottle ostentatiously. Reversing his grip, he swings it hard against the hospital wall. The bottle shatters; the man proffers its jagged neck.

"In a hurry to bleed, Hinjuman?"

Kandri shakes his head. "I don't want to fight at all."

"Who does?" says Skem brightly. "Waste of a nice fucking evening." He taps the dagger against the boy's cheek, then bends to kiss the small round forehead. "You'd like to get this over with, wouldn't you? Tell him, boy. Go ahead."

The child's bare legs are shaking. His eyes lock on Kandri's own.

"You can't save them all, Hinjuman," says Skem brightly. "Now if you'll kindly—"

The boy's head jerks. His teeth close on Skem's hand below the dagger, and despite the gag in his mouth, he draws blood. At the same instant, Kandri moves, striking Skem's face dead on with all his strength. Three blows, half a second. Skem drops like a sack, and as he does so, Kandri whirls to face the larger man.

The soldier hesitates; Kandri does not. Right elbow to jaw. Left arm swipe, bottle blocked. Right fist. Left knee. Down.

"You fff—"

Kandri kicks the bottle away, battling the urge to be sick. He hates fighting, but he is very good at it. He has killed six times in his three years in the army, but managed to finish his last deployment without killing anyone. He wants to believe he can finish his life.

Skem is wheezing, spitting blood. He claws at the boy, whose teeth are still locked on his hand.

Kandri puts his boot on Skem's neck. Bending, he takes a firm grip on the dagger. *"Palejek,"* he says to the boy. "It's all right. Let go."

At first the boy is uncomprehending, or perhaps unable to respond. Then his mouth opens and he flings himself away and is gone instantly in the darkness, a fish thrown to the sea. The big soldier lies curled in a ball. Skem cradles his hand, eyes bulging, mouth agape. Twisting his neck, he looks up in horror at Kandri.

"Yatra," he says.

⁖

Last week Skem had held forth from his bunk. How he paid whores only in wax. How he'd massage the drug into their scalps as he took them from behind. How days later they'd crawl back to him on their knees, give him anything, their bodies and gold besides. "And who are you to judge me?" he demanded, although no one said a word. "I'm the same as anyone. I get pleasure where I can."

From women too hungry or frightened to escape you. From girls so worn out from hauling water or firewood, they fall asleep by the brothel door. From boys like that Faru, fleeing with the gag still in his mouth. Kandri's hands are shaking. He touches the machete he never bothered to draw. Men will sleep with village women, or foreign women from the war zones, or any women they can buy with scrip or coin or half a cabbage. Those with money even go with the *Kistrela* courtesans, who ride in like dreams on their slate-grey stallions, galloping along the perimeter fence, swords aloft, twisting in the saddles to reveal a dark thigh, a naked midriff, taunting the men with their unbearably suggestive songs.

Lust is currency, lust is a common tongue. Kandri himself has spent money on women: you can't refuse without declaring yourself a *lulee*. But he cannot fuck them. The moment he is alone in their brothel chambers, their squalid huts, their tents half a mile from the killing fields; the moment they light a candle and he sees their gaunt cheekbones, their fingers cracked from years at the washtub; the moment their thin flanks and worried nipples emerge from threadbare clothes, his desire makes a blushing exit, his lust vanishes like a breath of song. He's not indifferent. He wants to be there, to sit and rock these women in his arms. *But to take from them.* To take the least thing, a sigh, a shadow, the stroke of a hand—no, that is unthinkable. He pays what they ask for, endures their bafflement, hopes they will not talk.

Later, he boasts with his comrades: *That girl Annuli with the melon ass, oh brothers, she has fire down there. And that tongue, I shouldn't be talking, forget I spoke will you, leave her to me.*

He has not touched a woman since he joined the army. It is his secret agony, his private shame. *But a child.* He could have killed Skem tonight with one swing of his machete. A braver man would have done so.

❧

The weapons shop is always brightly lit. There is the yellow glow of oil lamps, dangling on chains from the roof beams; and there is the furnace, smoldering like the throat of a dragon. The broad front doors stand open, letting a little of the dragon's breath escape.

Kandri pauses at the threshold: he does not wish to blunder in on an officer. Tonight, however, he sees no one, not even Chindilan. Only the small desert bats come and go, improbable acrobats, feasting on the insects drawn to the light.

He steps within. The heat of the fire welcome, the night already cold. He whistles for Chindilan—they are friendly enough for whistles, though the older man will pretend to be annoyed—but no answer comes.

Arranged near the furnace are the anvil, stacks of raw iron, cooling tubs, and a rough table on which Chindilan lays out his tools. Kandri moves carefully between these objects. Where can the smith have gone? The furnace is roaring; in its mouth, a length of iron glows red upon the coals.

Then Kandri sees the knife.

It lies on a clean blue cloth at the center of the table. He knows it at once for a mattoglin, one of the huge desert knives of the Parthan nomads. It is almost as long as a machete, and it broadens near the tip, where three vicious teeth curve out like bending flames. A weapon made for beheading, disemboweling, for killing with a single blow.

This mattoglin, however, was clearly made for a prince or sartaph, or some other ruler of men. The steel blade is inlaid with gold in a beautiful swirling script that races from the pommel to the teeth. The pommel itself is a smooth, cream-colored wood bound with rings of gold. Small rubies like droplets of blood encircle the hand guard, and at the base is a pale blue stone the size of a quail's egg. Under the lamps the stone gleams like enchanted ice.

Kandri's heart is pounding. He has never been alone with such wealth. How can it be lying here? Why is it not under guard?

He glances left and right, then starts to turn away. But the blade is fascinating, and he will never again see such a thing. Not once. Not ever. He reaches out to touch the stone.

"Little bastard. Get your filthy paws away."

Kandri nearly leaps out of his skin. The smith is seated at the far end of the building, copper jug in hand, broad buttocks tipping back on a stool.

"Uncle! I was just—"

"Trying to get your head snipped off. That knife belongs to the Enlightened One."

Kandri shivers. Of course it does. Who but the Prophet could possibly afford such a treasure?

Chindilan rolls to his feet and saunters near. He takes a towel from around his enormously powerful shoulders and mops his face. He is Molonji by birth; his family comes from the great cattle-herding lands of the south, but he has spent so many years among the Chilotos that only his bulk and pure-chocolate blackness hint at his origins. A leather apron covers his torso like a suit of mail; his jeweler's glasses are high on his forehead. There is no smell of liquor on him: he drinks only water, gallons of water, when he works.

"She left you alone with this knife. The Prophet trusts you, Uncle."

Chindilan scowls at him, cockeyed. "Stop calling me Uncle. I'm not that old."

Kandri smiles. He will always be Uncle. In point of fact, they are not blood relations, but the bond between Chindilan and his family is absolute. The smith is his father's best friend, and godfather to all six of the Old Man's children. Before joining the army, he had eaten at their table three or four nights a week.

"I don't know why they left me alone," he says. "For a while, the men who brought it were standing around like goons. They wanted it sharpened, nothing else, and I was nearly finished when their commander showed up and took them away. He said a new team would be along any minute to collect the knife, but I've been waiting over an hour. I wish they'd fucking arrive."

"Is it old?"

"Old? Is the ocean large? Is the desert hot at noontime? That's a Kijinthu blade, from before the Empire of the Kasraj. It's ancient. Why are you here?"

"Can I touch it?"

"No, imbecile, keep your Gods-damned distance! Step over there by the door."

"It's cold."

"So is a spear through your belly button. Why are you here, Kandri?"

"I want to know about the Spring Offensive, Uncle."

Chindilan glares at him again. He is, in fact, old enough. He pulls off his jeweler's glasses and slides them into his pocket.

"You look starved. Like a rat."

"I'm all right," says Kandri.

Chindilan sighs and walks to the table. He lifts a small wooden box and brings it back it to where Kandri hovers by the door. He lifts the lid.

Inside are sausages, glistening with oil, lined up like cigars. Kandri's head swims. He has not tasted sausage in years.

"Take one. No, take two, but eat them both right now."

"They're fresh, aren't they? Who the hell gave them to you—?"

"Ojulan."

Kandri's hand snaps back as if from a live coal. Ojulan is the Prophet's third son. Also a gleeful killer, a maniac. Unlike his elder brothers, he has no military rank, and takes little interest in the War of Revelation. He is mercurial; he can be found drinking with the troops at sunset, and whipping their backs to ribbons before the rising of the moon. He is not clever like his brothers. His speech is notably less refined. But for all this, the Prophet dotes on him, cherishes him, perhaps more than all the rest. Consequently there is no more dangerous man in the camp.

Chindilan gestures at the knife. "That's his mattoglin you wanted to touch."

"Devil shit. You said it was the Prophet's."

"She's making a present of it to the Thirdborn. He wants to use it in war, can you believe it? That thing belongs in a museum, or mounted on some sartaph's wall. And not just because it's priceless. There's a history behind that knife, I gather. Dark sins and curses. Rubbish, if you ask me, but Ojulan believes it will make him a hero on the battlefield. Take the sausage, Kandri."

The meat is so delicious it hurts. For a few precious moments Kandri cannot think of knives, pushers, Ojulan, Mektu's terrible rumor. Chindilan laughs and pokes him in the chest.

"You mention these to anybody, it's your ass. He had a whole wagonload of dainties. Wine, brandy, licorice, seed cakes, honey cakes, hams. Straight from the Valley. He gave me these with a big smile. It's true what they say about his teeth."

"Gold?"

"Solid gold. Six or eight of them, anyway. Jekka's hell, but that smile gave me the creeps."

Kandri gestures at the mattoglin. "It won't be damaged. Ojulan never goes anywhere near the fighting."

Chindilan's smile fades. "He's going north with the Third Legion."

Kandri is speechless. North is the largest, hottest front, where the Važeks resist them still. *The depraved and bloody Važeks*: that is the phrase all children learn. Merciless occupiers before the Prophet drove them out. Lunatics, liars, believers in a single God.

"Why now?" says Kandri.

Chindilan leans close. "Ojulan had to have the knife," he murmurs. "They say he was squirming, begging. That he promised to become a war hero, if only Mommy gave him this toy."

His uncle's disrespect chills Kandri's blood. What has gotten into everyone? To call Her Radiance—*that*. Even to whisper such words in confidence. Even to think them.

He puts the rest of the sausage in his mouth and chews. The meat seems almost flavorless now. He wipes his hand on his trousers.

"Mektu says we're going to attack the Ghalsúnay. Just our legion, just the Eighth."

"He's right," says Chindilan. "There was talk of it this morning. In a day or two everyone will know."

The chill deepens. "Are they hurt somehow, the Ghalsúnay?" he asks.

Chindilan shrugs.

"Maybe their crops failed? Or they've suffered some disease?"

"I couldn't tell you, boy."

"Because otherwise it's madness," says Kandri. "The Eighth Legion's too small. You know what happened last time."

The smith rubs his face. All at once he is reluctant to look Kandri in the eye. "Not as well as you do," he says.

೮೦

Just past midnight a team of soldiers comes for the knife. They are led by Ojulan's deputy, a ferocious officer named Idaru. A colonel and a terror in his own right, Idaru stands six foot ten. On his cheeks are the ritual burns of the Mesurat clan: spirals that look as if they were made with heated wire. He storms up to Kandri and screams in his face: what in Jekka's hell are you doing here, who are you to gaze at the Prophet's gift to Lord Ojulan, were you planning to steal it, you dog?

Kandri's uncle lifts his hands. "I asked him to be here, Colonel. I didn't know what was happening. Lord Ojulan told me he'd be back within the hour."

"Lord Ojulan is"—Idaru stammers—"busy, detained. Lord Ojulan has a thousand cares!"

"Yes, sir. And I knew Corporal Hinjuman would fight to protect his property, just as I would. He's like a son to me, sir."

The colonel's nostrils flare. "That is good, then. That is excellent. Why did you not speak up for yourself, Hinjuman? The Prophet requires boldness of her men."

Kandri promises, with great contrition, to be bold.

"See that you are." Idaru's eyes shift to Chindilan. "Your man here could be out drinking and fornicating, smith, but instead he is here with you, guarding the Thirdborn's property. I am pleased with you, Hinjuman."

"Thank you, Colonel," says Kandri.

"Your breath is somewhat foul, however. Do you brush your teeth?"

"Twice daily, sir."

"Show me."

Kandri opens wide. Before he knows what is happening, the colonel's hand is in his mouth.

"Close gently. That's right."

The colonel withdraws his hand. Kandri stiffens: Idaru has placed an object in the pouch of his cheek. And his men, all of them, have aimed their spears in his direction.

"Speak through your teeth," says the colonel. "Don't move your jaw until I say so. Your life depends on your obedience."

Sweat breaks out all over Kandri's body. The thing in his mouth is light and brittle, like a hollow egg. A hint of sugar teases his tongue.

"Colonel, what in Ang's name—" Chindilan starts forward, but Idaru's look stops him cold.

"Keep still," he says. "This is no punishment. Corporal Hinjuman is among the first to be honored with this chance to prove his loyalty. And to place a new tool in the arsenal of the Prophet. We hope to use this test often in the future—if all goes well."

The new test, Kandri thinks. *It's real. Ang all-merciful, I'm going to die.*

"There is an insect in your mouth," says the colonel. "Or more precisely, a chrysalis. The vermin itself is dormant, but the warmth of your blood will change that. Any moment now—"

Kandri gives a distorted cry. Something has twitched inside the shell.

"Do not touch your cheek!" snaps Idaru. "Stop that shaking at once."

"I'm loyal," Kandri pleads through locked teeth. "I love the Prophet, her feet walk Heaven's—"

"The insect is an ash locust," says the colonel. "It has neither bite nor sting. But the fluid inside the chrysalis is a contact poison. Should it touch your flesh, you will be paralyzed. First your facial muscles, then your throat. Eventually, your lungs and heart."

Kandri starts to plead again, but the colonel silences him with a gesture. "If you are loyal, you have nothing to fear. The chrysalis alone is almost too fragile to touch, but we have glazed it with another substance. A rather extraordinary substance: a sugar that dissolves more quickly in a liar's mouth than that of an honest man. Do you follow? Speak falsely, and the shell will rupture before I finish my questions. Speak the truth and live."

Kandri stares at the colonel, rigid with horror. He can distinctly taste the sugar now. His uncle's chest is heaving, his big hands forming fists.

"Kandri Hinjuman," says Idaru, "are you a loving servant of Her Radiance the Prophet? A nod will suffice."

Suffice to kill me? He cannot help the thought. He dares not hesitate. He nods.

The locust twitches, and so does Kandri—every part of him, save his face. "And are you a willing soldier in this war?" asks Idaru.

Sweetness coats Kandri's tongue, but in his mind a strange cold has descended. *Is* he willing? Is any part of him still true?

He nods. The locust is squirming violently, now; the shell quivers and jumps.

"Colonel Idaru," pleads Chindilan. "This is a flawless soldier you're experimenting on. He nearly met his death in the Ghalsúnay campaign. He had an audience with the Prophet herself. He's one of us. I'll stake my life on that."

The colonel turns to Chindilan with deliberate slowness. "If you value him so, why delay me with these outbursts? You may doom an innocent man—*if* he is innocent."

Another extravagant pause. At last, his gaze returns to Kandri.

"One more question," he says. "Is there any person in this camp—anyone at all—whose loyalty you doubt?"

Kandri closes his eyes, and in the darkness, Mektu's face appears like a sallow bloom. His crooked grin, his provocations, his hopeless dreams of escape. The insect writhes; the shell bulges. He shakes his head.

"Spit it out!" snaps the colonel.

Kandri doubles over. The chrysalis drops from his mouth, slick and translucent. Even as it strikes the dirt it ruptures, and a barbed, black leg twitches free. Then it's gone, crushed by the colonel's boot. Idaru sets a hand on Kandri's arm.

"Rejoice," he says. "This too is part of winning the war. You have both faith and courage—and from this moment, no one may question them. Our Prophet shall hear of your strength today, Corporal Hinjuman. That's a promise."

৩

He is seated in the dust, knees raised, head thrown back against the wall. Chindilan is cleaning his tools, hands shaking; he has yet to breathe a word. Idaru and his men have departed with the golden blade.

The test failed. Kandri dares not say it, even to Chindilan. But in his mind there is no doubt. Perhaps, in some wildly unlikely way, he was truthful in his first two answers. But not the third. Mektu is no more a loyal soldier than he is a lamb chop. Kandri has just lied for him. By rights he should be dead.

Kandri looks at the flattened insect. *A new tool in the arsenal of the Prophet.* A useless tool, apparently. How many times has it been tested? Has it killed true believers, just because their nerves betrayed them? Or did something more than blind luck save Kandri's life?

"Uncle," he says, "my brother wants to bug out."

Chindilan leans hard on his workbench.

"He said the same to me this afternoon. I kicked him right out of the shop. You can't fucking run, I told him. You can bitch, drink, use wax, chew gumroot. You can fight and whore around with village girls. But not run. A man who runs is a man who's stopped believing, and that can't be overlooked. Now go and straighten out your head."

"He didn't listen, did he?"

The smith turns, his upper lip curled in anger. "Do you know what he was doing, the whole time I spoke? He was staring up at the mountain. And when I finished, he said, 'With a fast horse, I could be there before anyone missed me. In two days, I'd be home.'"

Kandri shuts his eyes. Mektu would never make it home. And if he did, he could only bring death to their family and friends. The Sataapre Valley is still beautiful, still green. But its rulers serve the Prophet now, and every street has its spy.

"That's what he meant when he asked if I was with him," says Kandri. "Gods, what can you do with such a fool?"

He locks eyes with Chindilan, and there is a wariness between them, sudden and immense.

"Because you know, even if someone thought they had a *chance*—"

"Not that way," says Chindilan.

"Not that way, exactly. Any idiot could come up with a better plan—I don't mean *better*, I mean smarter. A more cunning plan."

"As a pastime. As a game in the head."

"The smartest way to run off. I mean for a traitor to run off. We're just thinking, for the sake of a game."

"No crime in that," says the smith.

They cast nervous glances at the doorway. Kandri can feel his own face, his false smile, like something carved out of wood. "You'd . . . have to run east, I suppose."

Chindilan nods, looking strange and miserable. "Straight east," he says, "like fire-walkers running through coals. Across the Windplain, down the cliffs, through the wastes of the Stolen Sea, if that's even possible. And then, Gods help you. Because—think about it, now—where could you be aiming for, ultimately? The desert, Kandri? The *Sumuridath Jal*?"

"You'd have to be crazy," says Kandri. *Sumuridath Jal:* the Land that Eats Men.

"And what about your eyes?" asks Chindilan. "The whole world knows what the Prophet pays for deserters. What's the first thing a bounty hunter looks at?"

"The eyes, Uncle. I know."

New soldiers in the Army of Revelation are taken to a darkened hut where the extract of a certain cactus is dribbled into their eyes. The pain is terrible but fades within hours. What never fades is a slight purple staining of the eyeball. The stain is invisible beyond a yard or two, but up close, it is unmistakable. Every last soldier bears the mark.

Chindilan shakes his head. "Bounty men, bandits, slavers. They'd pounce on a deserter like cats on cream."

"You'd have to run far," says Kandri. "*Impossibly* far. South of the Blue Mountains, maybe. Or Kasralys City, where the desert ends. Is Kasralys as magnificent as they claim, Uncle?"

Chindilan shrugs. "It's a wonder of the world, boy. Everyone knows that."

Kandri's voice quickens. "Our captain says that before the Quarantine, people crossed the ocean just to see Kasralys. Which means there's nothing like it anywhere, not even in the Outer World—"

He jumps. Chindilan is scowling, as though visited by a dreadful thought.

"Uncle," says Kandri, "you know I wasn't really—"

"Shut the fuck up. Of course."

Their mouths close like drop gates. They watch the bats fly in circles. A lamp abruptly winks out.

"Mektu saved my life," says Kandri. "At the end of the first Ghalsúnay campaign. We were fleeing, the bastards had chased us to the river, someone cracked my skull with a stone—"

"I heard all about it," says the smith. "Not from Mektu; he never boasted about that day. It was that friend of his, old flappy-ears."

"Betali."

"Right," says Chindilan. "He said that when you fell, the others left you for dead. That they were trampling you."

"I can't remember a thing after the stone," says Kandri.

"Mektu carried you for five hours, on his back. They tried to make him abandon you. One man even seized your arm and tugged. I guess he thought that if Mektu dropped you, he'd never have the strength to pick you up again.

"Mek didn't drop you, but he did lay you flat. Then he turned to the man who had grabbed you and beat him until the man curled up, begging for mercy through his broken teeth. Mek lifted you up again and carried you another four miles, to the field camp."

"He did that? For me?"

The blacksmith nods. "You had better learn to talk to him, Kandri. Now give me a hand."

They lower the chains, extinguish the oil lamps one by one. When the last flame dies, only the glow from the furnace remains. They stand before its scarlet maw, warming themselves, two shadows reluctant to fade into the night.

"I promised the Old Man I'd protect you both," says Chindilan. "I swore it the day you enlisted. But there's nothing else I can do for your brother. I've tried, Kandri. I've tried more than you know."

"Never mind," says Kandri. "I'll make him listen, or I'll break his legs. The crazy fuck. He shouldn't be here at all."

Chindilan looks up sharply. In his eyes, further treason, another glance at the abyss. None of us should be here, says the look.

The half-brothers were born three days apart. For over a decade neither suspected the other's existence.

Kandri lived in a ramshackle house on Candle Mountain, in the Coastal Range, with his mother and a blind cook and a stream of orphans delivered without comment by the Old Man. Kandri could not see the ocean, but late afternoons he could see the sunlight glancing off the ponds, streams, and fish tanks of the Sataapre Valley. Turning east, he looked up at Green Pass. That name was a stale joke: nothing was green at those altitudes save the lichen and the mold on the flatbread.

The house wheezed and shifted in the constant winds. In plain truth it had once been a horse barn, and was still divided into stalls. For years Kandri slept under the words SPECKLED HEN, painted in a ghostly blue above his bed. He supposed it referred to a particularly favored horse.

Kandri's mother Uthé kept goats rather than horses. She made goat cheese for the mountain farmers and sold their wool in fine black bolts and worked their dung into the stony soil. Kandri held her in awe. She wove snares for grouse and partridges. She fried goat intestines with salt and chilies. She coaxed beans and root vegetables from their fragile garden, and somehow, even in the dead of winter, the food never quite ran out.

But she drew the line at the orphans. "Not one night," she told Kandri's father. "You bring them with coin enough to pay for their food, or don't bring them at all." Lantor Hinjuman grinned and shrugged his shoulders, but he never crossed Uthé in the matter.

The orphans came from the east, from the desert or its margins. There was fighting in those lands, and also something that drew his father, who crossed the pass several times a year. Kandri dreamed of these visits. His father was no good, of course (all the mountain folk concurred in this), but when he stomped into the yard and sought them out with his gaze, something kindled in Kandri's heart, and his breath came easier for a time.

In his earliest memories, his father brings gifts. If he had come from the Sataapre it was fruit and sweets—and occasionally, astonishing toys he built himself. These creations were the pinnacle of wonder in Kandri's first years and left him in no doubt that his father was a magician. There was a delicate spider—bone, wire, bristle-covered feet—that could scurry across a floor and, meeting a wall, ascend it all the way to the ceiling. There was an iron dragon with a water reservoir in its chest and a space for live coals in its belly; it whistled, blew clouds of steam from its nostrils, opened its jaws and spat sparks. Most beloved of all was a gleaming, articulated copper snake ("A sidewinder," said the Old Man) that slithered with a strange hypnotic pattern when set on the hot stone of the winter hearth, and wound itself into a perfect coil, as if going to sleep, as it cooled.

"Our secret," his father would proclaim with a hard but happy glance before presenting one of these marvels. "Never a word about these to anyone, save your mother and the orphans, you understand? And never outside the house. And hide them all away if a visitor should call."

Kandri promised, but disaster struck all the same. In his sixth year, on midsummer's day, he yielded to the temptation to see if the patio stones, throbbing with heat, might bring his snake to life in the same manner as the hearthstone. The question was answered in a matter of seconds: the snake took off across the patio, a wriggle of copper lightning. Kandri laughed and gave chase—and then the old tomcat that roamed the fields appeared out of nowhere, pounced on the snake, and vanished with it into the sloughberry thicket behind the house.

Uthé Hinjuman turned pale when Kandri admitted what he had done. The wild sloughberries ranged over six acres, giving way eventually to brambles and gorse. Kandri's mother slashed her way through the thicket for days in search of the toy—and not, Kandri knew somehow, out of any concern for his loss. When Lantor Hinjuman paid a visit a fortnight later, she made Kandri stand before him and confess. The Old Man stood frozen for a few seconds, then turned and left the property. An hour later, he was back with a neighbor's ox and plough. He spent the next day cutting a wide furrow around the sloughberries. When nothing flammable remained in the furrow, he set the berries on fire and burned the whole six acres to ash.

He never told Kandri whether or not he had found the snake. He never grew angry or spoke a word of reprimand. But that night he searched out every wondrous toy in the household, and took them away when he departed, and never brought such things again.

With the years, Kandri began almost to wonder if those little miracles had been a dream. Had the dragon really belched fire? Had the spider truly climbed? It grew hard to insist on the reality of these toys when no one would speak of them, or even confirm that they had existed.

His mother grew silent and troubled. She and Lantor Hinjuman talked less and less, but he still smiled his wolfish smile for Kandri, and he still, after a fashion, came with gifts: weird artifacts of his travels (square coins, sharks' teeth, lizard eggs turned to stone), and once the blind cook—and often, as the war crept nearer, orphans.

But the orphans never stayed. After a month or two, strangers would appear in the evening, share a quiet tea with Kandri's mother, and lead the children off by the dry mountain trails. Kandri wept at these partings, even though it meant more food for the rest of them. Never once did these frightened, stick-thin waifs show the least disrespect to him or his mother or even the cook. Some spent whole days in corners, staring at the nearest window or door. Others woke howling as though stabbed in their sleep. One girl fled the house without waking and was fetched home the next day by the dog.

∞

So, life. Fourteen years in this vein. Then came a day when Kandri found his mother seated at table, stone dead, her left hand swollen and purpled like some obscene fruit by the bite of a rare plumage viper. Chin on chest. The book she'd stolen a few minutes to read before the day's work began still open on the table. Steam rising from her teacup.

The viper, an undeniably beautiful coil of feathery, silver-white scales, lay in the iron cauldron near the fireplace, where it had apparently crawled for warmth.

Kandri walked to the adjacent farm, and the old couple there hired a messenger. The next day his father came from the Valley with a shovel and a mule. He chose a spot with a view of the lowlands, and with his own hands he assaulted the stony ground. Kandri watched, sick and stupid with grief, an orphan girl on either side of him clinging to his hands. Slowly, impossibly, his father cut a rectangle, a narrow wound in the earth. Kandri bethought himself and asked to take a turn with the shovel.

"Damned right you will," said his father, scrambling out of the grave. "Go on, the last foot is yours."

He slid into the hole; the earth was hard as a dish. This was where his mother would rest until the day the Gods returned.

"No tears in the grave, boy. That's for later, when we've had some rum."

"You'll let me drink rum?"

"If you stop digging like a girl, I might. Oh, quit bawling, it's a joke. You're a fine strong boy, she'd be proud. You can help carve her gravestone, too."

They buried his mother as the scriptures required: without a coffin, in a shroud of undyed wool. The stone was a mere fieldstone, dragged into place behind the mules, but when the chiseling was done, her name looked beautiful and permanent, and his father said they could come there and talk with her for the rest of their days.

After sunset men came for the orphans. It was the last time Kandri would ever watch the strange ritual unfold. Their father paid them, something his mother had never done. No names were spoken. Kandri's father told him to give the older girl his shoes.

"What will I wear, then?"

"Cow pies, you rascal. Now take those sorry things off."

Later they sat at table and gnawed the flatbread his mother had baked the week before. The Old Man produced a flask and shared it with Kandri, not bothering with cups. He told stories about the dead woman, who had come west with her people out of the Great Desert of Urrath. He poked Kandri in the chest: "You're part sand panther, boy. In all the four hundred clans of Urrath, you'll find no tougher stock. And one day you'll prove it." But he would say not a word about his courtship with Kandri's mother, or why they had lived here like squatters on the chilly mountainside, while he came and went.

Kandri had never tasted alcohol. He found himself babbling, then angry, then simply undone by grief. He lost the thread of the Old Man's words, which meandered over scores of subjects without revealing very much.

One last remark did emerge through the haze of that night, however. Kandri recalled it later because it seemed so baldly untrue.

"Your home," said his father. "Don't speak ill of it, Kandri."

"I just said it was cold."

"Not the mountaintop, you fool. I mean the continent, all Urrath. There's hunger here, and too much bloodshed—and ignorance, Ang knows. But there should *never* be shame. We lit the fire that warms the world today. Architecture, writing, music, mathematics, law: do you know what made those things possible?" He tapped his forehead. "Urrathi minds, boy. We were dancing before the Outer World learned to walk."

"Mathematics?" said Kandri.

His father nodded. "You heard me."

Kandri looked down at the cracked plate his mother had repaired five or six times with a weak glue of bone marrow and mud. The wind moaned over the desolate fields.

"What happened?" he said.

The curve of his father's mouth flattened into a line. He took the flask from Kandri's hand.

"Many things happened. Plague happened, and the world blamed Urrath. And there was more to it than that—violence, plunder. But go to sleep now."

"Someone plundered our mathematics?" said Kandri.

His father's fist smashed down on the table, making saucers jump. Kandri jerked away. He did not quite believe that his father would harm him. But he was appalled by the misery on the Old Man's face.

"I would ask you," said his father, through his teeth, "to respect the land you come from. Can you remember that?"

"Yes, Papa."

"Then go to sleep."

Kandri went, his eyes moist again. He hated the Old Man—for lying about Urrath, for leaving them here on the mountain, for shedding no tears of his own. But in the dead of night, he snapped awake, imaging that some-one had whispered his name. Finding himself alone nonetheless, he rose and looked out the window, and there was his father, kneeling in the dirt, rocking by his dead wife's grave.

The next morning, Lantor Hinjuman brought Kandri and the cook down into the splendor of the Sataapre Valley, with its lilacs and humming-birds and smells of the life-giving sea. Kandri was frightened. Everything was decadent and damp; frogs croaked in gullies; the wooden signs at the crossroads trailed beards of gray-green moss. The village names were odd and menacing. Wolf Kill. Bittermoon. Blind Stream.

"This is the one," said his father. "Blind Stream Village. Welcome home."

The place was anything but blind. Faces peeped at them from cane thickets, curtained windows, over garden walls. Dogs snarled, roosters hurled war-screams at the sky.

"Papa," he said, "can I tell my new family about the toys?"

The cook hissed through her teeth. Lantor Hinjuman stopped the cart and put his hand on the back of Kandri's neck. It might have been a loving gesture, but the hand, the whole arm, were as rigid as wood.

"Absolutely never," he said.

ဆ

The house, when at last they reached it, loomed impossibly large. There were outer gates and inner gardens, breezeways, porches, a copper sundial, a balcony with a cast-iron rail. Kandri heard laughter, doors slamming, bare feet on stone. Through the nearest gate he saw brown faces, young and old, assembling in a row.

His father opened the gate and dragged him into the courtyard. "This is Kandri, your brother," he told his six other children.

"WELCOME, BROTHER," they screamed, impassive, obviously coached. Two ancient aunts mumbled prayers; an even more ancient man tapped his cane upon the stone. Kandri's stomach churned. His old cook was led away into the house. A hound sniffed at his crotch. A smiling, slender-cheeked woman gave his cheeks a ritual dab of rosewater. His father cleared his throat and said that Kandri should call her Mother now.

Stepmother, he thought. Replacement mother, fake.

But the woman scolded her husband: "That's not up to you, Old Man." Then she fixed her big, lambent eyes on Kandri. "My name is Dyakra. I'll be your mother if you'll have me. But we have a duty to your birth-mother as well, child. You must honor her memory; I must honor her place in this family, and the gift she's given us today. So call me *Mother* if you want to. But sometimes also call me *Sepu*, second mother. It will help us remember the one who came before. She will be a bond between us, not a wall."

Kandri bowed his head, astonished. It had never occurred to him that such kindness could exist. "Lovely, charming," said his father. "Now come and meet your *Sepu's* pack of weasels."

Six new siblings. Four girls, all younger. One boy still in diapers. And a second boy a little taller than Kandri, though slightly crooked at the ribs.

This boy stepped out in front of the others. His upper lip curled. His eyes locked on the newcomer, this novelty his father had produced from thin air. Kandri could not tell if he was elated or appalled.

"You and Mektu are the same age," said the Old Man. "From now on, we'll celebrate your birthdays together. Lend him those shoes, Mek, until we go shopping in town."

"What'll I wear?" said Mektu.

☙

Morning: a smell of bile and cinders haunts Eternity Camp. Kandri is climbing the ladder of an eastern watchtower, which happens to be at the center of a camel stockade. The animals churn below him under a mantle of flies, bellowing and screaming for their morning meal. Kandri feels strong and clear-headed: to his surprise, he has slept like the dead.

It is midwinter, the gentlest season in central Urrath. The light is crystalline, the savage heat still many weeks away. The crescent bushes that surround the camp have opened flowers small as melon seeds, and swarms of stingless wasps have appeared to lap the bounty of their juices. It cannot last, Kandri knows. Already this morning, the wind is flowing west out of the infinite desert, slow and determined, a foretaste of that scorching wind the villagers call *amiuk*, the dry-mouthed kiss.

He pushes open the trapdoor. The two soldiers on the tower platform have to shuffle aside. One is a youth of no more than eighteen. He is fresh from the Sataapre, his skin still flush with the Valley's abundant water, his expression one of perpetual, if muted, shock. The other soldier is Mektu. He scarcely glances at Kandri. He is rolling a cheroot on the rail.

"Corporal Hinjuman," says the new recruit to Kandri. "I chewed a silverwood twig like you told me, sir. For my throat. It stopped hurting. Thank you, sir."

"Don't mention it," says Kandri. "You're relieved."

"Corporal Alar's supposed to relieve me."

"We traded posts. Go on, get some breakfast."

The youth takes a dubious glance from the rail. "I'll wait until they feed the camels, sir. Those sons of bitches, they bite."

"Only if they think you're a *lulee*," says Mektu. "You have to stand your ground. And if one of them bites you, take a stick and beat the shit out of him. It won't happen again."

They bustle the youth down the ladder. Alone, neither brother finds his voice. The camels bump and jostle the tower. Mektu smokes. Kandri picks up the telescope and trains it on the south.

"Dust on the road," he says at last.

"That's the Fifth Legion," says Mektu.

"Is it, by damn?"

"The last of them, anyway. Most crossed the Obic in the night."

Kandri has them in focus now: a few thousand men trudging south along the distant river, in ragged clothes but tight formation. Bound for Kiprifa, a rain-blessed land of green pastures and rice paddies, taken with ease four years ago. Kandri feels a burning envy of the Fifth Legion's soldiers. They would see nothing of the Ghalsúnay campaign.

"Betali's applied to join a mounted division. The *Shessel* cavalry, he says."

Kandri shakes his head. "No one's going to put that man on a horse. Listen, Mek—"

"I know," says his brother. "I have to stop talking about an escape. Well, quit your worrying. I can keep my mouth shut."

Kandri sighs. *No, you can't.*

As if on cue, Mektu grumbles, "Not as if you have a better plan."

"Suicide's a better plan," says Kandri. "Find a mirror. Take a look at your eyes."

"You can only see the stains up close," says Mektu. "And the Valley's a big place. We can stay away from Blind Stream. Ma can say she doesn't know where we are."

"While they're tearing out her fingernails."

Mektu's body twitches. He hides his face in the crook of his elbow, a gesture he has made since childhood when overcome with feeling. Then he lowers his arm and blinks down at the camels. "You're right," he says.

After a moment, Kandri says, "You were right about something too. The Offensive—"

"I'm right about lots of things," Mektu shouts. "I'm right about the yatra. You don't believe in them, that's fine, be a fool. But you, you have to laugh—"

"Lower your fucking voice," hisses Kandri. "I won't laugh anymore. But promise me you'll drop this shit about desertion."

Mektu's cheroot has gone out. He sucks at it anyway, then flings it down at the camels. After a moment, he says, "Do you still think about her?"

"About Ma? You have to ask?"

"Not Ma."

Kandri grows still. He lowers the telescope. He feels as though Mektu has just turned and kicked him in the gut.

"Of course I do," he says.

"I dreamed of her last night," says Mektu. "We were on her cousins' porch. She was playing the bandalia. I think her feet were in my lap."

For the first time that morning, he turns and looks at Kandri. "Do *you* dream about her?" he asks.

Kandri is seething. "What kind of shit question is that? Yes, sometimes."

"She said she loved me. Did she ever say that to you?"

"I don't want to talk about her, Mek."

"She said it more than once."

"Then I guess she loved you. Now shut up."

The second silence is deeper. All the wellbeing Kandri brought with him to the tower is gone. Love is an illness, a savage enchantment. He raises the telescope again.

The lands about him are beautiful, blinding, cruel. Eternity Camp squats at the center of the Mileya, or Windplain. A sparse grassland, dabbed here and there with stands of brush, solitary vylk trees like giant crones buried to their necks, button cacti, villages of thirsty Chiloto goatherds. The Prophet rules the whole of the Mileya. She rules the lands beyond it also, in every direction, as far as the eye can see. It could not have been otherwise; heaven has singled her out. Ang and Surthang, supreme Gods of Life and Death respectively, have jointly informed her of her fate. She will be Empress and Lawgiver to the continent of Urrath. She will restore this land to glory and see it mocked no more by Outlanders, nor starved by their Quarantine.

East of Eternity Camp, the grasslands start to die. There is a palsied twelve-mile swath where a few villages scratch out a living. Then dead earth. Then clay. And finally, sixteen miles off, the glittering white of the Yskralem, the Stolen Sea. It is a place of death, the Yskralem: a monstrous canyon that was once a true sea, until the rivers that fed it were diverted by the Kasraj. Beyond it somewhere are the nations of the Lutaral, still unconquered. And beyond that the desert, wider than the reach of any tales.

Kandri swings around to face west. The mountains of the Coastal Range, the high wall between him and home. His gaze lingers on the peaks: white mists, here and there a wink of snow. He picks out Green Pass, where the road leaps the ridge and starts its winding descent to the Sataapre Valley and the sea. The pass Mektu claimed he could reach "on a fast horse" before anyone noticed that he was gone.

A fast horse. The thought rekindles Kandri's anger.

"Has no one ever told you," he says aloud, "that the Rasanga's stallions can outrun any other horse in this army?"

Mektu grunts, a concession. The Rasanga are the Prophet's elite commandos and the deadliest killers in the Army of Revelation.

"If you think for one instant that you could steal one of *those* horses—"

"I don't," says Mektu.

"You couldn't steal a sandcat, either—the damned thing would kill and eat you. You *might* be able to steal a camel or some common horse, but even then, they'd catch you soon enough."

"Kan," says Mektu, "do you want to stay here until we die?"

To Kandri's irritation, he has no ready answer. Mektu glances at him, fidgets, tries to straighten his spine.

"I thought Ariqina—"

"You bastard."

"We have to talk about her someday, Kandri. I thought she might have gone to Loro Canyon, or the Cotton Towns. If we went there together, if we asked around—"

Kandri could throw him from the tower.

"She didn't go either of those places. We'd have heard. She went"—he forces the words out through his teeth—"somewhere *very far away.*"

"Do you think she's dead?"

"Gods damn it! No!"

"I don't know why you're so certain. Did she tell you something?"

"You're fucking cracked."

"The Old Man was strange too, wasn't he, when he learned that she was gone? You remember, he looked guilty, we should have stood up to him then. But we could try again with her cousins. Or the people at the clinic, or her aunt. Someone knows and isn't talking. A person doesn't live her whole life in a place and just disappear. She had no enemies, everyone loved her; what's the matter with you, brother, are you sick?"

"Mek," he says, turning away, "nobody knows where she went."

℥

After his shift in the watchtower, Kandri's captain puts him to work on the perimeter defenses. Beyond the wall of fishhook-thorns, an earthen trench encircles the camp. The trench is divided into sections, each of which is filled waist-deep with palm fronds dipped in thick black oil. If the camp were ever besieged, any section could be set ablaze with little more than a match.

Such barriers discourage the Prophet's enemies, but not so the yellow mole rat, whose relentless digging crumbles the walls of the trench. Kandri and his team are walking the trench floor, stuffing arsenic-laced bread into the rodents' burrows and sealing them with clay. It is a job he detests. The rats have other exits; some crawl out to die twitching in the moonlight. Kandri's clothes, his skin, will reek of oil for a week.

Mektu, as usual, has been sent to the kitchens. Kandri can picture him, grating yams, shelling palm nuts, sweating over cauldrons of soup. This morning they had parted bitterly. "You used to care about her," Mektu had accused. "You used to grin like a fool every time she walked into a room. I was almost jealous."

"Almost?"

"I should have stopped you. Told you to find your own girl. But now it's like she never existed. You won't even say her name."

The last jab is true enough. For three and a half years, Kandri has avoided speaking her name in Mektu's presence, anyone's presence; he has tried not to say it even to himself. And for three and a half years, Mektu has respected that silence. As well he fucking should.

Now the truce is broken, the silence gone. He will hear her footfall everywhere, hear her breathing when he breathes. At night she will speak his name with quiet laughter, drive him over hills and swamps and badlands until he wakes, bereft, groping at the air or holding his dick like a talisman, watching her fade with those sordid dreamscapes in an eyeblink or two. Even then, he will not say it. Her name, Ariqina, will be the word that dances on the tip of his tongue, the clear note above the harangues and recitations, the sour trumpets, the curses and cackling and threats, Ariqina, the name that stitches all the scraps of him together into something he admires, something worth the trouble to recall.

Too late, he's smiling. Broad daylight in this stinking trench and yet she's here with him, leaning close, forcing him to meet her eye. *The spark, Kandri. You can't hide it from me.* The twitch at her lip's left corner, so small and private. He will pay for this memory with tears.

"Hinjuman's thought of a joke," says the man to his right. "Either that or he's cracking before my eyes. Make it a joke, will you, Valley boy? The filthier the better?"

He stuffs poison into the earth. He slaps in clay. This morning he lied to Mektu. A lie he has often repeated, a lie of which he cannot repent. Ariqina did vanish, of course. Vanished utterly, and the Sataapre Valley grieved. Hundreds of men and women searched the countryside, from the lowlands to the peaks and even beyond. Her aunt consulted oracles, offered a reward. Her cousins wept; the priest who had tried to prevent her from studying medicine wept; nurses at her clinic for indigents wept; patients rose from their sickbeds to join the search. Doctors who had tried to seduce her wept on the shoulders of their wives.

Mektu's tears were open taps. He shouted at anyone who would listen that he had planned to marry Ariqina, that she was "the blossom of the Valley" and the woman of his destiny and dreams. And Kandri wept in secret, his grief walled in like these rats.

He never once told Ariqina that he loved her. Not when he first understood. Not when they began to lie about their walks in the hills, hiding from Mektu, hiding the stains on their clothes. Not when her eyes grew moist and she spoke of her own love, saying she trusted him with her weakness, her ugliness, the parts of her she couldn't love herself.

Not when Orthodox Revelation swept the Valley, and the hour grew so obviously late. Not when Ariqina took a copper ring from the neck of a fever-syrup bottle and slipped it onto his thumb with a laugh:

"Now I have you, Kandri Hinjuman. That's a totem ring. I'm the master of your soul."

Not when they kissed a moment later and he thought, *My soul? Keep it, why else would I need it, I never noticed it before.*

Not on their last night together. Not when she told him, a matter of hours before she vanished, exactly where she meant to go.

ဆ

The shift ends at sundown. There are barrels of water for the trench crew; Kandri strips and scrubs, racing against the night's oncoming chill. Racing too against the time of evening prayer. The great bell in the Palace of Radiance will toll at any moment, and he is still far from his unit. He is in no danger of reprimand (prayers may be offered anywhere outdoors), but he is in danger of going hungry—again. If his comrades beat him to the dinner line, he will be left with scraps.

Kandri jogs across the camp, searching for landmarks. He barely knows this sector. Latrines, armories, endless identical tents. A lumber yard. An archery range. The horror of the blackworm pits somewhere off to his right. Already men are gathering in the open areas, facing north, hushed before the evening rites. Kandri weaves among the warehouses, the drab canvas triangles. The orange sky has faded to gray.

"Oh, flaming shit."

Wrong turn. A high brick wall blocks his path. Desperate now, he follows it north, wondering what it encloses, how much of a detour it entails. Then his luck turns: just ahead is an iron gate, heavy and imposing, but ajar. Perhaps they will let him through just this once.

Inside, a wooden stool, but no sentry. No one at all. Kandri pokes in his head and sees a great dusty courtyard, entirely walled. The yard is a curious shape: an octagon, in fact. It is quite empty save for an ornate little structure at the center, with a gabled roof and narrow windows. Kandri squints: a shrine? A carriage stripped of its wheels?

Well, there are the guards, anyway: half a dozen, straight across the courtyard, by the only other gate. Kandri waves, but they do not see him. They are assembling for prayers themselves.

To hell with this. He's famished. He steps into the courtyard and makes right for them. *The gate was open, brothers, no one was there. And I couldn't shout to you at prayer time, could I?* That is what he will say if they are angry. But perhaps they won't be angry; perhaps they are people he knows.

CLANG. The brass thunder of the first bell, the summons. *I'm so hungry, brothers. I've not even tasted any boar. Have mercy. One day you'll need kindness too.*

His path brings him closer to the ornate structure. It is neither shrine nor carriage but something odder still: a palanquin, such as one sees in drawings of the bad old days of the Occupation, or even the Empire. Something for sartaphs to ride about in on the shoulders of slaves. The object is lavish, with faded gilt trim and stone inlay that must surely gleam in the daylight. The windows are barred. Heavy bolts and padlocks secure the doors.

Faint lines in the dust of the courtyard. Vague chalk shapes: circle, triangle, square. All of them centered on the palanquin. And by its locked door, fresh flowers. Something he has never seen in Eternity Camp.

He should stay well clear. He does not. His running feet have their own ideas. A quick look, that's all. Then the far gate, his plea to the sentries. One glance. He will not even stop. Or perhaps for only an instant, just long enough to see—

There is no glass in the window, only those heavy bars. Inside, there is no finery, nor even any seats. The palanquin contains just one object: an urn, lidded, massive, carved from cold white stone. The urn has no markings of any kind.

All at once Kandri knows that he has made a terrible mistake. Nothing has visibly changed, but a dreadful unease has pounced on him, like the moment before a massacre. He wants to run, but something (is it guilt, is it fear?) slows him to a wobbly march. And now the guards see him. They are leaping, waving. Not one of them makes a sound.

He slows still more. He is walking underwater, against the current, very nearly adrift. The silence is hideous. Something behind him does not want him to go. Then a sound does reach him—*but is he dreaming? Of course, Gods of Death*. It isn't real; it's his fancy. He has not just heard the scraping of stone.

Why has he stopped?

Another sound from behind him, now: a child's voice, high and meandering. The voice of a small girl talking to herself.

CLANG. The second bell. Instantly free of whatever madness afflicted him, Kandri races to the gate in a transport of joy. "Brothers—" he starts to whisper: but no, that is forbidden; it is the moment of prayer. They are on their knees, arms raised to the northern sky, murmuring the first words of the evening canticle. Kandri joins them, melting with gratitude. He is safe; he is kneeling with his thirty thousand comrades. What does a Soldier of Revelation have to fear?

For ten long minutes, peace reigns in his heart. Then the prayer is over, and the guards explode to their feet. Two run headlong for the gate by which Kandri entered—steering well around the palanquin. The other four, among them a lieutenant, lift Kandri and slam him against the wall.

"You little fuck," snaps the officer. "What in Pitfire are you doing here?"

"That's Kandri Hinjuman," says a private. "He's the brother of that cuckoo bird."

"The gate was open, sir," says Kandri.

"The padlock's faulty," snarls the lieutenant. "We were repairing it, filing it down."

The other soldiers are whispering together, and all at once, Kandri knows that they are not only furious but afraid. "I'm sorry, Lieutenant," he says. "I don't know anything about this place. I just needed a shortcut."

"A shortcut. Why you prick."

"What's in the urn, sir? Is it the yatra? Did Her Radiance trap it? I won't tell."

"Listen to him, Gods, he thinks we have the fucking yatra."

"Hinjumans," says the private. "I know that family, sir. Back in the Sata-apre, they're always in trouble. His brother Mektu—"

"Shut up." The lieutenant's eyes scan the courtyard. "Did anyone see you, Corporal?"

"No, sir. Not one soul."

The lieutenant reaches behind his back and unsheathes a knife. Kandri stiffens; the men holding him tighten their grip. The lieutenant rests the point of the blade on Kandri's neck.

"That gate was not left unguarded," he says.

"Yes, sir."

"That gate is always locked. You saw nothing. You were never here."

"Yes, Lieutenant. I mean no, no sir, never."

"Look me in the eye, Hinjuman. Can I count on you?"

"I was never here, sir. I swear on my mother. I swear on the mother of us all."

The lieutenant draws a deep breath—and suddenly smiles. "That's just fine, then. Let him go. On your fast fucking way, Corporal Hinjuman."

෪

He is very nearly the last to arrive. As the dinner line inches forward, he sees his brother through the open side of the kitchen tent, washing dishes under the moth-crowded lamps. Mektu is in fine form. Laughing, shouting: *What about the afterlife, brothers? Will there be nipples, do you think, and will we be allowed to touch them? And what about our scars, our dirty nicknames, belching contests, tattoos?* The other workers cringe, avert their eyes.

Anyway, Mektu adds with a shrug, *we'll know the truth soon enough.*

When at last he is served (more than scraps, but not much more), Kandri sits on a stump and wolfs his food. He is still shaking, and his mouth feels numb. Something horrifying has occurred. But did it happen in the palanquin, or in the dark box of his mind? Is he feverish? Did he swallow rat poison somehow? These are comforting thoughts, given the alternative.

But even if he was temporarily mad, and the white urn's lid never scraped open, and that singsong child's voice never called out—even then, something must explain an antique litter in a walled courtyard, and the fear in those men.

He decides to take himself in hand. *No business of yours, Corporal. Not your sector, and you've just sworn to hold your tongue. Besides, you have enough to worry about. Your brother's death-wish, for starters.*

He cleans his plate with a last bit of flatbread. He will have to threaten Mektu into silence; he has tried everything else. But that will not be easy. Mektu is no coward and does not take well to threats. He hears his brother's whinny of a laugh. An irritating laugh: and that too is a problem. Some men die for heresy, others because their mannerisms grate on the nerves. Mektu could die for either. A mid-level officers' mess is just a few yards away.

෪

But luck is with Mektu tonight, for as the meal ends, there are cries of alarm. Plates are dropped, orders howled, buckets filled from any source whatsoever, including the soup cauldron. Everyone breaks into a mad stampede. The yatra has set fire to the Prophet's house.

Kandri, bucketless, races to the scene. The rumor is horrifying, thrilling. Could she possibly be in danger? If the building collapses, what then? Surely, the Gods will let her pass through the fire unscathed?

The gate of the palace compound stands open to the wider camp. Loud cries of *Odulche pam di Ang!*—Ang loves the Enlightened One!—echo among the walls. Thousands have squeezed already into the Old Gallows Courtyard, cheering and chanting, surrounding the Prophet's tiny house. Atop its thatched roof, twenty men with empty buckets dance and cheer, as if at some great victory. A little smoke hangs in the air, but the fire is dead. From his spot at the edge of the courtyard, Kandri can see no damage at all.

One of the roof-dancers lifts his hands in exaltation. "Yatra, yatra!" he shouts. "Flee our Mistress, who scours evil from the earth! Flee Eternity Camp! Flee her anger, and go your lonely way!"

The soldiers below give an answering roar: *Flee! Flee!*

Kandri cannot bring himself to shout. There are no yatras, the whole army has gone mad. Then his nose wrinkles at a familiar scent. Clove oil. He looks over his shoulder: the pusher Skem is an arm's length away.

For a moment, they are both quite still. Then the Waxman speaks. Kandri cannot hear him over the roaring, but Skem enunciates slowly, letting Kandri read his lips.

Dead man.

Kandri flashes him a bare-toothed snarl. Now that he has a mortal enemy, he knows he must be taken for a lunatic, a man capable of any horror, a man the practical Skem will choose not to provoke. An eager killer, that is: the opposite of the truth.

The crowd gives a violent surge, pressing Kandri against the wall. Twisting, he sees that the Prophet herself has stepped into the courtyard. She moves at the center of her phalanx of Rasanga commandos, gripping the chain of her cherished white baboon.

The roaring stops, a snuffed candle. The Enlightened One moves with mincing steps. As always, she wears a wrap of blood-red wool, stripes of white greasepaint on her face and forearms, and the necklace of dog's fangs that symbolized the martyrdom of her people. Short, thin, wrinkled: a woman slight enough to be carried away on the breeze. Her eyes are wandering, her dry lips slack; she might well be unaware of the crowd. It is a face both haunted and frail, but the whole world knows the speed with which those eyes can awaken to deadly purpose, those lips form words of holy rage.

The crowd squeezes farther back. Forty Rasanga with spears and swords, crossbows and mattoglins glare at the soldiers as if daring them to look at their mistress askance. Up close, they are terrible to behold: enormous, scarred from old battles, shoulders like the haunches of bears. *Rasanga*: Innocent Dreamers. Each one chosen personally by the Prophet, and each entrusted with a glimpse of her ethereal visions. Strangest of all, about two thirds of the Rasanga are women. Kandri has never understood this: everyone knows that the Gods disapprove of women soldiers. The barbarous Važeks send their women out to kill, but Chilotos tolerate no such obscenity. And yet here they are, women Rasanga, the deadliest fighters alive. Once, greatly daring, Kandri had asked his captain to explain the contradiction. The man's response was cryptic.

"Rasanga are more than human, corporal. They are changed by faith, by their encounter with the holy mysteries. Our rules don't apply."

The tightest ring around the Prophet, however, is reserved for her sons: the Sons of Heaven, Lords of the Orthodox Dominion. No father sired these boys; Revelation alone kindled life in her womb. The elder sons are the Prophet's ministers, war counselors, interrogators, and executioners at need. The Chiloto people pray for them, and cry out in joy or terror when they pass, knowing they will one day rule the continent.

Kandri stands on his toes. He cannot tell just how many of the eleven sons are here in the crowd. But there for starters is Lord Jihalkra, the First-born. Tall and severe, with bright eyes and a broad, chiseled forehead, he wears a salt-white desert tunic fastened with ebony pins. Jihalkra the Silent, he is called: each of the Sons has such a title. He is the army's field marshal, the manager of all the war's far-flung campaigns.

Jihalkra studies the men on the roof with grim disapproval. Instantly, like whipped boys, they turn and rush for the ladders.

Then the Prophet speaks. Not in her terrible war-voice; this is a murmur, audible only because no one is breathing.

"Little one," she says to the enormous baboon, "what has happened to my men? Something has stolen all their tongues."

A rebuke. The soldiers freeze for an excruciating instant. Then a frightened voice cries out: "Her feet walk Heaven's Path!"

The Prophet allows herself a smile. The crowd erupts, repeating the blessing seven times. Kandri shouts as loud as anyone: he stands just yards from her, after all. The white baboon puts its head back and screeches. Its mistress studies the creature with concern.

"Gently, Sleepyhead. I'm not leaving for heaven just yet. And you shall go with me when the time comes."

The baboon's name is Sleepyhead. It is rumored to have developed a taste for human flesh. Kandri knows for a fact that the creature attends executions, crying and leaping and running circles on its chain. The Prophet is rarely without it. Her servants, regularly mauled by the animal, taste its food for poison as they do the Prophet's own.

The Enlightened One steps closer. Kandri curses himself for letting the mob sweep him into the courtyard. With great effort, he slides one foot in the direction of the gates. He sees the hard, flint faces of her younger sons, the medals on their chests, the savage eyes of the Dreamers, who seem enraged to find no one to kill among the soldiers.

And there, by damn, is Garatajik. This is a much rarer sighting: Garatajik the Merciful, the learned son, the mystery, the one who reads. Even now he is clutching several books to his chest: perhaps they were in his mother's house, and he feared to lose them in the fire.

Garatajik is the Secondborn Son of Heaven. Like Jihalkra, he is over forty years old. He is perhaps the least dangerous of the brothers (out of eleven rattlesnakes, one must be least dangerous), and the only one not to serve in his mother's wars. He has returned but recently to the camp, out of the distant east, along with a few strange, bookish men and forty emaciated nomads. The Prophet had shed tears of joy, embraced him in public, made him gifts of gold and horses and weapons and wives. Garatajik had been missing for two years.

Now the frail woman stops, and her entourage with her. She raises a spidery hand, glass bangles dropping past her elbow, and the hush that falls is total.

"I do not fear this thief of souls," she says. "Nor should you, believers. Fear is idleness, fear is sand blown under the door. But are we helpless, that we cannot seal the crack beneath the door?"

A pause, in which the men dare no more than slight shakes of their heads.

"Like that whisper of sand," she continues, "death seeps in through the crevice of fear. But for those who know Revelation, there is no final death. True, this yatra is a mighty one. I sensed it, away there beyond the Stolen Sea, raging in the desert, among the dry wells and wastes of sulfur and the tombs picked clean by ghouls. This yatra drifted for centuries. Bodiless, it cursed the winds, cursed the sun, burrowed under dunes by daylight. It thirsted. Not for water, not for wine or even blood. It longed for green grass, my soldiers. It thirsted for the west. But it erred when it invaded my camp."

She twists her body, waves a hand at the roof. "The little stings it has dealt us? Nothing, nothing: they were inflicted in our sleep. But we are awake now, and we will slap and crush this yatra, or drive it back into the sands. It is the will of heaven: no man or spirit or plague or storm can turn us aside. My son Ojulan—he is not here tonight—my son takes any woman he wants, the virgins, the most fertile, they praise the Gods when he enters them, and the force, the force of his love—"

She stops, gazing at them almost with accusation. The mob holds its breath. Kandri fights the urge to glance at his fellow soldiers: to do so, even to shift his eyeballs left and right, would be unutterably dangerous. But some of them, surely, are seeing what he sees? For never before has her madness been so plain, exposed like a boil on her cheek. He feels ashamed for her and wishes he could run.

My son Ojulan. Not here tonight. That's one blessing, at least. For Ojulan, her favorite, worst of the rattlesnakes, would have found some excuse for bloodshed in the chaos of the fire. But where is the maniac, anyway? Is he indifferent to his mother's fate? Is he up in the palace, surrounded by courtesans, fondling that golden knife?

"Radiant mother," cries Garatajik (his schoolmaster's voice, water dashed in all their faces). "Night has fallen, and the great boar is roasting on the spit. May we send your loyal soldiers to their feast?"

The Prophet gazes at him, startled, then slowly lowers her hand. "You may go," she says. "My son is right, this night is for feasting and joy. So go, go and find some. Eat the pig. The day comes all too soon."

Uncertain shuffling. Kandri takes another step toward the gates. They are dismissed, surely? They may quit her holy presence with a murmured blessing and a bow?

Then it happens. The Prophet's eyes grow wide. The hand stabs skyward again, and her body straightens and stands tall. A wild passion lights her features. The voice that comes from her now is a shriek that rends the air.

"On wings of flame that day is coming, and the flame that is our cause will scour clean this land, and all lands everywhere, all the known and secret places, the forest depths of Bathia, the castles of the heretics, the Mountains of the Kasraj, the dark floor of the sea. And those who cling to false ways will earn oblivion. Are we to wallow in their filth? Do we wait for pigs to shamble from our path? Our path is molten silver. We strike no bargains. We sweep the animals aside. The earth shall vomit up her dead, the White Child shall awaken, the land suffer the torture of the wind, flesh melt from the bone, and the small blind beggars will crawl to us, sobbing, and the Twin Abominations dwell in Urrath once more. No matter. They will know our strength when we are done. Go and feast, you men."

She is breathless, swaying. Unsurprisingly, no one moves so much as a finger. Then her eyes flash with rage.

"I AM THE KEEPER OF THE IMMACULATE LAW! GO AND FEAST!"

In less than a minute, the courtyard is deserted.

⊘

Kandri lives with a double certainty: no one could possibly love the Prophet; no one could fail to love the Prophet. She is a diseased and monstrous animal; she is the Liberator, mother and father to them all. She ignores the most sacred beliefs of the Chiloto nation; she is that nation's holy core. She is the Giver of Shelter, the Voice of Love; she kills with a tireless commitment.

It is her love which makes her kill. Before her, the Chilotos had never once found a leader who was not soon slain, or put in irons, or devoured by leprosy, or bought. They assumed contempt; they were a dirty, dung-collecting, artless people of a vast but marginal land. The source of slaves and foot soldiers. Goatherds, horse thieves, "warlords" who were lords of nothing and made war mostly on themselves. True, their coast was green and fertile, but in the eyes of Urrath, this splinter of land was the exception that proved the rule. *Chiloto:* the people themselves knew the word meant "The Honest Ones" in their own language, but they were helpless to deny the common Kasraji meaning: disorder, a mess or accident, something spilled.

They were the accidental people, the stain on Urrath. Whom the great southern clans would not allow even to tend their cattle, and northern princes and sartaphs ran down for sport, as they did antelope or deer. The ones all armies hacked their way through, languid and complaining, on their way to worthier foes.

The Prophet declared an end to all that. She was the Gods' chosen instrument and never flinched from the task. She united the people no one could unite. In her prisons are Važeks who castrated Chiloto men with hot irons, who burned the vylk trees that housed the souls of Chiloto ancestors, who sorted Chiloto women according to their suitability for rape.

Or so her troops are told. Kandri has witnessed none of these things, and in recent years, as declaring love for the Prophet changed from a collective impulse to a mode of survival, it has been hard to tell memory from fancy. An old man sells you matches and speaks of Važek crimes: are they what he remembers, or what he knows he is expected to remember? And how long before the two begin to merge?

Of course, Kandri too has loved the Prophet. All his life. On Candle Mountain, his birth-mother Uthé told him to thank the Gods each night for the gift of the Enlightened One. When his father appeared in the household, he reminded Kandri that if the Prophet had not led the fight against the Važeks they would all be enslaved, or conscripted, or dead. And just days after Uthé's death and Kandri's arrival in Blind Stream, Mektu took him aside and whispered:

"We're not Orthodox here. But that doesn't mean we love the Prophet any less. Some pigs in school are jealous because we're sophisticated people. They lie. They say Hinjumans think they're above religion, that we're too proud to pray. But that is horseshit, we pray sometimes. Don't you?"

"Every night," said Kandri. It was the truth, and yet it felt deceitful. He prayed because his birth-mother had prayed beside him. He meant to go on doing so as a way to keep her near.

Mektu looked unsettled by his "every night," as though Kandri had issued a challenge. "Praying doesn't make you superior," he said. "We know what the Prophet's done for our people. She freed us. The Chilotos were slaves. Have you ever seen the face of a slave?"

"Of course."

"Liar," said Mektu. "Where, up on your mountain? In your barn?"

"People pass on the road," said Kandri.

Mektu sighed expansively. "Come upstairs."

He led Kandri into his new mother's dressing chamber. Above a table littered with combs and bangles hung a portrait of a couple in wedding finery, seated and holding hands. Their faces smiled, but their eyes were deep-set and haunted, as if searching some desolate vista for a trace of whatever they had lost.

They were his mother's parents, Mektu explained. They had been raised in slavery under the Važeks, suffered unspeakable cruelties, watched nearly everyone they knew die of starvation or abuse, watched the sick or wounded tossed into mine shafts, alive. When the Prophet's army liberated the slave camps, they had come to Blind Stream, built the family home, raised children and dogs.

Their lives were peaceful enough, although the war raged on east of the mountains. But in time, their oldest child, Peyar, came to understand how wounded, how broken his parents remained in their hearts. The boy swore vengeance. He wanted to join the army and fight the Važeks, but no one would hear of it: he was only thirteen.

One day word reached the Valley that the enemy had made a lightning advance and were closer, in fact, than at any point in years. Then Peyar knew what he had to do. He stole his father's machete and slipped away in the night. The next morning, the parents found the note he had left and gave chase. And not one of them returned.

Kandri looked at his brother, aghast. "What happened to them?"

Mektu hesitated. "You can never speak to Ma about it. She lost her parents and her brother in one day."

"I won't talk," Kandri promised.

Mektu lowered his voice to a whisper. "Uncle Peyar must have gotten close to the Važeks. He was captured, and so were our grandparents. They died horribly, Kandri. They died in the Theater of Bones." He squinted at Kandri. "You *do* know about the Theater of Bones?"

"Of course," Kandri lied.

Mektu waited for him to prove it. Cheeks burning, Kandri stammered, "What's the matter, what do you want me to say? I love the Prophet as much as anyone."

After a long moment, Mektu nodded, and even patted his brother awkwardly on the back. "That's the main thing," he said.

❧

So it was: the main thing. At least for as long as love was enough, and worship something you could take or leave. For in fact, the Hinjumans were indifferent to the faith. The only exceptions were their other grandfather, Lantor Hinjuman's father, who had fought in the worst battles of the Sataapre and made a pact with the Gods at the time; and Nyreti, Kandri and Mektu's eldest sister, whose devoutness nobody could explain. These two prayed together at dawn and dusk, and went to temple together; otherwise, Kandri rarely heard so much as a mumbled prayer. He himself prayed less often with each passing season.

But from that day, standing before the portrait of the grandparents slain before his birth, Kandri's love of the Prophet grew. He saw the lines of sadness enclosing Dyakra Hinjuman's eyes, and love for this new mother became commingled with love for the Mother of All Chilotos. He listened to the priests when they visited the school, and the love blazed stronger. At last it simply dwelt in him, warm and nourishing, a bed of embers against the cold. *The Prophet saved your people. She freed the slaves, she freed the Valley, she routed the shits who killed your second mother's family and left her grieving for life. The Prophet fights for you still. Although you fail her, she never fails you. Even when you pray for selfish things, she prays for you. Morning and evening, each day without exception, all her life.*

She herself said it often: *My people are the reason I draw breath.*

Tonight, her delirious words still ringing in his ears, Kandri flees the palace compound with his comrades. Desperate to obey her, to be worthy of her prayers. Is it gone forever, that warm embrace? Has any shred of it survived the Ghalsúnay massacre, his cracked skull, these sickening displays? Is love for that jangling, shrieking creature, that woman scrawny as a boiled stork, that murderer who spawned eleven murdering sons, even possible?

How can he doubt it?

How can he feel anything but doubt?

※

Mektu is waiting for him outside the gate. Kandri, appalled at his thoughts, storms by without a word. His brother falls into step beside him, snickering, pawing at his arm.

"'Go and feast,' she tells us. As if all of us had a great cut of boar to look forward to. Did you get to taste it, Kandri? Do you want me to sneak you a bit of fat?"

Kandri shakes him off. There is a strange light in Mektu's eyes. His head makes little bobs in Kandri's direction. He is not so much walking as leaning over him, making them jostle and bump. He reaches for Kandri's arm again.

"I have an idea, brother."

"Sorry to hear that," says Kandri.

"Do you know who comes and goes from Eternity Camp without apply-ing for leave? Without even carrying a pass?"

"The mole rats."

"No, fool. The Xavasindrans."

Kandri has to close his eyes.

"They're the answer we've been looking for," says Mektu. "They can free us. Don't they claim they're here to help?"

The Xavasindrans are a medical mission from the Outer World, beyond Urrath, beyond the Quarantine. Under the Plague Protocols, they are the only ones allowed to come or go from the continent. Urrathis are generally immune to the World Plague, and that is strange enough. But the foreigners also claim that *every last Urrathi* carries the disease—dormant and harmless to themselves—in their lungs, of all places. One cough, it is said, could kill millions in the Outer World, and so the Outer World has made a jail of the continent. Urrathi princes never meet their foreign counterparts. Urrathi ships are sunk on sight.

But there is a softer face of Quarantine. Xavasindran doctors are sprin-kled across Urrath, treating lesser diseases, binding wounds, drawing parasites from the blood. And above all, hunting for the secret of Urrathi immunity.

"We can reason with those doctors," says Mektu. "We can explain that we don't want any part of this war."

"And then?"

"We get one of them to say that we're ill. That we need to be taken to one of their special hospitals."

"You're a genius," says Kandri. "I'm sure no one's thought of that before."

"Don't be nasty, it's a decent plan. And you have the imagination of a stump."

"The doctors take an oath of noninterference," said Kandri, "and they travel with army escorts. Also, they're not here."

"Not here?"

"The captain told us last week. Not one Xavasindran left in the camp, and none expected before midsummer. Otherwise it's an excellent plan."

Mektu, silenced, walks stiffly at his side. Kandri considers whether or not he has been cruel. One hides certain crushing truths from children; why not from soldiers? Are they any more likely to know what to do with them? Are they any stronger, in the end?

"Forget the Xavasindrans," says his brother at last. "They're not what I came to tell you about. Listen, I have something for you."

"No, thanks."

"And one for me, of course. We'll need them. It was worth the risk."

"What risk, Mek? What the hell are you talking about?"

"I took two bush kits," says Mektu.

"You *what*? Devil's rectum."

Kandri's cry turns heads. The brothers march, frightened as two beaten dogs. But no one approaches, and after a few paces, Mektu is buoyant again, prancing, smirking. *I will never be rid of you,* Kandri thinks.

Bush kits are survival packages, kept ready for couriers or commandos: anyone the army might dispatch in haste on some urgent errand. Kandri has never touched one. They are more an idea than a physical presence in the camp.

"No one knows, no one knows!" hisses Mektu. "We were unloading fifty wagons from the north. The kits were at the bottom of a mountain of loot from the siege of Misafa Palace: rugs, silks, leopard skins, lady's slippers. But when we cut off the tarp, we found it was infested with blackworms. They told me to burn it all."

"Stay away from me," says Kandri, "until you wise up. I'm sorry, I just can't—"

"The worms never reached the bush kits, Kandri. They're sealed, they're absolutely fine. I burned the rest, but I put the kits in a sack under my bed."

Under his bed.

Kandri twists on his heel, drags his brother into an alley between two tents. When he is sure no one can see them, he grabs Mektu's uniform just below the throat.

"You shit. Listen close. If you can't stop this nonsense, I'm going to report you myself. Do you hear me? I'll tell them you're a nutcase. What else can I do? Maybe they'll just lock you up instead of feeding you to the fucking dogs."

His brother's hands are in fists.

"A nutcase," he says. "I want to get out of here. You want to stay and serve Her Radiance until she sends us off to the Ghalsúnay slaughterhouse. But *I'm* the nutcase, am I?"

"I don't know what the hell you are. But I swear on our mother—"

"My mother. Yours died in a barn."

Kandri is speechless. Once again, that blow to the stomach, that pitiless assault. He looks his brother coldly in the eye. "I swear on our mother," he repeats, "that if you run for the Valley, I'll denounce you. I'll tell them our family's not responsible, that they didn't know your plan. I'll tell them I did everything I could to make you stay."

Mektu stands frozen. Then his eyes move, up and down Kandri's body. It is a look no one accustomed to violence can mistake.

"You wouldn't really do that."

"I just swore to do it, Mek."

⅏

Late evening. Kandri has purchased a bottle of fine cane liquor at the cost of six days' pay. A moment of weakness, or inspiration perhaps. He has tried to share it with such friends as he has in Eternity Camp, but they are suddenly busy at his approach, recalling promises to be elsewhere. Well, fuck them. He takes a long first swig: bliss and pain commingled, sweet honey and a blow to the skull.

He has become a pariah—but why exactly? Has Mektu's chatter reached an officer? Has Skem been talking of his plans to put a knife in Kandri's ribs?

Whatever else is happening, the Feast of the Boar rolls on. Tonight, the pig's organs and viscera have been fried with chilies and scarlet palm oil; the smell wafts through the camp, irresistible, driving men mad. Kandri, his timing lucky for once, queues for an hour and receives three inches of intestine and a grape-sized cut of lung. The men ahead and behind him keep their distance. Not even the server meets his eye.

He wolfs the meat and chases it with liquor: a private feast, a celebration of solitude. Then he goes in search of Chindilan.

In the two hours since his standoff with Mektu, Kandri has felt a burning need to speak with the smith. Their last meeting shook Kandri to the core, and somehow, he knows that their next will change everything. What he does not know, however deeply he probes his own heart, is what he will say to Chindilan:

Uncle, I'm on my knees now. You have friends among the officers. Call on them.

Uncle, I am no longer joking. I will shatter his foot, leave him crippled but alive.

Uncle, I'm abandoning the fool.

Chindilan is not in the weapons shop, however, nor any of his usual haunts. When Kandri inquires with the men in his unit, they shrug. Only when he refuses to leave does one of them face him directly.

"The Master Smith went off to the village. Hours ago."

"The village? What for?"

"What the fuck do you think?"

From the back of the tent, another soldier says, "Pussy, Hinjuman. Some of us like it. We're strange that way."

Kandri walks. The village begins a quarter mile east of the camp, just beyond the barren security zone declared by the army. He is deeply unsettled, but not by the soldiers' derision. Something is wrong: Chindilan does not go whoring. He has occasional liaisons with a widow from Dholédd, a fruit vendor who supplies the officers' mess. "She's trouble enough" is all he says if the subject arises. Kandri has never once seen him on Brothel Row.

Tonight, for the first time in months, the East Gate stands open. Twenty sentries guard the narrow exit, glumly sober, patting down the revelers for contraband, for theft. Press-ganged Chiloto boys stagger across the drawbridge over the pit. Grabbing their crotches, jingling coins. Once outside, prostitutes descend on them like crows.

Kandri too is quickly surrounded. "Bargain, bargain," say the women, their labor-roughened hands traveling his skin. He keeps a grip on his coin purse, but he passes the bottle around. Have they seen Chindilan, the blacksmith? The women shake their heads, cooing and sighing over the liquor. When he takes the bottle back, it is two-thirds drained.

No, he's not buying sex. Their smiles harden into scorn. *Lulee,* they mumble, predictably. But a young woman in a tattered sarong puts her arms about his neck and kisses him, long and deep.

"Thanks for the drink," she says.

The village is almost lightless. Most of the huts are closed tight as drums, the dogs cringing and slinking back from the soldiers (village dogs learn quickly), the chickens caged for the night. Chickens, daughters, sons. Because of his injury in the Ghalsúnay campaign, Kandri has not seen the village on a feast night in over a year. Now it all comes back. The shattered bottles, discarded bones. The silent paths between these homes of mud and straw. The Kiprifani merchant in the village center, hawking drugs to promote virility, ward off disease.

Between the huts he has a glimpse of the badlands, stretching east to the Stolen Sea. Nothing out there, beyond the first few grassy miles. Nothing but death.

Brothel Row is merry, however: no bloodshed, the night is young. A fat man with a pushcart winks at him, lifting a bottle. "One sip a night protects your privates, friend! Why gamble? You know where those girls have been."

He moves from house to house, seeking Chindilan. In the first three, no luck at all. But in the last and largest business, Aunty Boom-Boom's, a soldier nods. Smiling and very drunk, he points Kandri down a long, narrow passage.

"Last door on the right, Hinjuman. Don't knock; it's another waiting room. Give us that bottle a minute."

Kandri passes him the liquor, has to wrestle it back. He moves down the hallway. Painted words on the floor read No REFUNDS. No PAIN GAMES. No BOOTS IN BED. The hallway darkens as he goes, however, and by the time he reaches its end he is practically groping. When he opens the door, he sees

Colonel Idaru, Lord Ojulan's deputy, being serviced by a slender woman kneeling on a pelt. Idaru turns him a furious scowl, and Kandri, panicked, slams the door with a bang.

His helpful comrade has fled. Those who remain smirk at him over their tankards.

"Hinjuman," says one, "is it true that your brother once crawled into a smokehouse and tried to cure himself like a ham? Did he do that? We've got this wager, see."

Kandri's first thought is to break the man's teeth. But Idaru could emerge at any moment. Furious and ashamed, he stalks from the brothel. In the barren yard, men are splurging on plates of *uitik*—hairless mice drowned in batter and fried—while a boy with a tin whistle kicks at a small chained monkey festooned with girlish bows, trying to make the creature dance.

He crosses the yard, forcing himself not to run. In the alley, he quickens his pace, turns one corner and then another, losing himself. Coward, fool. The night air cold in his chest. Retreating to a darkened doorway, he lifts the bottle to his lips.

Uncle, can I truly maim my brother? Crush his foot with a sledgehammer, an iron cartwheel, the anvil in your shop? And would even that be enough to save him? Would they send him home or just chain him to a work station, to a sink?

Footsteps. Swift and heavy. Kandri swallows his mouthful and takes another, the hell with everything, this night has a feeling of doom.

But the feet pass him by. He lowers the bottle and sees four soldiers, almost running, locked in a whispered argument. Clearly, no one's seen him. But before they vanish around the corner, one man raises his voice.

"I told you, didn't I? This is the *last* place he'd go."

Kandri steps from his alcove, thinking: *that* was strange. Huge brutes, all four of them. Akoli Militia, perhaps, or even Orthodox Guard. But who could they be searching for?

In any event, they are gone. And all at once Kandri realizes that his fear is gone as well. It can't be him they want—for the simple reason that Idaru cannot have seen his face. The chamber was bright, but Kandri himself had remained in the shadowy hall. The colonel was squinting in his direction, not scowling. And Akoli Militia aren't summoned to chase down a man for opening the wrong door in a brothel.

No danger, then. No one after him at all.

He drinks, feet and mind wandering, thinking of the kiss of the young prostitute, thinking of Ariqina Nawhal. She was only two years his senior, but even in their teens, he rarely thought of her as a girl. She felt too much, knew too much, she had a fullness of heart that left him shocked and sorry for lesser people, grown men and women included. She wasn't normal. She was Ariqina, a category of one.

On their last night together he had given her his cap. An old thing of uncombed wool, round, plain, faded from scarlet to fish-gill pink. She adored it. On cold nights she wore it beneath the hood of her *shemlad*—but only in the hills, when the two of them walked alone. Kandri had tried to make a gift of it many times. Ariqina refused, and took care that no one but Kandri ever saw it on her head. A woman did not wear a man's clothing unless they were lovers. It was unwritten Valley law.

Of course they *were* lovers by then: the peasant and the genius, Kandri the tree pruner and Ariqina the doctor, the healer, the unstoppable force. That night she'd worn the cap only briefly, then returned it, saying she wasn't cold. Kandri had crushed the hat into his pocket. But later, on an impulse, he'd slipped it into her shoulder bag, under the medical kit she was never without. It was easy; Ariqina was sleeping with her head on his lap. She stole many such naps on their night walks, pulling him down with her in some distant meadow or shed or cedar grove, holding him, gone in mid-sentence, pinched out like a flame. She was so often exhausted. Sleep was a fugitive thing in the household she shared with two elder cousins anxious to marry, an aunt who took in street dogs, an insomniac rooster forever shrieking of doomsday. And at any hour, a summons might come for Doctor Ariqina. From the clinic, or from any house in any village, up or down the Sataapre.

This is where I'm safe, Ari would whisper. *Here in the darkness with you guarding my sleep.*

A gust of wind blows sand along the alley. He wonders if it is possible that she doubted his love. On Brothel Row his comrades are laughing, fucking, maybe haggling over the bill. Why shouldn't he find some pleasure there? What is wrong with him? Ariqina likely gave his cap to the first indigent she met on the road.

He hears a child, weeping.

Kandri turns, puzzled. He has walked right out of the zone of festivities. Dark walls surround him. He is entirely alone.

But the child—a little girl, probably—is somewhere quite near at hand. Not crying, exactly, but whimpering, and he thinks: *Is that fear?*

He calls out: "*Elu, elu.* Who's there?"

No answer. But to his left there are thumps, shuffles. And the child's voice again. Yes, that is fear, that is terror in fact. An abominable sound.

"Whose girl is that? What's the *matter* with you people?"

Suddenly, a door creeks open. An old woman stands there, shriveled, naked to the waist. She gestures at him frantically. *Away, go away!*

Then Kandri smells it. Clove oil.

Skem.

He moves to the next hut. It is distinctly crooked, listing on its dirt foundation like a man in a stupor. The door, out of true, cannot quite close. A dim light flickers there in the darkness. Kandri sets the bottle down, slides his fingers around the handle of the machete.

"Skem. You Gods-damned shitting animal."

He tries to shout the words, but his voice has withered in his chest. His skin is cold and his hands are trembling. Pointlessly, he reaches out in the direction of the door. "Skem! I'll fucking kill you." The words no louder than before.

From the doorway comes a man's low grunt of pleasure. In the same instant, a child screams in pain.

Kandri feels himself go mad. He is through the door with the machete raised. By one candle he sees a man's rutting hips and the naked child on the bed, and then the man is up and flying at him with a long, bright knife. Kandri sees his death in that knife; the man is viper-quick, but his lunge is hampered by his lowered trousers, and *There, dead,* Kandri's machete takes off his ear and splits his throat wide open, *dead, dead,* two more blows and the man falls in twitching pieces and Kandri's legs are drenched in blood.

He staggers, drops the machete. The man is not Skem. The girl, twelve at the oldest, has risen to her feet. Bloodied, cradling herself. Kandri looks around for something to cover her, but when he turns, she shoves past him and flees through the open door.

By the guttering candlelight, the dead man's blade gleams like gold.

Voices, gasps, men and women flitting past the doorway. Kandri curses in a nonstop whisper. He must get out of here, back to his tent; he must somehow clean the gore from his pants. Drunken fights are one thing, murder of a fellow soldier another. If they learn who did it, if someone, anyone talks . . . .

The corpse lies face-down. *Who are you? Why the fuck do you smell like Skem?* But in fact, the reek of cloves is gone. Has he imagined it? Is he truly going mad?

He slides his boot under the man's ribcage, lifts. The corpse flops over— and Kandri hurls himself back with a moan, not believing what he sees.

"Oh fuck. Oh fuck."

The dead man is Ojulan. He has killed the Prophet's favorite son.

II. A VOID

Wicked child, by whose leave do you play with those embers?
Were you not raised in a village of straw?
CHILOTO FOLKSONG

He picks up the machete. He lurches over the corpse, deeper into the shack. As though it were big enough to hide him. As though he could wait this out under the bed. The man's half-severed neck is almost in the doorway. The blood is steaming in the chill night air.

Ojulan had lunged with the mattoglin. His severed hand still clutches the priceless weapon, blood smearing the golden script. Mouth and eyes both open. His bare legs look strangely contented.

The candle goes out.

Kandri gropes in the darkness. Something clean. On the straw mattress are underthings, a doll, and a reek of different blood, the girl's. He turns and plunges across the room. A bucket. A stool. At last a second bed, and a rough woolen blanket.

In the street, a woman calls out, her voice low with terror: *Sadina, where are you?*

Kandri wipes furiously at his arm. Then he crouches and begins to swab his boots.

There is a blaze of lamplight: half a dozen figures are crowding the door. Villagers, silent and gaping. The one with the lamp, an old man with a face like a shriveled plum, bends to peer at the corpse. Then his eyes stab up at Kandri.

"You son of a worm-eaten bitch! They are going to kill us!"

"Help me," says Kandri.

"Help you! We should cut off your balls! Or lock you in here and burn the place down. Save your army friends the trouble."

"The girl," says Kandri, "is she—"

"What girl, you talking turd?"

Kandri's head is reeling. "He was fucking her."

"And for that you kill him? Was she yours or something?"

"Not a whore. A *girl*. Didn't you see her?"

The change that comes over their faces is something he will never forget. They look at one another, naked with horror and revulsion. A woman hides her mouth in her hands.

"Sadina. Where is Sadina? *Athiri Ang*—"

Hers, the voice that had called in the street. She breaks and runs. Kandri points a finger: the doll has fallen to the bloody floor.

"I had to," he says. "She was screaming. Can't you see I had to?"

Silence. The old man passes the lamp into another's hands and steps up to Kandri. His eyes are streaming but his movements are precise. He looks at Kandri's blood-spattered clothes.

"Boy," he says, "you should kill yourself. Hurry and do it. For your own sake, not ours."

There are murmurs of agreement. *Kill yourself, kill yourself. Someone fetch him a razor, better this way than*—

A jolt, a whisper. Suddenly everyone is fleeing for the lives. Someone is coming; there can be no other explanation. In seconds, he is once more alone.

Except for one figure. A thin, sharp-elbowed woman, his age or slightly younger, has pushed forward while the others fled. Now she tears the blanket from his hands and spreads it on the floor. She takes the corpse by the ankles.

"Lift!"

He obeys, grabs Ojulan under the armpits. A bad dream. The head dangling, the mouth still open, the gleam of golden teeth. They place the corpse on the blanket, toss in his clothes and the doll and the mattoglin, the girl's clothes, the bloodied sheets. They fold the blanket shut and lift. The woman gasps, and he recalls the first time, his first body, the shocking weight of the dead.

They step out of the shack. The old man is waddling toward them with a bucket of water. He waves at them, frenzied.

"Run. Run. Take it away."

"Is the girl with her mother?"

"How should I know? *Harach*, Eshett, just get out of here!"

They run, Kandri and the woman, the leaden corpse swaying between them. Down alleys, through gates, over the tilled earth of lightless gardens, the young plants crushed beneath their feet. The moonlight weak and watery: he can barely see the woman, let alone the path ahead. Voices blow on the night breeze, clipped oaths, muffled cries. He braces for the roar of soldiers, the sudden barked command.

Or nothing. Arrows. We're obviously stealing, and thieves are shot on sight.

The walls about them vanish. Tall grass sighs around his legs. They have left the town and are thrashing across some fallow field. The woman falls, curses, rises with a groan. He can't recall if she has shoes.

He understands why they must do this, why they must bear Ojulan far from any home. The old man will be furiously cleaning, tidying, trying to wash away the blood. It will not be enough. The Prophet will have vengeance. If she cannot blame someone, she will blame everyone; she will put the whole village to the torch.

The grass turns to thickets. They pass through a dry wash and over a low hill, and then the woman drops the blanket, letting the corpse fall to earth. She bends double, utterly winded, her gasping so loud he fears it will give them away.

But there is no sound of pursuit, only the distant croaking of frogs about some wallow or water tank. And by the dim moonlight he sees why she has stopped. A shoulder-high barrier stretches across their path. It is a wall of beaten mud.

After a moment, she gestures at the wall. "This is the place. We'll heave him over. No one lives nearby."

"They'll find him."

A snorting laugh. "You think?"

He could almost laugh himself: the hopelessness, his idiotic words. This is Lord Ojulan. They will find him *anywhere*. They will peel the skin from the earth.

Now he can smell it. Ojulan's blood, soaking through his trousers, drying on the hairs of his forearms. He is shaking, he is damned. He sets his back to the cool mud wall.

They are common, these walls, the remains of cattle stockades from a time when the Mileya enjoyed more rain. The woman staggers about, catching her breath. After a moment, she nears him and brings her square-jawed face close to his own.

"Did he shove his prick in her?"

Kandri cannot speak, and so his silence speaks. The woman turns and kicks savagely at the corpse. She drops, stifling a scream, both hands gripping her foot. Kandri winces: she was shoeless after all.

"You kicked his mattoglin, I'm guess," says Kandri. "You're lucky you didn't break a toe."

"Maybe I did. *Togra katakuch!* The shithog. That girl is nine years old."

Kandri gropes for the edges of the blanket. Still cursing, the woman rises, and together they lift the body and tip it over the wall. A soft thud and a crackle of underbrush. It is done.

"I'm sorry," says Kandri.

The woman snorts again. "You just threw your life away, for a girl you don't even know. We call you names, threaten you, tell you to take your own life. And then you help with the corpse. You're sorry? We should be kissing your feet."

Kandri thinks of those moments of stillness, of cowardice. Staring at the cracked door, whispering his threats.

"The Pilgrim is returning," she says.

Her words startle him, although he already knows. The Pilgrim is the world's second moon. A nomad, it appears in the skies every twenty-one years, and stays barely a month. But in that brief season, nature loses her mind: darkness never falls, things weigh less than they should, ocean tides swallow the shore. Kandri has seen the Pilgrim only once, as a child of three. But he can still recall that reddish eye over the mountains, the trembling of the earth, and the feeling of precarious lightness, as though at any moment his small body could take to the sky.

This time next year it will all be happening again.

"What does the Pilgrim have to do with Ojulan?" he demands.

"Nothing, until you killed him," she says. "But there's talk of ruin next year, of madness. And there are signs already. People say the yatra strangled a man in his bed. Maybe that's a lie, but what about the other stories? A blue dog outside the temple, scratching at the door. And a rattlesnake, a sidewinder, curled up in the alms bowl, behind a locked door. The villagers are out of their heads with worry. They brought in an old priest to bless the town, but he just pissed everyone off. Instead of telling them how to stop the bad luck, he said it had barely started; he raved about death and blood and fire from the Gods, until no one could stand it anymore. We couldn't sleep. That old man had no mercy."

"What did you do?"

"Stopped feeding him. The next morning he was gone."

What is that accent of hers, singsong and bitter at once? Kandri cannot place it, but he knows he has heard it before—years ago, or decades.

In the darkness, a slurping sound: the woman is sucking the loose end of her sarong.

"Why are you doing that?" asks Kandri.

"Blood spots."

He's impressed: this woman means to survive. They get to their feet, and she leads him south along the wall. Somewhere ahead he hears the clanging of goat bells.

"Listen," he says, "was there a drug seller in the village tonight? A mean bastard, pushing wax?"

"You mean Skem?" she says. "Of course he was there. He arranges everything for Ojulan when that pig wants a young girl. Wanted, I mean."

Kandri draws a hand over his face. All so simple. A whiff of clove oil, a death. But what if he hadn't thought he was fighting Skem? Can he even pretend he would have found the courage to fight a Son of Heaven? Or would he have pretended to hear nothing, walked right by?

The image of the girl rises suddenly in his thoughts. Naked and so very tiny, like something skinned. What if they come looking for her in the morning? And this woman—

"You should get away from me," he says aloud. "Go back to the village and say nothing. I can find my way."

"To where? Back to the camp? You look like you've just slaughtered a bull."

He follows her. The mud wall ends and the land flattens out. Ahead, a low triangular structure looms out of the darkness. It is a simple sun-tent, for goats and their keepers. At their approach, five or six animals leap up and scramble away.

They are northeast of the village: he can see the brothels' glow. But no emergency beacons, no running torchbearers, light up Eternity Camp. "They haven't sounded an alarm," he says, amazed.

"They don't dare," says the woman. "Oh, they'll be sniffing around. But if they raised a stink and later find that he's just out whoring—well, Ojulan would slit their throats. He isn't supposed to screw around until six days after the feast."

"Why not?"

She shrugs. "None of the sons are. Don't you know? The Prophet told them it would bring bad luck."

Gods, thinks Kandri, maybe she *can* see the future.

Suddenly, the woman tenses. Kandri's hand flies to his machete. But it's just a boy, a village boy, running toward them like the wind. His bare feet spray earth at them as he slides to a stop.

"Eshett," he gasps. "Hurry, hurry, *je.*"

Under his arm is a tight bundle of clothes. The woman turns to Kandri. "Strip those things off, the boy will get rid of them. Faru, you run west to the short grass. Find a rat hole, a deep one. Stuff them in with a stick."

Faru?

Kandri steps closer. It really is the boy he rescued from Skem. He looks at Kandri with a mix of gratitude and fear.

"You have a wicked bite," says Kandri.

The child kneels and touches the ground with his forehead, a gesture of deepest respect. But his eyes are still fearful. "Oh, Gods," says Kandri. "I'm not the yatra. Skem just wanted another way to fuck with us. It was all he could think of to say."

The boy offers him the folded clothes. In broken Chilot, he says, "I kill Waxman, Uncle. One day in his sleep."

"No, no. Don't try."

"I curse him to burn, have pain forever. I stick the knife up his *mulit*."

"You want to curse him? Stay alive. Grow up and fight all the Skems in this world. Fight to stop them from existing. Eshett—that's your name, Eshett? Explain to him, will you?"

The boy nods vigorously. "Yes, Uncle, yes and thank you. Grow up, fight, stop existing. But first, I stick him dead."

"Gods damn it," says Kandri. "In a few hours, *I'll* be dead. A lot of people will be dead. Stay alive, you little shit. That's an order."

He takes off his clothes, reaches for the folded shirt and pants. *Uncle*. It is normal, an everyday honorific for an older man. But Kandri can't recall ever hearing the term applied to him. Most villagers call soldiers *Ghifi*, Protector, even if they've never witnessed a single act of protection. For Kandri, it is a source of abiding shame. No doubt Faru was still calling his attackers *Ghifi* even as they dragged him behind that wall.

Kandri freezes. The rough weave of the fabric, the weight, the feel of the buttons in the dark. "This is a uniform," he says.

"Of course it's a uniform," says the woman. "What did you expect, pajamas?"

"But where the hell did you get it?"

"From sisters," says the boy.

"Sisters?"

The woman looks out over the lightless plain. "I have a lot of them," she says. "I'm a whore."

Now it is she who is naked. The fury in her voice, the struggle. She forces out a laugh. "We help each other. One of your comrades is passed out drunk beside his girl. Ang knows what *he'll* wear back to the camp."

"And will your sisters cover for you tonight?"

"Fah," she says.

"Where will you go tonight? Where are the rest of your people?"

"My people? Get your pants on. Are you losing your mind?"

With that she leaves him, running back along the wall. Kandri dresses, looking down at the village. From where they stand, he can round it easily, in darkness, then follow the thorn fence back to the gate.

"Don't let them see you out here, Faru. Faru?"

He turns in a circle. The boy is a shadow, racing over the grasslands with Kandri's clothes, that burden of holy blood.

ᛒ

At the gate the sentries have been doubled. He walks straight for them in the center of the road. Empty-handed, terrified. Certain he looks deranged. *You're walking like an imbecile, a drunk.*

And suddenly, salvation. *That's perfect. A drunk.*

He twists his face into a smirk. He works his mouth, then forces out a song, lewd and low.

> *Oh, to warm my hands at midnight*
> *In the pockets of my girl*
> *In the sweet, secret pockets of my girl—*

They wave him by, scowling. They are worried, but not about Kandri Hinjuman. Once more, hope flares in his breast. He's a slob. He's enchanted. He staggers all the way to his tent and no one spares him a glance.

In the tent, there is no light whatsoever. A few men are murmuring; a great many lie asleep. He feels his way to his cot. How many soldiers went to the brothels tonight? Maybe two hundred? What if they never suspect him? What if no one fingers him at all?

He pulls the uniform shirt over his head. As his head emerges, the obvious answer materializes, a fiend's face in the dark. *What will they do? Burn the village, torture the villagers, torture the soldiers until they cough up names. False names, true names. Your name. Anyone's.*

Slowly, he puts the shirt back on. The few men awake have noticed his stillness; he can feel their unseeing eyes. Before Mektu's rashness started, they were never hostile. One or two were almost friends.

"Well. Goodbye."

He has not really spoken, only moved his lips.

☙

"You're serious."

"Do you still have the bush kits?"

"I think so. Yes, I have them. You mean it, Kandri? You're not fucking around?"

They stand in the darkness outside Mektu's tent, squinting, barely perceiving each other's faces; the only light comes from a distant security lamp at the end of the tent row. Kandri has a thick canvas bundle under his arm. His right hand grips a lanyard, to which are tied four leather faska, heavy with water. His left hand is twitching. His whole body aches with fear.

"I took a sunshield from the unit reserve," he tells Mektu. "And a long coil of rope—we'll need it for certain. I have three gold, true gold, from our Mother. All my pay's in *gham* coins; it's heavy, but we can't help that now. And we can't use the gate, of course: they'd never believe we were heading to the whorehouse with all this gear. But we can slide under the fence near the Pikers' latrines."

"Under the fence." Mektu blinks and rubs his forehead, perhaps still tempted to think this all a dream.

"The village dogs have scratched a hole there," says Kandri. "I saw it yesterday, on trench duty. They won't have fixed it so soon. It will be tight, but there's no other way."

His eyes are darting. He must not let them dart. Something is wrong, something is changing; the shouts of late-night revelers are too few. At the end of the tent row, two officers pass through the cone of lamplight, rushing somewhere with urgent frowns.

"Your boots?" says Kandri.

Mektu stares at his bare feet.

"Put them on. But wrap your feet first, we can't stop to deal with blisters. How much water is there, anyway?"

"In the tent?"

"Wake the hell up, Mektu. How much water in the kits?"

"Six faska each. Kandri, what time is it? We must be too close to daybreak. Unless—"

Mektu suddenly freezes. His eyes widen with disbelief. Kandri's chest tightens. *You know, don't you? You can see it in my face.*

"Brother," whispers Mektu, aghast, "have you stolen us some horses?"

"Oh, Pitfire, Mek. Get the Gods-damned kits. Now, please."

"Or camels? Camels are no good in the mountains."

"Get the kits."

"You know when we should run, maybe, brother? Week's end, just after dark, when everyone's bellies are full and the whole night's ahead of—"

Kandri grabs his brother's face with both hands, pulls him close, feels his nails biting flesh.

"Now," he says.

ॐ

The astonishing thing is how little it takes to seal one's fate. A blind fumbling around the wall of a latrine. A ground-hugging slither under the fishhook-tree fence, a scramble through the oily brush in the bottom of the trench. A few moments of almost suicidal blundering, their packs caught on brambles, items falling from their pockets, sticks loudly snapped underfoot. Curses, hysterical giggles. *Shut up, brother. You fucking shut up. You want to live or don't you? I'll be quiet if you—*

Mektu stops in his tracks. Kandri has started walking east. The desert? says Mektu's silence. Not the Valley, not home?

Kandri turns on him, growling: "We've *talked* about this."

"I know," says Mektu. "But I was just thinking, we could—"

"If you say 'draw straws,' I'll break your teeth."

"I wasn't going to," says Mektu.

And yet he stands there, wonderstruck, impervious to words. Kandri's stomach is churning. He is on the verge of tears.

I'll leave you. Ang as my witness, I won't stand here arguing until they wake up and surround us.

Then Mektu starts and looks at him anew. "We could get away."

"Yes! Come on—"

"I mean *entirely away.*"

"Yes, yes, yes! That's the fifty-times fucking idea!"

"Well, let's do that."

And suddenly his brother is running, and Kandri is beside him, laughing with terror and relief, and they are Soldiers of Revelation no more.

ဆာ

At fifteen, they went mad for a girl named Ariqina Nawhal.

Neither brother had yet spoken to her, but what of that? This was true love, and only one boy could claim her, and so they fought with fists and words and mocking laughter and lies. Kandri has forgotten much about that foolish war, but he distinctly recalls dragging Mektu's best pants through the filth of the chicken coop, and spotting his own school compositions book at the bottom of the outhouse hole. And the fistfight behind the kennel, egged on by four friends and nineteen hunting dogs. His swollen lip, Mektu's black eye, the fight's sudden end when one of the bystanders stepped backward into a rubbish pit and broke his arm.

Their feud was a nightmare for the family. Their sisters briefly took sides, then settled for even-handed contempt. Dyakra Hinjuman (who Kandri had by now come to cherish) implored the Gods to reveal how she'd earned such punishment. Their baby brother wept. He was large and plump and his voice was astonishing. At table, if no one else managed to break the tension, he would rest his face in his food and just howl. The family dogs bayed in sympathy. The Old Man would look from Kandri to Mektu and back again in bewildered rage.

One night, he exploded from his chair. It was so unexpected that both boys leaped up in alarm. Lantor Hinjuman grabbed them by the arms and hauled them out into the courtyard, scattering dogs and chickens. He made the brothers stand side by side. He ran his fingers through his hair.

"How many real sons do I have?" he demanded. "Just one—that screaming butterball. As for you two: I think gremlins came and snatched my two eldest from their cradles, and left me a Northy and a Southy in their places."

"Kandri didn't *have* a cradle, he had a pig trough," said Mektu.

The Old Man smacked him sideways.

"Horse trough," he said. "And that isn't true either, there was bedding, so shut up. Southy."

Mektu's eyes filled with tears, more from the insult than the blow. It meant the lesser of two bad specimens. The weaker of two runts.

Eighty miles south of Blind Stream, a deep rift called the Loro Canyon slashed through the Coastal Range. During the fall of the Empire, the central span of the great Loro Bridge collapsed, leaving two stone arches yearning for each other in vain. In like fashion, the villagers on either side of the abyss lost all contact with each other. Neither wall of the canyon allowed for a descent, and restoring the bridge was as unthinkable as learning to fly. So the villages turned their backs on each other. "Northies" married and traded with the folk of the Valley; "Southies" kept to the high country and married each other and devolved into crude, cruel dimwits—or so the Valley folk contend.

For well over a century, the two peoples grew apart. Then the Prophet arrived, and her army set about proving itself the equals of the vanished Empire. Five years and three hundred lives later, the bridge reopened, connecting the village for the first time in eight generations.

One might have predicted a joyous reunion. Not so. Competition for trade led to the first quarrels, but soon other conflicts arose. The slang of both groups had changed. Often these mutations were weird, but harmless. The Southy word *Eku?* ("What?") had come to mean "When?" north of the Loro, whereas the Southy *Eef?* ("What?") survived among Northies only as a request to speak up ("Louder, please?").

But sometimes, the confusion went deeper. Certain Northy phrases had changed among Southies into terms for sexual lust. This delighted just about everyone. In Eternity Camp, teasing Northy and Southy recruits was one of the durable joys of army life.

Northy woman: Is your husband thirsty? ["Would your husband like a fuck?"]

Southy woman: What?! ["When?"]

Northy: Right now, of course.

Southy: Are you insane?

Northy: Well! Forgive me for trying! And it's so hot today. ["I'm so horny today."]

Southy woman gapes, sputters.

Northy: See? You're looking flushed yourself. Maybe *you're* thirsty?

Southy: You damned dirty whore!

Northy: What?! ["Louder, please?"]

Southy: YOU DAMNED DIRTY WHORE!

And so on. The jokes no longer depend on linguistic truth; they have taken on a life of their own. But the mutual hatred of the Loro Canyon peoples is (and was) quite real. Kandri can still hear the Old Man's final rebuke:

"They were a family once. Now they're the laughingstock of Urrath. Is that how you want to end up?"

With that, he had gone back to his dinner, leaving them alone. Kandri will never forget the shame of that evening. But for his brother, the incident has always meant something else. *Southy.* That one word. Had their father chosen at random? Or had he known exactly what he was doing, when he labeled Mektu the lesser of his sons?

&

This is freedom: the stinking camp vanishing behind them, the pitch-dark Mileya underfoot, morning cold like a snakebite, the silence broken only by themselves. Sweet odor of gingerweed, memories of mountain dawns. Their path, due east. The faintest dab of milky light on the horizon, better than a guiding star.

But that light will grow into an enemy, Kandri thinks. Mektu is perfectly right: they have started hours too late. How far can they hope to get before the day reveals them, reveals everything? Before the Rasanga issue from the camp like devils on horseback?

They run parallel, long straight strides. The packs are enormously heavy; the water alone adds thirty pounds to each. Still, they are riding a wave of fear and elation, and Kandri feels he could run this way forever.

Mektu shoots him a sudden glance. "The Yskralem," he huffs. "The fucking Stolen Sea. That's your plan, isn't it?"

Kandri nods as he runs. "We have plenty of rope. The cliffs won't stop us, but they'll damn sure stop a camel or a horse."

"They might follow on foot."

Might. Kandri winces.

"Doesn't matter," he says. "We'll find places to hide. If we make it to those cliffs, we lose them."

"But we won't make it."

"Yes, we will. Shut your mouth."

As a soldier, Kandri has developed another useful schism: *That way lies death* can coexist in his mind with *That way I must go.* The ability has saved him more than once, given him the clarity to charge the enemy or to flee over swollen rivers, burning fields. He knows also that they are fast, both of them. Running, fighting, fleeing: they do it all with impressive speed. It is one reason, besides blind luck, that they have survived three years of war.

But horses are faster, and the cliffs lie sixteen miles off. Mektu is right again: they will not make it, unless no one bothers to look east, or the sun fails to rise.

He wrings more speed from his legs. *Idiot. Face facts.* Someone will look east. Wolfpacks (the army's term for death squads) will ride out on their trail. He and Mektu will be captured, miles before the cliffs. Before the day's end, they will be flung at the Prophet's feet. They will die screaming, mutilated, mauled. For the sake of a village girl, a stranger, a naked child in the dark.

"Mek," he cries into the wind, "we'll buy horses in Balanjé."

"What?"

"Balanjé, the village. We have to run through it, almost—"

"I know where Balanjé is! What kind of horses are we going to find in that dump?"

"Kind with four legs. What do we care?"

Balanjé, the last settlement, lies just three miles ahead. They can hope to reach it in darkness, or at worst half-light. And with horses, they will reach the cliffs in time.

There, already: the spur trail leading into the village. The ground is firmer, better for running. A whiff of a cookfire. Mektu, a few paces ahead, calls to Kandri over his shoulder:

"We'll steal the horses. We won't pay them a *gham*."

Right again: better to rob the villagers, leave them blameless. The thought brings Kandri another flash of understanding: they have not just become the Prophet's enemies. They have become enemies of all who love her, or try to love her, or pretend. Yes, this is freedom. They have escaped the madhouse by leaping from a high window, barely glancing at the earth beneath them, laughing as they fall.

☍

Balanjé. A village shrunken into itself, an ancient spot that never flourishes or dies. They hear the dogs first, then the wavering call of a milk-seller urging mothers to rise and unbolt their doors. *Pegri na clannet!* White and fresh! In the Sataapre Valley, the same cry announces daybreak. Once more, hapless fool, Kandri breaks into a grin.

The town rises before them, a congregation of humble rectangles and domes, mud-brick walls, goat pens, hayricks waiting for spring. And there are the dozens of low, squat towers that are Balanjé's only fame: prayer platforms, their flat roofs blazing in the first light of the sun. But Kandri sees no one atop the platforms, no sign of the morning prayer at all.

"*Pegri na—*"

Strange: the milk-seller has fallen silent in mid-cry.

They leap over a brush fence, and are at once in the heart of the settlement. Nothing moves. They turn in a circle, gasping. Not a soul to be seen. A door booms shut. A child cries out and is quickly silenced. Mektu looks at Kandri in distress.

"We startled them," says Kandri.

Mektu nods uncertainly. They walk along the main row of houses. Their footfalls ring loud in the empty air. A white cat flees before them. Windows go dark as they approach.

Kandri has been here before. All told, there might be two hundred homes, but some stand empty, for life is hard in Balanjé. The well is meager, the water tastes of mud. A twisted bonewood tree marks the village center. Standing near it, you can throw a rock beyond the last house in any direction.

"Where are the stables?" asks Mektu.

"I don't recall," Kandri admits.

Mektu steps up to a rude wooden door, smacks it with the flat of his hand. "*Daro, daro!* Come out, brothers. Don't you want to earn some gold?"

Silence; then a soft thump from within.

"I heard that," cries Mektu.

When Kandri tugs his arm, Mektu launches himself across the street to an adjacent house. This time he beats harder.

"Wake up, wake up! We're Chilotos, Chilotos like you. Help your brothers, for Ang's sake! I don't care who you're sleeping with."

The light is growing. Kandri glances over his shoulder, and sees a face draw swiftly back from a window. *Why are they so terrified? They can't possibly know.*

His brother, too, has begun to look frightened. Kandri points down the rutted lane: the old bonewood tree stands fifty feet ahead. They hurry toward it, and to Kandri's immense relief, he spots a figure seated beneath the twisted canopy.

It is a frail old man, bald and brown. His face is mushroom-shaped, cheekbones so much wider than chin. Shirtless, he sits on a rock beneath the tree, both hands gripping the knob of a battered cane. As they approach, he does not move so much as a finger. He is gazing up into the last of the dark.

"Hello, grandfather," says Kandri. "Please, can you tell us—"

"Stables!" blurts Mektu. "Are there any stables in this town? Any horses at all?"

The man sucks his dark lips into his mouth. His bony hands writhe on the knob of the cane.

Mektu bends over him and shouts: "Horses! Can't you hear me? Horses, or even a camel. We can pay, if that's what you're worried about."

Kandri crouches down. The man could well be four times his age. "Please, grandfather," he repeats.

The dry lips part. The old man speaks for half a minute, then taps the earth with his cane. The brothers look at each other. Kandri has not caught a word.

"He doesn't speak Chilot," says Mektu. "Son of a junkyard bitch!"

Kandri repeats their question in Kasraji. The old man responds in the same language.

"No horse can help you," he says. "It is *Darsunuk*, the Time of Madness. When the wise fall silent, and armies march against phantoms, and the Gods weep tears of fire." He lifts the cane and points at the sky. "I watch them, boys: the stars that wander, the stars that spin on heaven's wheel."

"Horses," says Mektu.

"Some call it the Everlasting Wheel," the old man continues. "They are ignorant. Nothing lasts. The spokes rot, the axle breaks, the cart is overturned, heaven's bounty spills by the roadside. And you"—he lowers the cane, pokes Kandri in the chest—"know this better than anyone. You can sense the fall of night."

Kandri stares at him, chilled. "The night's almost over, Uncle," he says, gently removing the cane.

"No," says the old man. "The night is just beginning. Save yourselves."

Mektu stamps his foot in frustration.

"He has to urinate," says the old man, "or perhaps he knows the truth. Run fast and run far, children. *Darsunuk* has come."

A thought flashes in Kandri's mind: the old priest the villagers brought to Eternity Camp, the one who frightened them half to death with his doomsday talk? Could this be the man?

What does it matter, though? "Let's get out of here," he says, and the brothers start away from the tree. But suddenly, Mektu turns on his heel and lunges at the old man. Seizing his arms, he shakes the old man like a gourd.

"Where are the *stables*, you daft, dried up, gibbering—"

"Pitfire, Mek, leave him alone!"

The old man, squirming, lifts his cane and points. The brothers whirl: thirty yards away by the settlement's edge is a mud-brick structure behind a listing fence. Mektu is off and running in a heartbeat. Kandri helps the old man sit up, mutters words of apology. Then he sprints after his brother.

The ground within the fence is hoof-churned mud. There is a sharp, comforting smell of dung. Mektu kicks open the gate, flies to the door of the building and wrenches. Then he curses as a rusty padlock rattles on its hasp.

Seething, he hurls himself against the door. It appears flimsier than the lock, mere scrapwood nailed to a frame. Inside, an animal snorts and stamps.

"Help me," growls Mektu.

Kandri steps up beside him, and together they throw themselves at the door. The wood cracks audibly; mud bricks shudder around the frame. They try again. And again. Kandri is painfully aware that dawn has come.

On the sixth attempt, the door bursts to pieces. Mektu falls into the building; Kandri tumbles to his knees, and rises just in time to see Mektu borne out again into the yard, his body folded over the head of an enormous bull. The creature bolts with him through the open gate, blind and bellowing, a long horn to either side of Mektu's ribs. When it throws him at last, he strikes the road with a doughy thump.

The bull careens off into the village, and Kandri rushes to brother's side. Already Mektu is struggling to stand. Kandri grips his arm, but his brother shakes him off. His mouth forms frantic, soundless words.

Kandri shakes his head. "Lie still, fool. The wind's knocked out of you."

He runs back to the barn. *Piss of the Gods!* Four goats and a rabbit hutch. He steps outside, retrieves his brother's pack. Mektu is on his feet now but remains doubled over, wheezing.

Kandri curses: the bottom of Mektu's pack is wet. "Broken faska," he says. "Well done."

Mektu is stamping his foot with the effort to speak.

"That bull could have killed you, brother. All right, what's so important? Just whisper."

Mektu stands straight.

"YOU MOTHERFUCKING SHIT-EATING PIG-ASS-FACED FUCK DOGS! GIVE US SOME HORSES! WE'RE YOUR FUCKING FRIENDS!"

He bends over and heaves. "That should work," says Kandri.

"Fuckers."

"We have to move," says Kandri. "We need more water, sealed faska or—"

He breaks off. Mektu straightens again, following his gaze. A figure is running toward them from beyond the northernmost houses. A woman. Mektu leaps and waves, but there is no need. She stumbles to a halt before them, gasping.

"You," says Kandri, not believing his eyes.

It is Eshett, the woman who helped him carry Ojulan's corpse. She has changed into a white *kanut* tattered and caked with dirt. In her hand is a rusty machete. Her eyes are wild with accusation.

"You hog," she says. "You followed me."

"Like hell I did," says Kandri. "What in Ang's name are you doing here? Are your people here?"

She is staring at his brother, her face appalled. Mektu, speechless, looks from one to the other.

"Why did you come?" Eshett demands.

"That's what I asked you," says Kandri.

"I have a friend here, a widow who needs help. I have a *reason*, something I can explain." She wrings her hands and shouts: "*Echim baruk!* You're dead men. They'll skin you alive."

"Kan," says Mektu, "what's going on here?"

"I can't hide you," cries Eshett. "This isn't my town. My friend's house is the size of a crate."

Kandri feels an explosion building in his chest. He holds out his hands, one palm facing each of them, begging for silence. "All we want," he says quietly, "is a horse. Just a horse, Eshett. There must be one. We'll pay for it, generously."

She shakes her head. "No horses. No camels either. One man had a mare but it was stolen. Tomorrow, merchants will be here for market day. Nothing sooner."

"We'll settle for a plough horse."

"No!" cries Mektu. "We can't outrun a Wolfpack on some lame old nag! What's *wrong* with you, Kan?"

"No plough horses either," says Eshett. "There's a salt wind from the Yskralem; they don't grow crops here anymore. You can't outrun a Wolfpack. You are going to die."

"Kandri, who the fuck is this bitch?"

Kandri thumps his brother in the chest. Eshett gives an exasperated hiss.

"There's a dust cloud on the western plain," she says, "It's not you the villagers are afraid of, it's that cloud. Death comes from that way, from Eternity Camp."

The brothers swear and start to run. But they do not know where to run. The woman stands watching their futile lurching. Mektu draws his knife. "How far, how far?" he screams.

The woman shakes her head: not far at all. Kandri's heart sinks into his boots. Then, wordlessly, Eshett takes his hand and tugs. Stunned, Kandri goes with her, and Mektu follows. What else is there to do?

They rush north out of the town. Mektu prances beside Eshett, spouting questions. Did you think of a hiding place? Who are you really? Are you sleeping with my brother? Are you pregnant, did you marry him, is that why you're here?

Eshett does not respond or even look at him. But when Mektu furrows his brow and cries, "I know you—don't I know you?" Kandri feels the convulsive tightening of her hand.

಄

Half a mile north of Balanjé is a plain of round stones, massive things six feet or more in diameter, all raised on earthen mounds and tilted to face east, like dead flowers still yearning for the dawn. Many are broken; some lie half-buried in the soil. Kandri sees a few dozen at a glance.

A chill travels his body. He is looking at a graveyard.

"Why are you slowing?" snaps Eshett, pulling him on.

"I don't see a hiding place. We can't lift those stones."

"Lift them?" says Mektu. "Why would we bother? That's a Tohru graveyard. No tombs under those things."

Kandri knows he is right: the Tohru people drain the blood from their dead and mix it with meal for their animals. They remove the organs and crush the bones inside the emptied flesh. Then they tie the corpses into small packages and bury them deep.

"The Tohru built this village," says Eshett, "but they've been gone for forty years. The Važeks took them north, starved them to death in the Theater of Bones. A few survived and tried to return, but by then, the Prophet had given their houses to you Chiloto. Hurry, come."

"Eshett," says Kandri, "let's talk about this."

"Talk?" She jabs a finger at the western horizon. There it is: the dust cloud. The Wolfpack on its way.

"But—it's *huge*," stammers Mektu. "There must be fifty riders." He looks hard at Kandri. "Tell me the truth, brother: does the Prophet *know* we're running east?"

"Of course not."

Mektu screws up his face in confusion. "When Terek ran, they only sent three riders to check the east road. Nobody runs this way. There's no water, nothing to eat. If she's sending fifty riders to check the crazy way, how many has she sent out overall?"

"I don't know," says Kandri, pleading. "How could I know, Mek? Who do you think I am?"

"You know something," Mektu insisted. "Just confess. Why is she trying so hard?"

"Keep standing there," says Eshett, "and you'll be able to ask them yourself."

She stalks away; they trail behind her like kittens. When they enter the graveyard, she moves from stone to stone, row to row, cursing and clearly more frightened with every step. At last her eyes find what they seek, and she runs to a large, crooked stone.

"In there, one of you. The other will hide with me."

She points: there is a hollow at the base of the stone. Little more than an animal's burrow. At the sight of it, a whole new fear blossoms in Kandri's chest. "What the hell is this?" he says.

"Graverobber's tunnel," says Mektu.

"Of course," says Eshett. "What did you think?"

"Never you mind what he thought," says Mektu. He is almost as afraid as Kandri, though for different reasons. It is shameful: on the battlefield, they have faced cutlass-wielding Važeks with blood to their armpits. And yet they stand shivering before a little hole under a grave.

"Isn't there someplace else?" Kandri asks.

"No, no!" cries Eshett. "Gods of death, can't one of you *move*?"

"What about—"

"Oh, shit." Mektu drops his pack and begins to wriggle, feet-first, into the hole. "Don't say that word, brother. Just don't say it. Go hide."

They crouch down, and Eshett smooths the earth behind him, hiding the struggle. "Keep going," she says. "At the very back they won't be able to see you at all."

"Unless they climb inside," says Kandri.

"Nice thought." Mektu's voice from the hole is strange and small. "Fifty riders. It just doesn't make sense."

He gives Kandri a last, puzzled look, then slides deeper and is gone.

ຂ

The mouth of the second burrow is several inches wider. Eshett enters first, holding her *kanut* tight against her body as she squirms. Kandri backs in behind her, dragging the backpacks in by their straps.

Do not panic. Do not scream.

The earth is cool and slick and much too close. It is too dry for worms, but there are spiders, beetles, whip scorpions, the rasp of an old hornets' nest.

He kicks her, apologizes. She guides him deeper, until the tunnel mouth disappears. With each least movement, a rain of dirt. It fills his clothes, his hair, finds its way into his mouth and eyes.

"Hush," she says, "You're breathing too hard."

And that is true: his own gasping will give them away. With a supreme effort, he slows his breath. They are at the back of the tunnel, as deep as they can go. Eshett pulls him tight against her, shameless. He can feel the whole shape of her body, and the cruel thought comes: *After all, she is a whore.*

In a whisper, she asks, "Is he really your brother, that shit?"

"He's my brother," says Kandri, "but he's not always so terrible. He has a good heart, when he shows it."

"He belongs in a cage."

"He carried me," says Kandri. "Off the battlefield, I mean. The others had left me for dead. But he falls to pieces when he's scared, and right now, he's scared out of his mind. It's not just the Wolfpack. He's afraid of flesh eaters, ghouls. And evil spirits—those above all. This yatra business at the camp—"

"You're afraid too."

"Not of yatras," he says. "Tight spaces, traps."

"Choking, drowning."

"That sort of thing."

"Something bad must have happened to you."

"Maybe we should talk *all about it*," says Kandri.

If she hears the reprimand, she gives no sign. "I am afraid of ghouls," she says. "Everyone fears them, even the Rasanga, even the Children of Death. And some ghouls do dig tunnels like these. But not here. The Tohru people do something to their corpses, once they've been drained and bound. Something ghouls hate. They're wise, the Tohru; they learned some tricks from the desert clans. Kandri, why didn't you tell Mektu about Ojulan?"

He jumps, and fresh dirt rains down on them. "That's my business," he says.

"All right."

"I couldn't tell him. You don't know him. We had minutes to get out."

"And maybe he would not have come with you?"

"Maybe not."

"All right. Be quiet now."

They lie there, two dusty spoons, her arms about him still. "Eshett," he whispers, "has my brother seen you before?"

Her body abruptly stiffens. "He fucked me," she says.

A long silence. He feels a sharp, unreasonable guilt, as if it were he, Kandri, who had gone to the whorehouse and bought this woman's flesh. And then forgotten.

"Sometimes," he whispers, "I could just about kill him."

Behind him, Eshett shrugs.

"It's true, what the madam tells us. Some men never look at your face."

∞

One day they drew straws for the right to love Ariqina. Needless to say, it was Mektu's idea.

He asked the gravedigger's hulking son to hold the straws. The older youth had one white eyebrow and a goiter like a potato on the back of his neck. He was considered slow but trustworthy; he had once found a gold coin in the shoe of a dead man and returned it to the widow.

They met behind the gravedigger's shack. The son warned them: "No good will come of this." But Mektu insisted, and even Kandri urged him on, hoping that the contest would deliver him from agony, either by granting him exclusive (albeit entirely hypothetical) license to kiss, copulate, marry, and grow old with Ariqina, or by killing him outright with the shorter straw.

It was the start of his third year in Blind Stream. He had a school uniform and a coin purse and a good pair of riding boots. He had kissed several girls and spied on others bathing, caught fish in Ashfield Lake, joined the brigade that beat back a wildfire threatening the school. He had even learned to swim.

But when he spoke to Ariqina, these triumphs vanished like dreams. She was a witch, he suspected. She had only to look at him, with that benign blazing intelligence, and he became witless with longing. She rarely blinked. She noticed if he twitched a finger. Her smiles were withheld until he gave her some reason to smile; then they took possession of everything: her dark lips and unkissed cheeks, the corners of her enormous eyes, the space between her and Kandri, his flesh, the daylight, the air in his lungs.

His brother claimed such feelings too, but Kandri refused to believe him. Mektu's hands groped at the bed sheets, or his thighs, whenever he lay back speaking of girls. It was no different when he spoke of Ariqina.

Face to face with her, he was amusing and chattered easily. He could make her laugh. Kandri mostly stood paralyzed, listening to her speak with quiet passion about something astonishing she had read. *There's a spider in the Nfepan jungles that cures leprosy with a bite.* What could you say to that? *There's a whale that lives on fish too small to see. In Dresheng, there are no royal families: when a sartaph dies, they choose a new one from the poorhouse. I was poor back in Nandipatar. I stole bread, I found things in the street. Have you tasted the cider this year, Kandri? My aunt gave me a little, I thought I'd die of happiness, I just shut my eyes and held it on my tongue, like this—*

"Draw, if you're going to," said the gravedigger's son, holding up a fist with two straws.

They drew. Kandri won. As the longer straw emerged, he felt a brightening of the skies.

Mektu demanded to see both straws, then accused the gravedigger's son of cheating.

"W-what? How?"

"You broke my straw with your thumb."

"Don't be an ass, Mektu," said Kandri, his heavens already darkening with crows.

"We can flip a coin," said Mektu. "There's no way to cheat with a coin."

Kandri shook his head. "Sore loser. Marry someone else. It's what you'd say if I'd lost."

"But you know he cheated!"

"Cheated! Why would I?" cried the big youth, stamping his foot.

Mektu glowered, as though the question were unfair. Finally, assembling the theory as he spoke, he said, "You . . . want her yourself. And so you want me out of the way. Ariqina doesn't care about Kandri, but if I'm the winner, you don't stand a chance."

The older boy's mouth fell open. His huge hands rose in fists. Kandri, taken by a strange impulse, jumped between them. But the gravedigger's son only turned, moist-eyed, and stomped into the house. Kandri had a moment to wonder if the young giant really might fancy Ariqina, who was kind to him as she was to everyone in the Valley, and then the boy's mother stormed out of the house and beat them both with a cane.

—

Somewhere outside the tomb, there is a shout. Eshett's arms clench about him. The voice is muffled by earth and stone but almost certainly a soldier's.

They lie rigid. Kandri is shivering slightly. Without her words to distract him, the panic tries to return. No air. Too little light. He should fear the Wolfpack, but what he fears is this dead soil around him, the black jaws of the earth.

Time passes. He grows desperately thirsty. He muses on the danger of opening his pack, digging out one of the remaining faska. Impossible; any small sound might give them away. But they could be here for hours! The sun will climb; its ruthless heat will inch along the tunnel, drill down from above. Could they last until nightfall? He will have to piss before nightfall. How can she have failed to think of such necessities?

He turns his head, whispers: "Eshett, I—"

Something with legs drops into his mouth. He gags, spits. But he has inhaled soil along with the creature, and now he is coughing uncontrollably, great body-shaking heaves. Eshett claws at him, begs him to stop. He thrashes. The air is full of falling soil and dust.

At last the fit passes. Eshett whispers curses in her mother tongue, then catches herself and stops short. Kandri's throat is burning. His eyes are full of grit he cannot clear.

A few terrible minutes pass. The panic waits in his stomach. Then they hear it: the dry earth pounded by approaching hooves. Men's voices, murmuring. The hooves slow. A shadow flits over the tunnel mouth. When it comes again, it remains. There is a sound of breathing.

"All right, soldiers. Come out of there."

The man's voice is soft and precise, and definitely familiar. Someone from the camp beyond all doubt. They do not move.

"I have four men with me, and sixty more in the village. You can't escape us. Come out."

They lie like the dead. The man sighs, and the shadow moves away. Then a new voice speaks into the hole.

"Kandri. Mektu. Get your asses up here *now*."

"Oh, Gods," says Kandri. "Oh, Ang's sweet tears."

Eshett gasps in horror when Kandri speaks, but he only laughs and starts to squirm from the tunnel. The voice is Chindilan's.

He wriggles forward. The Master Smith is kneeling by the hole. Beside him stands another soldier in riding boots. Two more, mounted, stand a few paces away.

"Uncle, how—"

"Just hurry, you fool."

Kandri emerges, grub-like, and Chindilan takes his arm and wrenches him from the hole. Kandri grins at him, almost weeping with relief. But Chindilan is not smiling, and the soldier on his left has drawn his sword.

"Steady," growls Chindilan, not releasing his arm.

The man beside him wears the insignia of a sergeant of the Shessel, the Prophet's lightning cavalry. Chindilan too is holding a weapon, some hideous axe. The two mounted men are also Shessel.

His smile gone, Kandri twists to look over his shoulder. And cries out in despair.

Beside the mound stands Garatajik, the Prophet's Secondborn.

Kandri's hand flies to his machete. The sergeant pounces, throws him flat on his back. A heel comes down on Kandri's weapon. But it is Chindilan, his beloved uncle, who raises the axe over Kandri's head.

"Don't kill him," says Garatajik.

That lilt, that schoolboy voice. He should have known it at once.

He wears a spotless white headscarf and *kanut*, and like all the Prophet's sons, a great emerald set in a chunky silver ring. Eyes wide, lips full and troubled. A distressed and thoughtful face.

Kandri looks up at Chindilan. "Backstabber. Shithouse dog. I loved you like blood."

"Kandri," says Chindilan. "Get your brother out of that hole."

"He's not in there."

Chindilan starts to kick him, almost viciously. "Kandri! We do *not* have *time* to fuck around."

Garatajik props his fine leather satchel against the burial stone, then steps nearer to Kandri and draws a short, broad-bladed knife. He looks at Kandri with wry fascination, as if the man below him were some kind of outlandish insect or frog.

"Which are you?" he says. "The quiet one, or the lunatic?"

When Kandri doesn't answer, he glances at Chindilan. "Kandri's quiet," says the smith, "and his brother's not exactly mad, my lord."

"I know that also," says Garatajik, probing their bush kits with his toe. Once more, he catches Kandri's eye. "An abused notion, madness. Like cold. It is not really there, you know; cold is just a thing we feel when heat is gone. A void, as it were."

Kandri breaks into another fit of coughing.

"Madness too is a void," says Garatajik. "My position in life has given me occasion to look into that void. Rather longer than is strictly healthy. A foul netherworld it is, a maze of few hopes and fewer exits. And yet we shut the poor lunatics away in further cages: the asylums, the dark, infested wards. I can hear your brother squirming, Kandri. Call him out."

Kandri shakes his head. "Mektu's not in there, my lord."

Garatajik looks at him thoughtfully. "Sanity, in my estimation, is merely oil in a lamp. You burn it, you light your way. But there's only so much to go around. Your supply can be exhausted." He smiles, wide white teeth. "And then you're truly fucked."

He glances at the sergeant. In a quick movement, the man twists Kandri's machete from his grip and tosses it away.

"The quiet one," says Garatajik. "You had an interview with my mother. You're afraid of drowning, but you wouldn't tell her why."

The sergeant turns sharply, as though noticing a sound. He squats before the tunnel and peers inside.

"My lord, there's a woman in there!" he says. "*Harach*, get out here, you!"

"Keep her quiet," says Garatajik. "Tell her she won't be touched."

Kandri hears Eshett scrambling from the hole. She crawls into his field of vision, face clenched in horror, caked with mud. "Devil's teeth, she's one of the village floozies," says the officer. "Don't scream, girl. Kneel down."

She kneels; his sword is close to her neck.

"Where is that amusing Mektu, then?" says Garatajik. "We have searched the graveyard and found only a few empty tunnels. Has he fled?"

"My lord, we must make haste," says Chindilan. "The others—"

"Quite right," says Garatajik. He crouches, takes his knife in a stabbing grip, and lowers it, until the point touches Kandri's chest. His gaze is fierce.

"Did you kill my brother Ojulan, corporal?"

"No, no, my lord, I'd never—"

"Did your brother kill him?"

The poised knife. The heavy axe. Kandri shuts his eyes, but that is worse: a flood of dreams and faces, a path to the future, hopes too beautiful to bear. The temptation is a thousand times stronger than the moment with Idaru and the ash locust. To solve the problem of Mektu! With a single word. With a nod of the head.

He opens his eyes. The world is bright through his tears.

"I killed him," he says. "My brother ran with me because I asked him to. He had nothing to do with Lord Ojulan's death. He doesn't even know."

"You killed Ojulan?"

"Yes, my lord. With my machete, in the dark. This woman, she's innocent too, she's—"

"Enough."

Garatajik sheathes the knife and straightens. Chindilan lowers the war axe, and the Prophet's son extends his hand.

"My mother would not show us the corpse, you see. I don't greatly care who did it. Just as long as the beast is dead."

Kandri sits up. The world has gone senseless, the men around him are counterfeits, or ghosts. The sergeant releases Eshett. Chindilan is smiling now—a crazed smile like the grimace of a bear.

"Hinjumans!" he says. "Walking Gods-damned calamities, every one of you! Where's Mektu, damn your eyes?"

"I think," says Garatajik, "that I shall need a few minutes with this man."

He turns to the pair of riders. "Return to the village," he says. "Tell the Pack we have a lead at the gypsum mines. Take them all; we will join you presently. Hurry, now, and see that there are no stragglers."

The riders wheel their horses about and set off for Balanjé at a gallop. Then, as Chindilan watches from a few feet away, the Son of Heaven crouches down beside Kandri.

"Have no fear. Both the riders and this good man"—he nods at the sergeant—"are as loyal to me as your uncle here. *They* will not betray you. Alas, the remaining sixty riders I led to Balanjé would slay you in an instant. Their hearts belong to my mother, you see. Like most of the half-million Chiloto in this world."

"My dearest lord, you—"

"When my body came of age," Garatajik continues, "I kept the matter to myself. But not Ojulan. He woke the household, shouting about his wet dream, exultant at the stain on his bedclothes. He deserved women now, he told us, and would fight for his share. He sent word to our mother in Techerepind, demanding young girls to practice on. The next day her answer came: *Give him anything he wants.* Ojulan began to scream for his pleasure: 'Two brown girls, two olive. All clean, and none too skinny!' Our eldest brother, Jihalkra, had his men build wooden frames. Girls were tied to these frames with their legs apart. For Ojulan's safety, you understand.

"Later that year, his pleasures took a darker turn. He began to kill the ones who displeased him. Then he asked for a new job: to rid the province

90

of 'ugly girls' before they grew old enough to breed. My mother did not endorse this idea; she merely frowned and told him to be discreet. He was not discreet. He killed two girls that first evening, and only stopped when I convinced him that killing so many innocents put him in danger. That the helpless become just the opposite in death—in short, that their ghosts would shrivel his manhood. I spun the tale in desperation, over the body of the next girl he meant to stab. And that night I began planning my escape."

He spread his hands. "I have not escaped. Oh, I left all this behind for a while—studied the arts of the enemy, as I told my mother, though in fact I found more friends than enemies in the east. I came to love their great cities, their blessed libraries, their songs. I was happy in those lands, but my soul remained caged. The more I learned of the world, the less I could bear the thought of my family's desecrations. I grew ill, then almost mad for a time, and the madness only lifted when I resolved to come back and fight. Now I doubt if shall ever truly escape. But I will stop them, stop her. You will hear of it, no matter how far you run."

"My lord, we're still in danger," says Chindilan. "If someone sees us here, a villager, a child—"

Garatajik waves for silence. "Listen, boy: did you take my brother's mattoglin? If so, I should like it back."

"I don't have it, my lord," says Kandri. "I left it on his body. I didn't kill him for the knife."

The older man studies him a moment. "I'm told it was gone when they found him. It's worth a fortune, of course. But you'd be foolish to keep it. That knife is a legend, and could make you a target even for those who would never willingly help the Prophet or her cause."

"I left it, my lord! Jekka take my soul if I lie! Besides, Uncle Chindilan told me it was cursed."

Garatajik looks at Chindilan, who shrugs. "Ojulan believed it to be cursed, my lord. But he said that the Sons of Heaven were immune to such hexes."

"Evidently not," says Garatajik. "Well, that is a pity. Our mother will post a substantial reward for the mattoglin—nothing like the one for your heads, but substantial—and I might have arranged for it to go into the coffers of her enemies. They are mostly empty, those coffers. I have little funds of my own.

"But to your plight. I shall report that we found no trace of you here. I have already made arrangements for your family. They may not suffice to protect them, but they were the best I could do at a moment's notice. I can't give you a horse, either: how would I explain the loss of it? Besides, you have no means of lowering a horse into the Yskralem."

"Is *that* where you're going?" says Eshett suddenly.

The four men turn to look at her.

"You can't," she says. "There's nothing that way. Just salt, heat, ghouls, animals. And the ghosts of fishermen. You're not ready for the Yskralem. You'll die."

"I wish you'd stop saying that," Kandri tells her.

"Do not reprove her," says Garatajik. "There are Ornaq vultures in the Stolen Sea. And worse beyond, though you may find some respite in the green Lutaral. On the East Rim, there is an actual city, believe it or not. But unless you make nothing but wise decisions henceforth, you'll never live to see it. Do you hear me, boy? Never, except as meat in a vulture's stomach, or dust on the wind."

He turns and walks back to the satchel beside the burial stone. "Travel at twilight, or in darkness," he says, "If you walk in the sun, you'll sweat out your water before you're halfway across. Tell me, have you served in a desert campaign?"

"I've served in the Gathen Wastes, my lord."

Garatajik shakes his head. "Then you've seen nothing. That's unfortunate. You listen to this girl of yours."

"I'm not his girl," blurts Eshett. "I'm not going *anywhere* with these fools."

Garatajik looks at her with a hint of suspicion. Then he shrugs and waves his hand. "Get back in that hole, then, while we clear out. I can't think what else to do with you. As for the killer—"

His black eyes fix on Kandri. "You may think this first desert, the Yskralem, is far enough. It is not. The Lutaral beyond is not far enough, nor the depths of Misafa Wood, nor the distant peaks of the Baluk Range. My mother has lost her favorite son, and her wrath is beyond description.

"Still, you were wise to run east. I thought you might. Anyone clever enough to ambush my brother in a house where not even the Prophet knew to seek him is clever enough to flee in the right direction."

Kandri looks at Chindilan, beseeching. *Ambush?*

"For what is the alternative?" says Garatajik. "You could throw yourself on the mercy of the Važeks; but you are the Prophet's man, and they will show no mercy. You could make for the deep wilds of the South—but that journey would require weeks or months of travel in lands my mother now controls, and nothing but lethal jungle at the end of it—and again, no likely welcome from its peoples."

"My Lord speaks the truth," says Chindilan. "The forest clans already fear us. The Prophet wants lumber; they have trees. If they refuse to sell, she drives them from their land with raiding parties."

"We are years from conquering those people," says Garatajik, "but they have learned already that the price of freedom is constant terror. And terror has your eyes, young assassin."

Assassin. Kandri gazes up at him, wanting to deny the word, to explain his predicament. But how can he? And what does it matter who believes him? Assassin or fool, he has killed a Son of Heaven. There can be no forgiveness; he is a man marked for life.

"Your one hope," says Garatajik, "is to vanish into the Great Desert, the Land that Eats Men. Reach *that* desert, and you leave the Prophet's world behind you. It is winter. Caravans will yet be crossing, before the killing heat. Join one, I implore you. Reach the Great Desert, and live.

"And now get up. Make some room in those packs. I have some things for your journey, and one item you must treat as priceless. If you will consent to—"

A snarl, a gasp. Mektu has appeared out of nowhere. His face is exultant. He seems to be embracing Garatajik—but no, the Prophet's son is bleeding. Mektu has stabbed him in the ribs.

The older man claws at his attacker. Mektu pulls the knife free and leaps back from the blood. Garatajik sways. His knees bend. He drops sidelong against the stone.

For an instant, no one moves. Then Chindilan looks at the cavalry officer and drives the hilt of the war axe into his stomach. The man doubles over, and Chindilan strikes him again between the shoulders. As the sergeant falls, Chindilan whirls on Mektu in a rage.

"You dumb savage shit! You've killed us all!"

His words shock Kandri into action. Falling to his knees, he tears open Garatajik's *kanut* and fumbles for the wound. He cannot tell if the man is breathing. Chindilan bends and lifts Garatajik at the torso. Kandri rips the scarf from the victim's head and winds it around his chest.

Blood through the white cloth, a red flower opening—

From behind them, Mektu sputters, "I saved you, Kandri, I had to, I needed to!"

"You hear that?" says Chindilan. "Your brother saved us. He's a fucking hero is what."

"That's Garatajik," says Mektu. "That's her son!"

"Bastard!" Chindilan makes as if to smack him. "One dead and it's curses and Wolfpacks. Two, and I don't even fucking know. Holy war."

Mektu's hands are quivering. "I'm a dead man, I'm a stain in the dirt, I should just kneel down and—two?"

"Did you hear something?" says Eshett.

"Two dead, Uncle?"

"Be *quiet*, Mek," says Kandri. "Listen: we're not crossing the Stolen Sea. We'll head west, angle back toward the mountains."

"You know that's hopeless," snaps Chindilan. "You're sounding cracked as your brother all of a sudden."

"We can make it," Kandri insists. "We can hide in the mountains. Trust me!"

"It doesn't *matter* where I go," says Mektu. "They'll chase me down the throat of the devil. They'll chase me to the back of the moon."

"Someone's coming!" whispers Eshett. "Kandri, shut him up!"

Mektu stops his raving, and Kandri hears them: men's voices, calling for Lord Garatajik. Eshett scurries to the next grave and peers around it. Shock takes her instantly, and she flies to them, her terror as clear as any scream of warning. *Too many, too many, run!* They dive for their packs and the bag from Garatajik and flee west, darting from mound to mound. They leave the Prophet's Secondborn sprawled in his own blood beside the moaning rider.

But as soon as the scene of carnage is out of sight, Kandri veers north. "What's wrong, can't you decide?" cries Eshett.

Kandri doesn't answer. Speed now as important as stealth. Very soon, he changes course again, this time sharply east.

"Brother, what are you doing?" cries Mektu. "You're taking us back toward the Stolen Sea!"

Chindilan's face brightens with comprehension. "The rider. He was conscious, he was listening. And he'll say we're running for the mountains, if he talks at all. You devious bastard, Kandri! *Harach*, there's still a chance."

They fly over the barren Windplain, the parched earth and brittle scrub. Sometimes, Kandri is able to lead them down along a dry wash, hidden from eyes above. The heat like a poured resin. The miles slide by.

When they pause for breath, Mektu gabbles: "You can't blame me. I thought you'd been taken prisoner. I thought you were about to die." Kandri looks at him without warmth, without forgiveness. Chindilan does not look at him at all.

Mektu grabs at Kandri's arm. "I can hear them!"

"No, you can't. Be quiet, rest."

"What did he mean, brother? One is curses, two is war?"

"I didn't mean anything," mutters Chindilan.

"That's a lie," says Mektu. "Gods of Death, this whole family's addicted to secrets! Papa runs off to the desert twice a year. I get mauled by a yatra and they all hush me up."

"For your own sake, that was," says Chindilan.

"Some barefoot kid turns up on the doorstep, and they say, 'Here's your brother, sorry we never mentioned him.' Ari disappears, and Papa acts like he's the reason why."

"Ari?" says Eshett.

"Ariqina, my girl."

"Mektu," says Kandri, "shut your mouth."

"And now this," Mektu continues. "I heard you, Uncle. 'Two and it's holy war.' Go ahead and explain that one. I'm listening. Prove me wrong."

Neither man takes the bait. They share a faska, knock pebbles from their shoes. Flies swarm their hands, drawn to the blood of Garatajik the Merciful, and Eshett looks east and says they will be famous, hated above mere mortals, devils made flesh.

☙

It is true that the Old Man acted strangely when Ariqina disappeared. His mild swagger turned to melancholy; he looked like a man sentenced to death. Watching him, Kandri's thoughts flew to the worst. But Dyakra Hinjuman banished those particular fears.

"He never so much as glanced at her in that way, child. Believe me. I know the ones he did."

Nonetheless, his second mother had forbidden him to plague the Old Man with questions about Ariqina. Stranger still, Uncle Chindilan had come to Kandri the next day with the same command.

"He doesn't know what happened to her, Kandri. For the love of Ang, drop the subject."

"If you don't want me talking to him, talk to *me*," Kandri countered. "What's wrong with him? Is it just memories? Did he lose someone at my age?"

Chindilan's eyes flashed with rare anger. "Just memories, is it? Just the harmless fancies of the old."

"I didn't mean it like that, Uncle."

"Yes, you did. I know how this works. The young don't have the courage to see their elders as real. To see them at all, if we're honest. To admit that they're fucking alive."

"That's not true," cried Kandri. "How can you think that, Uncle? I never—"

"Forget it," said Chindilan. "Yes, he lost someone. When he was much younger than you."

The smith turned and cracked his knuckles, looking mad enough to spit. But his hands were trembling.

ॐ

Sand becomes clay. Their footfalls ring like uncertain applause. They are running straight into hard, white light: the eye-wounding brightness of sun on salt. Kandri squints but cannot see the edge of the Yskralem: the horizon is simply too bright to look at.

He mops his face with the tail of his shirt. His mind full of voices, nagging, severe. His mother weeps: *Ang, Great Goddess, you've made assassins of my sons.* The Old Man's rejoinder a verbal shrug, hiding his disappointment. *What did you expect of those two?*

Ariqina hides nothing. She whispers in his ear: *You can't be a killer. Not you. A part of heaven lives within us, Kandri, under the flesh and the stink and the shit. Our job is to find it. What good are we if we can't find it?*

They snatch two minutes' rest in the shade of a long-ruined hut. Gasping, light-headed. Salt rimes the stones about them like hoarfrost.

"Uncle," says Kandri, "what did he mean about arrangements for our family?"

"He sent his own man to question them," said Chindilan. "Beyond that, no idea. Maybe he'll try to bundle them off to Nandipatar, or someplace even further—the Cotton Towns, perhaps. At least they'll have some good whiskey in their old age."

"Be serious," hisses Kandri, miserable with shame.

"Serious?" His uncle shrugs. "Garatajik's man will likely burn the house down and tell the Prophet they're dead. That's what I'd do."

"When did Lord Garatajik—"

"Recruit me? Five weeks ago. Five damned-to-the-Dark-Gods weeks." He casts a smoldering glance at Mektu.

"And that rider you hit?" asks Eshett. "Wasn't he a friend?"

"Of course," says the smith, "but what could I do? Bring him with us? No, it was kinder to make it look as though he fell defending Garatajik. They may not believe it, but it's the best chance he has."

"We could have done the same to you," says Kandri. "We still could, maybe. You don't have to run."

"The devil's ass I don't. The Old Man was my best friend. Without Garatajik to vouch for me, I'd be thrown straight to the worms, boy. I'd be first in line."

And Eshett would be next. Kandri draws a hand over his face. She has no choice now either. With a Son of Heaven murdered in Balanjé, the army will seal off the village, search it house by house. Some soldier would recognize Eshett from the brothel; certain villagers, badgered long enough, would say they saw her go to the two standing by the vylk tree, screaming for a horse. If they had not marked Balanjé with blood, she might have stayed there with her widowed friend. Now there is nothing for her but flight.

Eshett seems to guess the drift of his thoughts. She points at him sharply. "If we live, you take me back to my village. Six days east of the Stolen Sea."

"That's fair," says Kandri.

"And when we get there, you stay hidden in the bush. I'll bring food, then you leave. That way, no one has to lie if the Prophet's men come calling."

"What's the name of your village, anyway?" asks Mektu.

Eshett's glance is hard as stone. "You've never heard of it," she says.

They race on. The salt coating the rocks begins to creep across the land like a skin. Where are the cliffs? He shields his eyes, but it's no good; he is dazzled no matter how he tries to look east.

At first the salt-skin cracks underfoot like brittle ice, but soon it grows stronger, smoother. And then Chindilan shouts out the words they've all been fearing: "Here they come."

Kandri does not look back. He can hear the hoofbeats, ringing as if on stone. The Wolfpack has seen through his deception—or guessed at least that they *might* have been deceived—and divided to cover all paths from Balanjé.

He takes Eshett's arm and pulls her faster: she is the slowest of the four. But why bother? They can't outrun horses, and at the cliff's edge, they'll need time to secure the ropes. Still, he shouts at them, *Faster, damn you*, and they plunge on into the dazzling light.

All the land is salt, now, a clean, solid skin. Like running on the surface of an egg. Kandri hears that strange falsetto cry, mournful and chilling, that has somehow become the army's prelude to slaughter:

Oorlulu-Kralulu-Kelulu-Lhor!

He sees his brother glance back, sees terror bloom in his face. "Six of them, Kan," shouts Mektu, "with bows."

Six riders, fresh from camp. Marksmen, possibly. Able to cut them down from a distance, without dirtying their hands. Kandri winces. He sees himself stopping Eshett, bending her over, beheading her with one well-aimed blow. Then Chindilan. Then Mek, who would watch him sidelong. Then his own life, his own stomach. If he can do it. If he has time.

Something ahead: a fractured line across their path. Are his eyes failing? Is that the cliff's edge he sees?

From behind comes the howl of a pursuer: "Death! Death to abomination! Let the earth drink their blood!"

The words break something open in Mektu. He stops running, whirls with machete raised, screaming a wildcat scream. Beside him, Chindilan too pivots heavily, raising his axe, hurling madness at their attackers with his roar.

No choice. Kandri lets go of Eshett and turns on his heel, whipping his own blade from his belt.

The riders are within a hundred feet. Their horses seem to fly above the salt-crust. Five cavalry, nocking arrows to bows. And at their center, one Rasanga, one Innocent Dreamer, huge upon his stallion, sword whirling overhead. The other five are howling, crazed for slaughter. The Rasanga's face is cold.

The riders take aim. Suddenly, Kandri is possessed by mad indignation: *to die full of arrows like a pig*. He doesn't know what drivel he is screaming, Kill fuck blood, or where he finds the strength to charge. But Mektu and Chind-ilan have found it too. They are attacking together, and will die together. No one will be tortured in Eternity Camp.

Arrows fly. Mektu screams in agony. The gap is nearly gone; the archers shoulder their bows and draw their swords. They will be ribboned, slashed to bits. Kandri's rage is also grief, he is choking on it, he says goodbye to Ariqina Nawhal.

There is a sound like the breaking of bone.

The horses vanish to their necks. They have fallen into the earth, and the riders are dashed with hideous violence to the ground. An air pocket, a cavity beneath the salt. Strong enough for four to have crossed without incident, but not six men and horses. Now the animals are thrash-ing, screaming, and the men are impaled, great salt fragments like window shards driven into their limbs, chests, faces. Some are crushed beneath their broken-limbed steeds. Others, luckier, are clawing at the edges of the pit.

"Kill them! Kill them *now!*"

Chindilan swing as he bellows, and his axe splits a man's grop-ing arm like a length of cordwood, hand to elbow. Then the Rasanga springs from the earth with a leopard's grace, blood-blinded but still attacking, still horrible, and Kandri and Mektu leap into the fray, and everything is simply hell. The Rasanga a blur, a flywheel, a madman with dagger and sword. Horses screaming, wild arrows from the pit, a severed arm gripping Mektu's ankle, new cracks spreading under their feet. The Rasanga prays aloud, and he is winning, he has reduced them to parries and retreats. His eyes serene. His every blow a little nearer the mark. *Her feet touch heaven*, he sings. His dagger kisses the corner of Kandri's eye.

Then it's done. They're the victors. Chindilan's axe has missed Mektu's face by an eyelash, but not its target. The Rasanga twitches, spraying them with blood. His head lolls back on a flap of skin.

When he falls, no one speaks. They are numb with amazement. The three of them still standing, and Eshett untouched.

ॐ

One of the horses, having somehow extricated itself, limps away across the plain, dragging a dead man by one stirrup. They slaughter the other animals, ending their agony.

"The Gods must truly love you," says Eshett, pointing at the body of the Rasanga. "What a monster. I didn't think he could be killed. And look at you, you're just fine."

Fine. The men bark with ugly laughter. They're in agony, shaking with it, nauseous: every wound is full of salt. But it's true, they're not dying. The cuts are mostly superficial; they have traveled with worse.

"He almost took us," says Mektu. "All by himself, and wounded. If any of those other bastards had climbed free—"

"They weren't Rasanga," says Chindilan. "I'd rather have fought all five of 'em than that son of a devil's whore."

"That one the horse is dragging?" says Mektu. "That was Ithim, from Sharp's Corner. The one who bet me I couldn't spell 'Mektu Hinjuman' backwards after drinking a whole bottle of—"

Kandri grabs Mektu's elbow. His brother twists and looks down. An arrow is snapped off in his ribs.

Eshett hisses through her teeth.

"What, didn't you *notice* it, you mad jackdaw?" says Chindilan.

"I noticed, of course I noticed, I forgot," babbles Mektu. He gazes, fascinated, at the shaft in his side. Cautious, he reaches out to brush it with a finger—and howls in agony, face raised to heaven. Kandri clamps a hand over his mouth.

"Gods of death, brother! They'll hear you at the gypsum mines."

When the fit passes, he is gasping, but his face is oddly calm. He takes a firm grip on the arrow and shoves.

His skin stretches at a point behind the wound. The other three hold him steady. Mektu howls again and a bronze arrowhead splits his flesh from the inside. Kandri leans in awkwardly, clamps his teeth on the arrowhead, and pulls.

By Ang's mercy, the head is not barbed. Out it slides with nine inches of shaft—*all* the remaining shaft, Kandri prays. He spits. Mektu is grinning. When they flush out the wound with spirits, he does not even scream.

"You were angry when I stole the bush kits," he says. "Are you still angry, brother?"

Eshett threads a surgical needle. Mektu, looking triumphant, watches her begin to sew his flesh. "They're full of medical supplies, did you know that, girl? Wound spirits, bandages, limb splints, scurvy powder, spider gall. And waspwort. And tooth powder. We wouldn't last a week without the bush kits. I'm right this time. Why can't anyone say it when I'm right?"

'You're right," says Kandri, turning away.

"And tooth powder. I know when I'm right! You think I need you to tell me?"

"Sew his mouth shut when you're done there," says Chindilan.

"Girl," says Mektu, suddenly sly, "I know why you look familiar. You have a vegetable cart."

"Stop moving!" snaps Eshett. "Kandri, make him behave!"

But Kandri has begun to loot the corpses. Some coins of fine, unalloyed gold. Dry meat wrapped in fish skin. And seven faska, more precious by far. He selects one, lifts it, hesitates. The prayer flows unbidden through his mind:

Beloved Prophet, envoy to the Gods.
By your intercession their wrath becomes tenderness.
By your grace I fill my cup.

He wipes away the blood and drinks.

ಬಿ

Only three persons know the truth about his fear of drowning. One was with him at the time. Another, the blind cook who came down with him from Candle Mountain, listened to the tale and then wrapped him in her arms, as she had done years before when he was frightened of nightfall.

It is very big, the darkness, she had murmured. *But it is only a stomach, not a mouth. It cannot swallow you without your permission. I know this, child. I am in the dark all the time.*

The third person is Mektu, who had tried for years to wear him down with questions. "It happened after you came to live with us, right? You weren't afraid at the seaside, when I taught you to swim. Did those Sharp's Corner bastards hold you down in a cattle trough? Did you fall into the Sataapre, hit your head on a rock?

To such pestering Kandri never yielded a word. But one day Mektu inquired with such unusual gentleness that Kandri decided to tell him everything. Mektu had stood speechless, which almost made it worthwhile. He never raised the subject again.

Nor had Kandri ever again shared the story. Dyakra Hinjuman asked and learned nothing. His inquisitive sisters, nothing. He even managed to hide his secret from the Prophet.

Kandri's stubbornness on that last occasion had terrified his father. It was on their third full day at Eternity Camp. The Old Man had accompanied the boys from Blind Stream and was still lingering about the base, mostly in Chindilan's shop. Late that afternoon, he and Kandri were summoned to the Prophet's house in the palace compound. She kept them waiting outside for forty minutes, watching the light bleed from the Gallows Courtyard, listening to the shrieks of her baboon.

Such interviews with the Prophet were not unheard of. She had an extraordinary memory and liked to stock it with details from her soldiers' lives. Where had they lived? What foods were they raised on? Had they fished? Had they ever skinned a coyote? How often did they rise to urinate in the night? How long did coitus last? Did they ever think of the Gods during coitus? Did they dream of the victory of Orthodox Revelation?

No one knew just how much she retained of their answers. And perhaps that was the point: she asked everything; therefore she might know anything. Safer to assume that she did.

When the doors opened at last, a half-dozen enormous Orthodox Guard had searched them head to foot, confiscated their shoes and headscarves, and slipped red mittens over their hands. The mittens were famous in the camp: made of thick cowhide and joined at the wrists, they were fastened with fine chain and padlocks. One could, with difficulty, grip a bowl or cup, if the Prophet should honor you with an invitation to dine. But little else.

The mittens were just one security measure, of course. Another, darkly rumored, was a silent dwarf from the Opapku clan, a being without name or tongue or genitals. This dwarf was said to lurk unseen in the shadows whenever the Prophet had visitors, and to possess some means of killing so swift and certain that no other bodyguard was needed.

They entered, alone, and Kandri almost stumbled: the room was dark enough to hide any number of dwarves. The Enlightened One sat on the floor behind a low table upon which three small candles burned. Sleepyhead, the white baboon, was chained a few yards to her right. The doors closed. They sat down awkwardly before her, mittened hands in their laps.

"This is the eldest, Lantor?"

His father inclined his head. "Kandri Hinjuman, Your Radiance. My son and your proud servant."

Kandri, astounded, suppressed an urge to turn and stare at his father. *She knows your name*, he thought.

There were no further pleasantries: the Prophet turned to Kandri and launched into a string of questions, which he tried in good faith to answer. *Why do you wish to be a soldier?* To hasten Urrath's liberation, Your Radiance. *What weapon feels best in your hand?* The machete, Your Radiance. *Could you kill a man with your machete?* Yes, if Your Radiance requires it. *How do you know that? Have you killed already?* No, never, but your Radiance, for our people, I'm certain that— *Yes, so am I. What is your birth sign, corporal?* The Well of Fire, Your Radiance; I was born under a red full moon.

"The Well of Fire!" she said. "Auspicious indeed. Tell me, have you seen it in your dreams, or in a waking vision? Have you drunk from the blessed Well?"

"Not yet, Your Radiance. But I will find it one day. Every hour in your service brings it nearer my lips."

So it went, faster and faster, while his father sat rigidly beside him and the baboon chewed and slobbered over a platter of bones. When the Prophet asked him to name his greatest fear, the answer came without hesitation.

"Drowning, Your Radiance."

The scrawny woman looked up in surprise. "Drowning? A curious fear for a boy raised in the Valley. Where could one drown?"

Kandri's nails bit into his palm. "There are deep clefts on the Sataapre River, Your Radiance. And our cousins live by the sea."

"Did you fall into one of those clefts?"

"No, Your Radiance."

"Let yourself be swept offshore by the tides?"

"No, my Prophet, no."

"Well, then?"

A silence followed. The baboon cracked a bone. The Prophet gazed at Kandri with a look of some annoyance, and Kandri found himself staring helplessly back, thinking of the murderous dwarf. The Old Man began to squirm. "Answer our Prophet's question!" he hissed at last. "Your Radiance, with all my heart I beg your pardon, the boy's in shock at your benevolence in granting this interview. And he has always been clumsy in speech."

"Not this clumsy," said the Prophet. "He is in the grip of memory, Lantor. Look at him sweating, smell that ecstatic fear. He is recalling something that left his mind bruised, and his heart in pieces. That copper ring on his thumb is part of the story. Am I right, Kandri Hinjuman?"

"In this and all things, Your Radiance." *But I won't tell you about it, never, some things are mine.*

"The Xavasindrans might like a word with him," said the Prophet. "They are intrigued by sudden fits of this kind."

His father turned him a blazing look: *Proud of yourself, jackass?*

"Those foreign doctors," the Prophet continued, "are exceedingly clever in matters of the flesh. But of our minds they know little—and of our spirits, nothing at all. They would speak of this or that portion of the brain, or certain salts and humors therein. But they would not understand this boy as I do. Shall I tell you, Lantor, why your son does not explain his fear?"

His father was pale. "I—Your Radiance—Kandri, bethink yourself, by all the Gods!"

"Because he cannot," said the Prophet. "This break, this rupture in his soul: he has recalled it from a previous life. It is hidden from his waking mind, though it taps every night at his dreams. *Tap tap. Tap tap.* Am I correct, my child?"

A previous life. That was it, exactly. A life before the Valley was lost to him, before religion was hammered into his heart, before Ariqina fled and this war claimed him, this meaningless march to a sterile future in a country emptied of love.

Kandri bowed low. "You see through me, Enlightened One. Truly, your feet walk Heaven's Path."

His words satisfied the Prophet, and let his father breathe again. But Sleepyhead, the white baboon, looked at him with cunning, as if he understood that Kandri had not truly bowed in spirit, had not submitted to the Prophet's will. The animal bared its teeth, blew bubbles of spit in Kandri's direction. The old woman laughed fondly at her pet. The monkey began to shriek and throw bones.

III. YSKRALEM

"Six years and thirty have I ruled Urrath from this throne," said Ut'xing to the magician. "Men have come with daggers in the night and I have killed them. Other kings have opposed me and I have laid them waste. I slew the tiger of the Thrukkun Marshes and the Ogre of Chahiyin. I have drunk from the Well of Fire and glimpsed the Mountain of the Gods. Now you say that a new foe, this yatra, will challenge me. Very well, I care not. Only tell me when I should expect it."

But the magician continued to bow, unmoving, and when the guards nudged him they found him already a corpse. And a voice was heard from the shadows, saying, "No one foresees my visits, Prince of Nations. Does the oak foresee the lightning, when the night is clear and still?"

ANNALS OF UT'XING

F our fugitives on a clifftop, overlooking the Stolen Sea.

Kandri shades his eyes, gaping at the monstrosity. A dazzling white canyon, blurry with heat, descending by a series of shelves to the old sea floor, many miles from where they stand. The land is scabrous, reflective, like the shed skin of some doomsday reptile. There are vast protrusions and pinnacles of rock, hazy and shimmering. There are boulders, trenches, rippling undersea hills. Over everything, the salt. In some places it is a slippery egg-white glaze, in others solid enamel.

"Gods of death, it's big," says Mektu. "I can't see the other side."

Chindilan raises his hand and gestures vaguely. "That way, somewhere, on the far East Rim, is the city Lord Garatajik spoke of. Mab Makkutin—that's *Ghost Port* in the local tongue. And it was a port, when the Yskralem was still a sea. Hardly an ideal refuge, but it's all we've got."

"You've been there?" says Kandri.

"Years ago. Her Radiance sent a team of us to inspect their ironworks. Strange place, it is. A great city in Imperial times, and the old wall's mostly intact. But the city's shrunk inside it, like the flesh of a gourd."

"Due east, you say?"

"Well, now, I couldn't swear to that. We reached the town from Loro Garrison, not Eternity Camp. It was a hellish long march up the East Rim, but exactly where it stands, well—"

"So this Mab Makkutin could lie straight across the Sea," says Kandri, "or fifty miles north or south along the Rim."

Chindilan nods reluctantly. Mektu's shoulders slump.

"It doesn't matter," says Eshett. "This is the only place to cross. If all goes well, we could do it in six nights."

Mektu turns to her, eyebrows raised. "How would *you* know? Have you been down there, or do you just like to talk?"

"I remember things," says Eshett.

"For example?"

Eshett's mouth twists. *Gods, how she must hate him*, Kandri thinks.

Chindilan makes a gesture of impatience. "Mektu," he says, "what do you see back there, to the west?"

Startled, Mektu squints at the horizon. "I can't see anything, Uncle. There's a mirage."

"That's right, genius: a mirage. And the next Wolfpack could ride out of that mirage while you stand there yipping like a pariah dog. Come along, all of you. And stop calling me Uncle. You're too daft to be my blood." He starts to walk, gesturing even as he goes. "Look ahead, where the cliff juts out. What am I seeing, bricks?"

Bricks, indeed: a round, low ruin of some sort, very close to the precipice. "Come on, Mek," says Kandri, taking his brother by the arm.

But Mektu's feet are planted. He crosses his arms, looks his brother fiercely in the eye. "I'm not going anywhere," he says, "until you tell me the truth."

❧

So Kandri tells him.

Mektu makes a small sound in this throat. For the first time in living memory he has nothing to say.

"You'd have done the same to help that little girl," says Kandri.

"Would he?" says Eshett.

Mektu looks from Kandri to Eshett to Kandri again. "You killed Ojulan."

"Isn't that what I just said?"

"I don't believe it. Kandri. You're a mad fucking dog."

Chindilan, already exploring the ruin, turns and shouts for rope. They walk toward him, Mektu's expression changing with every step: denial, suspicion, confusion, rage. The mood that finally claims him is sheer blazing excitement. He starts to cackle, then to whoop.

"Ojulan, dead! Her ass will split open! She'll piss herself a lake!"

"Stop it, fool," says Eshett. "Your wound."

Kandri is pleased to see her smile—a small, dazed smile, but a smile nonetheless. His brother has noticed it as well. He stares at her, works his lips. Finally, he clears his throat.

"I'm sorry I called you names. Bitch and things. It's not you who's the bitch, it's us soldiers, we're dogs. I mean we're all taught to behave worse than dogs."

When her smile does not entirely disappear, Mektu is deeply moved. "We'll protect you," he blurts. "That's a promise, vegetable girl. I myself will protect you with my life. From insult. From the groping hands of men."

Kandri shuts his eyes. When he opens them, Eshett, little wonder, is marching stiffly away. Mektu turns to Kandri, ecstatic. "I understand now. I don't mind."

"About Ojulan?"

"About everything. She's beautiful, that Eshett. I'm glad she helped you hide the body. I'm glad we're running away."

Some knot or tangle loosens abruptly in Kandri's chest. He has dreaded this confession more than he knew, and can barely look Mektu in the eye. "I should have told you," is all he manages to say.

"That's all right. Shake my hand, brother. Gods of Death, you killed the Thirdborn! And then I killed—devil's prick."

"Maybe you didn't, though," says Kandri. "Garatajik was still breathing when we ran. Mektu, listen, there's more to all of this—"

"She likes me," says his brother, "can't you tell?"

❧

Brothers should never serve together. So said Kandri's legion commander, a thick-necked colonel who had died on the banks of the Shev. The colonel believed this so strongly that he had taken on the task of separating such pairs throughout Eternity Camp, usually by dispatching one brother to some distant campaign.

Kandri and Mektu had escaped this fate when his aide revealed that they had only a father in common. The colonel had snorted, contemptuous: "Half-brothers? What's a half-brother, can anyone tell me? Absolutely nothing, that's what. The hell with it, let them stay."

Kandri has never quite understood the colonel's meaning. But he recalls those words whenever Mektu disgusts or repels him. Which is often enough.

The groping hands of men. Bastard. You can start with your own.

Of course, the true bastard in the family is Kandri himself. Chiloto men take but one wife. When Kandri still lived with his birth-mother Uthé, the people around them had assumed that she was that wife. But who were those people? Ragged farmers and herders. Gap-toothed, unschooled. You couldn't expect them to grasp the truth.

Blind Stream was a proper town, and a part of the larger world of the Sataapre. They had laws, teachers, rooftop water tanks, a store with hours written on a sign. Astonishingly, they had a man who lived by nothing more than cutting other people's hair.

Naturally, the wife from Blind Stream was the real one, then. Even Kandri was sure of it, once he glimpsed the splendor of the Valley. But what did that make his birth-mother? There were words, he learned soon enough. *Concubine, kissing maid, spare sandal, bush wife.*

"Bush wife?" he had asked Mektu on their first night as brothers.

"Pay no attention," said Mektu.

They sat side by side in their shared bedroom. An hour before, it had not been shared. All his life Mektu, had enjoyed the privilege of a room of his own. When his new mother declared that he and Kandri would be sharing it from now on, Kandri had quickly offered to sleep on the floor. Mektu had screamed in indignation: *But I need my floor!*

"Bush wife." Mektu shook his head. "I suppose you'd better get used to it. You'll hear much worse at school. If people learn about you, I mean. If someone tells."

His face was brightening. He rocked on the edge of the bed.

"But what does it mean, *bush wife?*" asked Kandri.

"Oh, nothing." Mektu rocked faster.

"Tell me."

"Nothing, really." Mektu laughed and shrugged. "Absolutely nothing. Almost nothing. I mean, it's not actually an insult, just the word for what she was, a nobody out there, someone you could screw—"

Kandri hit him. It was a clumsy rabbit punch to the stomach, but delivered with all the strength of his pent-up misery. His mother was but three days dead.

Mektu collapsed, and Kandri thought he had killed him. He bent low, touched Mektu's shoulder. Mektu reached up and slammed Kandri's temple against the bedframe. Ten years later, he can still feel the scar.

⋈

"The *rope*, you pair of clowns! Why the hell are you dawdling?"

The brothers hurry to catch up. The "bricks" Chindilan has noticed are in fact great blocks of crumbled granite, arranged in a circle on a tongue of rock protruding from the cliffs. In the canyon beyond, the spires of rock Kandri had noticed earlier rise like gnarled fingers from the seabed.

"This is where we'll descend," says Chindilan. "The cliff's low, no more than sixty feet to the first shelving. But I can't work out what used to stand on this spot. A lookout tower? Why here, where there's no sign of a town?"

Kandri shrugs. "Grain silo?"

"On a sea ledge? Makes no sense at all."

Mektu looks from one to the other, as if amazed at their stupidity. "It was a lighthouse," he says.

Chindilan snorts, and Kandri represses a smile. But then he glances again at the stone formations rising from the canyon, and suddenly everything is clear.

Islands. Ang's blood, those are islands.

The first two rise gently, wind-smoothed hills of naked stone. The third is tall and sheer, with a flat summit like a tabletop. Others, more distant, run in a straggling line from north to south. They are facing a small, perished archipelago.

Kandri looks at the back of Mektu's head. Drooling idiot, buffoon. And the one who just might see what no one else does. He turns to help Chindilan with the rope.

The heat is fierce now, but the descent is a simple matter. One bend of the rope around a solitary stone, the two ends braided together and dropped over the cliff. Mektu scurries down without incident and stands waving at the bottom. Chindilan follows. But when her turn comes, Eshett goes suddenly stiff. She says she is afraid of heights. Always has been. Her nails bite Kandri's arm.

"I thought you would lower me."

"We can't do that," says Kandri. "The rope is shit. The rocks would slice through it in no time."

"Then it's not safe!"

"*Harach*, sheathe those claws! It's perfectly safe if we're not grinding the rope over the rocks. Go on, there's shade at the bottom. And there's no other way."

"I can't," she insists. "I'm not strong enough. I'm afraid I'll let go."

Kandri all but shoves her over the cliff. She does not let go. She just looks up at him, furious, and descends with surprising ease. From the bottom she flips him a gesture he assumes is obscene. Smiling, he follows her, grimacing at the heat already throbbing from the cliff wall. Once his feet touch the earth, they unbraid the rope and pull the whole length down.

"Now we've done it, boys," says Chindilan. "No turning back. And no more dawdling. They could be here any time."

They stand on a broad shelf of salt-poisoned scree descending gradually into the canyon. The heat is savage, and the glare is far worse. Much of the Yskralem is simply too bright to look at, reflecting the sun like shattered glass. Already his eyes are watering. He calls the others together.

"Garatajik told the truth," he says. "We don't have enough water to walk in this heat, and we couldn't carry it if we did. We'll have to move in the darkness and sleep through the days. But heat or no heat, we have to get out of sight. Those—islands, they'll have shade on the far side. We should make for those before we rest."

"What if they lower horses over the cliffs?" asks Mektu.

Chindilan frowns. "Now, there's a happy thought. Any more for us?"

"What if they lower *sivkrin* and turn them loose on our scent? What if we get lost? What if the Army's seized the eastern rim? And what if there are cliffs on the other side and we *can't* climb out?"

"The East Rim is not abandoned like this one," says Eshett. "There are cliffs, but also staircases. People come and go."

"So you *have* made the crossing," says Chindilan. "Why didn't you tell us before?"

Once again, her face closes to their scrutiny. She rounds her shoulders, withdrawing into herself. "Climbing out is not the problem," she says.

Sudden movement: the men's hands jump to their blades. But it is only the shadow of a carrion bird, wheeling silent overhead.

"Vultures," says Mektu. "What if there are big ones in this place? I mean the *really* big ones. So big"—he gestures, conjuring—"so big they're huge?"

"You mean Ornaqs," says Chindilan. "That's another silly fear. They're big, but not big enough to threaten us. Your head's full of the Old Man's bedtime stories."

Mektu looks relieved. Then strangely disappointed. "Anyway," he mumbles, "we can't set out before nightfall. They'll see our tracks."

"Jekka's hell," says Kandri, "you're right again."

And you, Kandri, are a Gods-damned fool. You won't last another day with blunders like that.

"We can't stay here, either," says Eshett. "We need somewhere to hide."

But there is no such place: they are at the foot of an ancient lighthouse, and for miles around the wastes are laid open. After a brief agony of indecision, they start north, making for a spot some four miles away where the cliff juts out like an elbow. They hug the firmer ground by the foot of the cliff, jumping from rock to rock. They leave no obvious sign of their passage, but it is slow work, and all the while, they are utterly exposed to the cliffs behind.

The heat grows. They pass in and out of shadow, in and out of the scouring sun. Kandri begins to slip, to miss his jumps. His head is throbbing and his eyes hurt when he blinks. Vague swaths of color invade his vision.

At last they reach the elbow bend and scurry around it into hiding—and out of the glare. Kandri urges them on a few hundred more yards, to a place where the cliff is more severely undercut, and some large, jagged rocks provide still deeper shade. There at last they stop. Chindilan throws down his pack.

"I thought we were dead men," he says. "I swear I could feel their eyes."

Mektu turns sharply. He clutches the older man's arm. "Eyes?" he whispers.

Still irritable, Chindilan shrugs off his hand. "Yes. Eyes. You've heard of 'em, then."

"You felt eyes, Uncle? Dead eyes?"

"*Dead?* Who said anything about dead? Sit down, you blasted hysteric, you're not even listening!"

Mektu's lips tremble. He bites them. Kandri knows what has spooked his brother: a tiny detail from the ghost stories of their childhood. The gaze of a yatra, studying the living from behind, is said to feel like "the gaze of the dead." Whatever that could mean. You could always count on Mektu to remember the useless.

"*And why are you such an unholy ass about women?*" hisses Chindilan, as if he's been harboring the question for days.

"I'm not," says Mektu. "They just don't understand me."

Chindilan gives a despairing laugh, and even Eshett giggles. Seeing her, Mektu flushes. He turns to Kandri, imploring.

With tremendous effort, Kandri guides his hand to Mektu's shoulder. "Sit down and be quiet," he says. "None of us is carrying a yatra. There are no fucking yatras."

Mektu looks as though he expects Kandri to drop dead on the spot. Kandri cuffs him on the cheek: equal parts affection and reprimand.

"Those islands are still our goal," he says. "We'll start walking as soon as darkness falls."

They settle into the shadow of the cliff. When Mektu opens his mouth again, Kandri raises a warning finger: *Not another word.* And yet on that mad run along the base of the cliff, Kandri had, damn it all, felt the same sensation as Chindilan. A watching mind, a scrutiny. Eyes drilling into the back of his skull.

ॐ

Kandri cannot sleep: the heat is too fierce, his cuts too inflamed. When he lies down, a black bruise on his forehead starts to throb. He crawls to the cliff wall and props himself against it. After a time, Chindilan comes to sit by his side.

"What the hell's wrong with you? Go to sleep, or you'll be useless tonight."

"I will, Uncle. Soon."

Chindilan shakes his head, but he stays and talks to Kandri anyway. He says that Garatajik had watched him for months. That the rebel Secondborn had no more than half a dozen men he trusted, and none among the Prophet's inner circle. His secret fight was in its infancy. One mistake, one instance of misplaced trust, and his campaign would end before the first blow could be struck.

"Except that you've just struck it," he adds. "Ojulan was the craziest, the most useless of the lot. But he's sure as hell useful now. He's a fucking martyr to the faith. And she'll go back to playing the game she loves best, which is vengeance. Double vengeance, two atrocities in a matter of hours! You and idiot boy over there"—he looks at Mektu with contempt—"have just added years to her life."

"Uncle," says Kandri, "Mektu thought we were prisoners. It was an honest mistake."

The smith glares at him. Then he sighs and leans back against the cliff. He says that after Garatajik recruited him, he recalled his promise to the Old Man: to do all in his power to safeguard the boys. "I thought I could get you sent home," he says. "Not out of the army, but home. There's a liaison office in the Valley now. You'd need to be promoted to sergeant, but that too was in the works."

Kandri turns slowly to face the smith. He can scarcely believe his ears.

"Until Mektu started jabbering about yatras, that is," says Chindilan. "I might still have gotten you transferred—you alone, I mean. But there was no hope of sending him anywhere, except jail or a madhouse."

Home. The word suddenly so bitter, so very cruel.

Chindilan bites his thumbnail, gazing out at the white expanse. "It's a terrible place, the Yskralem," he says. "We'll need the Gods' own luck to pass through it alive. Even if we do, though, we'll have gained nothing more than a breather. Ang knows we'll need one by then."

"But the Prophet will keep coming," says Kandri.

Chindilan nods. "She'll keep coming. Garatajik spoke the truth. There's only one place to lose her, boy."

"The Great Desert," says Kandri, "I know."

The smith nods again, runs a hand through his hair. Then he gestures with his chin at Mektu. "That arrow could have killed him. It still might, if the wound doesn't heal clean. We'll have to keep an eye on it. You can't trust him to notice."

"What do we do if he worsens?"

"Pray, or find a brilliant doctor. A Xavasindran, maybe. They have tools we've never dreamed of. Your father used to say that next to the Xavasindrans, we were savages in skins."

"You look the part."

Chindilan doesn't smile. "Do you know why they're not welcome in Eternity Camp anymore?"

"I heard they killed someone, bungled a surgery."

"That's a lie," says Chindilan. "It was just the opposite: they were too good. One of their patients was so delighted with his recovery that he called them 'miracle workers,' and his words reached the Prophet's ears. She couldn't stand the competition, see? No one is allowed to work miracles but Her Radiance."

"Of course," says Kandri. "But can we afford a Xavasindran?"

"Afford? They don't ask for a gham, boy; they're medical missionaries. *Harach*, you know nothing of the world."

Kandri bristles, although it is a simple statement of fact. They sit in silence for a time. Mektu is snoring. The white wastes shimmer like a dream.

"Let's have a look, then," says the smith at last. He leans over to his pack and tugs out Garatajik's leather satchel. Propping it on his legs, he frees the buckles and folds back the protective flap. Inside are a jumble of objects wrapped in waxed paper, heavy canvas, or leather tanned to softness of silk, each item tied firmly with string. Chindilan removes a folded parchment envelope. Upon it, in a neat, fussy hand, are two words:

PACKING LIST

Chindilan breaks the seal and removes a sheet of linen paper. He spreads it open, and Kandri leans close to read.

~ Sixty Gathen sovereigns (value 1 Kasraji true gold apiece)

~ Eight Imperial sovereigns (40 k.t.g. apiece)

~ Four bloodstone rubies (500 k.t.g. apiece)

~ Compact field telescope

~ Antivenin for the acuña sidewinder (vial 1a) and the marble scorpion (vial 1b)

~ TEMPORARY army eye-stain suppressant (about three one-hour applications. Will cause pain and irritation) (vial 2)

~ One antidemonic expectorant pill (enormous, yellow; take with food)

~ Two suicide capsules (instantaneous) (vial 3)

~ Letter of introduction to Dr. T. R. Fessjamu (waterproofed envelope inside stitched calfskin sleeve. DO NOT LOSE THIS LETTER. Deliver it to Fessjamu's hand; guard it with the utmost care)

The men look at each other, stunned, then dive into the satchel.

"The gems are here," says Chindilan, "and the coins as well. Two thousand . . . sixty . . . forty times eight . . . Ang's Tears, he's given you almost twenty-four hundred true gold!"

"How much is that in *ghams*?"

"Lots, boy! Not a fortune, but enough to get us a long way from the war, if we're frugal." He gives Kandri a stern look. "Not a word to your brother."

"Hell, no." Putting gold in Mektu's hands is like tossing steak to a street dog.

"Antivenin. Suicide capsules. Everything he names is here. Including this."

Chindilan is holding a second envelope, quite different from the first. It is a single piece of rugged leather, folded in half and stitched shut with rawhide. The stitches are almost comically numerous, as though meant to keep out anything humankind or nature might throw at the envelope. Stamped in dark indigo on either side is a small, inscrutable mark:

Chindilan sets his finger on the mark. "That's one of his Lordship's seals. Plain on purpose: nothing you'd stop and think about, unless you were looking for it. The resistance has scores of these little signs. We don't dare use any one of them too often." The smith rubs his beard in agitation. "Lord Garatajik was starting to talk about this letter when your brother stabbed him. *One item you must treat as priceless*, remember?"

"Of course I remember. It was the last thing he managed to say."

"He finished the letter just before we saddled up. His valet was still stitching the envelope when I brought his horse around. And he mentioned it on our ride to Balanjé. 'I should have dispatched it months ago, smith, and with better couriers,' he said. 'Fear stayed me, and later, the net began to close. These fools of yours may be my last chance.' 'What's it's all about, my Lord?' I asked. 'Don't question me!' he snapped. 'Ang forbid that you should ever face my mother's inquisitors. But if that black day comes, you must be ignorant. Your nephews, too, would best be kept in the dark, but how can I be sure of their commitment unless I tell them the truth? That letter *must* reach Dr. Fessjamu. If I could trade my life for its certain delivery, I should do without hesitation. My life or theirs, smith—or, for that matter, anyone's.' He meant it, Kandri. Lord Garatajik never said a thing he didn't mean."

Madness, free fall. Kandri cannot catch his breath. "What's in the letter, Uncle?"

"Weren't you listening? I have no Gods-damned idea."

"Dr. Fessjamu." Kandri rubs his temples. "Don't I know that name? Is he one of those foreign doctors?"

"She. And no, she has nothing to do with the Xavasindrans. She's from the east, and a person of great influence, I understand. She came to the Valley once, years ago while I was off with the legion. I don't know where she is today. Garatajik must have planned to tell us."

T. R. Fessjamu. Kandri swears under his breath. The mystery will gnaw at him. He slips the letter back into the satchel.

"His Lordship was damned generous, anyway," says Chindilan, sealing the buckles, "and we thanked him with a knife in the chest. But do you want to know something funny? Bad as things are, they might have been a whole shit-pillar worse."

Kandri turns him a battered grin. "Please," he says, "tell me how."

The smith reclines, hands behind his head. He tells Kandri that a feud has long simmered between Garatajik and the Prophet's Fourthborn, Etarel. For a long time after the disastrous first assault on the Ghalsúnay, Etarel had lain low, surly and fearful. The Prophet herself had interpreted the defeat as the result of witchcraft, and had blessed Etarel as "Savior of the Legion"—he had, at least, brought half his men limping home. But among the Sons there were whispers: her all-seeing eye was on the Fourthborn. Etarel dared not fail again.

Over time, he had recovered some of his standing. The Prophet was exceedingly glad of a certain poison he developed that could be released as a smoke; she foresaw a day when the enemy might be killed merely by lighting fires upwind.

"And then Garatajik returned. And she went mad for him, her long-lost Secondborn. And Etarel too went mad. With jealousy and fear."

Beside Garatajik, Etarel looked like what he probably was: a vicious, simple-minded lordling without an original thought in his head. Among the first things Garatajik did was to reveal, quite innocently, that the smoke-weapon Etarel had claimed as his own was in fact an invention of the Važeks—and that they had abandoned it, because the poison broke down swiftly in storage, and killed too many of their own on shifting winds.

Etarel did have some cunning, however. He grasped his mother's obsessions far better than Garatajik: the mad understand the mad. Little by little, he had chipped away at her joy in Garatajik's return. Wasn't he the only one who never took up a sword for Orthodox Revelation? Did it not harm the family's image, the solid ram of fear with which it battered its enemies, to have a Son of Heaven who preferred archives to armories, books to daggers and swords? And how did she know what he had *really* done with those two years? How many secrets had he traded, how many of her plans had he betrayed?

It was a crude campaign, and the Prophet, no stranger to cunning, had surely guessed why Etarel waged it. And yet it had an effect. She began to look at Garatajik differently, to ask more questions, to shuffle his Rasanga guards. She placed a tight watch on his servants, especially those sent on errands beyond the camp. She had not yet guessed that he was her committed enemy. But like Etarel before him, Garatajik felt the weight of her eye.

"He spent more time in uniform," says Chindilan. "Started playing the soldier, the proper Son of Heaven game. But he *wasn't* a soldier, and it was late to make amends. The resistance he'd built was in danger—not because we stumbled but because Etarel wanted a greater share of the Prophet's love. And it was getting worse all the time."

Now everything would change. Garatajik would be a martyr; doubts would vanish like the dew. And those whom Garatajik had favored would benefit as well. They would hold a place of honor, like the vassals of a murdered saint.

"He might live, you know," says Kandri.

"Yes," says Chindilan, "wouldn't that make things interesting?"

You know nothing of the world. His uncle's statement is more true than he suspects.

Kandri and Mektu stayed in school through the eighth primary, but by their fifth year, many subjects ceased to exist. History, geography, politics, the classic Urrathi tales: none of these were taught any longer, save by private tutors. When Kandri asked for such a tutor, his second mother agreed at once. "We have gold enough, Gods be praised," said Dyakra Hinjuman. "And you're on fire to learn; any fool could see that. Your lessons won't be wasted." But his father, shockingly, refused outright. He fought his wife with rare obstinacy, and eventually prevailed. Kandri was stunned by his unkindness. The memory hurts to this day.

By sixth year, not only subjects were disappearing from the school. One day the brothers arrived to find the music master gone. A month later, the teacher of rhetoric and civics. The replacements, if they came at all, were invariably priests, brought in from Gathen or Nandipatar. No one explained, or even mentioned the missing instructors. Those who did not vanish had a knack for avoiding certain themes.

Kandri filled his school days with what was still allowed—math, sport, the Kasraji language, and of course religion. The latter subject was by then almost purely Orthodox Revelation, but the teacher was one of the old philosophers for whom the Prophet had a curious soft spot. Kandri loved his meandering lectures, which touched on everything from the moral superiority of animals to the wailing in the desert that was the voice of the Goddess Kumnai, Daughter of the Wind.

Kandri was strong and excelled at sport. He liked farming, too, and above all the care of useful trees. But he knew very well what was missing from his education.

One morning he brought his father breakfast in his study. Poached eggs, warm bread and butter, half an orange, coffee with a splash of rum. Lantor Hinjuman smiled, closed his book, and began to wolf the bread.

Eyes discreetly lowered, Kandri asked for some lessons in history. Lantor's chewing slowed as though the bread had turned to caramel.

"What does a farm dog like you need with history? Learn a trade, boy. Find a wife."

"A wife?"

"Don't you dare say, 'Or two.'"

"I'm just sixteen, Papa."

The Old Man blinked at him, startled. "Whose fault is that?" he said at last. "Anyway, who'd be fool enough to teach history these days? I mean honest history. What if someone found out?"

"You could teach me."

"Bugger off. Learn a trade."

"Then teach me a trade," Kandri begged. In a lowered voice, he added, "Papa, teach me about machines."

From his first day in Blind Stream he had obeyed his father's edict, never mentioning the walking spider, the iron dragon, the beloved copper snake. Even with Mektu he held his tongue, tempting though it was to take just one person into his confidence. Nor was there any trace of Lantor's mechanical genius about the house. Everything was well built; nothing was remarkable. The only proof of what the Old Man could do was in Kandri's head.

His father locked eyes with his eggs. "Listen to me, boy. It takes a rare mind to build machines, and a rarer one to use them correctly. That's not the sort of mind you're equipped with. You're a farm dog, nothing more. And one day you'll thank me for saying so."

"I could have been smarter," said Kandri, blinking back tears. "I could have started school with Mektu years ago, if we'd lived in Blind Stream. Why did you make us spend all those years on the mountain?"

"Your birth-mother chose that place."

It could only be a lie; Uthé Hinjuman had detested Candle Mountain. "What could make her do that, Papa?" he asked, trying to keep the scorn from his voice. But the Old Man had turned away from him, back to his breakfast and his book.

A week later, Kandri had lingered after school with several friends. He returned home to an astonishing scene. His sisters were flailing about the courtyard, screaming as if deranged. His baby brother was hiding under the chicken coop. Rushing into the house, Kandri found Mektu backed into a corner of the kitchen, holding a large green musk melon above his head.

The Old Man, shirtless, stood in the middle of the room, his face dark with fury and his belt dangling from his hand like a whip. And between them stood Dyakra Hinjuman.

"I dare you, bastard!" she shrieked at her husband. "Go on, do it! See what happens!"

Her words frightened Kandri to his marrow. Lantor would go through her like a bull. "Run, Mek!" he shouted, preparing to do the same. His father's breath was deep and loud.

"I forbid it," he said. "Do you hear me, boy? I forbid it, as your father and master of this house."

"Go upstairs, Lantor," said Dyakra.

With a terrible quickness, their father swung the belt over his head, cracking the buckle against the floor so hard Kandri could feel it through the floorboards.

Then his pants fell to his ankles. "Go upstairs, you stupid man," said Dyakra again.

Lantor raised his trousers, stunned by his own violent gesture. He went upstairs. Dyakra sighed and brushed past Kandri into the yard. There, for the first and last time that Kandri would ever witness, she lit a cheroot.

The brothers looked at each other. Kandri struggled to find his voice. "What's the melon for?" he said at last.

"To defend myself."

"Put it down. Come here."

Mektu was shaking; Kandri pulled him into a hug. "What the hell did you say to him?" he asked.

"That we were going to start a troupe."

"A what?"

"An acting troupe. You know, for plays? Betali and I and Sar and Ubrin. I want to be a performer, I told him."

"That's all?"

"He's crazy, isn't he, Kan? What if he stabs us in our sleep?"

The Old Man was late for dinner that night. When he finally shuffled into the dining room, all six of his children took fright: he was a wreck, and still quite angry. But rather than shout he spread his arms like a man facing execution by archery.

"Mektu my son, I've wronged you. I'm ashamed."

He dropped into his chair and began to eat, and said no more to anyone that night. And although Mektu never again dared to speak of his "acting troupe," he woke the next morning to find nine musty volumes of epic poetry on his bedside table. His father had plucked the books from one of his tall, locked bookcases in the study. Just poetry, nothing else. The other books, all six hundred of them, remained a forbidden land.

Kandri hated that poetry. Talking rats, hysterical lovers, fairies born in buttercups. The only book he could stand was the *War Choral*, a four-hundred page reminiscence about a seaside kingdom torn apart by jealousy and greed. It was an awkward poem, swinging from gruesome accounts of battlefield slaughter to abstract and interminable philosophies. Their sister Nyreti called the book a sacrilege, but Mektu fell in love with the *Choral* and declared his intention to commit it to memory.

Kandri gazed at the shelves with longing: were those the sort of books Ariqina read? Travelogues and histories, true life accounts? Books about the whole of Isp'rallal, beyond Urrath's shores? About what really happened in the world?

One morning as Kandri was feeding the chickens, his father stepped out into the courtyard to light his pipe. Kandri took a deep breath and turned to face him.

"It's other people, isn't it? Any other people, except the ones in fairy tales. You don't want us learning about them."

Lantor Hinjuman started; the box of matches spilled in the dust. He spoke without lifting his eyes.

"If you don't like the arrangement, go and find yourself another family, another roof over your head."

Kandri stalked away, too furious to speak. *I will, you know. Even sooner than you think.*

But that night, after the younger children were asleep, Lantor Hinjuman approached his eldest sons again.

"Meet me in the barn in five minutes," he said. "Bring warm clothes, and some drinking water. It's going to be a long night."

∞

The Hinjumans' barn was a tall, narrow structure, built for cattle long since sold. The Old Man lit an oil lamp and handed it to Kandri. He produced a ring of keys and unlocked a storeroom from which he dragged the expandable ladder. They climbed to the second floor and pulled the ladder up behind them. Kandri had occasionally been sent to this second floor, to retrieve a tool or to hang bunches of longstaple tobacco to dry. But on those few occasions he had never noticed the small trapdoor in the ceiling, also padlocked, to which they ascended next. It could only lead to the hayloft, which Mektu had assured him was long abandoned.

His father unlocked the trap door and climbed through. Mektu followed. Kandri handed the lamp up to his brother and pulled himself into the loft. And with a single glance, he knew his father had made an irrevocable choice.

The hayloft was a secret workshop. There were long work benches, saws, planers, boilers, pedal-driven grinders and sharpening wheels, an anvil, a kiln. There were also smaller work stations, with tiny precision tools dangling in neatly ordered rows on the walls. But every surface was blanketed in dust.

"Six years," said Lantor Hinjuman. "That's the answer to the question you were about to ask me. Six years, except for winding now and then."

"Winding?" said Mektu.

Lantor Hinjuman checked the windows: all tightly shuttered. Then he led them to a table near the center of the room and hung the lamp from a hook above. Something lay on the table beneath a dust cloth; it was about the size of a raccoon. Kandri and Mektu started, glanced at each other for confirmation: yes, a noise—an almost imperceptible whirring and ticking noise—was issuing from beneath the cloth.

Their father cleaned the table meticulously, then drew the cloth aside. Before them stood the most extraordinary device Kandri had ever seen. It was a clock, nothing more—*but what a clock*. Four faces in pearl looked out from beneath a crystal dome. Below the faces lay an intricate wilderness of machinery, components of bronze and steel and silver, some thinner than the veins in a leaf. And it was alive! Covered with weeks, perhaps months of dust, its wheels and gears and cogs were nonetheless spinning, and second hands swept round the clock faces, silent and serene.

"You . . . built this?" Kandri said, barely breathing.

"Don't be a fool," said Lantor. "This clock was made for the Imperial Governor of Važenland, four centuries ago. I won it at cards."

He produced another key and wound the clock reverently. It was an astronomical clock, he explained, and told not just the hour but the precise day of the year, the phases of the moon, the positions of the three Sentinel Stars, and even the approach of the great second moon, the Pilgrim. "See there, that pinprick." He pointed at a small red dot upon a clock face. "As the Pilgrim nears, it dilates open, wide and wider. And when the moon is so close that its pull could damage something as delicate as this clock, it shuts itself down protectively—just long enough for the Pilgrim to pass. Once every twenty-one years." He shook his head. "No, I couldn't build such a marvel. I'm a tinker, not a magician."

But the next eight hours were magic all the same. For as they watched, Lantor Hinjuman dismantled the clock—ratchet and pinion, escape wheel and flywheel, gears light as flower petals, springs smaller than the legs of bees—and reassembled it, explaining every step to the boys, even letting them help. They screwed the dome back into place with daylight leaking through the slats on the barn's east side. Kandri was half blind but suffused with a joy beyond words. His father looked at them and grinned.

"You followed some of that, didn't you? Some part of it made sense?"

They assured him it had.

"We'll get your hands dirty next time. I'll teach you metals, show you what your Uncle Chindilan can do."

The brothers nodded, reeling with exhaustion, smiling like drunks. Lantor Hinjuman opened his mouth as though he might just start talking metals immediately. Then he checked himself, and his grin became a frown.

"You ever speak a word about this—so much as *hint*—and I'll strangle you. What you learn here, you hide away, against a time when the world's very different. Until then, you're not to let on that you can build anything more clever than a folding chair. I'm deadly serious, boys. And don't expect your mother to save you again. She might even help me. Let's lock up."

So it began: a secret education, dreamlike, unmentionable. They met once every three or four weeks, that autumn when the boys were sixteen. They discussed nothing but what was before them: engineering, properties of metal and water and stone and steam, leverage, momentum, the specific weights of various oils and extracts, the marriage of copper and iron in a furnace, the laborious tempering of steel.

Never in his life would Kandri see his father so happy, so intensely himself. And after the fifth such lesson, exhausted and glowing as ever, they stumbled from the barn at sunrise to find an elderly priest watching them through the courtyard gate.

Lantor Hinjuman froze. The priest's eyes narrowed to slits. Both men opened their mouths as if to speak, but neither did so. Later that morning Kandri would learn from his brother that the priest was Father Marz, the All-Shepherd, a great servant of the Prophet. And in later years, he would realize that their secret education had ended then and there. But at the moment he knew only that his father was afraid.

The priest touched the gate. He pursed his lips at their father as though communicating a warning, or a threat. But then, with a twitch of his crooked shoulders, he turned and limped up the road.

Kandri and Mektu never saw the inside of the hayloft again. They never had other tutors, or read a book from the forbidden cabinets in the study. Today, nine years later in the Yskralem, Kandri tosses pebbles at his brother until the snoring stops. *We're still farm dogs, Mek. The Old Man traveled Urrath; why wouldn't he share it with us? What was he afraid we'd find out?*

Night falls, a stone into a well. They rise and set off walking with scarcely a word, shuffling down the gentle slope. The darkness is deep, but they can still make out the islands before them, black silhouettes against the stars. The closest two are mere steep-sided hills. The third is far larger and stranger. The summit—the old island's surface—is rather flat, but the land beneath it is hourglass-shaped, narrower at the middle than it is above or below. It is an uncanny sight, as if the upper third of the island were weightless, balanced on its narrow midsection.

The air cools in no time, although the scree is still warm underfoot. Descending, they pass a broken helmet, a snapped oar, the perfect skeleton of an eight-foot fish. Ragged wind. Utter silence. The cliff looms behind them like a suspended wave.

"We really are on the floor of the sea," Kandri says aloud. No one answers, and he wishes he had not spoken. He is not sure why.

Deeper, lower. A rowboat, one oar and two boots inside, salt crystals coating the whole of it like frost. A bed of fossil oysters. A camel's skeleton, long legs, white cage of ribs.

It is almost cold by the time they reach the first island. It looms black and sullen before them, a round hill that outlived the sea. They grope and stumble around its base, littered with smooth stones and ancient driftwood. Mektu gazes up at the island.

"I smell bird shit."

"You're a crackpot," says Chindilan.

"He's right, I smell it too," says Eshett. "Something's nesting up there. Eagles or vultures. It would be a safe place to raise chicks."

Kandri can almost feel his brother's smirk.

They are rounding the second island when the moon peeks above the horizon. Soon a tattered silver ribbon gleams before them over the wastes of salt. *Our feet walk Heaven's Path*, thinks Kandri, mirthless.

The third, hourglass-shaped island is even taller than it looked from afar. Standing close to its concave sides, countless tons of rock and earth above his head, he cannot help but imagine it collapsing, burying them, although of course it has stood that way for eons. He leans his head back, gazing at the distant summit. Who lived there, before the rivers were diverted, the sea left to perish in the sun?

He collides with Mektu, who has stopped in his tracks.

A hundred yards ahead is a large cluster of men, passing swiftly among the boulders at the island's foot. By the moonlight he cannot see them well. They bear no lamps or torches, but Kandri thinks he sees the glint of steel.

It is almost funny, the way the four of them dive for cover, squeezing behind a barely adequate rock. "Gods of death, they got here before us!" says Mektu.

"It can't be a Wolfpack," says Kandri.

"Can't it?" says Chindilan. "Garatajik said that the Prophet was certain you had outside help. Maybe in her mind that meant horses, saddled and waiting to take you east. She could have sent a force into the Yskralem at full gallop, from the legions in the south."

"If she thinks we're assassins," says Mektu.

And Eshett says, "Thinks?"

Kandri, with infinite care, leans out from the rock. Nothing has changed: the men have not stopped moving, or sped up, or started in any new direction. He leans back with a sigh.

"Whoever they are, they haven't seen us," he says. "Ang's tears, let's keep it that way. But we also need to count heads."

More careful glances. Kandri cannot be sure that he has seen more than ten figures; Mektu puts the number at twenty or twenty-five. But even with the telescope, it proves impossible to say: the men pass in and out of view too often. Already they are vanishing, deeper among the rocks and ridges surround the great island. Within minutes, the last of them is gone.

But not far gone, Kandri knows. The open seabed between the islands is a paltry distance, something that could be crossed in one determined charge. "We should fall back," he says. "As a matter of fact, we should find ourselves a hole and dig in. We can't take another step until those bastards leave."

"What if *they* dig in?" says Mektu.

"Then we're food for jackals," says Chindilan. "If they dig in, it means they think we're somewhere close. We'd have to try to flee along the rim, north or south, until we find a staircase or ladder. And hope to hell it's not guarded."

"Or stay right here," says Kandri, "until more of them come up behind us, and they start turning over every Gods-damned rock." He shakes his head. "We can't wait for that to happen, and we can't just run. We need to move at the right moment."

"If it comes," says Eshett.

They retrace their steps, until the lower slopes of the island close around them. After half an hour of searching, they find a deep cleft in the hillside, out of sight from both east and west. It is no ideal shelter: by noon tomorrow, it will offer no shade. But noon is a long way off.

∽

Kandri takes the first watch. As the others roll themselves into blankets and cloaks, he climbs with great care to a ledge some twenty feet up the hill. There he crouches, hidden by a shoulder of rock, peeping out at the moon-washed island across the flats.

Nothing moves. The salt wastes make him imagine fields of snow. He has never seen snow, except for a thin midwinter gleam on some distant peaks of the Coastal Range. He has heard it said that there are mountains in the world where the snow never melts. It seems an outlandish claim, but then, he has never seen any other mountains. How many can he even *name*? There are the lush Blue Mountains of the north, which some call the Jewels of Urrath. There are the Teeth of the Dead, a dark rumor from desert stories, and perhaps no more than rumor. And there are the titanic peaks Ariqina had somehow heard of, and in which she passionately believed: the Night-fires, climbing range upon range behind the city of Kasralys.

Kasralys. The great city-state, the Invincible City, fortressed in unbreachable walls. The last living shard of the Kasraji Empire. Kandri tells himself that he is certain: Ariqina is there. No other place in Urrath could have drawn her away from her clinic, from her beloved Valley, from him. What has she become, in these years he has wasted on war? A surgeon? Possibly, but she could wield a scalpel before she left the Valley. Her passion was medicine, the science of cures. She would be serving the poor of Kasralys (they must have their poor; didn't everyone?) or testing their blood and bile in some old Imperial hospital. Perhaps she had found work with her hero, Dr. Tsireem, the one who inspired her with talk of the city in the first place.

Tsireem. Kandri sits up with a gasp. A puzzle-piece of memory has just snapped firmly into place. The satchel from Garatajik, the twice-sealed envelope. *Letter of Introduction to Dr. T.R. Fessjamu.*

Tsireem Fessjamu. *Gods of Death, they're allies. That letter is for Dr. Tsireem.*

ॐ

He had forgotten her last name. He'd only heard it once or twice. But *Tsireem*: that name he carries like a scar across his heart.

You could say they'd met. Kandri heard her speak before a large crowd in the Valley. She spoke of the Throat Rust—or as she called it, the World Plague. The crowd had liked her jokes: "So we're resistant to the Plague, here in Urrath. The world calls that a miracle. I don't. The Outlanders had to leave a *little* luck behind. If they'd tried to steal any more from us, it would have sunk their ships."

She spoke of grave things lightly, even irreverently. She had visited the bleak memorial to the thousands executed in the Theater of Bones, and reminded the crowd that it was "the noble, cultured, civilized Kasrajis" who had built that palace of death. "Your enemies the Važeks merely carried on the tradition when the Empire fell. Savagery is not the province of the poor alone, my friends. Never believe that. Never believe a man can't be a grotty little strangler, just because his nails are clean."

She was—save for the Prophet herself—the most charismatic person ever to bother with a visit to the Sataapre. When her speech ended, a crowd of ninety escorted her to the next town, all of them aglow with the vision she'd shared: an educated Urrath, out from under the Quarantine, taking its rightful place in the world called Isp'rallal," which only on that day did he learn meant "Island in the Stars."

His family was there. Dyakra sang a song about the triumph of the humble. The Old Man smiled without craftiness or irony, and the smile took twenty years off his face.

Only Kandri was miserable. In the doctor's presence, he felt a jealousy that left him witless, melting with rage. He knew why; there was no mystery. She had touched the one thing in all the world Kandri could not bear to think of sharing: Ariqina's heart.

Dr. Tsireem was brilliant, dedicated, strong. She barely reached Kandri's chin and had a face like a squirrel monkey, but her voice could blow the roof off a barn. She revealed nothing about her clan origins, but spoke of years spent among the Shôl—and they were enemies of the Važeks, so Tsireem was all right. Who could have guessed (besides the Old Man, maybe, who was nearly as well travelled as the doctor) that she had come from Kasralys?

She had stopped in Blind Stream for one reason: to meet a young nurse who was attempting something remarkable. An open clinic, where no one was barred from treatment, or beggared by the charges when the treatment was done. A clinic where you paid in proportion to your wealth: the most outrageous idea ever heard of in the Valley.

That nurse was Ariqina. Her clinic, just six months old, was already near collapse, for even the rich of the Upper Sataapre were not very rich, and the doctors were not pleased with what they took home. But Tsireem loved the idea, and since she had already impressed the best minds in the Valley as a genius, her praise transformed the clinic's fortunes.

Ariqina's, too: she and Tsireem had huddled for an hour before the doctor's speech. That night, after the great woman's departure, Ariqina came to Kandri and flung herself into his arms. Her eyes were moist but she was laughing. She was going to become a doctor, she was going to change the world. She would finish her studies in Nandipatar and visit the Xavasindran missions and acquire the new translation of the great *Anatomyca* of the Kasraj. She would become, thought Kandri, the Tsireem of the Sataapre Valley.

"I'll help you," he said. She took his face in her hands and kissed him, long and deep.

Kandri held her stiffly. He was frightened by her intensity, and at the same time aware that it was the very heart of why he loved her. Urrathi legends spoke of a well that led to the world's fiery heart, from which heroes came to drink before embarking on a journey, or attempting great deeds. Ariqina might be kissing him, but it was heart-fire she tasted.

And it was Dr. Tsireem, not Kandri, who had led her to the well.

You've gone to Kasralys, haven't you? Wait for me, look for me.

Ariqina would have laughed at such talk. *You don't even know if you're coming to Kasralys. You don't know where it is.*

I'll find it. Kandri can almost see her in the darkness: her slender shoulders, the mirth and joy in her gestures, hands never at rest until she dropped unconscious, dark eyes as urgent as a deer's.

If you're strong enough, she would have answered. *If you're ready to be wise. If all that lust and yearning has made you into someone the world could need.*

She was so much harder than his drill sergeants. They just shouted and punished. Ariqina challenged him with love.

Kiss me, he tells her.

I can't, fool, stop dreaming. I'm not there.

❧

So he does stop. Immediately, a thought of danger takes her place, and he knows he has avoided it too long.

Water. By his count, they are carrying twenty-five faska, including the seven from the soldiers they killed. It is a dreadful weight; Kandri has never marched with more. But can it possibly suffice? Even traveling after sundown, each of them will need a full faska daily just to keep moving. Any less, and the deadly fatigue that comes with thirst will slow their pace.

Kandri had hoped they might cross the Yskralem in five days. Eshett says six or more. Six days: twenty-four faska. If all goes smoothly, they should make it with one to spare. But what if they are forced to linger? A full day?

Two days? They will drink less in hiding than on the march, but they will still drink.

This time tomorrow, he thinks. *If we don't start by then, we'll have to turn back. Into the jaws of the beast.*

The wind rises. Its chilly hands probe his clothing, find a hundred paths to his skin. By the time Chindilan relieves him the moon has sunk low.

℥

"Kandri?"

"..."

"Kandri?"

"What is it, Mek? Why aren't you asleep?"

"The Prophet may think we're assassins, hired assassins. But that's not all. She thinks we're doing the will of the yatra."

"Oh, for fuck's sake."

"And what if she's right? I don't know why I stabbed Garatajik. There's no reason I should have."

"Of course there's a reason. You thought he was going to cut off my head."

"But I heard him talking. After he fell, I realized that I'd heard quite a lot. About his hatred of Ojulan. The things he'd learned in the east."

"You heard that?"

"And I stabbed him anyway."

"Piss of the devil. All right, you heard something, but you weren't clear about it, that's all. We were in terrible danger and there was no time to think. Anyone could have done what you did. I might have done it: is that good enough for you? Shut your eyes, Mek. Go to sleep."

"How did you know they were open?"

"I didn't."

"Can you feel my eyes, brother?"

"No. Idiot."

"..."

"*But don't you lie there fucking staring at me!*"

"What if I'm the one, Kandri? What if I've been carrying it all along?"

"Mek. How can you stand being you? I mean for even one day? If you were carrying the yatra, you wouldn't be talking about carrying the yatra. And if I had it, I wouldn't be talking to you this way either."

"Yes, yes, you would."

"Oh, Pitfire. So now you think it's me?"

"I think it's traveling with us. I can feel it pushing, sometimes. Like a thumb."

"A thumb."

"Like a dry thumb groping for my eyes."

෯

At daybreak, Eshett spots a hole in the side of the island, just yards from where they've slept. It is no more than a two-inch gap between hard stone and drifted scree, but a few minutes of digging with a chunk of driftwood reveals the mouth of a long, narrow cave. Chindilan makes a few exploratory stabs with Kandri's machete, then lights a match and leans inside. "No ghouls," he says. "In fact, there's not a blessed thing inside. A lovely little sea cave, that's what it is. Ang's handed us a gift."

The cave is less than three feet high. Kandri looks at the dark hole, and his old fear growls a warning. He turns and gazes across the seabed: the strangers have not reappeared. Survival before stupidity. In the cave, they will be out of the sun.

"I'll keep watch," says Eshett. "I can't sleep again so soon."

The men eat a quick breakfast, then crawl one by one into the cave. The floor of the cave is fine, cool sand, so comfortable that Mektu and Chindilan groan with pleasure as they stretch out. But to Kandri the space is almost as horrible as the grave-tunnel in Balanjé. His heart pounds; he wakes quivering, over and over, from whatever shallow sleep he achieves. Cries escape him, waking the others. Chindilan asks what in Jekka's hell he's so afraid of, and Mektu says with unusual sharpness to leave his brother alone.

At last it is Mektu's snoring that dispels his terror. All the years he fell asleep to that horrible noise, a pig drowning in its slops. At times, he would wake Mektu with a kick and then deny it; today, the noise soothes him as nothing else could. He shuts his eyes and imagines the deep water that once filled this cave, the tug and billow of it, the vanished fish and octopi and eels.

ೞ

After their fight over the "bush wife" remark, Kandri and Mektu opted for peace. It was a loveless, utterly strategic choice. Everyone in the household was watching them; Mektu even claimed that the Old Man would beat them if they didn't appear to be getting along. Kandri didn't want to believe that his father could be so dreadful, but he realized to his shame that Mektu was in a much better position to know. The Old Man had spent a great deal more time with his Blind Stream family than up on Candle Mountain.

So Kandri agreed to call his wound an accident: he had slipped in the bathroom, struck his head on the sink. And Mektu agreed to let him sleep on his floor.

In the presence of others, the boys put on a show: they were delighted with each other; they were friends. Kandri struggled with this performance. He was still furious with Mektu and disgusted with his snoring. And Kandri was an awful liar to boot. In the bathroom mirror, he forced his face into a smile, and recoiled at his own demented look.

But his brother was a natural. Everyone believed in his joy. Kandri can still recall Mektu's effortless transformations: bitter contempt in the hallway, warm goodwill and a hand on Kandri's shoulder when they reached the kitchen door. "Can I borrow three *roda*, Mother, if I make it up in chores? I want to buy Kandri a lemon roll. He's never tasted one, and you know the shop runs out."

Such easy kindness would last until the door shut behind them; then the coins and the smile would vanish into Mektu's pocket, and there would be no more talk of lemon rolls. Mektu was so convincing that Kandri caught himself feeling grateful. He had a new brother; he was loved. Until they were alone again, he could forget that it was a lie.

But a lie sometimes evolves in the direction of truth. Three weeks after Kandri's arrival, Mektu began to forget to sulk when they were alone. Then, very cautiously, he began telling jokes. Kandri laughed, even at the worst of them. He thought it was the least he could do.

One night, the brothers were lounging on the porch roof (gained from Mektu's bedroom window, another privilege that had been his alone) looking out over the Valley at the lights of seven villages, faint pools of lamplight in the darkening Valley. It was early summer; they lay back eating chaffa nuts, drowning in the tireless din of tree frogs, and catching whiffs of the water pipe the old man was sharing with his cronies below. The stars were few and hazy; the younger children were already asleep. Mektu told a long tale of their "war" with the boys in the village of Sharp's Corner, two miles downhill from Blind Stream. "They're older, and they fight better too," he admitted. "One of them kicked Betali in the nuts. His children will all have squeaky voices. That's how it works, you know."

Kandri winced. "Poor Betali."

"You have to stand up to them," said Mektu. "Always."

"I will," said Kandri.

Mektu studied him doubtfully. "Don't be frightened," he said at last. "Remember there's a lot more of us." Indeed, the Hinjumans were an enormous family: two adjacent houses belonged to uncles, and there were cousins beyond counting seeded across the Valley.

"We're all fighters, Kandri. The women too. You should see Aunt Ingla make a fist."

"I can fight," said Kandri. It was the simple truth; he had blackened eyes, and worse, among the hardscrabble mountains boys. What shamed him was the guilt he felt, the longing to beg forgiveness of those he punched or kicked or threw to the ground, to pray for them in the temple. It was an awful weakness. Small children felt such remorse, not men of fourteen.

The night deepened. Mektu plucked fireflies from the air, held their wings, licked their glowing abdomens until his tongue blazed green and ghoulish. He urged Kandri to do the same, and Kandri did. The residue of the insects tasted like soap and made his tongue feel dry and foreign.

Mektu was pleased. "Now I'll show you my treasure," he said, and pulled Kandri to his feet.

Like monkeys, they scaled to the roof of the main house, leaped light-footed into a cypress tree, and from there descended to the wall between their own courtyard and that of the nearest uncle. "Don't fall," Mektu whispered. "His dog will wake the whole Gods-damned town. Also, there's slugs."

Kandri had good balance and didn't mind the slugs, which oozed like butter through his bare toes. His only fear was that the fireflies might make him vomit up their dinner—a birthday dinner for their sister Dira, and the finest meal of Kandri's life.

They crept on. Mektu pointed to a small, neat house down the hill from them, where the road made a hairpin turn. "That's Uncle Chindilan's place. You know about Chindilan, don't you?"

"The Old Man's best friend?"

Mektu looked as though the question had never entered his mind. "I suppose he is," he said, "but that's not what matters. He makes weapons. He's going to make me a sword."

Kandri blinked at Mektu: a thin, crooked boy with glowing goo on his lips.

"When?" he asked.

"What do you mean, when? Soon enough. Don't be stupid."

The wall led to other walls, and then to a much larger structure, which Kandri had admired since the day of his arrival. It was a bridge connecting nowhere with nowhere, rising in great symmetrical arches over the folds and ravines of the Sataapre Valley. Greenery cascaded down its sides; bats whispered over and under its immensity. The boys stood some fifteen feet below its upper surface.

"Aqueduct," said Mektu proudly. "It used to bring fresh water down to the port. Now it's my secret road."

"Did the Kasrajis build it?"

"Must have. There's a heap of rocks near the sea called Old Palace, and that's where the aqueduct ends. Be careful, will you? Every year, someone falls off the aqueduct and dies. We're forbidden to climb it. Let's go."

There were footholds. They scaled the ruin and walked in darkness above the village, the pigsties and rice paddies, the great amphitheater of the Valley rushing down toward the stage of the sea. Mektu roamed ahead, impatient with Kandri's awe. Now and then he'd turn and whisper *Hurry* with a green flash of tongue.

Blind Stream Village ended, and the wild margins of an apple orchard brushed the foot of the aqueduct; Mektu said they would come back in autumn and scavenge for fruit. They passed the seminary and the fish farm. They passed the New Life Orphanage, where forty years earlier, the tiny girl who became the Prophet had learned to fear the tread of the priests. A dancing white ribbon was the moon on Moti Lake, and then the outskirts of the next village began. Its name was Sed Hemon ("Blessed Dell"), but Mektu called it *Chegemmon* ("Yawn of Boredom") because it was very religious and proper, and its girls were not allowed to climb trees or wade in the river or kick a ball in the road.

The first dozen houses were whitewashed, and joined together like cells in a hive. The aqueduct passed very close behind them, although it was choked along this stretch with more greenery than ever.

Kandri looked down through the tangled brush. "You could piss into their gardens," he said.

Mektu pulled him back from the edge. "Don't even joke about that," he hissed. "And don't make a sound unless I do. I've never brought *anyone* here, you understand? Not even Betali. If you mess this up—you're not my brother. I don't care what the Old Man says."

Shocked, Kandri could only nod. Mektu studied him another moment, as though reconsidering a gift. Then he nodded and smiled broadly. Kandri smiled back, suddenly aware that Mektu *wanted* to share his secret. Whatever it was, he was tired of guarding it alone.

They passed two houses, then dropped to hands and knees and crept, with infinite care, into the brush. A third house slipped by. Then Mektu stopped. Beside him was a narrow path through the foliage, right to the aqueduct's edge. He motioned for Kandri to look.

They were behind the fourth house, large and rather shabby, with few windows and a back garden in need of a trim. The wall about this garden was ten feet high and crowned with broken glass. Solid brick, it ran alongside the vastly larger wall of the aqueduct. The alley between them was some four feet wide.

Kandri glanced at his brother, lost. But Mektu was searching the weeds. A moment later, he placed a rope in Kandri's hand. Thick, wet, grimy. Mektu gave a sharp tug: one end of the rope was tied fast to something deep in the brush. Kandri ran his hands along the rope: it was knotted at intervals. Mektu took it back from him and fed it down the aqueduct's side, into the narrow alley between the walls. He descended, bare feet gripping the knots. When he beckoned, Kandri followed. He was afraid of making some noise, enraging Mektu, ruining his life. But seconds later, his feet met the ground.

The alley was weed-choked and damp. In one direction, it simply dead-ended; in the other, it ran some twenty feet and cornered left. Mektu put a finger to his lips. They crept to the corner and turned.

Now they were between two private gardens, and the ground at their feet was smooth stone. Thirty feet ahead was another dead end. Mektu led him forward, urgently now, and Kandri felt suddenly ridiculous. What were they doing here? What if they were discovered, mincing around puddles on tiptoe, two clowns pretending to be thieves?

A smell of woodsmoke met his nostrils. Then he saw that the last six feet of wall on the left-hand side were made not of stone but of wood: broad planks covering what must once have been a passage into the shabby garden. Mektu touched the planks with his fingertips, like something cherished. He tugged Kandri to his side.

There were small gaps between the planks, but Kandri could see nothing through them but darkness. His brother grinned and cupped his hands around Kandri's ear.

"Now we wait," he whispered.

Kandri looked at him, and shrugged: *What for?*

Another whisper: "It may be a long wait. Maybe until morning. But you'll thank me when it happens. You'll see."

So they crouched and waited. It rained a little, and Kandri grew wretchedly cold. It was then that he made the acquaintance of a doubt that would needle him for years. What if his father had kept them apart out of kindness? What if Mektu was simply mad?

Of course, there was no escape tonight: Kandri had given his word. He squatted, freezing, and even held his jaw to keep his teeth from chattering. The night was endless. Bells tolled, dogs barked and fell silent, fat toads hopped in the alley with a sound like flung mud. After a while, Mektu put his arm around Kandri's shoulder and they huddled together, cold as toads themselves.

"I didn't mean it," whispered Mektu. "You're my brother and I'll always take care of you."

"Thanks," whispered Kandri uncertainly.

"I was only nine when the yatra came. I thought it would kill me, Kan. In fact, it promised to kill me."

"What's a yatra?"

"Ask me in the daytime. The point is, I'm sorry. I'm ashamed of myself. Just remember I'm on your side no matter what."

He hugged Kandri tighter, and Kandri hugged him back, nervous but glad. Then voices sounded from behind the wooden wall, and Mektu looked up with a predator's eyes.

The voices were female. An old woman's rasp, followed by the low, lilting voices of two young women or girls. They were hushed, as though trying not to wake others in the house. Soft footfalls. Jangling keys.

A door creaked, and yellow lamplight blazed through the cracks in the wall. It slashed across the brothers' faces, and for an instant, Kandri felt utterly exposed. But they were quite safe, for the cracks were extremely narrow. Too narrow to look through at all, unless you pressed your eye to one of them. Which was, of course, exactly what they did.

Beyond the wall was a bath chamber. It was much like the outdoor chamber in their own house: wooden bench, smooth flagstones, a bamboo door that could be latched from the inside. And of course a raised water tank, with a horizontal pipe some seven feet off the ground, ending in a spigot. But there was something odd about this tank. A long iron box was built into its base, with a heavy door and small holes along the side. From a few of these holes smoke was drifting. *A firebox*, thought Kandri, astonished. *Hot water, for bathing! Why don't we have one of those? Papa could build it with his eyes shut.*

An ancient woman with a white nest of hair stood in the chamber, raising a lamp above her head. A servant, Kandri guessed, and none too happy about the hour as she struggled to hook the lamp over a nail on the wall. Succeeding at last, she hobbled from the chamber and returned with an armload of firewood. She opened the door of the firebox, poked and grumbled at the coals, and shoved a great quantity of wood inside. The flame leaped, and the old woman's face became visible, thin and crevassed like a wooden puppet. Then she slammed the door and walked out.

Soon, the other voices came again, murmuring and laughing. The door reopened, and two young women in heavy cloaks stepped into the chamber, carrying folded towels. They were dark and slender, with great gleaming eyes; and their cheeks and foreheads were nearly identical: sisters, Kandri thought.

They were older than the boys: one eighteen or nineteen, the other a few years her senior. They were recalling someone's antics, mimicking a ponderous male voice, covering their mouths when they laughed.

Moral correction!

He spilled the wine on my arm.

Did you see him? Did you see his face?

When they removed their cloaks, they were naked. Kandri felt as though he'd been flung into the sea. Breasts, actual breasts, and bellies, and four buttocks, and dark, mysterious hair! The younger sister sat down on the bench and drew her feet up and she was barely two feet away. The older sister raised her hand to the spigot. A fall of water, a puff of steam on the flagstones. She plunged into the water and gasped with pleasure, and Kandri thought he would weep. His face was flushed. His penis was larger and needier than ever before in his life, peeking like a bald infant above his pants.

The younger sister rose and shook out her braid, and black locks cascaded to her thighs. Stepping to the bamboo door, she called softly, *Aren't you coming, dear?* From the house came a muffled *Yes!* The younger sister turned back to the older: *Get out, you greedy thing. Save a little for Ari and me.*

They traded places. The older sister wound a towel about her head, then put her cloak on wet and left the chamber. The younger sister talked to herself as she bathed. When she finished, she moved nearer and dried so exquisitely between her legs that Kandri found himself communing with the Gods. If he moved or breathed or blinked, he would explode; his ejaculation would be accompanied by drums and trumpets that would wake the neighborhood, the village, the Valley, but the Gods kept him silent and he praised them, praised this holy bathing place, praised his dear brother and the invention of thighs and nipples and other beauties for which he had no name, and the Gods told him his life would be unbearable in its sweetness, and they scalded him in arms of living gold.

The woman put on her cloak. Kandri fell from the stars. When he caught his breath, he saw that a third figure had entered the chamber. She was still robed and her back was turned, but he thought she was younger, perhaps just a year or two older than the boys themselves. Like the old woman, she was reaching for the lamp.

What is it? said the one who had sent Kandri to heaven.

A moth, said the new girl, standing on her toes. *It's going to burn to death on the glass.*

Let it burn! Oh, don't—

The girl blew. The lamp went out. The older girl whined in protest, but the newcomer said, *Don't be silly, there's light enough.* She pushed open the bamboo door, and the older girl padded carefully toward the house.

My cousin Ari, savior of moths.

What if they feel pain? asked the new girl.

She undressed, but they could not really see her. Mektu wrung his hands in frustration. The girl was a flaw in the darkness, a tease of movement, a trick of the eye. And sounds. Kandri heard her small gasps, heard the water break and change against her body as she moved. And soon, too soon, the closing of the spigot, the slap of her feet on the stones, a sudden creak as she sat down on the bench.

There came a thump, which Kandri felt more than heard. She had flung herself back against the wall—against the very board to which his cheek was pressed. And in the same instant burst into tears.

Mektu gripped his shoulder: *Don't move an inch!* But the girl did not sense their presence. She wept a long time, hidden from her family, hidden from the world. Kandri still could not see her face; that first night, he never did. But he felt the storm of her misery, the board trembling slightly with each pitch of her shoulders, and the water trickling from her body passed under the wall and wet his feet.

&

Then it was over. The girl stopped crying and felt her way into the house. The boys retreated, shadows among shadows, and no one was ever aware of them, not even the uncle's dog.

Back in their room, Mektu was triumphant. "When they bathe at sunrise, you can see *everything*," he said. "But the old aunt goes first, and she's horrible, you want to scream. Oh, Gods, Kandri, we have to plan something, if I don't talk to her I'll die—not the aunt, I mean the sister with the braids, Ang have mercy, I must be the first man ever to see her naked, that counts for something, I'm going to write her a poem. Do you think you can put a dick in a poem?"

Kandri was only half-listening. Visions of naked flesh still danced before his eyes, but his thoughts were with the youngest girl. "What do you think she was crying about?" he asked.

"That one?" Mektu shrugged, pulling on his nightshirt. "How should I know? Girls cry. Maybe someone told her fortune and she didn't like what she heard."

"At the party?"

Mektu looked at him. Then he buried his face in a pillow and laughed. "You oaf," he wheezed. "Those are the Nawhal sisters. They don't go to parties. They were coming from the temple. From a destiny service."

Kandri's face was blank.

"Don't you know anything?" says Mektu. "Twice a year, the holy farts in Chegemmon make their daughters sit up all night praying for rich husbands—that's the 'destiny' they're after. The priest, Father Marz, will stay up too, if you pay him enough. He's a creepy old lizard, that Marz. He chants and tells the girls about married life and douses them in rice powder and cloves. That was Marz they were laughing about: *moral correction*, he says that a lot. Papa hates him, you know."

Kandri sank to his place on the floor. "But that last girl. She's not old enough for a husband."

"Old enough for you, though," said Mektu with a wink.

Kandri flushed, dropped his eyes. But after a moment, he gave Mektu a nervous smile. "Yes," he said. "I like her. I wish I knew why she was crying."

"I'll introduce you," said his brother, magnanimous. "But don't get your hopes up. She must be seventeen."

"I couldn't see her."

"Neither could I—that fucking moth! But I know all about that girl. Betali's sister made friends with her at school."

Mektu yawned enormously, snuggling down into his bed. "Her parents abandoned her in Nandipatar. She lived on the streets for years. She went hungry, she begged. Then an old nurse took her in and they lived together in a shack behind the hospital. The nurse tried to bring her parents before the law, to get some money for the girl's education. But the parents picked up and left for the Cotton Towns, in the dead of night."

"That's strange," said Kandri.

"Strange and bad," said Mektu. "Kids die on those streets. But the Nawhals are all right. When the nurse died, someone sent them a message, and the old lady went to Nandipatar herself. And they're well off, too. That girl's problems are over."

"It didn't sound that way," said Kandri.

Mektu shrugged again. "They say she's clever. I wish we could see in the dark, like foxes. Her name is Ariqina, I think."

ଞ

An urgent hand on his shoulder. Kandri wakes, bolts upright, strikes his head on the ceiling of the cave. He curses; she hisses her sympathy. He starts to lie down again.

"Don't," she warns. "Get up, come outside. The men out there are leaving. We have to decide what to do."

He rolls over. From the cave mouth, a weak gray glow. "Devil's ass, it's after sunset!" he cries. "Why did you let me sleep so long?"

"You looked tired."

Kandri squirms out of the cave. The others, still and low among the rocks, are peering east into the twilight. Chindilan points, and Kandri sees them, just to the left of the big island. Once again, they carry no torches. They are moving north with good speed.

"We almost missed the bastards," says Chindilan. "If they'd waited another ten minutes, we'd have never seen them at all."

"Still no idea who they are?" says Kandri.

"None," says the smith, "but at least we have a head count. Twelve of 'em out there."

"They move like *gradhynds*, like distance walkers," says Eshett. "And they are heading away from us. That's good. I do not wish to meet them."

"Damned right, darling," says Mektu. "*I'm* sure who they are. That's a Wolfpack."

Kandri gazes up at the sky. "The minute it's fully dark, we go," he says. "We should reach the next island by moonrise, and maybe get farther than that. Let's just hope they're alone."

"No landmarks after that next island," says Chindilan. "How do you plan to keep east?"

"By the stars, Uncle," says Kandri.

"You know your stars that well?"

Kandri nods. "The Old Man," he says, and Chindilan's mouth spreads in a smile.

"You should have heard Kandri complain when he dragged us out to stargaze in the cold," says Mektu. "'How could anyone get lost in this country, Dad? Uphill is the mountain. Downhill is the sea.'"

"And he said you wouldn't live in the Sataapre forever, I suppose?"

The brothers look at each other, and Mektu bites his lips. In fact, the Old Man had said that the Sataapre, like any place, would find a way to kill a dreamer or a fool. His eyes had fallen on Mektu as he spoke. But it was not Mektu who had nearly proved the truth of the statement.

"We should hurry," says Kandri.

They lace their boots, pass a faska around. Kandri watches their horselike drinking and feels a tightness in his chest. They have lost a night and he is leading them on. Into what pain, none can guess. But he knows that every mile they walk could be a mile they will have to retrace, defeated, sick and feeble with thirst. And that soon enough, they will cross that invisible line beyond which no return will be possible.

In the near-darkness, an object catches his eye. He picks it up: a long, heavy wooden brush topped with wiry pig bristles. "What the hell is this?" he demands.

"That?" growls Chindilan. "Why, that's a long-handled camel brush, of course. Because every fucking fugitive needs a long-handled camel brush. Or so your brother tried to tell me, when I went through our packs and took inventory."

"I didn't know it was there," says Mektu. "The bush kits were so well packed. I didn't want to pull everything out."

Chindilan points to a mound of objects near their packs. "Boot spurs, for instance—don't pull *them* out. Hoof picks—you'll miss 'em if they're gone." He starts to kick at the pile. "Riding crop. Leather punch. A spare saddle pad."

Kandri is stunned. "We just *ran* with all that?"

Mektu hides his face in his elbow.

"And see here, the best of the lot," says Chindilan. "A jar of tablets. What kind of tablets? Fucking salt."

∞

They bury the useless gear and smooth the ground above the hole. Then they set out. It is now so dark that they can see little more than the black outline of the island against the stars. As they draw closer, more and more stars vanish behind the looming cliffs. Great irregular boulders ring the island like forgotten toys.

But there are more than boulders, he sees now. Strange walls surround the island, knobby and misshapen, like hedges abandoned for decades. Some have crumbled to knee height; others rise ten or twenty feet above their heads. Only by probing with his fingers does Kandri realize what they have found.

"Coral," he says, awestruck. "This island had a reef about it."

Mektu laughs, incredulous, but the smith's voice is low with amazement. "Feel those sharp edges. Kandri's right; a reef's exactly what we've wandered into. *Jeshar*, it must have been beautiful here."

"What is a reef?" asks Eshett.

They move gingerly into the once-living maze, passing through gaps torn by boulders, now and then scaling the sharp coral walls to check their position. Kandri glances at Mektu. Does he remember those fishing excursions, with their cousins by the sea? The dark curve of dolphins breaching? Schools of lindfish turning the waves to sudden gold?

"Jekka's hell, look up there," says Chindilan, pointing.

To Kandri's amazement, there are buildings atop the island, framed darkly against the stars. "Didn't you know?" says Eshett. "People lived here, Chiloto people. There were fishing towns, temples. And older things—towers, fortresses—from the days of the Empire."

"I wish you trusted us, Eshett," says Mektu. "I wish you'd say why you know so much about—"

He stops dead. His head goes up and he sniffs. "Don't you smell that?" he says.

Now Kandri smells it too. Woodsmoke. Faint but unmistakable. He licks a finger and holds it high. "The wind's from straight ahead," he says.

"Gods of death, there's more of them," says Mektu.

At once, the specter is very real: more killers from Eternity Camp, close by, waiting to pounce. Where to flee, where to hide? How will they keep from being spotted in the moonlight once they light out across the flats?

"Maybe it's not the army," says Eshett.

"I'll bet it's not," says Chindilan. "Why would they light a fire? The Rasanga aren't that stupid. They want to surprise us, not warn us away."

"Then who's out there?" says Mektu, looking for some reason at Eshett. "Merchants? A salt caravan?"

Eshett shakes her head. "Salters have no reason to come here. Even if they're selling to the Prophet, they'd be a day's ride further south, where the cliffs are lower. They could be miners: some say there's gold under the Stolen Sea. Or looters, poking through the dead towns on the islands, taking whatever they can sell. Or just *Tirmassil*."

She speaks the final word with obvious loathing. Kandri glances at her, startled. "*Tirmassil?*" he asks.

"Bandits of the desert. Filth."

He waits, hoping she will elaborate. Mektu, oblivious, rakes a hand through his hair.

"The fuckers!" he blurts suddenly. "What are we supposed to do now? Turn back?"

"Like hell we will," says Chindilan. "We don't know one thing about them. But there's all kinds of death behind us—that's a fact. Let's have a peek at them. If they're dangerous, we'll double back around the island to the south. If not, we'll tip our hats and press on."

No one likes the plan. Or has another to suggest. They creep closer. As they move among the rocks, the smell of woodsmoke grows, along with a stronger smell. It is roasting meat, Kandri realizes—but some gamey, even slightly revolting meat. Dog, horse, camel? He cannot place the scent. But even as he wonders, they round a wide boulder, and firelight stabs their eyes.

They fall back instantly, then look again with great caution. In a large natural clearing in the crumbled reef, six men are standing beside a fire, drinking from tin cups, warming their hands. They are all armed—knives, clubs, a few battered scimitars—but they do not look like soldiers. They are lean and pale and obviously poor. Hollow eyes, short untidy beards. Their desert *kanuts* little more than rags. One man, slightly taller than the rest, wears twenty or more silver rings on each ear. The fire burns in a wide circle of stones. Above the flames, some animal, a bird it seems, is roasting on a spit.

"Scrawny fellows, aren't they?" whispers Chindilan. "That's a relief."

"They don't have bows," said Kandri. "How the hell did they shoot down a bird?"

"And what a bird," says Mektu. "It's the size of a goose. But it smells all wrong. But I want some!"

"Be *quiet*," hisses Kandri. "Fuck. They heard you."

But it is a false alarm. Something else has caught the men's attention: they have all turned suddenly to stare at a point somewhere off to the left. The man with the earrings makes an amused gesture with one hand, and the other men laugh aloud.

He's in charge, Kandri thinks. With great care, he leans out a bit farther. And silently curses.

Thirty feet from the campfire stand another four men. Three are very much like the first six, but one is a pale giant with enormous hands and an expression of casual menace. Their bearing, although slovenly, has something about it that reminds him of army constables.

He hazards one more inch. *There*, he thinks. *I knew it.* Beyond the four men burns a smaller fire, guttering and quailing in the wind. This fire burns in the lee of an overhanging boulder, but it is failing nonetheless. Beside the dying flames lies a man wrapped in a dark cloak, utterly still. And above him, gazing with fury at her guards, stands a girl.

She cannot be more than eighteen. She is short and broad-shouldered and quite obviously strong. She wears a man's tattered trousers and even more tattered coat: the right sleeve is missing entirely, revealing a powerful dark arm. Her face is wide, her eyes bright and slightly bulging. Her large mouth is curled in a sneer.

"*Spakad! Ku hali spakad?*" she bellows.

"*Taya,*" replies the man with the earrings, pointing at himself.

The girl makes a sound of contempt. "Oh, *you're* the doctor now? You lying pig. You can't treat your own fucking sores."

A general argument erupts, partly in Kasraji Common, partly in something Kandri cannot understand. The girl is clearly demanding aid for the man at her feet—and, by her gestures, more fuel for the fire. The men look both sly and uncomfortable. They show her their empty hands, or laugh, or point to the man with the earrings, who appears to speak for them.

Ten armed men, a crazed girl, another man dying at her feet. Kandri slips back behind the rock. "At least it's no ambush," says Mektu.

"I saw camel dung at the clearing's edge," says Eshett. "Fresh dung. It was steaming."

So there are more of them, somewhere, and camels as well. Mektu slides over, making room for Chindilan—and then it happens. Two metal somethings in their gear smack together, with an almost laughably audible *clink*. A shout goes up from the men in the clearing. Blades clash on blades, a challenge.

"Salt rats!" shouts one of them. "We have thirty men here! You want to try your luck?"

Kandri steps out from behind the rock, hands raised high. It is their leader who has shouted, but all ten have weapons drawn. The girl too is staring at him, rage and confusion in her eyes. She is not one of these ruffians, he decides. Her accent, her face and color all belong to some other clan.

"The Gods keep you," shouts Kandri. "We're not salt rats. Not a danger to you, either. We didn't know you were here."

"Atau, who the hell is that?" shouts the girl. She turns to Kandri. "Are you a doctor? *Idi spakad?*"

"All of you, come out into the clearing," shouts the man with the earrings again. "But keep it slow, or by the Buried Saints, we'll cut you down! There's thirty of us."

You're repeating yourself, thinks Kandri. *What are you scared of?*

The travelers step out into the clearing. Eshett raises her hands like Kandri; Mektu looks at the bird on the fire and grins. But Chindilan hefts his axe, staring ferociously at their leader.

"You want to think very carefully before you fuck with us," he says.

"Uncle!" cry both brothers, whirling. Eshett jumps in front of the smith. "Gods' peace!" she cries to the strangers. "My husband is very protective, but he means no harm! We bless you as trail-brothers. *Tam idi tam.*"

Kandri looks at Eshett, impressed. Husband. Quick thinking.

Her words, especially the final three, have an immediate effect. The men look at her with great surprise, and a few of them even smile. The man with the earrings turns uneasily to Chindilan. "Why didn't you say you were Parthan?" he asks.

Kandri looks the men over. *Parthans? These wretches?* He has never met a member of the deep desert clan, but those who have use words like *proud* and *formal*: neither quality is much visible in these men. Kandri turns to Eshett. *Is that what you're speaking, the Parthan tongue? Is that what you are?*

"My husband is not Parthan," says Eshett. "But *ey vrama, brother*s, peace! We have no quarrel with you."

"Nor we with you, unless you've come here to steal," says their leader. He gestures again with his scimitar, and several men ease reluctantly around the travelers to slip among the rocks. After a moment, they return, shaking their heads. "No one's back there, Atau," says one of the men.

"Just the four of you, lighting out across the Yskralem?" says the man with the earrings. "Are you mad? Where are your camels? Where the hell do you hope to get?"

Once again, he addresses his remarks to Chindilan, as though his status as "husband" leaves no doubt that he leads this band.

"Ah, well, just away," mutters Chindilan. "Away east. To the Lutaral, if we're so fortunate."

"But why cross the Yskralem? There's a fair path on this side as far as the Aricoro, and a road from there to Mab Makkutin. It's much longer, to be sure, but there are wells to drink from, and villages, and food."

"We're in a hurry," says Kandri.

"A hurry to die, maybe. This is a terrible place."

The strange girl gives a cry; the men jump and raise their blades. The girl is on her knees, talking to the motionless figure beside her, touching his face. One of her guards—the pale giant—crosses quickly to the group's leader and whispers in his ear. The giant is smiling. The man with the earrings listens, his face impassive.

At last he appears to reach a decision. Sheathing his blade, he turns and waves his men back from the fire. "Come here, then, warm your bones," he says to the travelers. "You're right, woman, we've nothing to fear from each other. *Tam idi tam.*"

They shuffle uneasily forward. When they are quite close, the man bows to them stiffly.

"My name is Atau. Forgive us this welcome; we have been dealing with madness and death."

"You're . . . Parthans?" says Chindilan dubiously.

Atau laughs with sudden force. "Come now, old man! You married a Parthan but cannot tell them from a mongrel like me? No, I am not of the desert blood. My roots run to six different clans, and not one of those people sees enough of themselves in my face to claim me as their own. Do not pity me. There is always a family for those without family, if you care to embrace it. That is where I choose to belong.

"For my boys, the tale is different. Many are the Parthans, whether settled in village or still drifting with the beasts and seasons, who have been slaughtered by the mighty of Urrath for the sin of taking no side in their wars. Half my men were so orphaned. They are loyal to me now as they would be to a mother or father. But they refuse to learn Kasraji, or any cultured tongue. So I have had to learn theirs."

"*She* spoke Parthan," says Eshett, nodding at the girl.

"Did she? Ah, yes, the doctor business." Atau looks bleakly at the girl. "That girl is no follower of mine. She is ill, and very dangerous. The man beside her is dead. She's been carrying his corpse for three days."

"Why would she do that?" says Mektu.

"I just told you, she's gone around the bend. Screams blasphemies, threatens to kill us. She nearly did kill my nephew here."

He throws a glance at the giant. Only then does Kandri notice the resemblance: the youth is like a crude, enormous copy of Atau. The giant smiles and shakes his head.

"She never rattled me. She pulled a knife, is all. From a place no knife belongs."

Atau looks at him sternly. "Watch your mouth, boy. Go on, get back to your post."

The giant shrugs. When he is gone, Atau turns to the travelers and grimaces. "My nephew is a bit of a fool. The girl fancied him, and he ignored my warnings that she was ill. I do not know what passed between them, but it ended with the girl very nearly slitting his throat. Make no mistake: she is deadly, and that knife is still on her person." He sighs. "We're all her enemies now. She thinks we're hiding a doctor from her."

"One of those thirty men of yours?" says Kandri.

Atau's dry face cracks into a smile. "We're not thirty, but there are more of us about than you've seen. I won't apologize for the lie, however. There are some fiends in the Yskralem. Tirmassil, they're called. Flesh traders, hawkers of women and girls—and small boys too; they fetch a good price with the militias."

"Tirmassil," says Eshett. "Very special people. With special rules just for themselves."

Kandri looks at her sharply. *There it is again: pure hate.*

"You know about the Tirmassil?" says Atau. "Have you been in the Yskralem before?"

"They are everywhere," says Eshett. "But yes, I was here once. I swore I'd never come near this place again."

"But a cruel husband's dragged you back all the same."

Chindilan looks at him coolly. "What brings you to this garden spot, friend?"

Atau considers him a moment. As if there are more decisions to be made.

"A gleaning," he says at last. "We heard rumors of an untouched island. A place no one had managed to climb since the sea was drained." He shrugged. "Well, someone has. The whole town has been looted. Nothing left up there but empty homes."

"You scaled those cliffs?" says Kandri, glancing up at the sheer wall.

"I did. Sometimes, the Gods love a fool. You need real climbers, professionals, for a wall like that. She"—he points at the girl—"is such a climber. Her friend there as well. They're human spiders; it's a sight to behold. And so we hired them at great expense. But then the man was felled by snakebite, and the girl lost her mind." He rubs wearily at his cheeks. "I managed to scramble up there myself. Devil's spit, what a waste of a journey! But that's a gleaner's life. If you hear ten stories of riches to be had, six will be bald-faced lies—spread by the competition, usually—three will be gross exaggerations, and the last"—he grins again—"will be an honest mistake. The wisdom of the desert, my dears."

Kandri and Mektu exchange an awkward glance.

"You haven't started begging," says Atau. "I like that. Not that begging would take you far. We can't spare any water, but you'd be welcome to a sip of wine. Just a sip, mind you—for friendship's sake. And I'll let you have a bite of that bird."

"It smells horrible," says Mektu.

Atau frowns at him. "Don't eat it, then," he says.

"Not horrible!" says Mektu, alarmed. "I don't mean horrible, exactly. Just different, putrid. And I'll eat anything. I could chew the ass off a cat."

Kandri turns from his brother in despair. The girl by the smaller fire is watching them again.

"You!" she cries suddenly. "Don't listen to that fucking Atau! He won't give us water, he won't share the firewood, he's just waiting for my sergeant to die!"

Is that sobbing Kandri hears? The fire is now too dim to light her face. "If you're not the doctor, who the hell are you?" she cries.

"Who's asking?" Kandri shouts.

"It's no good reasoning with her," says Atau. "Believe me, we've tried. Every word provokes her further."

"My sergeant is bleeding to death!"

Chindilan's brow furrows. "Bleeding to death? Thought he had a snake-bite."

Atau gives a twitch of impatience. "You want to hear it again? She's mad. The bite of the acuna viper can kill a man in three minutes. He howled for twenty; he was that strong, but he's dead and rotting now, and she won't face the truth. I'm guessing his howls broke her mind."

"Why does she call him *sergeant?*"

"Because she's insane."

"A bandage!" shouts the girl. "Just one bandage! I'll pay you for it. Damn me to hell if I lie!"

Now Kandri is certain: the girl is struggling with tears. He looks at his brother. "Give me the medical kit," he says. Mektu squats down, fumbling in his backpack.

"What are you doing?" says Atau.

Kandri doesn't answer. He does not know himself.

"Ang's tits, man, you can't treat a carcass."

"Maybe *she* needs help," says Mektu.

"She sure as Pitfire does. The Gods' help, or a priest's. And your friend will need a priest as well—to sing him the Last Prayer, if she pulls that knife."

Mektu hands over the kit. Atau moves in front of Kandri, uncomfortably close.

"Don't do it, boy."

Kandri steps around him. The four men guarding the girl seem confused by his sudden advance but do not hinder him. Atau's huge nephew mutters something that makes the others laugh.

The girl herself beckons wildly to Kandri. When he nears her, she makes a grab for the medical kit. Kandri smacks her hand.

"You try that again and I'll just walk away."

"You're no doctor," she says. "You'll just fuck him up."

"I'm a soldier."

"The fuck you're a soldier. Which battalion are you with?"

"Is he alive or dead, girl?"

"Which battalion? Whose command?"

They lock eyes, one belligerent staring down another, and perhaps she sees something she recognizes. For when he asks her to show him the wound, she does not curse or argue, only bends and rolls the big man carefully onto his back.

He is a few years older than Kandri. His skin pale in the flickering light. The girl parts the cloak and the tattered remains of his shirt.

Kandri winces. A jagged lesion, caked with dry blood, runs from his shoulder to the middle of his chest. The wound still bleeds slowly near the collarbone.

Snakebite?

His mind erupts. He turns and shouts in Chiloto: "They're lying! Get away from them *now*!"

Snarls and curses. Atau calls his men to his side. Kandri's companions fall back; Chindilan pushes Eshett behind him. Mektu, looking deadly, whirls his machete and screams.

The man's wound is not three days old, or even one. His flesh is dry and cold to the touch. Kandri looks again at the girl. She is really quite young.

"I'm sorry," he says.

She brings her face near his own and screams like a wildcat: "*Help him, motherfucker!*"

Kandri catches her wrist. Without breaking eye contact, he presses her hand down against the man's chest. The stillness there, the cold. The girl's face contorts. She breathes in deep shuddering gasps, choking on snot and tears.

"I'm sorry," Kandri says again.

She stares with disbelief, then hatred. Then perhaps no longer sees him at all. From her throat comes a sound that frightens him. She rises, turns to face Atau.

His men have formed a line some twenty feet away. Atau's voice when he calls to them is utterly cold.

"You were right, of course. The Tirmassil are everywhere. And we do have special rules, just for ourselves."

Two of Atau's men draw close to him, whispering. Then the whole group begins to fan out around the clearing. They look more cunning than deadly—no, these are not hardened warriors—but there are nine of them, and Atau has already proven that he is more than he seems. And there is his nephew. The enormous youth is staring at the girl with contempt. When he catches her eye, he makes a thrusting motion with his hips.

"My men," says Atau, "wish me to remind you to pray with special fervor. They listen to mystics, some of them. I do not. But they would warn you that the *Darsunuk*, the Time of Madness, is upon us, and that the world's end is in sight. Pray then for peace in the hereafter. Even dead souls lose their way in the Time of Madness."

Kandri looks across the clearing. His brother, Chindilan, and Eshett have drawn closer together. Atau's men are trying to slip behind them again.

"Leave your things," says Atau. "Water, boots, every stitch of your clothes. You're going to walk out into the flats and wait for sunrise. If you cause no further trouble, I'll leave you a pocketknife, and you can make the sort of end you choose. A blade to the throat's much the quicker way, but the sun will do the job as well." He glances at Chindilan. "Your wife stays with us, old man."

"What about the bird?" says Mektu.

Atau turns him a look of perfect bewilderment.

Then the girl seems to hug herself, reaching inside her tattered uniform, and when her hands come forward again they are holding knives. She twists backward at the torso, then snaps her whole body forward with a lunging step and flings her arm out straight.

"*Vahg!*"

And—

"*Vahg!*"

Two motions, two animal screams. Atau's men bolt in panic. Most vanish into the darkness beyond the clearing, but two, including Atau's nephew, lie twitching on the ground.

Mektu rushes after the Tirmassil, howling and brandishing his machete. "Stop, idiot!" bellows Chindilan. "Come back, get your pack on! Kandri, get over here!"

The girl stalks toward the enormous youth. He has managed to pull the knife from his chest and rise to his knees. "Cunt," he says. "Whore's cunt, fucking—"

The girl leaps high and kicks him savagely beneath the chin with the point of her boot. There is a sound like a stick snapped over a knee. She comes out of the leap already marching toward the next man, and this time, Kandri shuts his eyes.

Tirmassil, he thinks. *And we walked up to you like lambs.*

When he looks again, the girl has returned to the giant and is slashing open his leggings with a knife. The cloth rips and she grabs his privates like a handful of seaweed and lowers the knife and once again he cannot look.

Time to go. Time to lose this cursed place, before Atau's men find their courage, or their friends. Time to clear out before that mad girl can—

"You!"

Kandri gives a small, utterly emasculated scream. She is at his elbow, hand and knives dripping blood.

"Whose fucking battalion are you in?"

"Fuck, girl, can't you stop saying *fuck?*"

"Whose battalion are you in?"

She has two faska clutched to her chest. A muscle in her throat is twitching so hard, it appears to be affecting her breathing. Perhaps he won't mention his battalion.

Chindilan storms up to him, dragging his pack. "Put this on," he snaps. "Girl, you can't come with us. Not if that's all the water you have."

"It's not."

Chindilan glances at the others. "Where's your family, then? Where are you bound?"

"Siakmatarivak."

They blink: the name means nothing to them.

"Who the hell are you people? Siakmatarivak, north of Sendu on the Smoke Road."

"The Smoke Road!" says Mektu. "You're a long way from the Smoke Road. You'll have to cross the Yskralem, like us."

"Cross it? Who the fuck wants to cross it? Your head's so far up your ass you could kiss your liver."

"But you've crossed the Sea already," says Kandri.

Now the girl just stares at them.

"Sister," says Eshett, "what did they do to you? We're at least five days from the East Rim."

The girl's eyes grow wide. She raises a trembling hand to her forehead, leaving a smear of blood. "Never trust people," she says.

ಙ

Minutes later they are running again, the girl alongside, muttering and swearing. It is quite cold now; their breath puffs white in the moonlight. They see no more of Atau's men in the vicinity of the island, but as they move onto the wide white seabed, Kandri looks back and sees a dark figure on a boulder, watching their flight.

For three hours they do not speak, except to debate the path eastward, the signposts of the wheeling stars. When they rest at last, Kandri hands the girl a faska and she drinks it dry. Chindilan looks at Kandri and shakes his head. Kandri knows. They should have asked more questions. They should have demanded to see the water in her pack.

She asks again for his battalion. When he explains that they are deserters from the New Orthodox Revelation Army, the girl laughs so hard, the water comes back up her throat.

"Enemies of the Prophet," she says. "Now you tell me."

You don't know the half, thinks Kandri, but it is too soon to mention their crimes. "Listen," he says, "at nightfall, before we came to the clearing, we saw men heading north across into the scree. Were those Atau's men as well?"

The girl shakes her head, still grinning oddly. "I think you know who they were."

Chindilan swears. Mektu hides his face in his elbow. "Army of Revelation?" says Kandri.

The girl nods. "And not just any grunts. They were elites of some kind."

"Rasanga?" says Kandri, feeling his heart sink like a stone.

"Yes, that was what they called themselves. Real bastards, too; I'd hate to fight them. I wondered how Atau had convinced them to leave us in peace. Now I can guess. He must have promised to keep a lookout for you. If you had surrendered, he wouldn't have left you to die. He'd have delivered you to the Prophet."

"Or our heads at least," says Kandri, "packed in salt."

"Rasanga," says Chindilan. "They'll probably check the northern islands and be back at Atau's camp this time tomorrow. And Atau will have something marvelous to tell them."

A grim silence falls. More to break it than because he expects the knowledge (any knowledge) to improve their plight, he asks the girl if she overheard anything that passed between Atau and the Rasanga. The girl shakes her head and tells him that she was keeping her distance. That Atau's men were goatish and stealthy, always trying to come at her from behind.

Then she lifts her chin, frowning with concentration. "One thing," she says. "It was strange. All the time those big fuckers were speaking, they treated Atau and his men like spittoons. Wouldn't even look at them. But just before they left, I saw their leader's face change. Really change, like he was thinking of something that scared him. And so I listened for a moment, and he said, 'They have awakened the White Child. No one wanted this, not even Her Radiance.' I had forgotten all about it until just now."

"The White Child?" says Eshett. "What the hell is that?"

The brothers look at each other blankly. "No idea," says Kandri. Then he sees that Chindilan is staring at the girl, aghast. When he notices Kandri's look, he quickly drops his eyes, but the effort to hide his response only makes it seem stranger. *Ask him*, Kandri tells himself. But a part of him is afraid of what the smith might say.

"I know what it is," says Mektu. "Her fucking baboon. Has to be."

He looks to the others for support, finds none. The Prophet does love the animal inordinately, but she has not set it up as an object of worship, or suggested it might possess any special role in Orthodox Revelation. And the creature was always awake; it screamed half the night.

No one wanted this. Suddenly, Kandri's mind is racing. An eight-sided courtyard, a palanquin with fresh flowers by the door. A barred window, a white stone urn. The guards' unreasonable fear . . .

"Is something wrong, Kandri?" asks Eshett.

Kandri jumps. "Nothing's wrong," he says, wiping sweat from his forehead.

"A baboon," says the girl. "You're telling me that the Prophet keeps a pet baboon?"

The men just grunt. It's embarrassing. Mektu asks the girl where she learned to throw knives.

"From my grandmother."

The others smile. The girl does not. Kandri clears his throat and asks if Atau truly hired her to scale those cliffs.

"Hired?" She looks at him with sudden anger. "I'm not a whore, you know. I don't sell myself to anyone who chances by. I traveled with that pig because he promised there was a doctor where we were going. And because a God whispered in my ear."

Once more, she is perfectly serious. "Which God?" says Chindilan, and Mektu asks, "Which ear?"

Kandri waves at them in annoyance. "I didn't mean to insult you, sister," he says. "I just wondered how you came to be in the Yskralem at all."

The girl looks at him as though considering whether he merits a reply. At last, she says that she is part of the Lutaral-Lo'ac Unified Survival Forces, under a General Tebassa. The names mean nothing to Kandri. Chindilan, however, looks at her with amazement, and more than a little suspicion.

"Black Hat Tebassa? He's still alive, that old fox? The man who killed the Sartaph of Sendu with a brick?"

The girl's face is impassive. "He deserved death," she says.

"Did he, now?" says Chindilan. "Well, the Prophet has no love for your general, I'm afraid. Used to say she wanted his head on the end of a pike."

The girl looks hard at Chindilan and says she will not get it. But then she confesses that she has not seen her general in months. That his second battalion was massacred by Orthodox Revelation forces at a place called the Megrev Defile, somewhere in the northern Lutaral. That her unit was pursued into the Stolen Sea, attacked anew by night, and scattered. That she and her sergeant took up with Atau's band out of sheer desperation. He was bleeding to death, she says.

Chindilan studies her with narrowed eyes. "You brought a dying man across the Yskralem because they *claimed* to have a doctor?"

The girl looks down at her knees. Her eyes are moist, but her face is all fury. A twitch has begun in her left hand.

"I missed my throw," she says. "The second knife was for Atau. The first one had to be for his nephew, that giant prick."

Mektu is openly gaping at her. Kandri prods him with an elbow.

"I see it now," says the girl. "They tricked us. They made us drink foul wine, saying there was no water to spare. I thought I had a fever, but it was the wine that hurt me, or something in the wine. Maybe they marched us for a week through the Yskralem. I can't remember. Things are missing in my head."

"Well," says Kandri, "do you remember your name?"

"Trouble," says the girl.

Mektu cackles like a crow.

"Trouble," says Chindilan. "That's just dumb. 'Hello, Trouble. Good morning, Trouble.' I'm not going to call you that."

"Then fuck you."

"Fuck you *and* your tall tales," says Chindilan amiably.

"Uncle!" cries Kandri. "What's the matter with you? *Jeshar*, as if *we* weren't a bit—strange."

"Strange is one thing. Lies are another." He looks sharply at the girl. "I've seen faces like yours. Heard accents, too. You say you come from down the Smoke Road? Well, maybe that's right. Two thousand miles down the Smoke Road, in the Nfepan Jungles."

The girl's cold eyes are locked on Chindilan. "You don't know shit," she says.

Chindilan holds her gaze a moment, then turns and addresses the others. "I have nothing against this little killer," he tells them, "but she said it herself: never trust people. Why should we make an exception for her? And even if she's telling the truth—if she was really under Black Hat Tebassa—then she'll have a hell of a lot of enemies in the Lutaral. We don't need them, Kandri."

The girl leans toward Chindilan, unblinking. "You," she says, "don't need *mine*?"

Eshett touches the smith's burly arm. "Why don't we all just take a deep—"

"Trouble!" shouts Mektu. "Say, Trouble, is that your sister Calamity over there? You're not related to old Doc Disaster up in Nasty Town, are you? Or his understandably fucked-up wife—"

"Be quiet, Mek," says Kandri. "Listen, girl, isn't there something else we could call you?"

"Eshett's right, this is pointless," says Chindilan. "Let's have a look at that water you say you're carrying, girl, or else—"

"Call me the Wind," booms Mektu, spreading his arms, "for I am he who BLOWS and FLOWS and NIPS your little—"

"*Mektu!*" shouts Eshett, leaping to her feet.

Mektu buries his face in his elbow. The girl looks from one to another. "I can leave right now," she says.

"I'm sure you can," snaps Eshett. "You can walk out into the flats and be dead of thirst by midday. Or get cornered by more Tirmassil than you can kill with those knife tricks. And I'm sure *all* of you can get into a fight over nothing. Go ahead, do it! Stab each other, use your skills. The carrion birds will be impressed."

The girl looks at her steadily. With one hand, she frees the buckles of her pack and flings it open. Inside are five bulging leather faska. The men glance at each other, abashed.

"Get up," says Eshett, "and stop this foolishness. You don't have officers to think for you anymore."

No one argues. They march on, stomp-crunch-stumble, over the glittering seabed. Except for their footfalls, the hours pass in silence; not even the buzz of an insect cracks the night. It is now bitterly cold. The moon, well past its zenith, throws their shadows before them on the salt. Kandri thinks of Ariqina. Her hands are like this girl's hands, strong and capable, good at what they do. He can close his eyes and feel them. He can still his thoughts and hear her voice.

"I have a clan name," says the girl.

"Of course you do," says Eshett. "Well, what is it? Don't be shy."

"Talupéké Orolekitju ukka Ilammad uk Itri."

"How about 'Girl?'" says Mektu.

"My sergeant just called me Talupéké. You can call me that."

"See, now that's a lovely name," says Chindilan. "Talupéké. What does it mean?"

"Trouble," says the girl.

IV. VISION

"When the Gods return," said the yatra, "you and I shall both be judged, O Prince of Many Splendors. Your empire is great, and my life is very long. You dispatch envoys, soldiers, assassins to work your will; I slip in at the ear, and change the will in the place where it is born. You break bodies on the rack; I pinch souls. Oh, we are both very wicked. But my wickedness has earned me only the freedom of Urrath, her barrens to embrace me, her wastes to praise my name. Yours has brought you the obeisance of the four hundred clans, a vault of silver, meals of hawks' hearts and foxes' tongues, emeralds for your fingers, young men and women for your bed."

Ut'xing laughed. "That is because the Gods love me, their finer creation, above a cold spirit who tumbles on the winds. Their judgment? It is here already: they judge me fit to rule. My word is law from the shores of Važenland to the mouth of the Ghel."

"None doubt your strength," replied the yatra. "But the play has many acts, auspicious king. Are you so certain of the playwright's favor? Does not every story turn before its end?"

ANNALS OF UT'XING

I n what remains of the night they march unhindered. The moon lifts and fills the canyon with its radiance, but it reveals no man or any other living thing. Toward dawn, they find a boulder field and erect their sunshield in its midst: canvas above canvas, four inches of air between the two, a channel diverting the heat.

Talupéké lifts a bundle from her pack and throws it to Chindilan: "Red figs, old man." The smith grunts and chooses the smallest, but he cannot hide his pleasure when he bites into the fruit. Kandri grins. He unwraps a seedcake and cuts it into fifths. "Where will you go, once we climb out of here?" he asks Talupéké.

"Wherever my general leads our forces," she says, looking at him warily. "*I'm* not a deserter."

"Those Tirmassil must be wrong in the head," says Mektu "How do you take a goose and make it stink so badly? Did they stuff it with shit?"

"Not a goose," says Talupéké. "That was an Ornaq vulture. I told them they were fools to cook it. I told them to bury it far from the camp."

Roasted carrion bird: Kandri's stomach gives a tiny lurch. Although in fact, he's seen men eat worse on the battlefield. There is an art to putting things out of your mind.

"Didn't I tell you?" says Chindilan to Mektu. "Ornaqs are big but not monstrous. Ang's tears, though, what a filthy thing to cook!" Then he turns, feeling Talupéké's eyes on him. "What's the matter, girl?"

"It was a hatchling," she says. "It fell out of a nest on the clifftop. Atau's son found it and killed it with a stone. I tried to warn them. Don't handle the feathers, I said. They didn't believe me at all."

Kandri finds he has no wish to believe her, either. "That 'hatchling' of yours must have weighed thirty pounds."

"People will call anything an Ornaq until they've seen one," says Talupéké.

Roasted carrion bird *hatchling*. Now Kandri does feel ill.

"I told them the mother would return, and that she'd hit them like a demon out of hell." Talupéké tilts her head, perplexed. "But she never did return. She must have been hunting far from the islands. Atau's son was a lucky man."

"That's an odd way to put it," says Kandri.

Sleep eludes them for a time. Even beneath the canvas, curled into the shadows of the boulders, it is hellishly hot. They keep very still and say nothing. Under the midday sun, the salt wastes turn to sheets of fire, dazzling them at a glance.

Kandri lies with one arm over his face. Beneath his elbow he watches Talupéké furtively. She is flat on her back with her unsheathed mattoglin upon her chest. Seventeen, perhaps only sixteen. At that age, he was hiding cheroots, feeling up the girls who would let him, writing moony love letters to Ariqina. Those were quiet years in the Valley: the liberation of the heartland completed, the surge northward into Važek territory hardly begun. For Kandri, the war was barely visible, a monster prowling somewhere east of the mountains, nothing that could cross them to prey on his life. He'd never spoken to a soldier, excerpt Uncle Chindilan. He had never imagined the horror hidden in a blade.

Talupéké's eyes are red and puffy. Over and over he watches them start to drift close. Each time this happens, she awakens with a violent twitch.

ಐ

Nightfall. A lone splash of daylight on the horizon. Somehow they have all overslept.

Kandri staggers to his feet. He is about to wake the others, but a strange reluctance comes over him. He is dizzy and his thoughts feels strange; is he about to be sick?

He steps away from the other four. The wind is cold and the stars are infinite. No, he's not himself. His balance: all off. Small movements of his legs seem to propel him weightlessly across the land. When he turns, he finds that he has walked not the three or four paces he imagined but a good fifty feet, and the still forms of his companions are barely discernible against the dark. Alarmed, he starts to hurry back. He moves closer to the sleepers, but they are still far away. Not just fifty feet, then: he has ambled ten times that distance on these buoyant legs. What is happening to him? Dehydration, dysentery? Fever from a wound?

He stops in his tracks.

High above him, shapes are gliding through the sky. They are pale and soundless and scattered far and near over the Yskralem. Graceful, fluid shapes, white stencils, rocking and pitching in the air.

They are ships. Long-oared galleys, high-prowed fishing boats with bat-tened sails, massive carracks, tiny dhows. They move like mist, swifter than they first appeared. Some drag nets beneath them; others winch in hauls of invisible fish. Kandri turns in a circle. He can see men working the halyards, swinging from the braces, scaling the masts. A small boy dangles from a bowsprit, kicking his heels. A white anchor drops on a translucent chain. It is not one day he is witnessing but centuries. Not the wasteland through which they have walked but the home waters of a people. These people. The ones from whom the sea was stolen.

Raiders come. Warriors mass at gunwales as ship closes on ship. Over the gaps, men leap with soundless war-howls, feet thumping down on quarter-decks, swords driven through the chests of merchant traders and fisherfolk. A mainmast topples; ghostly flames consume a sail.

There above him: a man's legs are on fire. He drops his cutlass and flies to the rail of his ghost ship and leaps. The fire vanishes, but the man sinks swiftly, tearing at his boots and clothing, reaching hopelessly for the sky.

He has coins stuffed in his pockets: many pockets, many coins. He rips at them, desperate; the coins blink and flicker like the bubbles from his mouth. Deeper, deeper. His body jerks a final time. It reaches the sea floor ten feet from Kandri, bobs there, lifeless, a heel tracing patterns in the sand. His eyes still open. His short beard combed gently by waters vanished from the earth.

Ghost coins fall around him, winking. Suspended high above, a single boot.

He runs for his friends with all his might. In the skies, fleets are burning; dead men fall like snow. He cannot shout. He trips and rolls and finds his feet and keeps running. The others loom near at last: Mektu and Talupéké motionless, Chindilan twitching a little in his sleep.

Eshett, however, is wide awake. She stands apart from the others, reaching for the heavens. Her face is wild, exultant.

But no, he's deluded; she lies asleep with the others. And a new fear surges in Kandri: what if *they* are the mirage? What if he is of this place and always has been, and the journey across the sea floor only the fancy of a short-bearded man, a man with one boot and useless riches; what if he has drowned here, alone?

He closes half the distance. And half again. And half again.

ɷ

Later, as they march, he needs no one to tell him that he's had a nightmare. But what is uncanny is how well he recalls the vision. Every detail, every silent moment, except the one when he rejoined the others, either by running wild-eyed into their midst or waking with a gasp between his brother and Eshett. No matter how he searches his mind for that transition, he cannot find it. His leap back to the living world is gone.

ɷ

They walk all night into a chilly headwind, over land flat and bare as a blade. The moon glitters on the salt as if on polished marble; fine sand peppers their cheeks. It is such empty country that they are all startled by what the dawn light reveals.

It is another island, even taller than the colossus behind them, and once again shaped like an hourglass. But atop this island is an enormous structure. They stop in their tracks, pass the telescope around. Battlements, crumbling but massive, enclose the summit in a ring of amber stone. A broken tower stabs at the sky.

"A fortress," says Chindilan. "Imperial, or older."

As the light grows the scene becomes uncanny. Bands of color streak the cliffs, salmon pink, bruise purple. And the erosion of the cliffs is far more severe than in any previous island. In many places, the fortress walls rise above open air.

"When those stones come down, the whole Yskralem will hear it," says Mektu.

"Some kind of naval base," says Chindilan, passing the telescope on. "See how those cliffs fold in on themselves, around the corner? What could that be but a cove?"

"I don't see a path up to the walls," says Talupéké. "If that is a cove, maybe there's a way up inside. Or maybe no one's been there since the Theft of the Sea."

Kandri scowls at the island. There it sits astride their path, smug in its mystery and menace. Of course it offers shelter. They could do with another cool day, a solid roof overhead. And from those walls they could study the land about them for a day's march in all directions.

So, of course, could anyone else.

Predictably, an argument begins. "It's *getting* there that confounds me," says Chindilan. "Up close we'd find plenty of hiding places—hell, we could be directly underneath the walls and they'd be none the wiser. But we'd have to cross those flats in perfect darkness. Even moonlight could give us away."

"We should go around," says Eshett.

"Impossible," says Mektu. "If the army's up there, they'll have telescopes, and a man with a scope could spot us at twenty miles. We're nearly too close as it is. We'd lose days, and we don't even know that there's any reason. What we do know is that a Wolfpack is behind us."

"Close behind, maybe," adds Talupéké. "Your brother's right. Every hour we're not moving due east is a gift to your Prophet."

"Letting ourselves be seen would be a bigger gift," says Eshett. "We should go around."

Kandri's mind hurts: too many choices, too little sleep. He doesn't have the heart to speak of their water problems now. *We must stay cool,* he thinks. *Every step must be efficient.*

At last the debate tips in favor of avoiding the island altogether. Wearily, they shoulder their packs and fall back, a mile or more, to round the island on its southern flank. But as dawn approaches, they stumble upon an object that changes their calculations entirely.

It is the wreck of an old fishing trawler, demasted, wedged on its side among rocks. A long wound in the hull gapes at them like a carious mouth. Ancient barnacles still cling to the sun-bleached planks. The anchor chain, feathered with salt and rust, snakes across the seabed for some fifty yards before it dives beneath the salt.

"Found our day camp, haven't we?" says Mektu. "Couldn't ask for better shelter, from the sun or enemy eyes."

Kandri feels his breath grow short. He half-expects to see white wraiths spinning about the vessel in the last shadows of the night. But there is nothing of the sort, and he can find no legitimate reason not to spend the day in the boat.

Easy, child. You can't drown in an empty sea.

Kandri smiles. He isn't sure whose voice he's imagining—mother, birth-mother, father, friend?—but the words are comforting nonetheless.

They crawl in through a gash in the bow. Inside, the boat is merely a shell, earth-filled and odorless. A great oblong of daylight enters through the cargo shaft: something to block with the sunshield.

Chindilan moves to the stern and looks out through a porthole. "Beautiful," he says. "We can watch the fortress all we like from here. One flicker of movement—or a torch at nightfall—and we carry on around. But if there's nothing, I say we make straight for it, and have a look from those battlements ourselves."

"If we can find a way up there," says Mektu.

The telescope, when they train it anew on the fortress, answers one question: the folded cliffs do indeed form a cove. Other boats lie abandoned in its mouth, and farther in, rows of blackened stumps suggest the remains of a pier. In the deepest recess of the cove is a great mound of earth and rock. Directly above, the wall is shattered. It is the first real gap they have seen.

"There's a big arch standing yet," says Mektu, his eye to the telescope. "I suppose that's the main gate, or the remains of it. What do you think: were they sacked after the waters fell or before? I'll bet you three sips from my faska it was pirates, long ago."

"Don't fuck around with the water," says Kandri.

"I was only kidding, brother."

"Kid about something else."

Kandri sets his back to the hull. His eyes are in actual pain. Mektu notices his vigorous rubbing and asks why he spent half the night staring up at the skies.

"I was just . . . checking," says Kandri.

"Checking? What the hell for?"

Kandri stares him down. He would rather swallow nails than tell his brother about the ghosts.

"My eyes don't feel right either," says Eshett.

"Nor mine, come to think of it," says Chindilan. "They itch."

Kandri looks from one to another. Deep inside him, an alarm begins to sound.

Then Mektu says that his arrow wound feels warm to the touch. Kandri bolts upright. "What do you mean, warm? Why didn't you tell us?"

"I just noticed," says Mektu, taken aback.

Kandri drags him into the daylight. The wound has closed, front and back, but at the arrow's exit point, the skin is puffy and red. "Mektu, Mektu," he says, too alarmed even for anger, "you have to fucking *talk* when this sort of thing happens."

"I'm talking now," says Mektu. "It changed suddenly, that's all." He looks at Eshett. "I'm not a fool, although he tries to make me look like one. Especially when you're around."

"I'm always around," says Eshett.

Talupéké smirks. Mektu glares at each of them, as though he has discovered some cabal of ridicule. "I know as much about medicine as Kandri," he declares. "I worked in her clinic too."

"Whose clinic?" asks Eshett. "What are you talking about?"

"Never mind," snaps Kandri. "Mek, listen to me: there's still a chance it's not serious, just angry flesh trying to heal. But will you please, please watch it like a fucking hawk?"

"And stop poking at it, fool," says Chindilan. "And for Ang's sake, keep it clean."

Mektu drops his hand, too angry to look at them now. "I'll bathe it with rosewater," he says.

❧

After a quick meal they stretch out in the shade. Once again Kandri takes the first watch, propping the telescope in the fist-sized hole. This time Talupéké is almost instantly asleep. Watching her, Kandri finds a smile on his face. *Starting to trust us.* The thought lifts his spirits. By rights they should have died on the rim of the canyon. By rights they should have been murdered by Atau. Instead they are well into the crossing, and armed with bows, and the deadliest sort of wounds for runaways, wounds to the legs or feet, are something none of them have suffered. The Gods have not abandoned them yet.

Then Talupéké begins to twitch. A moan escapes her; one hand gropes beneath the coat she has rolled up for a pillow. Kandri is about to nudge her when Eshett opens her eyes. She crawls over to the girl.

"Wake up," she whispers. "Sister, wake now. It's just a dream." But the girl goes on twitching, her faced creased in rage or fear. Eshett taps her arm.

Talupéké explodes to her feet and lashes out with her mattoglin, which seems to appear out of nowhere. Eshett, astonishingly quick herself, twists and hurls herself away. The tip of the blade flashes within an inch of her throat, only slightly farther from Kandri's chest, and bites deep into the boat's rotting side.

178

Everyone howls. Talupéké gasps into full wakefulness, rips the blade from the wall, and brandishes it, consciously this time, as though expecting them to close ranks and kill her on the spot. Eshett reaches out for her; Chindilan hauls her brutally back. He points a thick finger at Talupéké and shouts: *You rabid dog! You butchering batshit savage!* Kandri, appalled, grabs his uncle by the shoulders and begs him to be quiet. Mektu does not appear to know what is happening. He waves his own machete and bellows wordlessly.

Kandri moves between the smith and Talupéké, arms spread wide. The girl herself has backed against the hull, reciting the Lone Soldier's prayer.

"To hosts of hell my brethren fell, but swift to Thee I fly—"

"Stop that," Kandri shouts. "No one's going to hurt you, I promise. Will you please, please drop that blade?"

"Drop it, bitch!" screams Mektu.

They are drowning; all the sanity has bled from this boat. Talupéké's eyes leap from face to face, her chest heaves like a bellows. "I'm offering again," she says, "to pick up and leave."

"Accepted!" says Chindilan.

"*Not* accepted!" cries Eshett. "Shut your mouth, you lard-headed old donkey! Think about the fate that brought this girl to us!"

"Think about *fate!*" screams Mektu, louder than the rest of them combined.

Chindilan snorts. "Don't talk to me about fate. There's blind chance and tough choices, and I'm fucking tired of choosing badly. No mystic fate made you a streetwalker."

Kandri seizes his hands. "Uncle, shut up! For the love of Ang—"

Chindilan stamps his foot. "That girl almost took Eshett's head off!"

"But she didn't," says Eshett.

"She didn't!" screams Mektu. "But she almost! What does it mean?"

Eshett takes the machete from his hand.

"Your uncle's right," says Talupéké. "I'm not safe to have around. Why do you think I tried to leave in the first place? I could kill one of you."

"Or," says Kandri, "you could stay with us, and sleep with your blade out of reach."

That, somehow, is the end of the argument. Not a resolution, but an end. The girl retreats to the stern of the boat and crouches, trembling, the matto-glin across her knees. The others mill about, waiting for their nerves to settle. Chindilan can meet no one's eye.

But they have marched all night, and the next march awaits them, and soon everyone but Kandri is asleep. When his watch is over, he lies down and wraps his headscarf tight over his eyes. He dreams of storms and the trawler underway, the cries of men and seabirds, boots on the top deck, a fierce wind tearing at the sails. He is there in the roaring darkness, hauling ropes, swaying, stumbling. A great city awaits them on the horizon but will not submit to scrutiny, it darts and whirls, and the glimpses he catches are from the corner of his eye. Likewise the sailors: no faces, only forms. Who are these people, these half-drowned, desperate souls? Warriors, fisherfolk, his family, the living and the dead. All of them exiles, riding forces beyond anyone's mastery, praying for dry land.

⁢

"Kandri?"

" . . . "

"Kandri?"

"*Jeshar*, Mek. I was sound asleep."

"That's all right. Isn't it strange, though? First Ari, then Papa. Two peo-ple we loved just disappeared. And now we're trying to do the same thing. Do you suppose we'll ever see them again?"

"Yes. Hell yes. We'll see them both before the end."

"How can you be so sure?"

"I don't know, Mek. I just feel it. Go to sleep."

"And now it's our turn to run. I wonder if that means we're as good as they are."

"Not yet, Mektu. But maybe we will be, when we find our true selves. Maybe we'll drink from the Well of Fire."

"Like Ari used to say."

"Right," says Kandri quietly. "Now that's enough, let's—"

"Or maybe we're all running for the same reason, Kan. Maybe when a place fills up with too much badness, you can spot the good people because they run for the hills."

"Brother, I'm begging you. Go to sleep."

"And with the yatra it's exactly the same. Your mind fills up with the demon, with all its tricks and lies and pokes and snickering, like an evil storm, black water pouring in through a hole in the roof, and you try to block the hole but it keeps coming, and your soul has to run, but where can it run to? It's a soul. It belongs where it is, and the yatra's there too and its arms end in razors, so your soul leans out the attic window and cries like a fool, waves its arms, cries for help, which is not easy for anyone to give if you think about it. Which is why I am like I am."

ဢ

Minutes later his brother is asleep and snoring, and Kandri is as wide awake as one thrown into ice water. His fury boundless and impotent. The Gods are sick bastards, to make people who snore. Mektu gets it from Lantor: a man whose snores could wake the dead.

He thinks of his last real conversation with his father. It was just after their interview with the Prophet, when Her Radiance had asked about his fear of drowning, and Kandri had defied her, keeping his silence. Father and son had left the palace compound and wandered a bit through Eternity Camp, too shaken to speak. Thirty minutes passed before the Old Man broke the silence.

"That was a risky hand you just played."

"I couldn't do it," said Kandri. "I tried to form the words but they wouldn't come."

"Don't start lying to *me*," said Lantor Hinjuman. "You didn't want to answer her question."

"Papa," says Kandri, desperate, "the last thing on earth I could want is to offend Her Radiance, the soul of our people, the mother of eleven future kings! I love the Prophet. You know that."

"Does *she* know you love her? That's what matters."

"I'll prove it. I'll show her with deeds of righteousness."

Kandri was parroting Revelation doctrine—but why not, if the doctrine was true? He was, in those few fleeting months, a believer: no one made it through Army training without at least *believing* that they believed. And the Ghalsúnay massacre was still a year away.

His father startled him by taking his hand. The Old Man's eyes focused on the copper ring Ariqina had placed on his finger. "Where *did* that come from, anyway?"

"A fever-syrup bottle."

"And to hell with my questions, too." The Old Man smiled as though in approval, but he had yet to recover his poise. He took a flannel from his pocket and mopped his brow.

"Well, she didn't punish you this time. Just keep your head down, for Ang's sake. And Kandri—" The Old Man looked him straight in the eye. "If you hear that I'm dead—some terrible accident, some brawl—don't you believe it."

"Dead?"

"I've told your brother the same, but I'm not sure he was listening."

"Papa, what in Jekka's hell are you talking about? I may be in uniform, but I'm still your son. You can tell me."

"Telling's the easy part. Can I untell you later? For my own sake? For yours?"

"Are you in trouble? Is something wrong back home?"

"I may not be home much longer. Your mother's provided for, and your siblings, and the help. My books will be hidden. And the library's a goner, your mother's after it, she wants a sewing room, why is every woman in the world obsessed with clothes—"

Kandri grabbed his shoulders. His father looked up, startled by the new, Army strength of Kandri's hands.

"Don't you pull this shit, Papa. We're grown men. Where are you planning to be, if not at home?"

His father pursed his lips. "Grown men. Yes, of course. Even your sisters are growing up. Emi has a young man in her life, can you believe it?"

"Oh, Papa, he's been hanging around for years."

"And Nyreti is devout," said the Old Man. "Very, *very* devout."

His voice was suddenly bitter, but why? His elder daughters' religious zeal was even older news than Emi's suitor. For as long as Kandri could remember, Nyreti had slept beneath a painting of Her Radiance, youthful and strong, leading her people along Heaven's Path through the Wilderness of Sin.

What was his father trying to tell him? Where did he mean to go, and what did Nyreti have to do with it? Lantor Hinjuman shook his head, muttering that he'd said too much. Kandri would learn nothing more on the matter for a year.

That evening the Old Man dined with his sons. Mektu chattered about the rigors of training, the survival tips passed on by Betali (recruited six months earlier), the terrifying spectacle of the blackworms at feeding time, how the Rasanga reminded him of figures from the *War Choral*. Lantor shot Kandri looks across the table. Finally, he interrupted Mektu's harangue.

"Your birth-mother, Kandri: she had an elder brother who still lived by the old ways, out in the desert. A real rough character, although his heart was good. We met just twice. I don't know what became of him, or if he's still above the earth. But when I look at you now, I see his face looking back."

Kandri was stunned. The Old Man rarely spoke of his birth-mother. He thought again to ask the name of her clan, but the question always made his father irritable.

A drum sounded, and the brothers shot to their feet. "Night patrol, Papa," said Mektu.

Their father rose and kissed them, then saluted with a touch of his old rascally grin. His hand tapped his forehead: *remember*. Before sunrise, he was gone.

Kandri was deeply worried about the Old Man. But a letter from Dyakra Hinjuman soon confirmed that he had ridden straight home, and was busier than ever. More letters followed, over several months, full of trivial news about the household, cheerful nothings about life in the Valley. Nothing changed. The Old Man labored on.

"It was just talk, all that 'Don't believe I'm dead' shit," said Mektu. "Fathers get nervous when their sons go to war. He wanted to impress us, to prove he's still a man."

Kandri disagreed. "Papa never tries to impress anyone. He's just . . . impressive."

Mektu shrugged. Then, with a loud laugh: "The old donkey! Where would he be without his secrets? He'd be nude."

In autumn, a grim-faced major pulled the brothers aside. Their father was missing, he said. The Prophet had sent him a summons the week before, calling him once again to Eternity Camp. "I don't know what the Enlightened One had in mind for him, boys. I do know he set out in this direction. We know he passed the first checkpoint in the mountains—his name is in the station log. But he never reached the second. The army's investigating. Don't lose heart."

Two days later the Old Man's pony was found wandering near Green Pass, and his checkered scarf was recovered nearby, snagged in weeds at the edge of a cliff. A fool could read the signs: the pony had slipped or shied, flinging Lantor Hinjuman over the precipice. He was decomposing in some crevasse, or in the foaming river a thousand feet below.

The boys knew better, of course. Their father had staged his death. He had needed to disappear, and so he had. Neither of them would entertain another version of events for an instant. But the mystery only deepened: why had the Prophet called him back to Eternity Camp? And why had he responded to that call with such a charade?

&

The answer came sixteen months later, when Kandri lay recovering from his skull fracture in the army hospital. Dyakra Hinjuman had been allowed to care for him. She came with Nyreti, twenty-two herself that year and immensely helpful on the journey from Blind Stream; and Perch, their little brother, who was not at all helpful but strangely insistent.

The three of them stayed a fortnight; Dyakra rented a shack in the village. Perch, now eleven, remained a troubled child and still slept with a knife, but his behavior in the hospital was exemplary. Day after day he sat with Kandri and their mother and sister, never complaining, listening to talk he was too young to understand. Mektu joined them when his duties permitted, entertaining and infuriating the family by turns. Kandri had thrown him out when he asked a burn victim if he ever expected to enjoy grilled meat again.

One morning Nyreti slept in, and their mother, after an hour at Kandri's bedside, excused herself to take a walk. No sooner had she left the ward than Perch leaned close to Kandri and whispered. "The Old Man's gone to the desert, Kandri."

Kandri grew still. He stared at his youngest sibling for what felt like an age. At last he cleared his throat. "He told you?"

The boy nodded sagely. "Only me. Just before he faked his accident."

"Why you, Perch?"

"Because no one thinks I know anything. So no one ever asks questions. But I have a question, Kan. Where's the desert? Can I walk there from Blind Stream?"

Kandri sat up and kissed his brother on the forehead. The effort sent a crazed bat of pain flitting around inside his skull.

"It's too far, Perch. Now listen: do you know why he left?"

Again, the solemn nod. "He didn't tell me, but I know. It's all Nyreti's fault." The boy looked over his shoulder, as if Nyreti might have snuck up behind him. Leaning close to Kandri's ear, he said, "I hate her. She says mother's a heretic and that Lord Jekka is going to claim her as a bride in hell."

"She said that?"

"And she was always nagging Papa. How he should be helping the war effort. How he should build things. For the army."

"Oh, Gods," said Kandri. "No."

"She blabbed about him, too—I'm sure she did. 'Ya ya ya, my Papa can build anything.' Until finally an army boss came to see him. A big man with medals on his chest. He wanted Papa to build war machines. He said, *Every Chiloto has a duty, Hinjuman. And yours is mechanical.*"

"What did the Old Man say?"

Perch gave him a funny look. "Papa was not very nice. He said the Prophet was *well supplied with mechanical servants.* I don't know what that meant, but it made the boss really angry. He told Papa to *get his clever ass to Eternity Camp* by the end of the week. Then he walked out without drinking his coffee. The next day, Papa left."

"And they really think he's dead, back home?"

Perch gave him a fragile smile. "Everyone but me," he said.

Kandri's headache was searing. He had not done so much thinking since the day of the massacre. He told Perch to wait for New Year's Day, and then to take their mother aside and tell her everything. By then, he reasoned, no one would be looking for the Old Man any longer. By then, it would be safe for her to know he was alive.

"But Perch, the desert's fuck—the desert's *enormous*, right? Didn't he say anything else about where he was going?"

"A little bit."

"Tell me, for Ang's sake! Before someone comes."

Perch fidgeted. "I was crying. I didn't want him to go. He said I'd been bellyaching since the day I was born."

"That's Papa," said Kandri.

"He said that he had to go to the desert to put an end to some nonsense. I asked him what kind of nonsense. Do you know what he said to me?"

"Something nasty, I'll bet."

"No," said Perch. "He said, *'The nonsense that started because I was afraid.'*"

⅋

Two hours to sunset. Chindilan, who has the last watch, is standing outside with his back to the ruined vessel. Kandri crawls from the wreck and stands beside him.

"Cooler out here now," he murmurs.

"So it is," says Chindilan. He gestures with his head in the direction of the fortress. "Five hours we've watched that island. No movement, no sign that anybody's home. Mektu says the shadow of a bird passed over us, but that was hours ago."

He stands straight and looks at Kandri. "Still no way to know," he says, "whether we'd save or doom ourselves if we go up there."

"True enough," says Kandri.

There is an uncomfortable pause.

"I don't want the girl to die, Kandri. But my first priority is you."

Kandri kicks at the earth.

"You think I'm a race-hater," says Chindilan.

"Are you?"

The smith frowns and looks away at the island. He begins to tell Kandri about his parents' years in the distant south, before his birth. How his mother worked the edges of the Nfepan jungles, keeping bees, tapping trees for latex, milling and boiling *tetemurih* vines into brilliant blue dye. How his father cooked for two hundred men on a logging crew gnawing its way through those same jungles. How they'd met at a dance.

Kandri, irritated, wonders how a single word of this addresses his question. He bends and looks back through the hole in the boat. His brother and Eshett are awake. She appears to be extracting a splinter from his foot.

"I'm not narrow minded," says Chindilan. "I've seen a fair bit of the world. Not as much as your father, of course, but a fair bit."

"Why didn't you two ever travel together?" Kandri asks.

Chindilan is startled. "Don't you know? Lantor asked me to keep an eye on all of you. He wanted me in the village whenever he couldn't be."

"Couldn't be?" Kandri snorts. "Didn't choose to be, you mean."

Chindilan gives him a careful look. "How much do you know about his travels, boy?"

Another irritating remark. "What do you expect me to know? Exactly as much as he wanted me to know, that's how much. The days he left and the days he walked back in the door."

"So you don't know *why* he went away."

Kandri's toe digs a recalcitrant stone from the ground. "I know he showed up with kids. He called them orphans, but half of them were probably his bastards. And I'm one more. He gave me his name because I was the first, maybe. Because my birth-mother was the first. She was lucky that way."

Chindilan shook his head. "They weren't Lantor's," he says. "You're the only one of his children not born to Dyakra's womb. I thought he might have talked to you about the orphans, and other things. Before you enlisted, I mean."

"We were a little distracted."

"By Ari's disappearance. I know."

Both men stiffen. The air between them is suddenly harder, more laced with fear. Kandri looks at his uncle, willing him to speak. This weapon-maker, his father's best friend. Whose side would he take, if it came down to choosing?

Then Eshett calls from the wreck, "Where is Talupéké?"

The men jump, bend to stare through the hole. "She was right there," says Chindilan.

"I didn't ask where she *was*," snaps Eshett. "Ang's tears, were you sleeping on watch?"

"No!" says Chindilan. "She didn't leave this way. I couldn't have missed her."

"She must have climbed out through the cargo shaft," says Mektu.

Kandri steps back. The girl is not atop the boat. He turns in a circle, scanning the horizon. Then, an awful thought descending, he rushes to the stern.

"Fuck a frog!"

Talupéké is a mile off, running hard for the island. A single faska over her shoulder, salt dust shining behind her in the evening sun.

"Idiot!" cries the smith. "Come on, boy, let's go after her. Your brother can guard Eshett; he'll love that assignment."

"No," says Kandri.

"What do you mean, no?"

"I mean you stay right here, Uncle. Haven't you done enough?"

Outrage and guilt in the eyes of the smith. Kandri has no time for either. He dives into the wreck, snatches up his machete and headscarf. Moments later he is off, the salt pan thumping underfoot like a whitewashed roof.

His stride is longer than Talupéké's, but she has a big lead. He can see now that she will reach the island long before he can catch her. But what the hell is she doing? Leaving them after all? Or taking on the fortress herself, to make up for nearly beheading one of their party?

She passes the first of the outlying shipwrecks. *Damn her.* If the army is up there, beheading is the best they can hope for. Darkness will fall in little more than an hour, but for now they are excruciatingly visible, their sharp shadows etched on the plain.

Footfalls behind him: Kandri's hand flies to his machete. But it is only Mektu, catching up, his loose scarf trailing behind him like a flag.

"Uncle's in tears," he huffs. "He's afraid she'll kill herself."

Kandri lowers his head and runs faster. The thought has already occurred to him. Some suicides drink poison; others fall on their swords. But Talupéké?

That mountain of rubble. She's going to climb it, climb it to the fortress and—

She reaches the mouth of the cove, vanishing at once among the black stumps of the fallen piers. Two long minutes later, they reach the cove themselves, and in a matter of yards, they are wading in sand—fine, wind-drifted sand, trapped like dust between the cliff walls. They flail on, weaving through the forest of stumps. High above, the fortress walls stand within feet of the eroded cliffs: horrible, to be running beneath something so vast and precarious, ants under the wheel of a cart.

Then Kandri sees her: already climbing the rubble mound. It is enormous, like the debris left by an avalanche, and at its top is the dark hole of the former gate. By the time they reach the mound's foot, she is halfway to the top.

Turn around, Kandri pleads as he climbs. *Just turn and see us. Don't force me to shout.*

And she does turn, a few steps from the broken gate. She does not appear surprised to see them. Kandri lifts his arms and shakes them desperately: *Wait there!*

She studies them, still too far for them to see her expression. Then she walks into the fortress.

"The bitch!" says Mektu. "What if she *knows* the army's up there?"

Kandri looks at him sharply. "Talupéké may be sick, but she's not evil. Two minutes with her should tell you that."

Mektu flinches at the reprimand. "You're right. I'm sorry. Sometimes I don't think it's me talking, Kan."

Kandri rubs his sore eyes. "Let's go and find her," he says.

The climb is steep and awkward. When at last they near the fortress, they drop to their bellies and crawl toward the gate. Kandri locks his eyes on the jagged hole. Among the many things it may confront them with is Talupéké's dead body. Or Talupéké gagged and beaten, in the hands of the Rasanga.

A bow, thinks Kandri. *Why didn't I grab a bow?*

What they find beyond the gate, however, is simply a courtyard, huge and stark. The outer walls of the fortress may be intact, but the interior, it appears, has been razed. There are knee-high rectangles of crumbled brick, the outlines of ruined storehouses or barracks or armories, remains of camp-fires, a shattered millstone, a rusted cauldron too huge and heavy for anyone to cart away.

"Pitfire," says Mektu. "This place has been dead longer than the Sea."

They move inside. The shadows are long in the waning light. Against the east wall, stone stairs climb to the battlements. To their left a square pit like a mine shaft plunges down into the hill.

Nowhere to hide, he thinks, unless one leaped into that pit, or curled inside the cauldron and prayed. But in the north wall are two stone archways, letting into another great court or yard. Beyond, looming high above over the fortress, is the broken tower.

A soft sound to their right. The brothers whirl, then swear. Talupéké is kneeling atop the battlements, sweeping the telescope across the land.

After a moment, she lowers the instrument and creeps toward them along the wall. The brothers meet her at the bottom of the stairs.

"No one to the east of us," she says. "The way is clear for you ahead."

"That all you have to say?" asks Kandri.

The girl's red eyes have a fierceness that shames him. What does he expect her to say?

She gestures at the twin arches. "We'll need to go in there for a view to the north. Of course, your enemies could be in there. I doubt it, though: nothing much to be gained from hunkering down in a closed courtyard. They could be in the tower, though."

"We watched that tower all day," says Mektu. "We watched the whole fortress. If they're here, they're not up to much."

"If they're here, they've seen us already," says Kandri. "Come on, before the sun sets. A look around is the only damned reason for climbing this rock."

They cross the vast courtyard as quietly as possible. Under the shroud of dust and salt, small objects resolve into view: a bent fork, a shoe buckle, a rusted length of chain—and suddenly, a human hand.

They stop dead. The hand is a ruin, scraps of flesh shriveled to rawhide on sun-bleached bones, two fingers missing, a bronze ring about the thumb.

"Ghouls," whispers Kandri.

Talupéké flips the hand over with her boot. "You know how to fight them, don't you? A stab with your mouth closed, then a leap back to breathe. Don't inhale their stench. It can wither you like a curse. Like a cold wind withers flowers, my grandmother used to say."

"I can smell them," says Mektu.

Kandri smells it too: rotting flesh, the most evil, most unendurable smell in all the world. In silence they approach the easternmost arch, and flatten themselves beside it against the wall. Inch by inch, Kandri leans out, until he can steal a glance into the space beyond.

Cold terror envelops him. Beyond the arch is a courtyard almost as large as the one they have just crossed, and almost as empty.

Almost.

Ranged along the west wall are four towering heaps of driftwood and brush, and atop the heaps are four nightmarish birds. They are twice the size of elephants. Their plumes are dust-gray, but their naked heads and necks are a slick, raw red, and their hooked bills are black. They shift and flutter stiffly, as though newly awake. Bones, human and otherwise, lie heaped around the nests. Dangling head-down from the nearest is the flayed-open carcass of a human being, mostly devoured, a skeleton draped in strips of cloth and skin.

As Kandri stares, one of the vultures stands and beats its wings, sending a storm of dust across the courtyard. Between its massive talons is an egg two men would struggle to lift.

People will call anything an Ornaq until they've seen one.

He pulls his head back, aghast. If they had chosen the west arch, they would be standing within ten feet of those birds.

No one breathes, or hesitates. They simply retreat, past the gnawed hand and the cauldron and the pit. The courtyard feels endless. Only at the gate do they pause to look at one another.

Mektu gives a whisper of a laugh. "Ghouls!" he says. "Couldn't it have just been ghouls?"

Talupéké's look is wild, hunted. "We need to get off this island," she says. "And then away, far away, as fast as we can. Those are roosting females. If they catch our scent they'll eat us alive."

"We shouldn't have come here," says Kandri.

"You mean *she* shouldn't have."

"Don't start that, Mek. If we're quick we can be back to the trawler before it's totally dark. And yes, girl, we want you to come back."

But Talupéké is holding very still, looking at a spot somewhere north of the ruined boat. She raises the telescope. Then she grins that same, unsettling grin she wore when she learned that they had come from Eternity Camp.

"What exactly the fuck did you do to the Prophet?"

Kandri snatches the telescope. A few miles to the north, three tawny, long-legged felines the size of ponies are gliding across the seabed, with two riders each upon their backs. He cannot see their faces, but he can see the white robes, the belts of scarlet, the weapons numerous and large.

"Rasanga," he says, fighting to control his voice. "Six of them, on *sivkrin*. Oh, Jekka's hell. Eshett and Uncle don't even know."

"Or," says Talupéké. "they're watching and know perfectly well. It's not as if they can run."

"Mek, we—"

"It will be over by the time we get there," says Talupéké. "Long over. And then they'll just kill us, too."

She speaks calmly. Kandri almost hates her for it, but her words are undeniable. Even alone, six Rasanga could slaughter a dozen fighters like themselves. And these six are not alone. The *sivkrin,* the sandcats, are trained to leap on a man and disembowel him at a word.

All true, and yet he runs. All of them run, sprinting through the last of the ruins to the slope, racing each other to their deaths. Even Talupéké, rushing to defend the man who called her a savage and a dog. Hatred, love, the Gods' great comedies. *I'm losing my mind,* Kandri thinks.

"Wait!" cries Mektu. "They've stopped!"

Kandri skids to a halt. The Rasanga have indeed reined in their cats. "The scope, use the scope!" hisses Mektu. Kandri raises the instrument, focusing desperately—and finds himself gazing at a Rasanga with a telescope of her own, trained directly on themselves.

"Oh," says Kandri.

The Rasanga lowers her telescope. Kandri lowers his. Then the riders turn the sandcats, abandoning the trawler, and begin to race like the wind toward the island.

ℛ

A place to hold. A corner. The broken gate is far too wide. The battlements? No exit from up there except a plunge over the cliffs, or a dive into the nests of the Ornaqs.

The Ornaqs. Will they rise, feast on hunters and fugitives alike? Or just circle, waiting for the slaughter to end?

There will not be much waiting: the sandcats are blindingly fast. Three minutes, maybe, and they will reach the mouth of the cove. Another five and the battle will be joined.

Talupéké wants to try their luck with the pit, and whatever caves or dungeons underlie the fortress. "Tie our scarves, make a rope, let go when the rope runs out. Maybe it's deep and we're killed. Or maybe we ambush them, or find another way out."

Kandri forces himself to lean over the shaft. Blackness, blindness. A fate worse than death.

Mektu seizes his arm, steadying him. "Forget it, girl. Next plan."

"I don't fucking have a next plan!"

They return to the gate. The Prophet's commandos are inside the cove, passing the last of the shipwrecks. He can see their weapons now: jaw swords, mattoglins, axes, bows. Perhaps the pit after all. He shuts his eyes, and his mind fills instantly with blackness. He's drowning. He doubles over, vomits on the stones.

"What, is he panicked?" asks Talupéké. "Some fucking soldier. Are you going to freeze?"

"Leave him fucking alone!"

"I'm all right, Mek," says Kandri, although he isn't. "We need to run. We need a place to fend them off."

"Underground," says Talupéké. "That's the only place. Except maybe that tower."

Kandri straightens, looking at her.

"The tower," he says. "It had one door, right? One . . . narrow door?"

Talupéké nods. "It was partly blocked. And the windows were high off the ground."

"How high?"

The other two look at each other, then at him. "What are you thinking?" asks Mektu.

The sandcats have begun to climb. The Rasangas' eyes are calm, unblinking. Their blades already drawn.

"Is it madness?" says Kandri.

"Is *what* madness?" hisses Mektu. "Talk, talk, for Ang's sake!"

They are halfway to the summit. Kandri says nothing, in the grip of a preposterous idea. Mektu, horrified by his stillness, slaps him hard in the face.

It is the right thing to do. Kandri seizes their arms and pulls them word-lessly into a run. Not for the pit or the stairs to the battlements. For the arches across the courtyard.

It must be the west arch. The Gods help us. The west arch and silence, or we die.

Twenty feet from the arch he stops them, turns back to face the gate. "Don't move until I do—no matter what. And don't either of you make a sound."

"Let's put our backs to the wall, at least," says Talupéké. "If they get behind us, we won't last a minute."

"We won't have to."

Kandri scans the rubble near their feet, scoops up three broken bricks. He gives one to each of the others. "Don't waste these on the Rasanga," he says. "Keep them until—oh, devil's ass. Steady, fuckers, steady."

The sandcats are padding through the gate. Three sinuous predators, hissing, baring eight-inch fangs. The riders on their backs have painted foreheads: white stripes for mourning, green for revenge. Three men, three women. All six enormous, muscled like Gods.

Without sound or hurry, they advance into the courtyard. They ignore Talupéké but gaze at the brothers like starvelings approaching a feast. At the lead is a woman bearing a war axe, double-bladed and black.

At a distance of some hundred feet, they rein in the cats, and two of the riders slide to the ground. Each carries a cruel, hooked mattoglin—and wears, strangely, a single iron gauntlet on the opposite hand. Before Kandri can even wonder at the purpose of these gauntlets, they burst into flame.

He feels his brother's twitch of horror. The flames, blue and orange, writhe like fistfuls of snakes in the Rasangas' hands, but the warriors show no sign of pain. Their eyes, unblinking, do not leave the brothers for an instant.

Their leader lifts her axe and speaks.

"Kandri Chamkarra Hinjuman. Mektu Malachat Hinjuman. You who shed the blood of the Sons of Heaven. You who spit on the Mother of Us All. You traitors to five hundred thousand Chiloto. You beloved of the Lord of Hell. Surrender. It is the last act of wisdom you may take in this world."

Kandri's grip tightens on the others' arms. The woman's voice is sibilant and low.

"You may say to yourselves, 'We are Chiloto also,' but that is not true: the Prophet has cast you from the clan. And she has ordained that every Chiloto man, woman, and child learn your names, the better to curse them, curse you, speed the punishment of your souls. Surrender. Embrace her justice. Name the foreign prince you serve, and your agonies will be reduced. There is no other path."

Kandri is cold and his flesh feels remote. He cannot control his heart. But in a slow, deliberate motion, he releases Mektu and lowers his hand to his crotch. His voice is barely more than a murmur, but in the windless yard it is enough.

"Her Radiance. I wish her death. She's a prostitute, a whore, she goes with animals, she gives diseases to her sons—"

The commander snarls an order. Spurred heels kick, and the great cats hurl themselves across the yard.

"Wait," hisses Kandri.

Mektu and Talupéké look feral, deranged. Once more, he grips their arms. *Do you see it? Doesn't matter.* Forty feet. *Wait for them, wait—*

"Now!"

They turn and sprint for the arch. Behind them, the Rasanga scream out the kill-song of the Army of Revelation:

Oorlulu-Kralulu-Ke—

And no more. Their voices obliterated by a hideous, torn-metal shrieking, so loud it is like a kick to the chest. Over the wall between the courtyards the Ornaqs rise, dark wings blocking the last of the sun.

Terror grips the sandcats. The Rasanga haul savagely at their leads. The brothers and Talupéké plunge through the arch, so fast that Kandri all but impales himself on the closest nest. No reason to throw the brick: he brings it down like a hammer, feels the eggshell crack. He spins away, flailing for the tower like a madman, expecting at any second to feel his spine snapped, his body lifted and torn like the corpse flashing by on his left.

The startled Ornaqs have risen high over the courtyard. Now they dive, screaming. The tower so distant. The narrow doorway half buried in stone.

Talupéké screams. Kandri whirls, she is lifting away from him, he leaps, they lock hands, they are both rising, *three* humans are rising, the vulture has pounced on a Rasanga and the warrior has Talupéké by the belt.

The ground falls away. Talupéké's clothes are burning, the Rasanga has seized her with a fire-gauntlet, she arches and kicks but he is behind her, Kandri cannot reach him, she is screaming, the Ornaq gulps and half the Rasanga vanishes into its beak, a talon rises long as Kandri's forearm, he swings his machete and just stops it from disemboweling the girl, the beak closes, the gauntlet goes limp—

They fall.

Black wings, bellow-churned air. Talupéké is torn from his grip. The head of the bird enormous and obscene as it stabs at him midair, and missing by so little that the dead man in its beak grazes his lips with a burning finger, but where's the ground, the fucking ground that will kill him—

Crack.

Driftwood shatters, brush explodes. He has struck a nest, it has saved him, he writhes in the bird shit and feathers, seeking solid ground—he's gone mad, a thing of slime and cinders rises wailing beside him, wielding two knives. It's Talupéké, yolk-drenched, no longer burning, she has shattered an egg with her fall.

"Get up, get up! Don't fucking stab me!"

They're on their feet, sprinting again. Somewhere a cat is screaming, blood is pouring from the sky. Then suddenly (he can scarcely believe it) they're at the tower door, Mektu gesturing from within, Ang still loves them, Talupéké dives through the gap—

A shadow. Kandri flings himself away as an Ornaq strikes the stone like a battering ram.

Within him, something accelerates. He sees nothing but beak and claws, the bird's great killing devices. He rolls, kicks off its leg, his machete is gone, the beak strikes, he twists away. When the vulture makes a hopping turn, he dives again for the doorway.

Agony. He's dragged backward from the tower. The reek of death envelops him, he is rising, he is in the vulture's beak.

For an instant there is nothing in the world but that beak, and the yellow pool of the Ornaq's eye. Then release, and the bird's sounds of agony. And Talupéké's knife buried deep in the eyeball.

He strikes the ground. He scrambles backward for the door. Hands seize him, lift him, drag him into the dark.

"Blades, blades!" Mektu is shouting. "If one of those shits fights his way in here—"

One of them does. The screams come from the floor above, mingled, indecipherable. They race up stone stairs into a scene of horror, a sandcat wedged in the narrow window, its hindquarters still outside the tower, and trapped against it a Rasanga, her cheek cut to ribbons and her leg caught in the twisted stirrup like a tourniquet, reaching back with her only remaining weapon, her war-axe, trying to saw herself free.

It is the leader, the one who spoke their names. *If she frees herself, we die—some of us, all of us.*

The mayhem is like nothing Kandri has ever faced. The whirlwind of claws, the spit and fury and feline screams. The astonishing skill of the Rasanga, holding off all three of them while being thrashed against the wall by her mount—and somewhere above, Ornaqs landing, ripping at the tower, trying to tear the structure apart.

They cannot best this woman. She fights them all, shouting *Dhagrii*, Abominations, as the walls tremble and the pool of her own blood widens on the floor. Above, the ancient timbers supporting the ceiling start to crack.

Stones plummet, dust blackens the room. For several moments, they are fighting almost blind. Then the sandcat gives a piercing wail: an Ornaq has seized it from behind.

The Rasanga looks over her shoulder, sees her death in the darkening air. Together with the cat she is hauled backward, one sharp jerk after another, her arms braced uselessly against the window, her mount's claws cutting grooves in the stone, and then she twists and brings the axe down and severs her own leg at the knee.

The cat is gone, its screams extinguished in an instant. The warrior keeps her balance a moment, even lifts the axe again—and then falls, thrashing in her own blood, the weapon gone from her hand.

"The Prophet"—she is frothing, spitting her final words—"freed us, freed your ancestors. Without her . . . you would not exist."

She lies still. Outside, the battle rages, stones plummet from the roof. They descend the stairs again, praying that the ceiling holds. Through the doorway they see the scarlet courtyard, the broken eggs, the bodies like rag dolls torn by spiteful children, and Mektu turns to Kandri with something like admiration in his eyes.

"Six down," he says. "Half a million to go."

⁊ა

They stand on rubble. The inner floors have collapsed: they can see right out through the stone funnel to the darkening sky. The Ornaqs scream and flap and take the spire in their talons, dislodging bricks that whistle down the shaft and explode. They press themselves to the walls. Splinters of stone pelt and cut them. In time, the Ornaqs' furies cease, but they can still be heard in the courtyard, ripping and feeding on the dead.

Jeshar, Kan," whispers Mektu in the darkness, "you called the Prophet a whore."

"I'm sorry," says Kandri.

"Why the hell should you be sorry?"

"I don't know. But I am."

It is the simple truth. He has completed a process that began with his wound in the Ghalsúnay campaign. He has torn out a part of himself, a shameful part, maybe, but what mortar will ever fill that hole?

He looks out across the courtyard. Halfway to the arch, a small fierce fire dances, blue and orange. It is one of the Rasanga's gauntlets, still attached to an arm, still fed by whatever arts or curses the Prophet lends these most faithful of her servants. He can almost imagine that the arm still lives, that those blazing fingers will drag it slowly toward the tower as they sleep.

199

"We're better off, aren't we, Mektu? Better with it all torn out by the roots?"

"Shut the fuck up, Kan, you sound crazy."

A long pause, then Mektu speaks again. "You had to provoke them, to be sure that they'd charge. And of course we hate the Prophet. I mean the thing she is today. Not what she was, the savior of our people, blessings on her soul."

"Now you both sound crazy," says Talupéké.

"It's something only Chilotos understand, girl," says Mektu. "And anyway, Eshett's a whore."

"You piece of shit," says Talupéké.

"Was, I mean. A whore."

"Be quiet now, Mek," says Kandri.

"No, I'll keep talking," says Mektu. "I can't say these things to Eshett, or when Uncle's around to call me a fool. But I dream each night of that Parthan. Don't laugh. For the second time in my life, I'm in love."

"What happened to the first lucky girl?" asks Talupéké.

Mektu ignores her. "She has a secret, Eshett does. You don't really think she just happened to show up when you killed Ojulan, do you?"

Kandri frowns at his brother. "Of course I do. What else? What the hell are you saying?"

"She's kept something from us," says Mektu. "She's not just a runaway whore. And don't lecture me, I don't judge think less of her for whoring. How could I? Look at the refuge *we* chose."

"The army?" says Talupéké.

"No," says Mektu, "belief."

∞

At dawn, Talupéké sheds her boots and scales the inner shaft with the ease of a gecko. Kandri sees her standing fearlessly atop the broken spire, leaning a bit into the wind. After a long look in each direction, she scurries down again.

"All clear," she says. "They must be scouting, finding out if there are more of us. But they'll be back soon. We should run."

And run they do, across the sticky flagstones, through the reek and the flies, stopping only to recover what weapons they can. Kandri tries not to look at what remains of the six who came to kill them. The black gauntlet has stopped burning at last, but they avoid it all the same.

When they spill out through the gate, they see one of the Ornaqs circling far away to the south.

"Do you know what's fortunate?" says Mektu. "If others come here, looking for us, it won't even matter if they recognize the scraps—the cloaks, the belts, the sivkrin hides. They'll blame the Ornaqs, naturally. They'll never know we were here."

"It won't make any difference," says Talupéké ambiguously. Then she looks hard at the brothers. "She can't do it, can she? Order every fucking Chiloto in Urrath to learn your name, and curse it?"

"Sure, she can," says Kandri.

"Where the fuck did she come from?" the girl almost shouts. "How did she dream up all this crazy shit? A path to heaven, Godlike sons, all Urrath ruled by one Chiloto family, madder than moon flies. You two are Chilotos, but you're normal people, too. Sort of normal. You say you hate her now, you don't believe in her cause. But do you believe in her powers?"

Who will answer first? Neither, as it happens: the silence holds all the way to the wreck. As they draw near, Chindilan emerges from the hull. An incoherent whoop, joy and disbelief at once, bursts from his chest. Eshett joins him, and the two rush out onto the scree.

The Parthan woman's eyes are bright. "You should be—"

"Dead?" says Kandri. "You don't know the half of it."

"We saw the Ornaqs," says Chindilan. "How in the flaming Pits did you escape?"

They sketch the events of the night before, and Chindilan hugs them, one by one. "Brilliant, brilliant!" he says. "Gods below, we were grieving already. Now come and eat something, and let's get the hell out of here. Together, of course—"

He is glancing at Talupéké, wringing his hands. Eshett watches him intently. Talupéké shrugs and brushes past him into the wreck. The smith's gaze drops to his toes.

Squirm, you old fool, thinks Kandri. *I hope Eshett chewed your ass off all night.* But her face shows only relief at their survival. When Mektu drops to the ground to empty sand from his boots, she actually tousles his hair. She lifts her eyes to Kandri, beaming, and touches his arm. But even as Kandri smiles in turn, her face hardens.

"Congratulations, Chilotos," she says. "It's your holy day."

Mektu freezes with a boot in his hand. Kandri, bewildered, turns to Chindilan. The smith gives a reluctant nod.

"She's perfectly right, it's Revelation Day. I'd lost count. Funny how that happens."

Revelation Day: the anniversary of the Prophet's first communion with the Gods. And her declaration of war.

"Not quite the same as last year, is it?" adds the smith.

Mektu lies flat on the earth, staring up into the cloudless sky. Kandri feels Eshett's grip tighten, helping him balance.

"No," he says, "it's not much like last year."

"Well, what the fuck happened last year?" asks Talupéké.

Kandri turns his head away. He does not want to see the girl, or Eshett with her accusing eyes, or Chindilan with eyes full of kindness. Only now does he realize that he has been dreading this anniversary, the fifty-first. Dreading the memories it will not let him avoid.

Talupéké turns to Eshett. "Why are *you* the one who remembered, anyway? You're no Chiloto. What's the Prophet to you?"

"An enemy," says Eshett. "Isn't that enough?"

Kandri walks to the far side of the wreck, trembling and ashamed. He's not weak. He's just come through carnage, spent the night in a tower full of blood and piss and shit and flies, scraps of dead men and animals. But this is different. Revelation Day. No, no, he can't look at anyone just yet—not even his brother, when Mektu shuffles up beside him and takes his hand.

ဆ

It had begun with mind-shattering noise. Steel hammer. Brass bell. Their captain was storming through the tent, issuing orders in a nonstop howl. The bell was the signal for mobilization. The fiftieth Revelation Day would not be a holiday in any ordinary sense.

The world was black and frigid; dawn was still far off. Nonetheless, in twenty minutes flat—dressed, armed, stuffed with food—his unit assembled and marched for the North Gate, heads held high.

Kandri was anxious. Their breakfast had included *sutsak*, a hot fermented drink normally reserved for mountain units. Brewed with honey and aromatic herbs, it went down easily, but the lingering taste was strange and heavy on his tongue. Adding to the strangeness was the behavior of his commanding officer. The captain was known for decency and a genuine concern for his men. But he had been irritable for weeks now, and had pushed Kandri's unit like never before. "The war front's waiting, you dogs!" he'd snapped just yesterday, without provocation. "You'll be back there before you know it, and the slow-arsed among you will be cut to shreds."

But this morning Kandri's greatest worry was his own heart. He knew he should feel nothing but pride and awe on this day. Fifty years of Revelation. Fifty years since the Gods allowed Her Radiance to perceive their greatest secret. Heaven's Path, the silver-paved road of glory that would transform the world. Fifty years since she swore on the Well of Fire that Chilotos would never again be slaves.

Pride, awe—and joy, of course. For the enemy was in retreat, the Chiloto heartlands were once more ruled by Chilotos. And the war's end surely could not be too far off. *So stop worrying, you fool. You're a good soldier. You feel everything you should.*

But was it enough? Did his joy truly match the greatness of the day? By the light of the security lamps he saw Mektu and his friend Betali, whose ears stood out from his head like the wings of a grouse. Both men were smiling, beaming. Suddenly aware of his own face, Kandri smiled in turn. It felt like donning a mask.

How would the great day be celebrated? No one in his unit knew a thing. Kandri imagined speeches, martial music, parades along the victory route. But nothing prepared him for what he saw outside the gate.

Countless thousands were on the march. Pike men, breachers, axe-wielding Jindits, lowly sandalmen with their chipped blades and rusted halberds, bricklayers, sappers, the Akoli Militia, the scarlet-sashed Orthodox Guard . . . and the Rasanga, aloof and terrible; and other elite forces Kandri could not identify. Everyone, in short: the Prophet was emptying the camp.

But the crowd was not limited to soldiers. Common Chilotos, farmers and townspeople, were everywhere. They had swarmed the local village and overflowed into the fields; they had erected tents of their own outside Eternity Camp. *Ang's blood*, thought Kandri, *they must have been arriving for days.*

The great throng flowed northward over the Windplain, murmuring like a river in flood. No orders were shouted; no officers addressed them at all. Far ahead, at the vanguard it seemed, a single kettle drum was booming, a lonely sound, a heart in a vault.

For many hours they marched to that drum. Fields were trampled, villages swallowed whole. Rumors buzzed like flies through the ranks. Some said that they were making for Hunger Cliff, where the Prophet came of age as the common-law wife of the warlord Bitruk Uslor, and later experienced the vision that would change the world. Others whispered that a great engineering project lay ahead, something at which thousands had toiled.

At daybreak, the whole throng knelt in prayer. In the vast, loving silence, Kandri asked the Gods to watch over the souls of his grandparents and the child Peyar they had tried to save: three martyrs, brutally killed by the Važeks. But his prayers were over before anyone else's, and long before the signal to rise. He waited, motionless. Once again he could taste the heavy sutsak—and once again his worries pounced.

The captain was right, of course: the front was waiting. At month's end, his legion, one of the smallest, was to march on a clan he'd never heard of before, a clan known as the Ghalsúnay. There were dark rumors about the mission. Several officers, without explanation, had been quickly transferred to other legions. Men were saying that they had requested—even begged—for the transfers. *They're afraid*, Kandri thought. *They know some-thing that's been kept from the ranks. They know what we'll be facing and want no part of it, they—*

No. He glanced at his comrades, still praying fervently, their faces serene. What was wrong with him? In his mind's eye he saw the face of the All-Shepherd, Father Marz, an enemy of the Hinjumans but a great favorite of Her Radiance. He thought of the way the hunched old man had squinted at them from the courtyard gate, as they stumbled from the barn after all-night lessons. If Marz hated his family, wasn't his family in the wrong? *Moral correction*: that was what Marz had always preached. True self-criticism in the deep stillness of the soul. Had he, Kandri, ever attempted it sincerely? What if he was too far gone even to try?

He panicked: faith was leaving him, the Prophet's love was leaving him, her holy eyes would turn away in despair.

No, no, no. With an immense effort he silenced his doubts. And in the void he recalled the words of her First Encyclical, committed to memory by every new recruit.

Study the mirror, my children. When you walk Heaven's Path, you must descend before you climb. Down it leads through lightless depths, through the Valley of the Gorgon, the Black Wood of the ghouls. Follow me, fearless, and you shall know the strength that is your birthright, and your true people, and the love that fear has kept from you. In the caverns of the soul, like the caverns of the earth, there is a well of sacred fire. Lift the cup with me. Dare to drink.

"Hinjuman!" His captain's voice was soft but imperative. "Get up, lad, we're moving out. And take the cup from your comrade there. Drain it. You're the last one to drink."

Kandri rose; a cup was thrust into his hand. More sutsak: he drained it dry. The taste was exactly like what had been served at breakfast, but this time he found it good—startlingly good. Instead of heaviness and dread, he soon felt a deep serenity. From across the ranks, his brother glanced his way and smiled, crazed and earnest. Kandri smiled back, and this time nothing was forced. As they marched on, he recited the rest of the First Encyclical and moved on to the second, and so the hours flew by.

Midafternoon, their numbers doubled. Four entire legions, recalled from the various war fronts, met them at a crossroads, along with still more civilians. The two throngs became one whispering, northward-gushing sea. Here and there among the common folk, songs broke out, but they died quickly. Only the lone kettle drum, that steady heartbeat, played on. The sun sank low. Kandri became light-headed—they'd eaten nothing since breakfast—but he didn't mind. In the Prophet's army, everything happened for a reason.

The drum fell silent. Kandri looked up and felt a tightness in his chest. Before them rose a hill: tall, barren, solitary; and on its summit crouched a sinister ruin. Whispers of awe swept the ranks. They had come to the Theater of Bones.

It was a coliseum, ancient and gigantic, six levels of tall stone arcades. Many were crumbling; a few had collapsed altogether: the place was long abandoned. The men of Kandri's unit nodded to one another: their captain had spoken at length about the Theater some weeks before—about the time his behavior started to change.

Now he beckoned his sixty men together, raked them with a manic stare. And to their astonishment, he screamed at them—he, their captain, a lone voice above that multitude.

"Are you going to be fit soldiers today?"

"Yes, sir!" his sixty answered, abashed.

"Come again? Are you going to make me proud?"

"Yes, sir!"

The man's lips worked in fury; a vein stood out on his neck. "Did I hear a fucking crow in the distance? Where in Jekka's entrails are your manhoods? This is where your ancestors were gutted, you prize pigs. This is where they tried to end us all. Now *speak the fuck up*: are you ready to stand proud under the gaze of everyone who's made this journey today—every widow, every grandfather, every last warrior in the Army of Revelation?"

In unison, they screamed at him: "YES, SIR!"

The captain whirled. A flag was thrust into his hand, and he set off, waving it in a great arc above his head. And the multitude fell back like parting curtains, and Kandri and his comrades advanced on the hill, and their fellow soldiers cheered. To either side, comrades rushed up to them, offering new uniforms: not hand-me-downs but pristine coats, never worn by anyone—and before they left the throng behind, all sixty had shed their tattered rags for these bright blue-and-golden raiments. They were not practical coats for warfare, but they were spectacular.

As if in a dream, they led the throng up the hill, right to the foot of the Theater of Bones. A moat surrounded the coliseum, twelve feet deep and bristling with spikes. An acrid smell, like oily paint or turpentine, wafted from the entire structure. "Circle round, ten-yard intervals, stand at attention!" their captain bellowed. "You're the honor guard tonight."

The sixty men raced to comply. They staked out positions and turned their back to the moat, weapons drawn, facing that sea of souls.

And then they waited. All of them. Two thirds of the entire Army of Liberation, it was said, and an equal number of common folk drawn by rumor and fascination. The sun set. The darkness deepened. Kandri and Mektu glanced at each other, smiling still, floating on the wonder of the privilege they'd been given. But an hour passed, and then another. And although Kandri fought it with all the strength he could muster, the sense of dread came for him once more.

The Theater was an abattoir, after all. Within those arches, the captain had explained, great rings of stone descended to a central fire pit: a crucible, with air shafts beneath it to feed the blaze. The Kasrajis had built the place to strike terror into the hearts of the fractious Chilotos. When the Empire fell, the Važeks seized control of the Chiloto lands, and saw at once how useful this circus of horrors could be. During the last years of their rule, the stream of arriving prisoners was almost constant.

The Theater's very shape was a blasphemy. Kandri's people built open tombs, much like the Theater but a fraction of its size. Every significant town built one; smaller villages shared a single tomb. Inside, upon those stone rings facing the skies, the Chilotos laid out their dead—washed, blessed, prayed for, unclothed—for the birds to pick clean.

Other clans thought it gruesome, but for Kandri's people the rite was holy, a return to the earth. At year's end, the bones were gathered and burned in the central pit. Ashes from the many tombs were exchanged, mingled, sealing the bond between villages far and near. And when the Pilgrim, that great second moon, next appeared over Isp'rallal, the ashes of twenty-one years of Chiloto dead were thrown to the wind, or spread over farmland, or poured with prayers into the sea. In death, the Chiloto people were one.

But their enemies brought no corpses to the Theater of Bones. Instead, Chiloto prisoners were marched to this hill, driven over flimsy planks spanning the moat, and forgotten. In that circular jail they were left to starve, or to make whatever end they could. Many climbed to the highest arcades and begged their captors for mercy. Finding none, they leaped. The able-bodied might get a running start and try to clear the moat. A few succeeded. The guards kept poles handy, to nudge their shattered bodies back upon the spikes.

Over the decades, ghouls infiltrated the structure, feasting on the dead and harrowing the soon-to-die. The Važeks had watched them at twilight, chasing men and women in circles round the arcades. It was an entertainment, this place. In some seasons, tickets were sold.

Three centuries of mass murder. Fifty thousand killed in this structure alone. Whole territories of the Chiloto heartland emptied of life. And their numbers not yet half recovered.

My Prophet, Kandri thought, *what if you'd never come?*

He was trembling with emotion. His head was not quite right. Then he jumped: a weird, thin sound, the hiss of some night creature perhaps, was issuing from the structure behind him. A cracking sound followed, like a stick broken over someone's knee. He looked at Mektu, but his brother still stood rigidly at attention, the perfect tin soldier, although his body trembled a bit.

Kandri glanced at the Theater with loathing. Most remnants of the occupation had been summarily destroyed, but not this one. "Her Radiance has something in mind for the Theater," their captain had said, "She's kept it sealed and guarded since the start of the war. *Totally* sealed, you understand? The bones of the dead are still in there, untouched."

That was the shocking thing: all those bones, the bones of their ancestors, still waiting for the end that was every Chiloto's due. Kandri tried to imagine them, ghoul-gnawed femurs and skulls, clavicles, ribs, in heaps and piles, bleached after decades in the sun. Why had they not been burned? Were they not taught as children that no ghost could rest easy until his bones received the dignity of fire?

His legs were numb from standing still. He thought of his mother's parents and brother. Their bones must be in the Theater too. Had they been part of the spectacle? Had Važeks laughed, placed bets, as the ghouls chased them down?

Slurp, hiss, snap. Kandri flinched again. *Jeshar, what's making those sounds?*

All at once the mob shifted, murmuring. *She is here, she is here.* Every head turned westward, and those not bound to duty stations jostled for a view. At the foot of the hill, a podium had been raised. Kandri could barely see it. The crowd was muttering: *Yes, someone is climbing a ladder. Yes, yes, it is Her Radiance! She is here with her sons!*

"Put out your torches, children. And your lamps. Put out every light."

It was her voice. Magnified by science or sorcery, it rolled like thunder across the land. Instantly the lights began to vanish. Kandri tried to breathe normally. Like everyone, he felt the dangerous thrill of her presence: the liberator, this destroyer of all enemies, this weapon of the Gods. But more than that, he felt her love—at long last, he truly felt it—washing over him, warm and sweet as rose nectar. A flood of certainties. A home.

The last fires were extinguished; the darkness was complete. Kandri let himself grin; he felt so good it was almost a delirium, like drinking wine with Ariqina, feeling her readiness for him, falling into her arms.

"Chilotos," said the Prophet, "I have not come here to speak many words. You have already heard me, heeded me: you are my beloved faithful. You know who guides my steps. And you know the ground we have walked together: the past that made us, the road washed in blood. You know how they used us, enslaved us, scraped out our land like a melon rind. Our land and our hearts."

Was he crying? Was that allowed? Kandri lifted his chin, straightened his back, begged the Gods to let him be the man he should be, just this once.

"You know how they tired of us, and sent us to the slaughter," said the Prophet. "How they toiled for a world where *Chiloto* would join *Nitani* and

Birlama, Edys Aqalat and *Srel*, the dark list of extinguished peoples, the dead forever, all this you know.

"You will take a private oath tonight: to tell your children this story. And you will nurture this pain we share, this burning in your blood and mine, and distill from it your essential selves. Do you hear me? You will make of it not the venom that weakens you but the elixir that makes you indestructible. They fear us, my children. But they will come to fear us more."

Motion on the platform. The Prophet's voice came more faintly, and with a hint of irritation. "That's enough, I'm finished. Help me down, Jihalkra. Bring my pet."

She is going, the crowd's whisper announced. *Her sons are leading her away.* But was it possible, could that truly be all? They were blessed, of course, blessed and grateful. She had made the journey, called them her children; it was enough. But what were her children to do now? Light the lamps? Wait in darkness? Begin the long march home?

No, not yet. Something else was happening. Soldiers were parting the multitude, driving it back, opening a bare, straight strip of land. Right up the hillside it opened, until it reached the Theater itself, a stone's throw from where Kandri and Mektu stood. Other troops coaxed the throng back from the moat's edge. Soon, no one remained near the pit's edge save Kandri and his comrades, the honor guard.

Even by starlight he could see the strip of emptied land, giving him a clear view of the platform in the distance, and a knot of people that must have been the Prophet's retinue. Farther, beyond the crowd's distant edge, the plain ran dark and flat all the way to the Coastal Range.

On the hillside, at the center of that emptied strip, something caught Kandri's eye. Something thin and faint but very long. A glittering scratch. Could it be a line of paint?

"Listen!" someone hissed. In the abrupt silence, Kandri heard it: a rising, churning sound. The roar of voices, many thousands of voices, a throng to rival this one in size. But this new roar came from the mountains, barreling across the plain and up the hill, to crack like a whip against the wall of the

Theater of Bones. A roar of triumph and pain and liberation and remembered rage. And as it continued, a light appeared.

It was a great bonfire, kindled in a notch of the mountains. The shape of the notch was vivid against the starry sky, and an excited murmur reached Kandri's ears: *Hunger Cliff! That's it, where the fire dances! Our Prophet stood right there at the moment of Revelation!*

The fire grew tall and red, like a devilish candle. Then—was he seeing things?—it grew a tentacle. A narrow thread, wriggling down the mountainside, following the contours of the land. The roar seemed to follow its progress, as though new voices were leaping up along the path of the flame. Eventually the burning thread detached from the bonfire, no longer a tentacle but a snake. It left the mountains, went slithering over the plain. The roaring grew and grew. The fifty thousand near the Theater held their breath as suddenly *boom* the snake exploded into a word, a holy word writ in burning oil, and the word was *Adradnin*, Imperishable Memory, and it lingered there, searing the darkness. But the fire-snake emerged anew and kept crawling, the roar still chasing it, growing; and Kandri's heart raced; he was laughing; he was scared out of his mind. Something had been loosed, something so vast that he could not glimpse its shape or purpose, but he knew it could annihilate him, sweep him unnoticed from its path.

The fire neared the Prophet's retinue. And then, as though tapping richer fuel, it simply *leaped* up the hill: straight up, like a sword stroke. Kandri barely had time to see the trench revealed by fire, and the braided wick of oil-soaked rags thick as a palm tree, before the flame roared past the honor guard, leaped the moat, and vanished down a dark stone tunnel into the Theater.

A full second's silence. Then the world went mad.

Every arcade belched fire. A volcanic howl rose to heaven, as though the Theater itself were in agony. Kandri was blown off his feet. All around the moat, the Honor Guard was running or crawling from their stations, the heat impossible, the air turning lethal in their lungs. Only when he was fifty yards from the structure did he dare to look up.

The throng was roaring, dancing, possessed.

The whole coliseum had become a torch. The army had filled the Theater with fuel as one might fill a bowl with bread crumbs, but these crumbs
burned like hellfire. Hundreds of feet above the wall the flames were climbing, illuminating the multitude and its sustained, feral cry. Kandri looked for
Mektu: there he was, two fists in the air, screaming, transported. And Kandri,
yes, he was screaming too, he could not ask why or think why, he could not
think at all. Someone doused him with water: his sleeve had caught fire and
he hadn't noticed a thing. Laughing, maniacal. They were not themselves any
longer. They were so much more than themselves.

"The ghouls!" someone shouted, and Kandri turned and saw them in the
flames: hairless, hunchbacked creatures, mouths too large, hands too wide,
eyes like greasy pools. They had swarmed the arcades, doomed of course,
leaping by threes and fours. Stronger than the men, they writhed and burned
upon the spikes, their yowls blending with the roar of the faithful, and they
seemed to fight on until the very moment their flesh turned to ash.

&

Silence. Windlessness. Five travelers crossing the white floor of the sea.

Kandri sways a little, dazzled by the sun, reeling with memory. That
night of collective lunacy, of fire, of oaths unto death. Imperishable Memory.
An army driven by a dream. What force could possibly stand in its way?

Then, underfoot: a sudden crackling and crunching. They stop dead.
Kandri shields his eyes and looks down.

They are walking on dragonflies, hundreds of thousands strong, black
pearl eyes and rainbow wings, desiccated, dead. All of them facing the same
direction, which happens to be their own. As if the swarm had set its collective mind on crossing the Yskralem and flown due east, low and purposeful,
moving as one. Until strength abandoned them, or the last trace of water in
their bodies, or simply their will.

No one speaks. But Kandri, walking beside Eshett, notes that her eyes are
bright. *Waste of water*, he can't help but think, though not without a certain

admiration. If no one were watching, if Mektu were not watching, perhaps he would have touched her hand.

For over a mile, they wade in this river of silver corpses. Then the wind starts to blow, and the insects click and clatter over the salt pan like a curtain of beads.

☯

"You haven't thought about it much, then?" says Chindilan.

"I try not to," says Mektu, blinking as he walks. "If I think about it, the dreams come, and that's never good."

Talupéké's eyes are inquisitive, she wants the story, chapter and verse. Eshett looks as though she knows it already, somehow.

"We were drugged, boys, you know that," says the smith.

"In more ways than one," Kandri says.

They walk a mile in silence. Their boots shed translucent wings.

"Well, that *is* the issue," says the smith. "How many ways? I told you before, what I overheard in the weapons shop. How they added something to our food when it suited them. I don't worry anymore about the *sutsak* we drank a year ago. Its purpose was obvious—to make us all maniacs for a night. No, I worry about the drugs we swallowed without tasting anything, without suspecting they were there. The ones that don't seem to have done a thing to us, yet."

☯

The sun is close to setting when they catch sight of the next pursuit. This time, there are no riders: just three men afoot, and one camel laden with supplies.

Chindilan whips out the telescope. "Pitfire, it's Atau!" he says. "I can see his silver earrings, plain as day! Atau and two cronies. We never shook them at all."

213

"They must have been guiding the men who attacked you," says Eshett. "The Tirmassil know the Stolen Sea better than anyone."

They quicken their pace to a jog. The Tirmassil do the same, drawing no closer but not allowing themselves to slip behind. "What the hell are they thinking?" says Mektu. "If they did bring the Rasanga, they can see how well that went. And back at Atau's camp, those little shits ran for their lives when they were still eight strong. Now they're going to try to take us with three?"

"Let's find out," says Kandri.

They stop and wait. The Tirmassil carry on for a time, but halt when the distance between them shrinks to half a mile. There they remain, squatting on their heels. Atau raises a hand and makes a sharp chopping gesture.

"You know what that means?" says Eshett. "It means, *I've come to kill you.*"

Kandri takes a turn with the telescope. He recalls the other Tirmassil from Atau's camp. The one leading the camel has a thick black-and-white beard: very black and very white, like a skunk's tail grafted to his chin. The other is a lanky bald man with a limp. Atau has his scimitar; the other two carry nail-studded clubs.

"We could walk right over and kill *them*," says Kandri. "That camel would be a blessing."

"I don't like this," says Mektu. "Why are they so fucking relaxed?"

Bewildered, the travelers resume their march. "They're dreaming about a reward from your Prophet," says Talupéké, "but they'll never see it. Those runts don't know how to fight."

Chindilan takes a last look over his shoulder. "Doesn't mean they don't know how to kill," he says.

☙

All that night and the next, the Tirmassil dog their heels, turning when Kandri's party turns, pitching camp when they pitch camp. From beneath their own sunshield, they laugh and hurl taunts in the Parthan tongue. Eshett says they are shouting, *Food for the worms.*

The wind is in their faces, as it has been since Balanjé, and this does nothing to help Kandri's irritated eyes. But a worse torment is his inability to guess Atau's game. An ambush seems impossible: the way ahead is clear for miles. Still, to quell their doubts, they veer north several times, adding miles to the journey. The Tirmassil make no effort to drive them south again. They do not seem to care where they go.

Midway through the third night, they find themselves on the edge of a great north-south rift. Before them, the land falls away to depths Kandri cannot gauge by moonlight. Far below, the land once more becomes smooth and flat, but what will it take to get down there? The downward slope, though comprised of the same loose salt-scree, is very steep. When Mektu heaves a rock over the edge, a great mass of earth breaks free and slides into the darkness. Eshett swears and turns her face away.

Kandri himself feels dizzy at the sight. "We can manage this," he makes himself say, "but for the love of Ang, watch your step. And if you do fall, keep your head uphill and lie flat. If you start rolling, they'll be nothing left of you at the bottom but a sack of bones."

"Under ten feet of dirt," says Chindilan. "Pull out that rope, Kandri, and we'll pass it around our waists. If one of us stumbles, the others might be able to stop him."

Mektu removes his headscarf and ties one end to his belt. He offers the other end to Eshett. "Hold this, too," he says. "I said I'd protect you, and I will." Eshett looks at him with great unease, but she takes the scarf.

The descent is slow and terrifying. Large masses of salt and earth sheer away with their every footfall, rushing before them like breaking waves. Kandri's boots are overflowing; the rope snaps and jerks. "At least we'll be rid of the Tirmassil," says Mektu. "No camel's descending this. Not in the dark, anyway."

"You're right," says Kandri. But he thinks: *Wouldn't Atau know about the rift?*

Then Eshett screams. Before Kandri can even turn to look, she and Mektu crash against him, and the three are borne together against Talupéké and Chindilan. Kandri stabs his fists into the earth but can find no purchase. They are tangled, choking, gathering speed. He flails over and over. So easy to die. So much unfinished. He sees his parents' faces; he feels Ariqina naked in his arms.

Then a flash of steel: Chindilan has rolled and swung his axe. *Snap*: the rope goes taut, tearing at Kandri's ribs. He can feel himself slowing, and claws at the earth once again.

The smith has done it, buried his axe deep enough to bite. The others too have regained some control. They never stop, but they are riding the wave now rather than being crushed. In a matter of seconds, they are all at the bottom, heaped atop one another, in a cloud of dust that hides the stars. Eshett clings to Mektu, shaking, too frightened to move. His arms are tight about her head.

ॐ

Eight more miles. Flashes of heat lightning. On the wind, faint curious smells: sulfur, citrus, pitch. Low in the northeast, the twin red stars called Jekka's Eyes. *Three in the morning*, the brothers' aunts used to whisper. *When all good boys are asleep. That's when the Lord of Hell peeks over the world's rim to search for sinners.* The Old Man would chuckle and say he doubted it was much of a search. The aunts would study him and scowl.

At dawn, the weather changes: a cold wind blows up from the south. The night's chill lingers, bracing and almost bewildering after so many days when the heat burst upon them with the sun. And as the light grows, they see an astonishing sight.

It resembles a broad river, meandering across their path. But this river is stationary and composed of pools, thousands upon thousands of irregular oval pools, each one a brilliant shade of green or turquoise. Some are enormous, others no larger than a child's wading-pool. From several a mist or steam is rising. The pools crowd together with almost no gaps, only diaphanous edges barely visible in the glare. Beyond the river, the land begins immediately to rise. Sharp hills stand on the horizon.

It is a scene of such weird loveliness that for a moment, no one speaks. Then Mektu comes to life. "Is that *water*?" he asks.

"Sort of," says Talupéké. The others look at her, bewildered. She frowns, touches her temple. "It's mud," she says after a moment, "and salts, spirits, minerals—"

"The biles of the earth," breaks in Chindilan. "Ang's grace, I remember! Garatajik talked about this place. He called it the Snakeskin."

Talupéké looks pleased, as though Chindilan has found a puzzle-piece lost in a corner. "The Snakeskin. That's right. We've reached the very bottom of the Stolen Sea."

"The part that never quite drained," says Chindilan. "Garatajik says that there are cracks beneath those pools leading down to the stomach of Urrath—that's how he speaks of hell—and that evil things bubble up from below. That explains the colors, maybe. What's certain is, we've made good time. Remember your nursery tales, boys? *The cold east depths, near the fair East Shore, bring me to harbor and I'll sail no more.* We're getting close. In short order, we should get a glimpse of the Rim."

"But how do we cross all those pools?" asks Mektu.

"Carefully," says Talupéké. "They have skins. Like ice, but made of salt and other things. You can walk on some of them, but others—" She breaks off, rubbing her temples again.

"What, what?" says Mektu. "Are they poisonous, is that what you mean?"

"Worse, I think. Something's very wrong about this place." She pauses, looks at them almost guiltily. "But I can't fucking remember. I was drinking Atau's wine by then."

"What do you remember?" asks Eshett.

The girl stares into the distance beyond the pools. "That there are only so many ways up the East Rim," she says at last. "The cliffs are taller on that side. There are a few staircases, but they're hard to spot. We need to find one of the old ports like Mab Makkutin."

"You've been there?" says Kandri.

"I grew up on the East Rim," says Talupéké. "But Mab Makkutin is barely a city anymore. The name means Ghost Port; but they called it Mak-kutharem, King's Port, before the Theft of the Sea. My grandmother says that a hundred thousand lived there in its richest days. But now?" She shrugs. "Nine thousand, ten? No one can tell you, really. No one counts anymore."

"How close are we, girl?" asks Mektu.

Talupéké scowls at him, struggling. "A day's march?" she says.

"A long day, maybe," says Eshett. "This time, it's all uphill—"

She stops abruptly. The others turn to her in surprise. "This time?" says Kandri.

Eshett's jaw is tight as she speaks. "I made the crossing once," she says, "in the other direction. A Tirmassil gang brought me to Eternity Camp over the Stolen Sea. They had too many Parthan girls in the east, they said. They had to spread us around."

"So you are a Parthan," says Chindilan.

Again, the hesitation. "Parthan, yes," she says at last, "but you Chiloto don't know the meaning of the word. There are many of us, far more than you imagine. And many kinds of desert blood. Some of us build great townships, grow grain where the land permits. Some are hunters only. Some follow the wild herds."

"What about your people?" Kandri asks.

"We are Nine-Year Parthans. We are nomads, travelers. But when we find a good place, we build a House for the Dead and live around it for nine years. My kin built their House three years ago. I have time to find them, time to get back."

"Atau looked a little frightened of you," says Chindilan.

"He should be," says Eshett. "Everyone fears my people, but the Tirmassil most of all: if we catch them, we slit their throats. But they keep coming, pretending to be merchants, bringing knives or lamp oil or other things we need. They cheat us, but that is not why we kill them. Everyone cheats us. Only the Tirmassil buy and sell us like dogs.

"They raise some of our children themselves, and teach them to hate their Parthan blood. To hide it, to be ashamed. They tell the children that their parents are cannibals, and would kill and eat them if they returned. By the time those children are half-grown, they are ready to go back and steal *more* Parthan women and children." She takes a deep breath. "That's how they got me. They sent a man with a Parthan face, who said he had come from Shefetsi. He seemed kind. We trusted him. One day he surprised me early in the morning, on my walk back from the well. 'I've come to save you from this life,' he told me, and threw a sack over my head."

She looks at Chindilan. "You and Talupéké are both right: Tirmassil are bad warriors but very good with disguises, with tricks."

"What happened to you then?" asks Kandri.

Eshett looks away to the west. "They locked us in a shed. We were there for a week, and two girls died of thirst. When they came for the bodies, they told us that we were going to Eternity Camp to work in the kitchens. The kitchens! I believed that, even though I'd been dragged away from my village by force. I didn't want to believe anything else.

"They brought us down the cliff by a long staircase, and then they stacked us on camels and brought us here. We were blindfolded, but I could hear the talk about the Snakeskin, and feel the camel wading across. Not all the pools are dangerous. The men walked ahead, smashing the salt-ice, searching. It took a long time. Then we traveled south to a hidden cave where the Tirmassil meet to do their business. You can get anything there. Wine, drugs, sapphires, holy relics, books. And children. And whores.

"I was lucky. The Tirmassil didn't rape me, because they wanted me clean." She looks at Kandri and Mektu. "The Prophet's warriors need new girls all the time. Fresh girls, virgins. They don't ever have enough."

Kandri drops his eyes. He feels ill; he wishes he had something to break or stomp to pieces. But Mektu is gaping. "You!" he says. "I remember! We made love."

Eshett looks capable of murder. "We did not," she says, "make love."

"You're wrong, we did," says Mektu. "You were a substitute for the chubby girl, I'd saved up for her especially, but it was all right, you were perfectly adequate, I decided then and there not to ask for a discount, and later we talked about—"

Eshett slaps him. The sound so odd and intimate. The silence that follows is different as well, out of place somehow, the hush of a bedroom in that vast open land.

ᙜ

The smells that began in the night grow stronger, especially the rotten-egg sulfur stench. But the wind remains cool. Talupéké says that she has known such days in midwinter: days that start with a flood of cold air from the southwest. Chindilan has heard of them too: *cold roars* is the army term. Blissful, but not to be counted on. The scalding heat could return in a day's time, or an hour's.

"And when it does, where are we going to bed down? Not much shade near the Snakeskin, and those hills must be eight or ten miles off. Garatajik knew what he was about when he told us to travel by night."

"Well, we can't wait for nightfall here," says Mektu. "There's no shade at all. We'll fry like shrimp in a skillet."

The choice is clear enough: to press on while the cool wind lasts, or backtrack more than an hour and dig in at the foot of the rift. Chindilan and Eshett favor a retreat; Mektu and Talupéké are for pressing on.

"If we run out of water, we die," says Eshett softly.

"Listen to her, listen to the Parthan!" says Chindilan. "We have water for two days and nights. If we're caught out in the heat, we could drink that much before the sun sets today."

"And if we're caught by the Rasanga, it won't matter how much water we have," says Mektu. He looks around for Kandri. "Brother, are you even listening? Why don't you say something?"

"I will, but you won't like it," says Kandri, pointing west across the flats.

Two men are walking swiftly in their direction. "Son of a bitch!" says Mektu. "It's the same Gods-damned Tirmassil, I'm sure of it!"

Chindilan whips out the scope. "Mektu's right," he says. "It's Atau, and that bald fellow with the club. They must have left the third man with the camel, looking for another way down."

The man in front makes the familiar gesture: *Chop chop*.

"No," says Mektu.

"What do you mean, no?" says Kandri.

Mektu turns him a dismayed look. "No, he's not looking for a way down. He's riding back to alert the Rasanga. Riding hard. They've finally realized that they can't fight us, and that we're not going to die before we reach the Rim. So they're going back to find the Wolfpack. And I'd bet my last *gham* they have a horn or a drum, something to call those bastards in."

"Then why aren't they sounding it?" asks Kandri.

Mektu bites the middle of his thumb, as he has always done when thinking furiously. Suddenly, his eyes light up. "Because they're waiting too! Waiting for a signal. They've already met the Wolfpack, right? So someone in the pack must have a horn as well, and he'll sound it when they're closing in. That's how they'll find each other. That's how they'll find *us*."

"Spotters," says Chindilan. "Why didn't we think of that before?" He looks at Mektu with grudging respect.

"If they are spotters," says Talupéké, "then we need to kill them. Right now."

Kandri looks across the glittering half-mile. "We can try," he says.

Covertly, they check their belts and weaponry, then turn and charge the Tirmassil. But as expected, Atau and the bald man turn tail once again. After several pointless minutes, Kandri calls a halt. "This is crazy," he says. "They're as fast as we are."

"We'll have to lighten our load," says Talupéké. "Two of us can kill those fools. The others can wait with the packs."

"They're cowards, no doubt," says Chindilan, "but which of us are the fools? Here we are, chasing them, wasting our water, wasting our strength—"

"Going blind," says Mektu.

"Damned right we are. And all the while . . ."

The others look at him, and the same thought is written in all their faces. The real pursuit, the Wolfpack. "Let's get out of here," says Eshett.

They turn east and run. The Tirmassil hoot and jeer: *Food for the worms, worms, worms!* Kandri fights down a tremor of panic. The sun is now directly in their eyes. He pulls his headscarf forward and lowers his gaze, but that solves only half the problem: the salt-glazed earth is dazzling enough. Worse yet, the wind is still rising, and carrying with it a fine grit, almost a powder. Each gust seems determined to fling the grit in their faces. Kandri's eyes are streaming. The world flutters when he blinks.

At daybreak, he had thought the Snakeskin close, but now it seems to recede the more they rush toward it. For two hours, they slog into the wind, increasingly dazzled, hands cupped around their eyes. When Kandri glances back, he finds that the Tirmassil have donned large, floppy hoods that hide their faces. It seems a poor solution—if the grit can blow up Kandri's sleeves to his armpits, it can blow into those hoods—but bandits too get desperate, don't they? Especially if they've nearly had you, nearly served you up for dinner with an apple in your mouth, only to find you've caught wind of their trick and might yet escape.

The ground goes soft: and there at last is the Snakeskin, blazing and shimmering before them. As Talupéké has said, the pools are topped with flat crystal skins, very much like ice. The rims of the pools are jagged walls of salt-scree, like irregular pie crusts. Some reach a height of several yards, but most barely rise above the pools. None are more than a few inches wide.

Kandri creeps to the edge of the nearest pool—a lovely, bird's-egg blue— and gingerly tests the ice. There is an audible *crack*. A web of fractures radiates from his boot.

"No way in hell," he says.

"They're all different, though," says Eshett. "Some have ice strong enough for a caravan to cross. Some are boiling, others very deep. The Tirmassil believed that the light green pools were perfectly safe: they broke the ice there and let the camels wade. But other pools scared them so badly, they wouldn't go near. Don't ask me which. They seemed afraid even to talk about them."

As expected, Atau and the bald Tirmassil have stopped again—this time somewhat closer to the travelers. With their hoods over their eyes, they look more foolish than menacing, but they go on laughing and jeering. "Fuck them," says Kandri. "Girl, do you remember *anything* about how you crossed?"

"We walked on the rims," says Talupéké, "but also on the ice. We did both."

"That's an enormous help," says Chindilan. "Lucky we brought you along."

Talupéké spins like a top and kicks the smith in the ass. Chindilan goes sprawling. As the others shout at her, she turns and runs along the shore. When she reaches the edge of the light blue pool, she steps out nimbly onto the rim. The top inch of crust shatters like fine crystal, but the rim bears her weight. She runs a dozen yards, pivots on one foot, and looks back at the others.

"Well?"

They follow. Talupéké makes the task look easy ("Circus freak," mutters Chindilan), but no one else finds it so. Kandri and Eshett move with some confidence, but Mektu sways and lurches, and Chindilan takes only mincing steps. Behind them, the Tirmassil move nearer to the shore.

Impatient, Talupéké roams ahead and tests the skin of the nearest pools. None will bear their weight. Kandri, at the rear of the procession, looks hopelessly across the beautiful, threatening mosaic of the Snakeskin. Which pools could a man wade if necessary? Which would kill him at a touch? Or draw him down into bottomless, slowly thickening mud? How many travelers were entombed there already, suspended forever, ants trapped in glue? He has seen a legion of ghosts in the skies above him; is there another trapped below?

Old friend Fear, he thinks. *Always turning up with gifts*. Churning stomach, wasteful sweat. But Gods, Gods, to die that way, in a closed, black trap. Kandri is almost grateful for the distraction of pain in his eyes.

That pain is real and growing. The powdery grit blows unimpeded over the salt-ice, and the wind is rising still. With each step, they must fight harder for balance; even Talupéké is concentrating now, fists rubbing brutally at her eyes. Chindilan is bent almost double. He looks like an old man fording a stream. *Uncle*, Kandri thinks, *how could I do this to you?*

The next three pools—pea-green, sky-blue, sapphire—also prove too fragile to cross. Some of the taller rims are impassable as well, walls of teeth as high as their chins. Time and again, they are forced to retrace their steps.

An hour into the effort, they are less than halfway across. The two Tirmassil have now reached the shore of the Snakeskin. They stand there facing

the travelers, deep hoods flapping in the wind. No longer bothering to gesture or to laugh.

"Brother?" says Mektu.

"What is it, Mek?"

"I was all wrong, you know."

"About crossing today?"

"No. Well, maybe yes. Or definitely yes. Of course, *you* never even haz-
arded a guess."

Kandri is fighting savagely for calm. "Will you please," he says, "just spit
it out?"

"They're not helping a Wolfpack," says Mektu. "They want the bounty
for themselves. And I think they might get it."

"What, by killing us? Just the two of them? Why the hell do you say
that?"

"Because I'm blind."

"Mek—" Kandri gropes for his shoulder. "Don't fuck with me. You're
totally blind?"

"Almost totally. And I know their plan now, Kandri. This time, I know.
Your eyes are going too?"

"They're going. I'm not blind yet, but—"

Waves of color, of mesmerizing light, travel constantly across his gaze;
he is seeing the world through schools of fish. Blinking hard, he looks at the
others. Eshett staggering, Talupéké furiously rubbing her eyes. Chindilan,
still creeping along with that exaggerated caution of his.

Exaggerated? Or the caution of a blind man?

Kandri looks back over his shoulder. And suddenly the whole game is
clear.

The two Tirmassil have thrown back their hoods. They are wearing tight
masks over the upper half of their faces. Masks, and goggles. A circle of
darkest glass for each eye.

"Salt blindness," says Mektu, "like snow blindness in the mountains. We should have guessed, Kandri. Eshett said they kept her blindfolded."

Salt blindness. And the Tirmassil have guarded themselves against it. Probably during every daylight hour, except when their faces might have been seen.

"We've got to run, Mek. Right now."

"No!" hisses Mektu. "We've got to keep up appearances. They're hungry, can't you feel it?"

"Hungry?"

"They're set to pounce, Kandri. They're just waiting on our blindness, waiting—"

Crash.

Talupéké has fallen through the ice. She rises, staggering, covered in turquoise mud. Chindilan and Eshett grope for her, pawing at the air.

"—for us to give ourselves away."

ↄ

All bedlam erupts. Talupéké climbs from the pool with a sustained howl of madness or agony. The Tirmassil step onto the rim and move swiftly toward Kandri and Mektu. The brothers try to double their speed and barely save themselves from a headfirst plunge. Talupéké backhands Chindilan, still reaching for her blindly, and when Eshett tries to steady him, they fall and vanish through the ice of the adjacent pool. Talupéké shows no concern for their plight, or no awareness. She draws her knives and slashes at random, screaming her bestial scream.

Kandri tries to shove his brother forward. "Move your ass, they're drowning!" But Mektu has told the truth: he is very nearly blind. Kandri could force his way past him—but what then? Leave him standing here, waiting for Atau?

Curtains of fire, sprays of orange stars. Kandri blinks furiously. There, thank Ang, are Chindilan and Eshett, surfacing, clawing at the pool's rim, breaking off large chunks of salt.

Behind them, the bald Tirmassil shouts with laughter. At the sound, Talupéké whirls, swaying in the wind. Then she lunges toward the sound, thrashing waist-deep through the turquoise pool she has just escaped.

Sudden, searing pain in his leg: one of the Tirmassil has thrown a rock. A second rock flies past his ear. What if they have bags of rocks? They could stand at a distance, stone the four of them to death. "Gods, brother," he says, "I'm going to have to fight them."

"We should split up," says Mektu. "They want both our heads. I can't fight; a six-year-old could kill me now. But I might draw one of them off."

"I'm not leaving you."

Talupéké wades closer, smashing ice with her fists. Kandri shuts his eyes for a precious moment. They can't have many rocks; the shore is all fine scree. *Nock an arrow. Hold them off.* He opens his eyes again: pain and fire. But for a moment, he does see more clearly. The effect is slight and lasts not half a second. But it is real.

He shuts his eyes for a full five seconds. Again, fleeting clarity, followed by deeper blindness, searing pain. As if his eyes have shed a burning garment and then passed naked, when he opens them, back into a flame.

"Kandri, why are you stopping? Talk to me!"

Red pinwheels, spools of burning wire. The Tirmassil are within thirty yards. *Forget the bow. If one of them gets past it, you're dead. Use the machete. Don't kill Mek on the backswing.*

Talupéké is closer than the men, still erupting with high, horrific screams. They reach the next pool, and Kandri kicks at it with his boot. The ice seems to hold.

"Step down, Mek. Hold my arm."

It is a large pool. The ice crackles ominously as they run across it (like invalids, like clowns). Kandri is nauseous with pain, every blink is a nightstick, what if his balance goes, what if he faints? Maybe they will hesitate. Maybe the crackling of the ice will give them pause.

"Kan," Mektu whispers, "we've got to fool them. Like they fooled us, only better."

Somehow, Kandri knows his brother is right. "I can still see," he says. "It's getting worse, but I can fight them, I can try. If they don't wait too long."

"They've waited for days," says Mektu.

Right again. The men are cowards. *Smart* fucking cowards. Kandri draws the machete from his belt. "I'll pretend I'm stone blind, then. I'll look in the wrong direction. That's what they're waiting for, isn't it?"

"Yes, but—" Mektu bites his thumb. "It's not sly enough. Not for a weasel like Atau."

"What would be sly enough?"

"I don't know. Something twisted. Think like me, brother, think like me."

Kandri wants to hit him. *Why don't* you *fucking think like you?*

Suddenly, Atau shouts at the bald man: "Go, kill the other two, before we lose the smith under the ice. Bring back his weapons and his head. I should be finished here, but if not, we'll use that bow of his. Get along."

"But that crazy bitch is coming this way!" cries the bald man.

"What do we care?" says Atau. "Just stay good and quiet when she passes. She used to throw those knives blindfolded, you know. It was part of her act."

Talupéké's roars grow louder. Kandri looks back and sees her barely twenty feet from them—staggering, striking at ghosts. *I could kill you*, she'd warned them. He tugs at Mektu's arm.

"Girl!" shouts Mektu suddenly. "Over here!"

"Shut up!" Kandri clubs him, hissing. "Oh, Mek, why do you do it, you stupid ass, every fucking time—"

Too late: Talupéké whirls and lumbers in their direction, thin ice breaking around her knees. Atau stands perfectly still. When she reaches the brothers' pool, she climbs up onto the ice and crouches low.

Kandri holds his breath. Talupéké flicks the mud from her knives.

"Girl?" says Mektu.

Talupéké charges, slashing at the air. Kandri shoves his brother from her path with all his strength and dives in the opposite direction. She lunges between them, screaming murder, and the knife in her left hand passes inches from Kandri's neck. Out of the blur of limbs and fire he snatches one glimpse of her face: madness, terror, an eye like a wounded horse. She doesn't see him. She rages on across the ice.

A few pools scared the Tirmassil so badly they wouldn't go near them. . . . Did one of those release a madness already latent in the girl, or inflict something new? Kandri watches her, a blur swiftly vanishing, a young girl seen through tears. Soldier gone. Killer, freak, fucked-up child: gone. Misery and rage clot in his chest, his throat. He staggers to his feet and draws his machete.

"Is that the blade that killed Ojulan?"

Atau's voice is casual. He is on the ice and starting to circle the brothers, his masked head like an insect's, his scimitar in hand. Kandri struggles to see him, a phantom among searing clouds. *Not sly enough*, Mektu had said. Right a third time. *You can't act stone blind unless you let Atau move behind you. And I'll be Gods-damned if I'll let him behind me.*

He pivots. Mektu crouches by his knee, staring in the wrong direction. *We have to fool him.* How, how? What trick do you spring on a master of tricks?

Kandri pivots again. Mektu clings to his leg. "Brother, kill me," he says. "Bring your hand down. Here, here's my neck."

The weeping has started; Mektu has snapped. In a burst of fury, Kandri kicks him away. Mektu falls hard, face smashing against the ice. When Atau makes a dart at him, Kandri swings his blade in a wild arc.

"Your brother has the right idea," says Atau. "It's better this way, honestly. When the Prophet collects you—think about it, now—you don't want to be anything but dead. The Rasanga could work you over for a year or more. They talked around our fire, you know. Small slashes, tiny tools like cheese graters, unimaginable pain. Then tourniquets, amputation when necessary. But worse than any of that—at least to judge by their own fear—would be simply to give you to the White Child. Can you tell me about this Child? What the hell is it? What makes a Rasanga's blood run cold?"

"Kill me," says Mektu again.

"But there's no need for your brother to kill you," says Atau. "I'll do you both if you can just get him to cooperate. Lie down on your stomachs. Or if you want to pray first, go ahead. I don't mind."

Kandri lunges again. What is he attempting? To kill Atau, to deceive him? Deceive him how? *I can't do this, Mektu should be doing this, think like Mektu, pretend you're—*

A kind of lightning grips his mind. He straightens, finds his balance. Then he leaps a third time—and Atau jumps back.

Kandri snarls at him: "I can see you, pig."

"Of course you can," says Atau. "You led your brother by the arm, didn't you? I know you're not quite blind. It's coming, though. Probably sooner than you think."

"Come and get me."

"Oh, I will."

"You're a shit-scared little eunuch," says Kandri. "If my dog fucked your mother, I'd say a prayer for the dog. Where did she have you, in a sewer, on a heap of rotting—"

Atau flings grit in his face.

"It's no good," says the Tirmassil. "I won't blunder to my death because you've angered me. Try again."

Stabbing pain: the salt-grit gnaws at Kandri's eyes. The streaks of light are expanding, crowding out what he sees. He moves through a halting, blinkered battle-dance, memory and practice guiding his feet. But Atau is maddeningly patient; he knows very well what to look for, it seems. Kandri has a momentary glimpse of his face: black mask, insolent grin.

"I like you, Chiloto," he tells Kandri. "You're about to make me rich."

The machete's grip is slippery. Kandri dries his palm on his shirt. One card left to play.

He swings—but makes sure that his blow falls short of Atau. He makes himself stumble, lets the machete bite into the earth.

"That's more like it," says Atau, delighted. "You're half-blind and worsening fast, but at least you're thinking. What to do? Feign total blindness and lure me in? No, no, that can't be done safely; I might not fall for it. Feign normal vision and scare me off? But you know I won't go far. So you make a bold choice: you *pretend to be pretending* you can still see well enough. And then you fake a slip-up, a tell. The very tell you think I'm looking for. You hope I'll rush in to finish you off and give you a last clean shot at me. Not bad, not bad at all. But let me say it again, boy: I can wait."

And for the next quarter hour, he does. Kandri leaps and stabs and never comes close to landing a blow. His eyes stream, his head is throbbing. His vision contracts to a few scattered points. He anchors himself on his useless brother, who has curled into a ball. Sobbing, crushed. Facing what Kandri cannot.

Beaten. Skinned and gutted. Outfoxed.

He makes a desperate lunge. Hacking at any hint of movement. Atau throws more grit at him. And the world goes black.

It is as if a piece of the sun has dropped and burst before his eyes. Brilliance and fire, then purest night. No grays, no shadows. He is blind.

A terrible silence has fallen. Atau gives him nothing, not a footfall, not a breath.

Kandri swings his blade in a circle. Two times around, three. The pain at the pit of his eyeballs, the burn. He thinks, *Blindness too is a sort of drowning*—and with that, his balance deserts him, and he falls.

Atau kicks the machete from his hand.

"Roll over, boy. Cross your arms beneath your chest. I'll make this clean; you won't feel anything. And the pain in your eyes, and the pain in your heart: all that will cease."

Kandri flails toward the voice. His fingers brush boot leather, close on nothing. Atau's second kick is to his face. He falls and his mouth gushes blood. The third kick is to his groin.

"Or if you're difficult," says Atau, rattled, "I'll just bleed you out. You fucking Chiloto dog! I make it easy for you, and what do I get? You ought to be *kissing* my boot, not—"

His voice is cut off with a sound like a slurp. Kandri flinches; blood sprays his face. He starts to rise and Atau crashes against him, lifeless, slashed open at the neck. A pair of hands seizes the body and shoves it aside.

"He should have waited a bit longer."

"Mektu. Oh, Gods, Mektu."

"You're a terrible actor, brother. Fortunately, I'm not."

രു

Mektu can still see. He has guessed the danger earliest, pinched his eyes shut the soonest, blinking only occasionally for the benefit of Atau. Now he is wearing the dead man's goggles. He says his vision is bad and blurry but getting no worse. He cannot see the bald Tirmassil or the other travelers. He can barely see the shore.

He mops the blood from Kandri's face, then winds a thick bandage around his head. "You could have told *me* what you were up to," says Kandri.

"Wrong," says Mektu. "It was you who made Atau believe in my blindness. You never suspected, so neither did he."

Kandri himself remains perfectly sightless. And strangely resigned. It feels almost good to be helpless, to be led along the jagged rims, across strong ice. But a new danger confronts them already: the wind has finally turned, and the heat is building. They shout for the others but hear no reply. "We need shade," says Kandri. "I'm sweating already. We can't make it to the hills."

"There is no shade anywhere," says Mektu.

"Then we'll have to get ashore and pitch the sunshield." He stops dead. "Oh, Gods, Mek. The sunshield."

"What about it?"

"The damned thing's in Uncle's pack."

Mektu begins to swear, quietly and steadily, as though urinating. He drags Kandri north—"Something different about the ice there—" and then curses again; it is only blue mud splashed on the rim.

"Maybe Miss Trouble waded through this one. Maybe it's the one that drove her mad. I don't know. I can't fucking tell where we are." He sighs. "At least we haven't fallen into one of these damned things. Just don't wipe your hands on your pants. There's green mud splashed up to your—"

He freezes, gripping Kandri's wrist. "A body," he says.

"What! Where?"

"It's the bald man, Atau's sidekick, and—oh."

"Be careful!" says Kandri. "The bastard might be faking death."

"Not likely."

Mektu's voice is odd. He leads Kandri closer, painting the scene in words. The Tirmassil is chest-deep in a small cobalt pool, arms stretched forward, hands clawing at the ice. Evidently, he had walked about six steps before it shattered, then tried and failed to pull himself free.

"The pool's not mud. It's a clear blue with lots of bubbles. It's very pretty, actually."

"Why are you so sure he's dead?" says Kandri.

"Because he's a gooey skeleton from the ribs down, and the bones are going too. That liquid's eating him, melting him away."

"Devil's Ass!"

"Steady, brother. Don't fall."

Which is worse: to see the corpse plainly, as Mektu does; or to imagine it, half-dissolved, a man turning to slime? "Let's get out of here," Kandri says.

"Hold on," says Mektu. "Something else on the ice . . . huh! Isn't that . . . curious. I suppose it's what he was after."

"What is it? Tell me."

"Big bloody knife."

"A dagger, you mean?"

Mektu releases him, crouches down. "No, not a dagger. It's a mattoglin. A beautiful mattoglin. All jewels and gold."

℘

Minutes later, Kandri is holding Lord Ojulan's priceless weapon, which his brother has knocked to the edge of the pool with a few well-aimed chunks of ice. Kandri feels the big stone set in the pommel, the gold tracery on the blade, the small sharp rubies, the flame-like teeth near the tip. He is dumbfounded. It is unquestionably the same mattoglin they tossed away with the body of the Thirdborn. But who has retrieved it—Chindilan? Eshett?—and why have they carried it all this way, only to abandon it here?

"Bait," says Mektu. "Someone determined that the ice was weak and tossed it out there."

"And the Tirmassil couldn't resist," says Kandri. "That's my guess, too. But did it help them escape? And how far could they possibly get—blind, in this heat? For that matter, how far are we going to get? We're in trouble, Mektu. We're sweating our lives away."

"Careful," says Mektu. "Here's the shore."

It is a great relief to stand on solid ground at last. They drop their packs, sip from a faska, then shout for the others again. At first Kandri thinks he hears a distant answering voice, but a moment later there is nothing but the low scrape of the wind.

He tells his brother to make a quick search along the shore, leaving him with their belongings. Mektu agrees; they both know how much faster he'll be without a blind man on his arm. "Ten minutes north, ten south," he says. "If I don't find them, maybe I'll at least find some kind of shelter. In any case I won't let you out of my sight."

"Just hurry," says Kandri. "I'm not going anywhere."

"Ha! That's a safe bet!"

Kandri looks at him—or rather, turns his head as if looking. His brother's laughter ceases. "I'll be quick," he says, and is gone.

Twenty minutes later, he returns and swigs from the faska. "Nothing," he says, "absolutely nothing." And without another word, he runs south.

Kandri sits under his headscarf, brooding. They *must* find shelter; the water won't suffice. And yet they cannot abandon Eshett and Chindilan. And Talupéké—was there any chance of finding her alive? Would she just try to kill them, if they did?

Poor fucked-up soldier girl. Nerves shattered and dreams full of death. Callous Gods, or sleeping. Beaten bitch of a world.

He knows why such savage thoughts are flooding him. Blindness, in a word. He is scared to death. What if it's doesn't wear off in an hour, in a day? What if it lasts forever?

"You're dying of thirst, Kandri Hinjuman. Forever is the last thing you should be worrying about."

Kandri leaps up, hand on his machete. "Who's there?" he shouts.

Utter silence. He draws the machete, recalling how quiet Atau managed to be when it suited him. No one attacks, however, and the minutes drag on. Was the voice in his head?

He laughs at himself: of course it was in his head. Where else?

But he knows the voices his thoughts come clothed in—his father's, his second mother's, Ariqina's, his own—and that voice is not among them. It is a stranger's voice. One he has never heard before.

ʕ

Mektu is gone much longer this time. When at last he returns, he is gasping and stinking of sulfur-mud. "What happened?" asks Kandri. "Did you see them? Did you find *anything*?"

Mektu collapses beside him, presses an object into his hands. It is a small, mud-caked shoe. "Eshett's," he says, spitting out the word.

He is struggling not to cry. He says that the shoe lay on the ice in the middle of a turquoise pool. No footprints: the blowing grit erased them all too quickly. But at one end of the pool, the ice was shattered. Mektu had leaped in, searching. He'd found nothing at all.

"That doesn't mean she's drowned," says Kandri. "You waded out of there, didn't you?"

His brother says nothing. Kandri gropes for his shoulder. "I know how to get us out of the sun," he says. "I don't know why I didn't think of it before."

He sketches the plan; Mektu sits like a stump. But for all his misery, he does not wish to die, and a moment later, they are both on their feet. They walk the shore until Mektu spies one of the harmless, light-green pools. As Kandri waits, he sets to smashing the crystal surface. Then, working together, they drag two enormous ice-sheets ashore, trim them roughly into squares and plaster them with mud. Finally, with much swearing and staggering, they prop the squares against each other, forming a tall triangle. "Good and dark on the inside," says Mektu. "Scoop out the floor, Kan. I'll build a windbreak so we're not drowned in grit."

Soon they are both in the shelter, lying side by side. Then the loss falls on Kandri like an avalanche: Uncle Chindilan, who guarded them in secret. Eshett, Talupéké. Clumsily, he recites a prayer for their safekeeping—*but why, Gods? I don't love you, I don't trust you; you'll do exactly as you like*—and Mektu crosses and uncrosses his wrists in the gesture of Holy Release. Kandri makes the gesture too: the shackles of hell torn asunder by the Eagle of Selulahi. One of the Great Tales of Urrath. Then Mektu begins to describe Eshett's ineptness at fellatio, and Kandri tells him to shut the fuck up.

"What's wrong?" asks Mektu. "I didn't complain. I never made her feel bad. I thought you might be interested, that's all."

"You fucker. She's probably dead."

Mektu falls silent. Kandri's hands are in fists. *Just wait, count the seconds. Eight, nine, ten—*

"I'm not actually concerned with what she did to my dick," says Mektu. "It's the broader picture that's interesting. Some girls just can't. Doesn't matter how you ask for it. You could draw a diagram, you could send them to dick-sucking school. But others get it right the first time. Ariqina, for instance."

Kandri grabs his own wrist: he is that close to striking his brother in the face. "You can be *such* an evil bastard," he says.

"I have every right to talk about her, Kandri. We were in love. We were engaged to be married."

"Goat shit. You weren't."

"It's true. You don't know everything. We'd be married already if she hadn't disappeared."

"She never slept with you. She probably never even kissed you. You dream shit up and then start to believe it."

Mektu answers by humming a tune. For a moment, Kandri simply cannot believe his ears. Then he elbows Mektu sharply. "So what?" he says. "You know that song, so what? You and everyone else in the Valley. What does that have to do with Ariqina?"

"You know."

"I know you're about to get your ass kicked like never before."

Mektu gives an odd little laugh. Kandri's arms are rigid, his heart pounding, his uniform drenched in wasteful sweat.

∾

The song is nothing special, of course. Except to a few hayseed Chilotos from the Valley. Except to him.

Grant me one last hour with my true love, and keep your cold Forever
I'll praise eternal life above her golden kisses—never.

The year is spent, the season chill, our heads are bowed in sorrow,
But in the hearth's an ember still to light a fair tomorrow.

If she's yet with me come the dawn, I'll live but for her smile
And bid a hundred years be gone before I stray a mile.

And if I forfeit heaven's joys, in barter for that hour,
In darkest hell I'll raise my voice, and sing of love's last flower.

What temple fair, what holy place, a sweeter secret's tending,
Then how we might in love's embrace go rowdy to our ending?

A song for closing down the tavern, arms around one's mates. Also a song for lovers, obviously. The Old Man had sung it for their mother, once, thinking himself alone with her, while Kandri and Mektu lay eight feet above on the porch roof, astonished. Years later, Kandri sang it to Ariqina—and they, too, had thought themselves alone.

It was on one of their walking-trysts, through the meadows above Blind Stream. Very late, that particular night, and the season chill indeed. All the same they had held each other, laughed; Ari twisted the copper ring she had placed on his thumb just the day before, and he had found himself singing that song.

They left the trail and climbed to a level place. Ari spread the blanket and rolled about like a schoolgirl, flattening the thigh-high grass. The place smelled vaguely of goats, but it didn't matter, nothing mattered; it was only their third time in life. She stripped everything from him but the copper ring; he drew his coat over both of them, and what magic he learned of a woman's pleasures then, of joys more elusive and harder-earned but earthquake-deep when they came. She had loved the song, impossible romantic Ariqina; and he, desperate to call the earthquake, thought *Well, Kandri, if your tongue can sing*—for his exhausted member was no help; it became a bystander long before her hands tightened in his hair and her head thrashed and one clear cry escaped her and flew over the Valley, like the whoop of some free heretic, the last unorthodox passion east of the sea.

They were alone, yes, but when they descended to Blind Stream Village, Mektu was waiting. He hadn't moved; he was still prowling the road where they had given him the slip. Ariqina panicked, dragged Kandri back into the shadows, one hand over his mouth.

It was her iron rule: Mektu must not learn of their union. *He's too loving,* she told Kandri. *Too loving, and too fragile. He would never forgive us.*

One day he'll have to find out.

Yes, one day. If you and I still—

But Ari, he interrupted (that was the *if* he would never contemplate), *Mektu's living in a dream world. This thing with you, this thing between you. It's all in his head.*

Ari had laughed at that. *Where else does love live, Kandri? In a milk jug? In a song?*

She demanded his word, and Kandri gave it: never to tell, never to crush his brother with the truth. *Don't strike him where he's weak, love. You'll never forgive yourself, and you'll lose your brother, too.*

Kandri was jealous of her affection for Mektu—he was jealous when a fly brushed her arm—but also humbled. More than anyone, Ariqina saw the good in his brother and drew it out. Mektu volunteered at her clinic; he cleaned the bedpans, swapped jokes with invalids as he swabbed the drool from their faces, sat up playing cards with addicts in voluntary lockdown, chattering to keep their minds off wax or skyseed or brandy. Kandri was a more dependable volunteer, but it was Mektu the patients loved.

There were mishaps. He brought hallucinogenic foxberries for the addicts once: "They looked so *bored*, Ariqina." True enough, but the second addict he approached had snatched the bag and guzzled handfuls of berries, and spent the next week talking to his thumbs. There were lost keys, outraged nurses. There was the night Mektu was sent to retrieve a package of bedsheets and surgical gowns from the station house in Bittermoon, and was found hours later in the Warhorse Tavern, snoring, the purse entrusted to him gone.

After that incident, Ariqina had not spoken to Mektu for two months. But he had repented and worked harder, and she had forgiven him at last. She loved his brother. And Kandri knew he loved Mek as well, in glum confusion. Keeping him ignorant of their trysts, however, was far from enough. People talked, and Mektu talked incessantly. They had to hide their love from everyone in order to hide it from him.

We sneak around like criminals, Kandri complained.

Ariqina just smirked at him. *Like lovers, you mean.*

That was true enough. In earlier times, lovers in the Sataapre had been left alone, provided they were discreet, but with the rise of Orthodox Revelation, *discreet* was fast becoming *clandestine*. Soldiers passed through Blind Stream every third or fourth day; there were barracks in Stone Gate and Wolf Kill, and the various constables, aldermen, barristers, and magistrates all answered to military superiors.

The resulting changes in Valley life were profound but not instantaneous. Human nature changed more slowly than institutions or rulers; in the shadows, things went on as before. Couples met, stripped, made love, made promises. By daylight, they did not even hold hands.

So: the long way home. A stumbling walk through the dark meadows above the village, over wooden stiles and bridges over the deep-cut streams. Kandri didn't mind. They were together that much longer, and at the last bridge, they crept down to the stream's edge and splashed their faces, their necks, each other, and she guided his wet hand beneath her shirt and arched her back. *What you did tonight, oh darling, what if I can't think of other things; what if I want it all the time?*

I do, he said.

I hadn't noticed. She laughed and reached for him. *What do you think about when I'm touching you? Do your thoughts race everywhere, like mine?*

He must have answered her. He could not have just sat there on the stones, lost in her hand's magic, breathing like a bull.

The closer you brought me, she said, *the more my mind flew away into the night. I could see the whole world, I was on the Gods' mountain, looking down on us and the clinic and the Valley all the way to the sea. I was happy, and so terribly sad. Kandri, what do you want to see before you die?*

The desert, he told her, for he had known it for years. *The deep desert, the great dunes, the stars at night reaching down to the sand. What do you want to see?*

You know already, she said.

Kasralys.

Yes.

To find your Dr. Tsireem.

She told me a secret, Kandri. A beautiful secret. Their work could change the world.

Spread the blanket, he said.

I'll go to that city one day, when it's time to leave the Valley.

The blanket, he repeated, then: *I'll go with you. To Kasralys, or anywhere you like.*

Do you know, she said, *I almost believe you would.*

ॐ

Kandri wakes in their shelter of salt-ice and mud, and lifts the bandage from one eye.

His heart soars. *Thank you, Ang All-Merciful.*

It's not much—a brown blur, his left hand—but he will take it. He can see. And when he crawls out into the red light of dusk, there is another blur that is his brother, kneeling, with his arms around a woman's legs. Kandri staggers close, squinting like some ancient grandfather. It is Eshett, beautiful Eshett, footsore and indescribably filthy.

"Stop that," she says to Mektu. "Give me something to eat."

Underneath her tattered *kanut* she looks like a ghoul. She has spent five hours standing chin-deep in green mud, hiding from the heat and the sun. Eyes clenched shut, more mud slapped on head and face, her bag lying near her on the ice, windblown grit filling her ears.

"I kept nodding off. I'd wake up sinking, my mouth and nose full of mud."

"How's your vision?" Kandri asks.

"Better for the rest, but still awful. *Togra,* I hate this place."

As the brothers guessed, she had used the mattoglin as bait, luring the bald man out onto the ice against his better judgment. "I slid it out across a pool and kept going. He was so close, and I was nearly blind. I didn't stop until I heard the crack."

"And it was you who took the blade off Ojulan's body," says Kandri. "You've had it all along."

Eshett nods. "I thought it would help me get back to my village. To start over and forget the camp. I thought I'd hide it for a month or two and then slip away from the whorehouse and sell it on the road. You don't have to tell me how hard that would have been."

Kandri steps close to her and takes both her hands. "What I have to tell you," he says, "is that I'm glad you're alive."

She pulls back a little, startled by his fervor. Mektu, still on his knees, is even more so. "I kept your shoe," he grumbles.

When she makes no answer, he nudges Kandri with his elbow. "Stop fondling her. Tell him, Eshett. Tell him about Chindilan and the girl."

"What, you've seen them?" cries Kandri. "When, where?"

"Midday," says Eshett. "They were running east. Talupéké was still crazy, wailing like a cat. Chindilan was running after her, trying to calm her down. They went right past me. I shouted, but the girl just stabbed the air with her knife, and Chindilan covered his ears. Maybe he thought *he* was going crazy, hearing voices from a pool. He was nearly blind, after all. In any case, he kept after her, begging and pleading: 'Girl! Talupéké! Girl!' He even called her 'Trouble.' She didn't stop."

"They must have run out of water hours ago," says Mektu. "If they're sane enough to stop and drink, I mean. And if they haven't lost their packs."

"Chindilan had his pack, and the bow too," says Eshett. "Not the girl, though. She was carrying nothing but her knives."

Kandri tries to picture them out there and shudders, hating what he sees. "They won't live through tomorrow. We have to find them. And we have to start now."

The others instantly agree. But as they make ready to depart, Kandri feels a deep ache in his chest. *Find them.* The idea is almost laughable. Two half-blind people, led by a third squinting through darkened glass. Searching a wilderness. Marching into the night.

"I'll lead you until it's pitch black," says Mektu. "Kandri, keep your bandage on, heal those fucking eyes. If I catch you peeking, I'll—say the kinds of things you hate."

"You will anyway," says Kandri.

He ties one end of his headscarf to Mektu's belt and puts the middle of the scarf in Eshett's hand. The other end he holds tight himself.

"That's good," says Mektu, "but keep your distance, and mind my shins. Ready, ducklings?"

At first the going is easy. They fall into a rhythm almost at once, and Mektu steers around the rare hole or obstacle in the scree. Kandri is surprised at his own confidence, the headlong way he lunges forward, the trust he still grants his brother, somehow. For a time, they even break into a shuffling run.

But more than ever, he feels the hopelessness of it all. Chindilan and Talupéké might have changed direction again. And even if they were sane enough to *try* to hold eastward, how could they? Even for Mektu it is growing harder as the hills fade from view. Their lost comrades could be ten miles off course, or even farther. *If we could fan out, cast a wider net . . .* But they cannot fan out. They are playing darts in a room with the lamps extinguished. Not even certain they are facing the target. And anything but the bullseye losing the game.

They shout and shout, but no answer comes. The wind whips their voices away like flakes of ash. The light dims; Mektu begins to stumble and swear. Somewhere on high they hear the scream of an Ornaq, angry and forlorn.

The plain begins to climb. Mektu, amazed, reports signs of life: bulbous cacti sprouting from hillocks of earth, tufts of wiry grass. Kandri too is stunned; they have seen no vegetation since Balanjé.

"Stop crowding me," says Mektu. "My eyes are in bad shape too. And those cacti have more spines than a fishhook tree."

They slow to a walk and fare better, but then the night grows deeper still. "No good," says Mektu at last. "I'm as blind as you are now. Until the moon comes up, we'll have to creep along like grannies. And not Talupéké's granny, either. I don't believe she learned knife-throwing from some old woman, do you? No, she must have taught herself; she must have natural talent. Kandri and I were just talking about natural talent, weren't we?"

Provocation, that's the word, Kandri thinks. And should they find two dead bodies waiting for them—more provocation, more sly little stings. Two minutes of crocodile tears. Then again with his fantasies, his hints about Ariqina, his lies. *One day you'll go too far, Mektu. One day you'll wish you hadn't pissed on everyone who tried to care.*

Hour after hour, they walk and shout. Kandri is plagued with visions of their missing friends, parched and sunburned, throats too dry to swallow, to speak. Their own water supplies are so low—four faska, maybe part of a fifth—that Kandri can think of no way of managing his thirst but to refuse to feel it. But what will they do when they reach the others? How can they possibly make it to the rim? *You won't face that problem*, says a voice in his head, *because you'll never find them.*

Shut up.

Throwing darts in the darkness. You'll never see them again.

"Gods damn it." Kandri halts the others. He throws his pack on the ground and slips the bandage from his eyes. Blackness, blurred shapes. A lamp seen through water: the moon. Ignoring Mektu's protests, he bends and gropes in his pack. Arrows. Matches. The medical kit. And within the latter, wrapped in goat skin, the glass bottle of wound spirits.

He pulls the jar out, then takes the end of his bandage in his teeth and rips off a three-foot length. He puts the bottle and the length of cloth in Mektu's hands. "Drench it," he says.

"What happened?" says Mektu. "Did you cut your foot?"

"Just hurry up," says Kandri. He gives the matches to Eshett, who has also lifted her bandage. When Mektu has soaked the cloth, Kandri ties it tight to an arrow shaft. He looks at Eshett, who nods.

"I'm ready," she says. "Aim high." Kandri nocks the arrow, points the bow skyward, draws. Eshett strikes a match.

A great flame springs to life by Kandri's shoulder. He lets fly. The arrow streaks upward in a dazzling arc. Three hundred feet above the wasteland, it goes out.

"Now look hard, pain or no pain," he says. "Uncle Chindilan has a bow as well. He'll answer, if he can."

Their eyes sweep the dark world, horizon to horizon. Minutes tick by, and the cold dread deepens in Kandri's chest. "Uncle's not the only one who might see that flare," says Mektu.

"You have another idea?" says Kandri.

Mektu doesn't answer. They wait on, but the darkness is unbroken. "Do it again, Kandri," says Eshett. "Do it until you run out of arrows."

Kandri shoulders his pack. "Later," he says, too miserable to elaborate. There are arrows aplenty, but the wound spirits will be exhausted much sooner. They walk another mile and climb the first of the hills before he sends a second flare into the sky. Again, there is no answer, and their shouts return only echoes. Kandri's mind ticks off the possibilities: the bow lost, the arrows lost, matches lost or soaked to uselessness, nothing that burns like wound spirits in his uncle's possession.

Or their faces turned away. Or their deaths already a fact.

They descend the eastern slope of the hill and climb another, much taller, and from its barren crown he sees dawn in the east. He thinks: *That dawn will kill them.* Very soon, mere minutes from now, their flares will be invisible in the light.

With great haste, they signal again. Mektu hisses a flat little tune through his teeth. Eshett's puffy eyes are on Kandri, imploring, and Mektu snaps at her, "Look for *them*, not at my brother!" His voice thick with heartbreak. Is there any torture like watching hope drain away, water through your fingers, dry despair on your tongue?

Dawn spreads from the east. Kandri shoots a fourth and final time; he has smashed the bottle and swabbed it out with the rag. As they wait, barely breathing, Kandri glances over his shoulder. And there it is: the East Rim. The sun is very clearly rising over a distant, jagged wall. It should have been a moment of joy, that first glimpse. The Lutaral is there; water and food and caravansaries are there. He and Mektu and Eshett will not die in the Yskralem. They will go on, devastated, toward that heartless sun.

In the Sataapre, we almost worshipped you, Samitra Sun-Goddess (look at my madness, talking to an ember in the sky). *You took so long to climb above the Coastal Range. You gave us long cool mornings for labor, for making love* (she does not listen, she does not care). *Here, a man could come to hate you. And you know it, bitch, you're still stabbing at my eyes.*

Kandri turns away—

A sputtering fire dances on a hilltop, two or three miles to the north. It waves fitfully in the half-light, two seconds at the very most, and dies. The brothers and Eshett roar as one, an appropriately hysterical sound, then fall dead silent, not daring to breathe.

Over the dead hills, a living voice: Chindilan's.

. . . eeeeeers . . . kuhhhhhhh . . . eeeeee!

Seconds later, they are racing northward down the hill. They have not understood the smith's words or stopped to worry about the fact. But the sounds reverberate in Kandri's thoughts until they sort themselves out. Tears and laughter burst from him, commingled.

We're fucking thirsty.

ॐ

For one terrifying moment, they fear they have aimed for the wrong summit, lost their friends in this sea of once-drowned hills. Then a flash of sunlight on metal. It is Chindilan, atop the next ridge, signaling with the side of his axe.

He comes reeling down the slope; they meet at the bottom and embrace. His eyes are sunken and his shriveled skin has a waxy sheen. Grinning, he takes the faska from Kandri's hand.

"Finish it!" says Kandri. "Just please be careful, Uncle. We can't afford to spill a drop."

The smith takes only a mouthful, dribbling the water through lips like cicada skins. After swallowing with concentration, he speaks in a pained, dry whisper.

"Saved . . . one mouthful . . . so I could yell . . . Ang's tears . . . glad to see you . . . come on."

He leads them west around the hill, to a small escarpment where Talupéké lies sprawled on Chindilan's riding coat, a rough bandage covering her eyes.

She is utterly motionless as they approach, but when the smith kneels and lifts her head, she frowns and starts to fight him. "Shh, dear," says Chindilan. "They've found us. . . . We're safe."

Her lips have dried together; Chindilan has to split them open with his fingers, like a rind. He whispers their story as she drinks.

Talupéké's madness had carried her almost to the hills. Then her legs had collapsed. She had lain in the sun, screaming and thrashing awhile, and finally slept. Chindilan (after taking away her knives) had dragged her on his riding coat through the worst heat of the afternoon. Up to that point, he had merely followed her voice; he was too blind even to make out the horizon. He prayed they were still making for the hills, where there would be some hope of shade. He had walked face-first into cacti and stumbled into holes. He had heard the chirrup of a deadly *khela* lizard, a poison-spitter, and felt a snake pass like the crack of a bullwhip across his boot.

"Then your flare . . . couldn't answer . . . had some arrows but . . . nothing . . . wanted to burn."

"But you found something finally," says Eshett.

The smith nods, makes a chopping gesture, then points at Talupéké. "Her braid . . . oily . . . as a wick."

"I'll bet she loved you for that," says Mektu.

Chindilan looks at Talupéké thoughtfully, and rasps, "Still . . . delirious . . . said they'd make fun of her . . . at school."

They drink the faskas dry, lavishing water on the smith and Talupéké. The big hill provides shade until almost midday, and again from midafternoon until dusk. Then Kandri climbs to the summit, and even without the telescope, he can see the lamps of villages along the Rim.

V. GIVE YOUR SOUL

After six hours, Ut'xing tired of the yatra's teasing. He clapped his hands, and his priests lit a fire of silphium, and the demon hissed and rattled the window casings. Throwing them open, the Emperor laughed: "How simple a matter it is to drive you off!"

The demon fled the palace as a whirlwind, never to return. But its parting words echoed in the courtyard, and long in the mind of Ut'xing.

"Simple as well to cast a stone, Prince of Nations. But who may retrieve it from the sea?"

ANNALS OF UT'XING

Mektu is bringing water to the pigs. Kandri, smoking under a persimmon tree, watches his advance across the blazing yard, the ghost-white farm dog padding at his heels. In the four days they have sheltered there, the animal has grown quite fond of Mektu, but bristles and growls at Kandri himself. No justice. Kandri even tossed it a chicken bone. The dog had shied from the offering, which later crossed the farmyard on the shoulders of ants.

Chindilan, near the fence, is hacking at a stump with a splitting maul. The old woman who owns the farm is a war widow and somehow indebted to Talupéké. She asks nothing of them, but they mean to earn their keep.

Kandri leans back against the tree. Swallows, grasshoppers, a blossoming vine along the fence. How can it be that they are fugitives? How can the world have little places like this one, and legions of men who want them dead?

Kandri lifts his gaze. The little homestead crouches on the rim of the Yskralem, half a mile north of Mab Makkutin, the city withering inside its Imperial wall. He can see the whole of the dusty road to the northern gate: deserted, save for a few children kicking a rag ball in the distance.

No Eshett. No Talupéké. He snuffs his cheroot against a rock and pockets the stub.

Damn the both of you. It's past noon. You promised to come back hours ago.

Four days since they crawled from the Stolen Sea. The first two given over entirely to sleep. This is the breather that Chindilan spoke of, that first day, while they still clung to the shade of the western cliff. But already, Kandri worries that they have stayed too long.

Yesterday, the women had set out for the city to bargain for the men's passage across the desert, and Eshett's as far as her village. The men had balked at the idea of sending them alone, but Eshett and Talupéké held firm: the last thing they wanted was an escort of deserters from the Army of Revelation.

"You want to protect us?" said Eshett. "Hide your damned tinted eyes."

And that makes sense. The eyestain would betray them to anyone close enough for a handshake. No one is safe in their company; even the war widow had come close to turning them away. They have the mysterious stain-suppressing ointment from Garatajik's pack, but so little of it, and who can say when their lives might depend on such a trick? Nor do they fancy the ointment's "burning and irritation"—not in eyes still recovering from salt blindness.

So the men had stayed behind, seething more than resting, while the women scoured the city. They had focused their efforts at the Dawn Gate, the east-facing gate, which in addition to having some holy significance was also the point from which all caravans set out. "There's a market for travelers heading east—the Desert Market, they call it—just outside the wall," Talupéké had said. "And the Dawn Gate brings good luck to everyone"—she glanced at Mektu—"if you're respectful."

But the Dawn Gate, whatever it was, had brought no luck at all, and at noon they had returned discouraged. Passage for strangers in hiding? No one had wanted to discuss the matter. Today, the women had set out at sunrise, steeled for a longer search.

Someone will need the money, Kandri thinks for the hundredth time. With the gold and rubies from Garatajik, they should be able to hire men to carry them on their shoulders. And then there is the mattoglin, a fortune in itself. No one contests Eshett's claim to the blade. But since the incident at the Snakeskin, she has been muttering about "that cursed weapon" and joking (was she joking? *Can* she joke?) about dropping it into a well. Kandri is not about to let that happen, but what to do with the thing? Fence it here in Mab Makkutin and hope it isn't recognized? Or carry it with them—heavy, desperately hidden, a temptation beyond words—and pray that they are never searched?

In any case, gold is clearly not enough. Desert caravans are not stagecoach services, apparently. And even a stagecoach driver will whip his horses past suspicious men on the roadside. What can the women be saying? *Gods' peace, stranger: how far can you take us, and how soon? One of us is a Parthan; will you pass close to her village? Will you ask no questions? Will you trust us, and the men we haven't brought along?*

No, it can't be easy. But for the moment, all he wants is to see Eshett and Talupéké emerge from the road's shimmering heat. They had promised to return by midmorning, and now his thoughts are full of dark conjectures.

He rises, crosses the farmyard, wipes his feet by the kitchen door. Within the house, the light is dim. He moves to the corner of the main room, where the four of them have spread their bedrolls, and retrieves the telescope from his pack. Then he climbs the stairs to the rooftop terrace.

The old woman, Yehita-Chen, is hanging laundry along one wall. She smiles vaguely at him, her eyes clouded with cataracts.

"Don't you fear for them," she says. "That soldier girl of yours was trained by General Tebassa. She knows how to stay alive."

"I'm sure you're right, mother," says Kandri, but his words are mere politeness. Talupéké's hints have made him wonder if the great Black Hat himself is alive.

He raises the telescope. Mab Makkutin's Imperial wall is vast and cold. Chindilan spoke of it as a ruin, but Kandri can see no breach in the massive structure, only the occasional crumbled rampart or turret in disrepair. But he can see over the wall: Yehita's farm stands on a bluff, and Mab Makkutin, the former port, straddles the lowest stretch of cliff for many miles. Dying or not, the city is strangely beautiful. There are barnacle-like clusters of tiny houses, smooth-walled and white and devoid of sharp corners, with round chimneys and windows like holes punched in dough. There are shops and teahouses crowded with customers, teeming schoolyards, dogs basking in the sun.

But between these brighter districts—looming over them—are crumbling halls and towers and warehouses built on an entirely different scale: the remains of the Imperial city, wreckage from the time of kings. They stand shunned, these monstrous buildings. Tomb-like, they look down on the living city with dismay.

And somewhere in that city, that Ghost Port, walk Eshett and Talupéké. *Merciful Ang, what's keeping them? What danger have they landed in for us?*

But Ang has no comment, and Kandri sweeps the telescope to the east.

The land is a fragile green. The rivers that fed the Yskralem are gone, but many thin, trickling streams still water the plain of the Lutaral. In the distance, Kandri spots antelope and wild buffalo, and farther yet, the steep Arig Hills that form another sort of wall: between this gentle country and the desert. *Sumuridath Jal*, the Land that Eats Men. Will they lose the hunters in that inferno, or just their lives?

Don't think about that. Study life while you can. Prancing colts in a barnyard half a mile away, carts heaped with winter oranges, red herons strung like jewels along a stream.

And to the north, a bamboo watchtower, new-built, soaring. Kandri frowns: why place it there? What danger does Mab Makkutin face from the north?

"Mother," he calls to the old woman, "how far off is the war front?"

"One hundred miles, give or take," she says. "Your Prophet's men are dug in north of Harul Makkut, last I heard. Now get down from here before you're spotted. The women will be along."

Kandri descends to the farmyard. Chindilan is leaning on the splitting maul, soaked in sweat.

"Take a rest," says Kandri. "I'll finish off that stump when the heat breaks."

"That's what I told him," says Mektu, emerging from the henhouse. Clutched awkwardly in his hands are nine or ten almond-brown eggs.

"You'd do better with a skirt," says Kandri.

"You'd do better with this egg up your ass."

Kandri giggles despite himself. The joke is less in the words than the voice Mektu has adopted: an uncanny impression of their mother, Dyakra, who even at swordpoint would never say anything so vulgar.

"Stop that, it's creepy," says Chindilan. "How are those eyes of yours, anyway? Still improving?"

"I found the eggs, didn't I?"

Kandri lifts a corner of his brother's shirt. He winces. The spot where the arrow pierced Mektu's side is healing swiftly, but the exit wound is another matter: red and tight as a blister. Closest to the scar, red flesh gives way to yellow. Kandri's fingers, hovering over the wound, can sense the heat without touching it.

"Charming," says his uncle. "Something you can brag about with the ladies."

His tone is light, but when Kandri catches his eye, he knows Chindilan feels the same dread that he does. The wound is festering. Mektu needs a doctor—a real doctor, not some village sawbones with grimy fingernails. *And that will be the end of secrecy. Unless the doctor is as good a soul as this old woman.*

A growl: the dog has heard something on the road. Kandri turns and sees a man in ragged uniform, still far off but coming their way. It is one of the sentries from the tower.

"What are they after now?" says Kandri. "This morning it was sweet limes. Yesterday too. They buy a lot of sweet limes."

"I don't think we need to hide from those kids," says Mektu. "They don't even come into the yard. If they're snooping, it's only because they're bored. You know what tower duty's like."

"Don't assume they're harmless," says Chindilan. "They serve at the pleasure of the Ursad of Mab Makkutin, and he is a ruthless man. Tight-fisted, charming, murderous when necessary. He was a soldier, then a warlord, and then he seized Mab Makkutin and made it his own private piggy bank. He's incredibly rich. They say he has a war elephant, and brings it out on special occasions to amaze the rabble. I don't know about the elephant, but I know he has spies. Every tenth man is a spy."

"How long ago did you say you were here, Uncle?" says Mektu.

"Don't call me Uncle. Eleven years, maybe twelve."

"Maybe he's grown gentler with age," says Mektu.

"Rubbish," says the smith.

"That's what happens to some men. They get gentler. Also slower, and fat."

Chindilan looks daggers at him. "The Ursad's a bit like that dog you're so fond of," he says. "He can sit quietly, play favorites, keep watch on his little kingdom. Or he can rip your throat out for looking at him cross-eyed. Or because you look like a nice slab of meat. And who do you think tosses him the sweetest morsels? The Prophet, that's who. You can bet your bread and butter that whatever his spies learn, Her Radiance learns soon enough. So get your asses into the house."

They know the drill. Close the shades. Sit in silence at the table. Wait for Yehita-Chen to fetch whatever the sentry is buying, to lie again about her guests. Wool merchants: that is the story they have settled on. Readying themselves for a journey by camel-train, south to Sendu where wool is in demand. No, they'd prefer not to meet anyone. They're a bit timid, you see. A bit ashamed of their rags.

The dog has slipped inside with them; it nudges Mektu, who smiles and scratches its ear. Kandri's nails bite into his palm. If he is ashamed of anything, it is that he hasn't found Mektu a doctor. They had to rest, he tells himself. Even with the Prophet seeking them everywhere, even knowing another Wolfpack might ride out of the Stolen Sea. Their eyes had to heal, their burned skin recuperate, their dry flesh take on water. To light out into the desert otherwise would have been unthinkable.

But for Mektu, lighting out untreated would be a death sentence.

ல

Late afternoon. Yehita-Chen has stopped telling them not to worry. The men put on the anonymous clothes she provided—her dead husband's, presumably—and set out for Mab Makkutin, surly and swift. The brothers have strapped their machetes across their backs, underneath their robes. Chindilan brings only a dagger: no wool merchant, he concedes reluctantly, ambles into town with a battle axe.

The smith chatters as they walk, betraying his unease. "We'll start at the Dawn Gate, and that Desert Market. You two should see the Gate anyway; it's a marvel. So old, even the Kasrajis couldn't say who built it, when they came here a thousand years back. They built it into their own wall, you see: whatever fortification it was part of was gone, eradicated, but the old gate's still sound. I passed through it myself, with my garrison. I still see it in my dreams."

"How close is the Great Desert, uncle?" asks Mektu.

Chindilan turns his face to the wall of hills. "Close enough to touch," he says. "From the peaks of the Arigs, you look right down into its jaws, and you can't believe this green country can go on existing. It's like a baby snuggled up to a crocodile."

The heat is lifting, the road busy again. Peddlers and farmers pass in both directions, leading horses and camels, fodder tied in enormous bundles on their backs. Voices like a lazy river: *Good day, brothers, Ang keep you. May fortune smile on your journey.* The three men return the pleasantries but keep their distance, hiding their eyes.

They near the wall and the city's north-facing gate. This close, Kandri can see the decay his uncle spoke of. The wall's great corbelled turrets are shedding their roof tiles; the iron gates are gnawed by rust. Still—

"It's so damned huge."

Chindilan nods. "And this was the periphery of the Empire, the lacy trim. Imagine the great cities at the height of Kasraji power. Imagine Kasralys, to this day. *Jeshar*, is that . . ." He points straight ahead at the city. "Ang's blood, lads, it's them!"

Eshett and Talupéké are running out through the city gate, making straight for them. Mektu gropes for his machete, but Kandri stops him with a wave. "Don't draw! No one's chasing them. Keep that blade out of sight."

The women skid to a halt before them. "What are you doing here?" hisses Eshett. "Are you trying to ruin everything? Have you forgotten your eyes?"

"Have you forgotten what *midmorning* means?" Kandri counters. "What did you think, that we'd stay back there shooting marbles?"

"Something happened," says Talupéké. "I had to go somewhere fast."

"Well, then, don't mention it."

"Let her explain, boy," says Chindilan. Since the Yskralem, he has become almost maddeningly tolerant of Talupéké's quirks.

"*Harach*, we can't just stand here," says Eshett, "and you can't pass through the gate until nightfall, or twilight anyway."

They look around, awkward as hell, and at last spot a man with a two-wheeled food cart making for the gate. Pouncing on the startled fellow, they buy five lamb skewers, and crouch in a circle by the road's edge, gnawing like wolves.

"Bad luck again," says Eshett through a mouthful. "Only three caravans preparing for the desert."

"How's that possible?" says Kandri. "I thought this was where they started."

"Mab Makkutin is the largest port of departure," says Talupéké, "and winter's the best season for a crossing. But they're not crossing this year. They're afraid."

"Of the desert?"

"Of course," says Eshett. "If you don't fear the desert, you're as stupid as a cow. But this year, they're also afraid of the *Darsunuk*. The Time of Madness, remember? Atau's men spoke of it. Today, it was the camel drivers. A night of blood is coming, they said. And tears of fire from the Gods. And senseless killing, neighbor against neighbor, clan against clan. It's a sweet little legend, the *Darsunuk*."

"And is the White Child part of that legend?" asks Mektu.

Both women start. Chindilan's response is closer to a gasp. "Of course not," says Eshett. "What put that into your head?"

Mektu shrugs. "I don't know. I just thought maybe."

"Because it sounds awful, and the *Darsunuk* sounds awful?"

"Because people are afraid of it," says Mektu.

"People are afraid of all kinds of things," says Talupéké. "I told you before, I'd never heard of the White Child before those Rasanga brought it up."

But you have, thinks Kandri, still looking at Chindilan. His uncle is shaken and trying hard not to show it. *What is this thing you're so afraid of? That the* Rasanga *are afraid of? And why the fuck aren't you telling us everything?*

"These days, most of us don't believe in the Time of Madness," says Talupéké. "But camel drivers are superstitious fools. They wouldn't even talk to us; they just waved us away. Or laughed, or tried to pinch us."

"Pinch you?" says Mektu. "*Harach*, those horny bastards. Let them try it when I'm around."

"Actually," says Talupéké, "it just happened once."

Kandri smiles at her, but Talupéké shakes her head. "Don't look at me. It was Eshett who cracked that fucker's jaw." She mimes a hard backward strike with an elbow. "Serves him right, the fool. You don't pinch a Parthan's ass."

"I was the fool, to strike without looking," says Eshett. "He could have been a nobleman. I might have been jailed. Fortunately, he was just a drunken pest. Men laughed and started joking with us, and when they learned our business, they introduced us to the owner of a caravan—one of the few preparing for the desert. They were strange folk. Nervous, and not exactly friendly. They kept away from the others at the Desert Market. From the south, they said, and trying to get east to Shefet Ang."

"They sound perfect," says Kandri.

"And you two look like someone pissed in your coffee," puts in Chindilan. "What happened? They turned you down like the rest?"

"Oh, no," says Eshett. "They're willing to take on passengers."

"So what's the matter?"

Talupéké gives a snorting laugh. "They're plain fucked, that's what. The mercenaries they hired for protection? They demanded half their pay up front, and as soon as it was in their pockets, they ran off down the Smoke Road. I told the owner that you three would be their protection. That made him laugh. *Come back when there are thirty of you*, he said."

Kandri's eyes widen. "Thirty guards?"

"Thirty soldiers, battle-tested," says Eshett. "Or else they won't move an inch."

"Pitfire, why so many?" asks Chindilan. "They're crossing the empty desert, not Važenland."

"'Empty desert,'" says Eshett, shaking her head. "No Parthan would use those words."

"Who the hell cares?" says Mektu. "Finish the story! You did something. You had to get somewhere fast."

Talupéké smiles broadly. It is so unlike her usual range of expression that she seems almost to become another person. *Ang's tears*, thinks Kandri, *she's a sixteen-year-old girl.*

"We'll show you," says Talupéké. "And we don't even have to cut through Mab Makkutin. We can follow the wall around to the market outside the Dawn Gate."

"The Desert Market?" says Kandri. "You found someone, then?"

"Oh, she found someone," says Eshett.

They walk north, in the wall's growing shadow. Blackbirds flash overhead, dark leaves in a whirlwind. Atop the wall, the crenellations stand in decay like rows of carious teeth. Grass and brush sprout between them: Kandri thinks of the aqueduct back home. The guards above seem tiny, and too few.

"Never trust people," says Talupéké, as if for the first time. "That's my weakness, that's what I do. One day I'll be killed because I've trusted again. I mean that: it's the way I will die."

"Nobody knows how they'll die, sister," says Eshett.

"If a God tells you, you know," says Talupéké.

Chindilan clears his throat. "Tal and I talked quite a bit in the Yskralem, boys."

Kandri's mouth twitches. *Tal.*

"The massacre of her general's forces was an ambush. Someone betrayed them."

"Someone inside Black Hat's ranks?" asks Kandri.

"Yes," says Talupéké, "someone deep inside. The general doesn't share his battle plans with many. Only senior officers would have known we were making for the Megrev Defile. I hope I'm the one who catches the traitor, whoever he is. I want to cut his feet off and watch him try to walk. I want to hold his gaze as he dies."

"Who could such a traitor be working for?" asks Mektu.

"How should I know? Everyone's betrayed us. The Ursad, who threw us out of Mab Makkutin. The Lo'ac royal family, who worship the Prophet now. And the worst shit-eating pig of all, the Sartaph of Sendu. He was a Chiloto, but we trusted him. He called himself 'the Last Free Prince,' said he would fight the Prophet to his last man. When he asked for contributions, my people paid. In cattle, in gold. And every year he asked for more."

"But then the rumors began: Sendu wasn't fighting the Prophet at all; they were in league, fighting together in southern lands. Of course we stopped paying that pig of a sartaph. He sent us presents, and a letter denying it all."

She picks her teeth with her empty lamb skewer. The letter, she says, ended with an invitation: send your military commanders to Sendu, see the fighting for yourselves. Black Hat Tebassa (only a major, then) smelled treachery and urged his superiors to refuse. But the letter guaranteed their safety, and bore the sartaph's royal seal. Days later, the entire Lutaral-Lo'ac War Council rode for Sendipre, capital of Sendu. And never returned.

Sendu abandoned all pretenses. It seized lands from the devastated Lutaral clans and mounted their leaders' heads on stakes. There was even a rumor that Jihalkra, the Prophet's Firstborn, had been waiting in Sendipre when the War Council arrived.

"But the sartaph was no match for my general," says Talupéké. "A year after the killing, he led a shadow team right into Sendipre. They dressed as rag-pickers, slept in the slums. And each day they kept watch on the sartaph. Everyone he met. Every festival and tavern and whore's den he visited. And one day—"

"This story's *much too long*," blurts Mektu.

"Be quiet, you ass," says Chindilan. "Tell us what happened, Tal."

"There were baths," says Talupéké, glaring at Mektu, "for rich people, but poorly guarded all the same. The general and his team slipped in through the laundry and killed the sartaph's men, and tied the pig himself hand and foot. General Tebassa took a brick from the fire where the bath water was heating, and wrote his name on it in charcoal and took the brick to the sartaph's skull. When he was done, he put the brick in the corpse's hands. 'I did this to you,' he said, 'but it is also true that you did it to yourself.' Then he led the whole assault team out of the baths and home from Sendipre, unharmed."

"That's a fine story." Chindilan turns her a crooked smile. "Didn't exactly change the world, though, did it? The sartaph's nephew was crowned before the corpse was cold."

Talupéké glares at the smith. "He stopped advancing. He doesn't dare cross the general."

"Who cares, who cares?" says Mektu, almost prancing with impatience. "All this old crap, what does it have to do with us?"

"Don't you understand?" Talupéké's gaze moves to Mektu. "He's coming, with all his forces. My general is coming here."

Chindilan stops in his tracks.

"Ang's blood, little sister. Black Hat Tebassa, here?"

"Keep your voice down. Yes. And if anyone can persuade a caravan master to take you over the desert, it's him."

"Is that where you're taking us?" says Kandri. "To see your general?"

"Only"—Talupéké gives him a piercing look—"if I can trust you not to ruin everything. And even then it won't be easy to arrange. You can't just drop in on him, like a visit to the fucking neighbors. The general's fought every evil bastard from Gathen to the River Shev. He's the most wanted man in Urrath."

Despite her ferocity, she is clearly pleased. But Eshett glances at the brothers and shakes her head. "Not anymore," she says.

℘

Chindilan spoke the truth: the Dawn Gate is a thing of beauty. An arch of wind-smoothed sandstone the color of sunrise, irregular in form but serene and graceful, it stands out sharply from the Kasraji wall that has subsumed it. That wall is centuries old, but somehow Kandri senses that the Dawn Gate's age is of a different order entirely, one for which centuries are scarcely the measure. He could almost imagine that he is looking at the tip of some vein of bedrock as old as Urrath itself—and rising, unbroken, from the heart of the world.

Within the stone arch, and built to fit its curious shape, are two doors of latticed iron. The bars are corroded but still massive, thick as a man's leg at the knee. Kandri finds himself oddly comforted by these relics. Mute, mysterious, their story long forgotten; yet all the same, they are here. Perhaps a few things do last forever.

But then again.

The gate looks down on a scene of utter transience: the desert market. There are tents beyond counting, tents of wool and canvas and sewn-together hides; and shops, thatched-roof and ramshackle. There are stockades of camels, horses, desert asses, goats; there are numberless men pushing handcarts, hawking dumplings and sausages, brandied olives, pickled eel, groundnuts steaming in their shells. Men just arrived or soon departing. Laughter, embraces, arguments. The rites of the open road.

The path along the wall crosses another here, cutting east toward the Arig Hills. For the first time, Kandri is struck by the size and severity of those hills, the mighty barrier they raise against the desert beyond. Once through the Arigs, will they find safety in those obliterating sands?

Right at the crossroads is a tiny hut—a model, really, barely three feet high—and in its open doorway stands a clay figurine. It is a shrine to Atalanith, patron saint of travelers. Offerings of nuts and flowers lie at Atalanith's feet, but his candles have succumbed to the wind.

Before the shrine is a flat stone plaque. Kandri brushes off the sand and withered flower petals, and reads:

By this road the modest traveler may
To fair Lupriz pass living.
And if his camel does not stray
And the moon of kindness light his way
And the sacred fire of love's first spell
Burn in that black and secret well
And the Gods be yet forgiving,

Then on to the blessed eastern lands
He may with faith aspire
To Shefetsi and Shefet Ang,
And Kasralys the Jewel Entire.

But woe to the man whose heart is proud:
For him the Bright Death, or the Shroud.

"Oh happy day," says Mektu.

"The Bright Death means thirst, or any death caused by the sun," says Talupéké. "I've heard of Kasralys, but not those other places. As for the Shroud"—she hesitates, glances at Eshett as if for support—"that's something out of a story book, isn't it?"

Eshett's gaze is severe. "My people do not speak of the Shroud," she says. "This way."

The women lead them deep into the warren of shops, the men hiding their eyes from the brighter lamps. The air is pungent: sweat and cloves, simmering onions, spoiling fruit. They slide, swim, squirm through packed isles of goods, much of it clearly for long expeditions. Wineskins, faskas, dried fruits, salted meats, fodder, tent stakes, whetstones, ghoul's bane, tea in bundles, molasses in rock-hard lumps. Boot laces. Prayer books. Playing cards to keep from going mad.

"Why is the market out here in the open?" says Kandri. "There's plenty of room inside the wall."

"There's *nothing* but room," says Talupéké, "but in the city proper you pay taxes, and bribes to the Ursad's treasurer. Out here, you just pay the bribes. My grandmother was still angry about them on her deathbed."

"Did she have a booth here?"

"A booth?" Talupéké snorts. "She had a circus. A real one, with eight wagons, acrobats, fire-eaters, spirit-summoners. And an elephant: Vuceku, she called him. Stormcloud. I used to ride him when I was small. But ten years ago the Ursad took him: unpaid fines, he said."

She pauses, as though weighing the value of saying anything more. Then she shrugs. "Our whole family was in the business. My uncles taught me climbing and such. And I told you already about Kereqa, my grandmother. She taught me knives."

The girl shuts her mouth, unsettled by this rush of confessions. Chindilan stands near her, almost protectively. Mektu just stares. "You really are a circus freak," he says.

Kandri wonders if the others catch the envy in his voice. Circus life: that is what Mektu has always needed, the life he should have had. Surrounded by onlookers. Swallowing fire, juggling swords, sticking his head in the tiger's mouth. Hidden in a tent, protected from the heartless world. Fearless, outrageous, loved.

Kandri's mind is churning. The last thing he wants is to get entangled with Talupéké's lethal general, this man who beat a sartaph to death. But the little farm will not be safe much longer. Word of Ojulan's death, and perhaps that of Garatajik, will reach Mab Makkutin, and the city will be gripped with bounty fever. Lethal or not, Tebassa is the only card they have to play.

After much searching, Talupéké stops at the intersection of two crowded alleys, between a tea stand and what Kandri takes for a barber's booth. Talupéké nods to the barber, then turns to Chindilan.

"Here you are, Uncle," she says. "Delousing. Sit down, wait your turn."

She points with her chin: a wooden bench, and two ragged men waiting, one of them scratching busily at his scalp.

Chindilan grows stiff, speaks through his teeth. "What is this?" he says.

"Go ahead, sit down," says Eshett.

"I don't have fucking lice."

"No lice, no charging!" shouts the barber, in broken Kasraji. "Only pay for the haircut. Yes, yes, you need it, sit down now, hair like wild monkey."

Both he and the women are strangely firm, and at last Kandri understands. This is a performance. Someone is watching, waiting for a sign.

Chindilan has caught on too. He lowers himself with dignity to the bench, keeping as far from the itchy customers as possible. Time passes. Talupéké orders tea. Somewhere, a voice is wailing above the throng. *Darsunuk! The Time of Madness! It is come, brothers and sisters, the end of all things and the breaking of this world. Who among us will find shelter on the Night of Blood? Who among us shall be spared?*

A beggar priest. Someone mimics him in high falsetto; a nervous laugh bubbles through the crowd. Many, however, do not laugh. *Darsunuk.* How many of these peasants, he thinks, lie awake at night worrying about the end of the world?

The priest moves on, his voice like a crank-siren. Mektu, Kandri notices with alarm, is surreptitiously probing his wound.

Who among us shall be spared?

Then he starts. An older man in a laborer's plain shirt and trousers stands before them. His bright green eyes study Kandri and Mektu over a pair of black spectacles. He has a face of sharp angles, the flesh stretched tight over cheekbones and chin. His hands are still powerful, his chest broad and strong; this is a man resisting the arrival of old age.

"The brothers Hinjuman," he says.

The travelers, men and women alike, are shocked. Mektu glares at the women, accusing. But the man makes a gesture of restraint.

"They told me nothing," he says. "They didn't have to. I knew you both at a glance."

The women look appalled: clearly, they expected no such encounter. Kandri feels the world closing in on him fast, as though the crowd surrounding them were bristling with hidden enemies.

"When did word reach Mab Makkutin?" he murmurs.

"Word?" The man's confusion seems genuine. "Word of what, my boy?"

Kandri looks at the others, bewildered. *If he hasn't heard—if no one's heard, yet—*

"How did you know our names?" Kandri asks.

"He didn't," says Mektu, twitching with anxiety. "He just knew to be on the lookout for us. He tried his luck. And you just stood there, you stupid ass, and let him look in your eyes."

"His . . . *eyes?*" says the older man. One emotion chases another across his face. Bewilderment. Suspicion. Comprehension. Fear.

"Get up," he says. "Hell's choir, I thought I'd seen everything. Go back, back to the crossroads. Wait for me at the shrine."

He is turning away already. "That's it?" says Kandri. "We just wait there until you return?"

The man hesitates, not looking back. "You might consider a prayer," he says.

☙

They wait a long time at the crossroads. Mektu buys a bottle of something; he and Talupéké pass it back and forth, taking small, grim nips. Kandri feels a dreadful unease. Everyone is watching them, everyone a potential foe. That beggar: is he faking his club foot, is he a spy? That man with the thick black beard: did he just look at Talupéké strangely? Have you seen him before?

Get a grip on yourself, Kandri. The man's leering. Talupéké has breasts.

He clears his throat. The bearded man, jolted from his reverie, turns and flees.

"*Lulee*," says Mektu, offering him the bottle.

"No, thanks," says Kandri. "And he wasn't a *lulee*."

"No? He stared at you longer than he did at her. Like you were a gold coin, or a puppy he wanted to scoop up and take home."

Talupéké peers after the man, though he has already vanished in the crowd. "Something strange about his face," she says.

"You're just jealous," Mektu tells her. He leans close to Kandri, makes kissing lips. Kandri thumps his cheek with an elbow, smiling despite himself. Then he leaves the others and walks over to the shrine.

He kneels down before the little clay saint. He even mumbles a prayer, but whether in hope of aid or merely to look less conspicuous, he does not know himself. Once more he reads the odd inscription.

And the sacred fire of love's first spell / Burn in that black and secret well.

It is his birth sign, the Well of Sacred Fire. He had always thought it simply a fanciful term for a harvest moon. But the moon is not black, or secret, for that matter. Could there really be some sort of fire-well in this world? Does it lead to the hell of Lord Jekka, where the damned find punishment? Or is hell some other place, and the world's heart reserved for love?

ଚଡ

By the time Kandri and Ariqina rose from the blanket by the streamside, it was very late, and no lamps burned in the village. They crept down past the aqueduct, the fish tanks, the black wall of the Sed Hemon Orthodox School.

It was the spot where they always parted: her aunt's house loomed at the end of the street. Kandri drew her close once more.

A hand clutched his shoulder, spun him roughly around.

"Uncle Chindilan!"

For it was he: *Sergeant* Uncle Chindilan, home two days for a goddaughter's wedding—the very festivities from which Kandri and Ariqina had slipped away. "Not a word!" hissed the older man, dragging them by the arms.

In the dark of a side alley he released them, but his gaze was more binding than his hands. "Where in Jekka's hell have you been?" he demanded. "Mektu was supposed to stop you. I told that little shit not to move!"

"He was there, we avoided him," said Kandri.

"Oh, Gods," said Ariqina. "You didn't say anything, did you? You haven't told him were together?"

"I didn't know that myself, Dr. Nawhal. As for Mektu, he just thinks Kandri's wandered off drunk."

"What's wrong, then, Uncle?"

"I'll tell you what's wrong. Someone's snitched on you two, and Ariqina's goose is cooked." He gestured in the direction of her cousins' house. "Father Marz is in there, screaming; her aunt is in tears. *Jeshar*, if you'd walked in on that priest!"

Someone, he said, had slipped a note to Father Marz, naming Ariqina a loose woman: that is, a woman who had taken a lover out of wedlock, in defiance of the Prophet's law.

"Law?" said Ariqina. "There's no law, Uncle, just a rule for Orthodox girls, and I'm not Orthodox. I'm not even practicing."

"Ariqina Nawhal!" said Chindilan. "Have you been living in some other Valley this past year?"

"I've been busy," said Ariqina.

"She built a medical clinic, Uncle. It's a wonder. You should go and see it."

"Yes, yes—astonishing, marvelous. But you live in the Orthodox Dominion now. Our Prophet decides which rules you follow—our Prophet and her anointed priests. I know you're a good woman and love the Enlightened One—"

"Her feet walk Heaven's Path," said Ariqina.

"Yes, of course, but some of her priests do stray. They're just men. They get angry. And Father Marz is at full fucking boil. The days of sneaking off to meadows are *over*, Doctor."

Ariqina's hands were in fists. "I've never once been late for work," she said.

"Late for work! You could be whipped, girl. You could be stripped naked in the square and forced to confess."

"Confess to what? To loving Kandri? I don't understand what you're saying at all!"

"I'm saying you can't sleep with him. You can't even make people *wonder* if you sleep with him. Do you hear me? It's not safe anymore."

She began to shake, to bite her knuckles. "The clinic," she said. "What will they do to it? What will they do to Kandri?"

"Nothing to him," said Chindilan. "Don't add that to your worries. Old Marz doesn't even have his name." He looked at Kandri sharply. "And that's damned fortunate. He's hated your father since that business with Mektu and the yatra."

"He'll find out," said Kandri.

"Why should he find out?" said Ariqina. "We were so careful, Uncle."

"Seems you weren't careful enough," said Chindilan. "But Marz doesn't care who your lover is, to judge by what he told your aunt. 'Men will rut,' he said. 'They are driven to the deed by nature, like goats in springtime. It is Woman's virtue that concerns us. That is what your niece is trampling, Madam Nawhal. And if she does this—a doctor, an inspiration to the young—what will become of less-educated girls? Where will it end?' Gods, you should hear the fellow rant."

Kandri felt as though the world were cracking open, no sturdier than a bird's nest, a thing of grass and twigs and droppings, empty smiles, lies.

"It's Mektu," he said. "He's the snitch."

Ariqina looked at him with horror. "Are you mad?" she said. "Your brother loves you. How could you even suspect him?"

"Who else could it be, Ari? He watches us. He won't leave us alone."

"Not Mektu," said Ariqina. "He might as well snitch on himself."

Kandri stared at her. "What does that mean? You haven't been with my brother. Have you? Have you?"

"Oh, *Kandri.*"

"Both of you, shut up." Chindilan drew a broad hand over his face. "Listen, Doctor: your family doesn't want a scandal. Neither does old Marz. There's a procedure for such situations. You pay an indulgence fee— Kandri will damned well pay it—Marz takes his cut, and the rest goes to the war effort. That's how it's done. If anyone titters, the priest can back you up."

They looked at him in confusion. "Back her up?" said Kandri. "How?"

"Well, with papers. She'll have to take a chastity vow, and there's a cere- mony. A ritual cleansing, I gather. That part is new."

"A cleansing," said Ariqina. Her voice was drained of life.

"I don't know much about it," Chindilan admitted. "But it ends with three days in which you're not allowed to speak to a man."

"It's not his fucking business!" Kandri snarled. "Tell Marz he can roll up his papers and—"

"Kandri," said Chindilan, "will you calm down and think? This doesn't have to end badly. Her clinic, for starters. That can be saved."

"Saved," said Ariqina. "From me. From the whore."

Kandri's chest felt tight. Waves were slapping him, trying to knock him off his feet. He took a deep breath. "Uncle," he heard himself say, "will you give us two minutes alone?"

"Kandri?" said Ariqina.

"Just two minutes, Uncle. Please."

"Alone?" said Chindilan.

"Yes," said Ariqina.

"What?" said Kandri.

"Yes, I'll have you, Kandri Hinjuman. We don't need two minutes to talk about it. I'll marry you." She put her arms over his shoulders, glowing, giggling. "I mean, if you'll marry me."

༄

Is the moment perfect? Yes. As perfect as they come in Urrath; as perfect as the Gods allow. Kandri kisses her, laughing, weeping; Uncle Chindilan looks abashed and grins, mutters, *I thought I'd have to lean on you, boy.* The three march into the waiting firestorm, the furious aunt and gaping cousins and old evil Marz, who cannot stop them, who must swallow his cud of indignation, for marriage is the honorable thing.

And the date is set, and the lovers still laughing say a chaste goodnight—chaste now, hilarious, both of them reeking of love. And he and Chindilan float home down the lightless road to Blind Stream, cackling like schoolboys, bonded by this moment forever. They collect his brother on the way, break the news to him with no hint of gloating: Kandri is suddenly a man. From Mektu, rage, accusation, rants, a pretense of a broken heart. And after a month of sulking, his own announcement, a brilliant and amazing catch, a girl from Bittermoon who paints and sings; he could never, of course, let the light shine on Kandri alone.

Perfect: like a passage of scripture committed to memory. And Kandri has indeed memorized it all. Every sacred detail. Everything that should have happened, and did not.

༄

For in truth, when he asked Chindilan for those two minutes, Ariqina touched his arm and said no.

"No to what?"

"No, I can't marry you. Not like this."

"I thought—"

"I do love you," she interrupted, blinking back tears. "Maybe too much. Let me go."

"I'll get a real job, Ari. I have skills—"

He was about to break his oath to his father, confess to all those nights of magic tinkering. But Ariqina was suddenly furious.

"You think I've just discovered that you're poor? You think *that's* the reason?"

"Perhaps if you just told him the reason, Doctor," said Chindilan. With a forced smile, he added, "You don't need me around for that, do you? I'll say goodnight."

Ari put out her hand and stopped him, never taking her eyes from Kandri. "I'll go to Father Marz alone," she said. "Then we'll see."

Kandri felt a clammy chill on the skin of his neck. For no reason he could fathom, the idea of his lover visiting Marz alone filled him with dread. "You don't have to do that," he told her.

"You're wrong," she said simply. "I do."

"In any event," said Chindilan, struggling to break whatever spell was descending on the pair, "I imagine he'll give his permission, if you're polite."

"Permission?" cried Kandri and Ariqina together.

"Of course," said the smith, taken aback. "He'll have to sign your marriage writ. He's All-Shepherd of the district, is Marz."

"He can go to hell," said Ariqina. "I don't want him involved in any marriage of mine."

"I understand, missy—"

"No, you don't," she snapped. "I'm not starting that part of my life with his pork-breath prayers, his greasy hands, his lectures about pleasing a husband."

"We can find another priest," said Kandri. "We can get married in Nandipatar."

Chindilan shook his head. "Not if Marz doesn't allow it, you can't. They'll ask for a letter from your home temple."

"A letter?" Now Ariqina was seething. "A letter saying what? That I'm a good girl? That I'll stay home and bear Kandri children, sons? Eleven sons?"

"Ariqina!" cry both men, aghast.

"Our Prophet went to war to free the Chilotos," she says. "*All* the Chilotos, women or men, young or old, married or not."

"Of course, of course," says Chindilan. "But this isn't about the war."

"What *is* it about? Just the flesh? To prove I haven't sold my body to some rutting man?"

"Yes," said Chindilan, "the flesh. The Prophet has spoken. Every Chiloto girl needs a priest to certify her chastity."

"Fuck all the priests!"

Her voice carried; from the nearby houses came murmurs of alarm. "Ang's entrails, girl, watch your tongue!" hissed Chindilan. "I took my soldier's oath from one of those priests. And there are tattlers everywhere—isn't that clear to you yet?"

"Ari," said Kandri, "let him have his stupid cleansing, and marry me. After that, we can live as we like."

"I'll live as I like *now*! I'll marry who I like—do you hear me? *Anyone I like!*"

Who else but me? Kandri nearly asked. But Ariqina was going to pieces. She leaned into him, weeping uncontrollably. Miserable, silenced, Kandri wrapped her in his arms.

ॐ

"You're deserters, aren't you?"

For an instant, gazing at the statue of Atalanith, Kandri fancies that the clay saint himself has asked the question. But no, it is the older man with the spectacles, from the market: he has crept up beside Kandri and knelt down, facing the shrine.

After a cautious glance around, Kandri nods.

The man is fumbling with a box of matches. He speaks around an unlit cheroot, which bobs with the motion of his mouth.

"Revelation Army. Stars and miracles. What's your first name, son?"

"Kandri."

"Call me Stilts. You must be hell's own fighters to have gotten this far."

"How did you know we were Hinjumans, Mr. Stilts?"

"Later," says the other. "Right now, listen carefully. I've just spoken to the man in the hat."

Kandri starts. He can only mean the general, Black Hat Tebassa. "He's here? In the market?"

"Don't be a fool. You five go back to Yehita-Chen's farmhouse. Lay low tonight, and all day tomorrow, but at half past midnight, come to Oppuk's Mill. No torches. No noise whatsoever. And if you make a mess of things, no second chances."

"Oppuk's Mill?"

"The girl knows the way. Here, help me light this fucking thing."

Kandri strikes the match, holds it up to the cheroot. The man called Stilts wears a curious ring, like a tiny rectangular pillbox, on his left hand.

Stilts notices his gaze, presses a catch on the ring. The lid of the pillbox snaps forward, revealing a half-inch razor blade. "Not a weapon," he says, green eyes shining with mirth. "It's for trimming a quill or sharpening a pencil. I write a lot, you see. I'm a Naduman."

Kandri looks at him, startled anew. He has never met a Naduman; the clan is little more than a legend in the Valley. Great scholars, they served sartaphs and princes throughout history, until they ran afoul of the last Kasraji emperor and were driven into the wilderness to die. The old religion teacher in Blind Stream had claimed that the Nadumans were all alchemists and sorcerers, dabbling in the occult. But Kandri's father had dismissed that as rubbish.

Stilts draws deeply on the cheroot, then exhales with a sigh. He aims the smoke very deliberately at the clay figure before them.

"Atalanith was a smoker too," he says. "But I don't see the point of all these candles—what does a saint need with them? By the way, leave your brother at the farmhouse tomorrow night. He's not welcome."

"Why not?"

"Talupéké says he's an ape, isn't that reason enough?"

"We have to reach the Great Desert, Uncle. And fast. And if your general's going to change his mind about helping us just because—"

"Whoa there, soldier. He can't change his mind before he makes it up to begin with. Besides, your brother's going to spend the night curled up with a chamber pot."

He slips a hand into the pocket of his coat, withdraws a small black bottle. "Purgative," he says. "Tell him to drink it all in one gulp before he sleeps. And he's not to have any food after sundown tomorrow. Doctor's orders."

"What doctor, Uncle?"

"The one who's going to treat his wound the next morning."

Kandri, overwhelmed, lets his eyes close for a moment. "Bless you, whoever you are. He's deathly ill—"

"Yes, Tal said as much. Be sure he rests tomorrow. After our meeting with the general, I'll escort him to the doctor myself. You'd better come too. He might need a shoulder to lean on afterwards."

"Ouch!"

The match has burned down to Kandri's fingertips. He could not care less.

℠

Stilts leaves them, and the travelers hurry back along the road. Halfway to Yehita-Chen's farm, they pass a spur trail to the east, winding deep into a ravine. Talupéké points to a listing barn and two knobbly stone silos, a mile or more down the path beside a trickling stream. "Oppuk's Mill," she says. "There was a river here once. Now they use donkeys to turn the mill wheel."

At the old woman's farm, the white dog is on edge, barking furiously at their approach until calmed by Mektu's voice. The woman herself is less easily calmed. "Come in, get out of the roadway!" she whispers. "There's strangers coming and going, on horseback mostly. Not an hour ago, a man rode by like the devil was after him. Something's brewing, and you can be sure it isn't anything nice. I'll ask you to bar the windows for me, if you please."

Even before they finish the job, Kandri hears the sound of an approaching horse. "Out of sight!" he snaps, and the travelers flatten themselves against the walls. But the rider passes at a gallop, and the sound of his steed fades to the north.

Once more, Kandri's nerves begin to fray: could these horsemen be the Prophet's forces? Is it possible that a Wolfpack has climbed out of the Stolen Sea? Has the story of Ojulan's murder been loosed on the town?

Yehita-Chen's eyes are a bit harder this evening, as if she is weighing the danger they represent against her debt to Tebassa. All the same, she serves them each a generous bowl of soup, which they drink standing in a circle in her darkened kitchen. "Drink up, and off to bed with you," she urges. "The quieter this house, the less attention it draws."

Tucked into the chamber he shares with Mektu and Chindilan, Kandri listens to the quiet voices of the women in the adjoining room. Noticing his stillness, the other men begin to listen as well. Talupéké is growling about the traitor among Tebassa's forces, of what she will do to "that backstabbing shit monkey" once he's rooted out. But Eshett tells her not to waste her thoughts on punishment and pain. That dwelling on loss is easy, and the harder task is to stay whole and upright, living with what's left.

"I love her," whispers Mektu.

"Don't we all," says the smith.

Eshett begins to speak of her village, her mother's goat's-milk cheese, the patterns of hunting, farming, foraging that keep the Nine-Year Parthans alive until the elders decree that the time for moving has returned.

The door across the hall opens and closes: the women creep down the hall to bathe. Chindilan sits back, shaking his head. "Eshett's seen more changes than any of us," he murmurs. "Life as a Parthan, a desert creature, eating cactus pulp and snaring birds and weaving bags out of goat's wool—those are the sort of things I've heard about, anyway. And one day the Tirmassil snatch her up and it's over, gone. She's not a person, she's a whore. Her life revolves around soldiers' dicks."

"I feel terrible," says Mektu. "I wouldn't have bought her if I knew we'd be friends later on. I wouldn't have made her do all those things. Do you think I can explain, Kandri? Do you think she'd listen to me?"

Kandri shudders at the thought of Mektu's explanations. "Just apologize," he says.

"But I want her to understand."

"The past is gone, Mek. Don't explain."

The men fall silent. A gust of wind makes the house crab and creek. Far away across the plain, some animal—dog, jackal, ghoul—cries out a lament.

"No, that's not true," says Chindilan. "The past is never gone. We're stuck with it, like our fingerprints, our eyestains. Like the shape of our heads."

The brothers wait, saying nothing. Their uncle's voice is strange in the darkness.

"You get a girl with child, you have to live with that forever. Deny her, and it rips out a part of you. Oh, you may get away with it, as far as the world ever learns. But you'll feel it inside. The spoiling, the rot."

"Uncle," says Kandri carefully, "are you talking about something in particular?"

"Why do you ask so many questions?" snaps Chindilan. "Try listening for once. Can you manage that?"

"I'm listening," says Kandri, stunned.

"It's the same if you harm a girl in some way," says his uncle, "or if you stand there and watch while harm comes to her. You have to live with your choices. Sometimes your children do also. Sometimes, the whole world."

⇒

Mektu wakes up screaming. The yatra, the yatra. In his head, in his thoughts, chewing on his memories like a rat. He is shaking violently. Kandri and Chindilan grab hold of him and tell him to breathe. Eshett and Talupéké stumble into the room, blinking and cursing. Mektu stares at them without recognition.

"I felt it move," he says. "I felt it wriggle like a worm. And I told it to get out, but it just laughed at me. I ran all over Blind Stream and Sed Hemon and all down the Bittermoon Road. I told it I'd kill myself, that I would run until I fell dead and it would have nothing, no home, it would just blow away on the breeze. It dared me, brother. It just went on laughing the longer I ran. Then suddenly I was at Betali's place and the smokehouse was right there in front of me and I went in. I slammed the door and started choking but I swore I wouldn't go out again, that it would have to let me go because I'd rather die than carry it around like a tapeworm, like a tick."

"Breathe, Mek," says Kandri, gripping his shoulders.

"It thought I was bluffing. It laughed and laughed. But then it looked in the right part of me and knew I *wasn't* bluffing, that I really would die. It grabbed at my legs, tried to make me walk out. I fought back, it used pain, nothing ever hurt like that again, not blades or fists or fire, it screamed *Get up, walk out*, I fought and fought and it bit down and my mind was bleeding GET OUT, GET OUT OF THE SMOKEHOUSE—"

The last words are a roaring, his voice something torn from him, alien. Kandri pulls his brother against his chest. Mektu gasps like an invalid.

"I wouldn't go, Kan. I drank the smoke and tried to die."

"It was a dream, Mektu. A dream."

Mektu's body starts to shake. "I'm sorry," he says. "Fucking coward."

"None of that," says Chindilan softly. "You're troubled, but it's not your fault. And it doesn't make you a coward for one minute, do you hear? In point of fact, you're one tough son of—"

In the doorway, a shadow—huge, haggard, armed with a knife. Mektu leaps up, screaming again.

"What in the sewers of hell?" says Yehita-Chen, pointing with her blade. "Shut him up! He'll bring every rogue in this country to my door."

Kandri embraces his brother again. Is it a dream or a memory he's been telling? Or the memory of a dream? And what does it matter, finally, if the inner torture is the same?

"I've killed people," his brother is babbling. "Kandri? You know that? I've killed in the Prophet's name."

"I know," says Kandri. "We both have, Mektu. Now hush."

Eshett reaches for Mektu's hand, and the change that comes over him is almost instant. His chatter stops, and the violent shaking reduces to a twitch. He releases Kandri and leans into the Parthan woman, his face soaked with tears. Over Mektu's shoulder, Eshett locks eyes with Kandri. And Kandri finds he can't look away.

&

All the next day they lie low, as Stilts insisted. Mektu sleeps fitfully, scratching the flesh around his wound. The others mostly remain in the house, venturing into the yard for short spells only, when they can be sure the road is clear. The old woman wants nothing from them anymore—nothing but a rapid departure. Kandri and Chindilan sharpen their weapons. Eshett cuts a reed in the yard's boggy corner and fashions a flute, but never once raises the instrument to her lips.

"It happened, you know," says Chindilan, breaking hours of silence. "The fool did almost die in that smokehouse, where Betali's father cured his hams. Lantor found him balled up in a corner, as far from the door as he could get. Stone cold dead by the look of him. But he woke up when your father dragged him into the yard—with a gasp, like he'd been stuck with a pin. Within a day, he was himself again: foolish and patience-testing, that is. Lantor asked us not to talk about it. I never did learn what made the boy go in there."

&

Toward sunset, a dust cloud appears in the east. Through the telescope they discern a group of fourteen riders, flying south like the wind along the edge of the Arig Hills. No one can make out who they are: the light is already failing. Still, Kandri watches them for as long as he can, from the shelter of an upper window. Just before darkness swallows them entirely, he sees them veer in the direction of the city.

The sight leaves him rattled. *We're hiding in plain sight*, he thinks. *Jekka's hell, we're barely even hiding. How can we and still arrange for passage out of here?*

A fine dinner—lamb, turnips, broad beans, bread—relaxes him somewhat, although they eat by a single candle, with all the curtains drawn.

Mektu, barred from the meal by the unknown doctor, watches them with the eyes of a famished dog. The real dog, concerned, watches him.

"Whatever you're up to this evening," says Yehita-Chen, "I hope it takes you far from us, and soon. This is a terrible year to seek refuge in the Lutaral. The whole country is on edge. The rains failed in the hills, and the streams are running dry. There's fighting to the south, open war to the north, and the Tirmassil stealing children, and ghouls under the wall at night."

She tears off a heel of bread, hands shaking in agitation. "Ghouls at the foot of the cliffs, too, and other places they've never dared to prowl before. I've seen them at dusk, snuffling along the edges of fields. They don't even wait for proper darkness."

"My father used to say that ghouls are like birds before a storm," says Chindilan. "When something big is coming, they're on the move before anyone else. Somehow, they know."

"Doesn't the Ursad protect you?" asked Kandri.

Yehita-Chen looks at him sourly. "The Ursad. He claims as much. It suits his picture of himself as the big man of this country, with his riches and his elephant. But the big men are elsewhere. And the biggest man of all is that woman of yours, that Prophet." She shakes her head. "Yes, perhaps the ghouls see more than we do."

"Ever since we escaped from the camp," says Kandri, "we've heard talk about a Time of Madness."

"The *Darsunuk*," says Talupéké. "Someone was wailing about it in the market, and others laughing."

"No one should laugh!" snaps the old woman. "I don't know if the legends are true, but why tempt fate? The Goddess Ang does not rule this world alone. She saves one soul, and her brother Surthang flings another down to hell, where Jekka tends his flames. Yes, we all grew up with stories of the *Darsunuk*. How those same Gods of Death bring it about to renew their power in Urrath, by leading us to destroy one another. Those who believe say it comes just once in three centuries, and that each time, the ruin is more terrible and the years of recovery longer. And one year, there won't be any recovery. The *Darsunuk* will mean the end of the world.

"Now the priests and astrologers say the *Darsunuk* has rolled around again. Not all of them, no—but enough to scare the wits out of simple people."

"Then what have *we* been worrying about?" says Mektu. "Those riders aren't looking for us. They're just extra patrols, because of all this superstition, and because the ghouls and Tirmassil are getting out of hand." He looks from face to face, settling at last on Kandri. "I'm right, aren't I, brother? Whatever's going on here has nothing to do with us."

Kandri draws a deep breath. Mektu's argument is sensible enough. Why, then, can't he believe it? Once more in his mind he hears those galloping horses: *For you, for you, for you* goes their thunder on the road. But is it caution he is feeling, or cowardice? Is he simply unable to believe that one can keep secrets from the Enlightened One, even for a matter of days?

Yehita-Chen turns to his brother. "Nothing to do with you? Perhaps not, soldier. But doesn't your Prophet have her own vision of how the world will end?"

"That's different," says Mektu. "That's Orthodox Revelation. There's no Time of Madness or Night of Blood."

"But there is a time of punishment," says Kandri, "when the earth vomits up her dead, and the wind strips flesh from the bone."

"And the Twin Abominations," says Chindilan, frowning, "dwell in Urrath once more."

Silence around the table. The brothers look at each other. Mektu's stomach growls so loudly that the dog cocks his head.

ॐ

There was no changing Ariqina's mind: she would go alone to Father Marz. And there was no dispelling the mysterious horror Kandri felt at the prospect.

"Did you know," she said when her tears subsided, "that he leads a special prayer service for girls who want rich husbands?"

"I've . . . heard rumors," said Kandri, scalded with guilt. He had never told her of his bath-house spying with Mektu, the night that started it all.

"Destiny services," said Ariqina. "My cousins took me to one, weeks after I arrived. We had to go barefoot on the stone. It was freezing. We wore these little white shifts, nothing else; the mosquitoes bit us through them. And that priest—"

She stopped, eyes blazing. Kandri and Chindilan dared not speak. At last, shedding silent tears, she leaned forward and brushed Kandri's lips with her own. Then she turned and walked down the lane to her aunt's house. She entered, and the men heard the shouting begin. When it was over, they headed for home.

Just outside Blind Stream they found Mektu, waiting in the road. He studied their faces and seemed to grasp something—or perhaps the absence of something, of candor. Kandri could barely stand to look at him. He remained convinced that Mektu was the snitch, but how could he say so? Ariqina didn't believe it and had sworn him to silence. How could he accuse Mektu of spreading a story that he, Kandri, had promised never to tell?

Back in their room, Kandri groped for his pillow, dropped to the floor like a sack of wheat, closed his eyes. Mektu squatted near his head. *What the fuck happened to you? Are you ill?* Kandri said, *Yes, very, I've had too much to drink.*

Mektu poked him. *Where did Ariqina go? She was there at the party, and then she wasn't. Did you see her? We were going to talk.*

I couldn't tell you, said Kandri, truthfully enough.

But where were you?

I don't know, said Kandri. *I got lost in the dark.*

Mektu sniffed. *Maybe she did too.*

The next day was agony. Kandri felt as if he had indeed spent the whole night drinking. Mektu brooded, snapped at everyone; what Kandri saw in his face was simple guilt. He did not lay eyes on Ariqina.

Among his places of work that summer was an apricot orchard on the Bittermoon road. The days were blazing hot. The other workers were chatty and kept trying to draw him out with jokes. *When a Važek woman has twins, do you know what they call 'em, Kandri? Do you?*

He knew one thing only: that he must be with her. But that was madness; Ari had been perfectly clear. *Stay away until I've seen him.* It was her last request, there in the street before she entered the house to face Father Marz. *Whatever lies he makes me speak, about my heart or my sex—I won't be able to say them if I'm thinking of you.*

You're going to lie? said Kandri. *He'll invoke the Prophet's name, Ari. You'll lie?*

I don't know! How could I know? Ang's tears, just leave me alone!

Kandri was filling his tenth basket of apricots when Mektu appeared. Breathless, sweating, enraged. He demanded to know what was wrong with Ariqina. He had seen her in the market; she had treated him strangely. She would not look him in the eye.

"I felt terrible. As if I'd done something wrong. Did you say something to her? Something bad about me?"

They were nose to nose. Kandri felt his promise to Ariqina like a chain on his arm. The arm that wanted to swing at Mektu as hard as he could.

"Whatever she thinks of you," he said, "is your own doing, not mine."

The air was motionless, the sun a heel pressing down. Only the orchard bees carried on as before, a multitude of tiny fiddlers, tuning.

❧

Kandri reaches across the old woman's dining table. In his hand is the vial of black medicine from Stilts.

"Off to meet our fate," he says, "or Black Hat Tebassa, anyway. You should go to bed the minute you drink this, Mek."

His brother nods. He takes the vial and sets it on the table.

"Go ahead," Kandri urges. "All in one gulp, like the doctor ordered."

"What's the matter?" says Mektu. "You don't trust me? You think I'll pour it in the yard?"

Kandri nudges the vial closer. "One gulp," he repeats.

"This is insulting," says Mektu. "You should trust me to drink it. The fact that you don't trust me makes me *not* want to drink it. That's the only reason I might not."

Kandri waits.

"Go on, get out of here," says Mektu. "You're not my father, you know."

Chindilan sighs, and Talupéké grins her secretive grin. Kandri waits.

Mektu cracks his knuckles. He opens the vial and brings it close to his mouth, then stoppers it again. It smells, he declares, precisely of piss.

"You unbearable fool!" blurts Chindilan. "We're trying to save your life. Pinch your nose and toss it back like a man!"

"Hell, no," says Mektu cheerfully.

A row ensues. Kandri calls him a fucking coward; Mektu points out that none of them have even seen this doctor, that they don't even have a name, and why is that? Didn't they ask? Do they expect him just to slurp down any quack's fermented piss?

At the height of the cursing, Eshett rises from her chair, and the others fall silent. She leans close to Mektu, and her eyes are deadly.

"Drink it," she says.

Mektu hides his face in his elbow. He taps his foot, squirming. He snatches the bottle and drinks it dry.

"*Glah*," he croaks. "You'll be sorry when I'm dead."

"That's assuming a lot," says Chindilan. Then he stiffens, listening. "Devil's spit, I hear horses. Blow that candle out."

Kandri hears them too: six or seven horses, galloping hard. But this time, as they near the farmhouse, the horses slow. The dog growls deep in his belly. The horses move slower, and slower yet, and finally come to a standstill, snuffling and stamping on the threshold of the yard. The riders begin to murmur among themselves.

Hands slide to weapons. Yehita-Chen rises and creeps to the sideboard, where she crouches down on swollen knees. Kandri feels a sudden pang for her—this frightened, half-blind creature who has offered them her home. Does she think herself hidden? She might as well have placed a lampshade on her head.

Then, just as suddenly as they have come, the riders thunder off. The travelers heave sighs of relief. As the old woman rises, she drags something heavy from beneath the sideboard. Kandri starts: the object is a black and battered mace.

She gestures at Talupéké with the weapon. "Girl," she says, "you're my sister-in arms, and my door is always open to you. But I can't declare war on the whole Orthodox Dominion. If the Prophet learns that I'm harboring deserters, this farm will be a heap of ashes before you can shout *fire*."

"We've endangered you," says Kandri. "I'm sorry, mother. We've stayed too long."

"Help us for a few more days, Yehita-Chen," says Talupéké. "These men are heroes, you know."

Kandri gives her a long-suffering look. "Don't deny it," says Talupéké. "Chindilan told me: you carved up two of the Prophet's Sons."

"They *what?*" cries Yehita-Chen.

"You proved they're just mortals," the girl continues. "That they bleed and die like the rest of us. And if they do, maybe that she-bitch does as well. She's no demigod, and one day the whole world will understand that."

"I wish I'd done nothing," says Mektu. "I killed a good man. If I killed him."

"I thought I was killing someone else," says Kandri.

"And 'she-bitch,' is redundant, you know," Mektu adds.

Talupéké looks from brother to brother. "You two," she says, "are the most confusing fuckers I've ever been around. And that's a big fucking accomplishment."

The old woman laughs. "And you, girl, are still the most foulmouthed. Gods below! Boys, if you've killed two Sons of Heaven, all Urrath's in your debt. Let them come and tear this house apart: you'll still be welcome. But they *will* tear it apart, that's the trouble, and when they do, you'll be found. You must leave soon or die soon. If you have nowhere to go, run off into the bush and say your prayers. Maybe Ang listens closer to the prayers of a hero."

"She doesn't," says Mektu. "I've tried."

ප

Kandri left his orchard job at dusk and ran all the way to the clinic. It was simple: he must see Ariqina or die. But when he arrived, the duty nurse told him that she had left early that night and was not expected until midmorning on the following day.

He ran to Sed Hemon and tugged the rope at the Nawhals' front door, but no one answered the frantic bell. He ran to the side of the house and tossed pebbles at Ari's window, then called out her name. She did not appear.

He searched the darkening village. Was she avoiding him? Was she going to break with him altogether? Or had she gone through with the cleansing ceremony after all, and begun her three days' isolation from men?

Abject, he stumbled home. He was quite late for dinner, but no one scolded him; wordlessly, Dyakra Hinjuman filled his bowl with parsnip soup.

Kandri sat, sweaty and rank, feeling the weight of their eyes. *You know, every one of you. You're laughing at me.*

Eventually, talk resumed. His baby brother Perch had named the six new kittens in the barn. The Old Man discussed weevils. Mektu's friend Betali had sent a letter from Eternity Camp. "He's learned to fire a crossbow," said Mektu proudly.

"A crossbow!" Dyakra Hinjuman made a blessing sign. "Ang's mercy, that boy's not safe around a spoon." She looked at her eldest daughter, Nyreti. "And what kept you out until dark?"

Nyreti had spent hours with Father Marz, she said, copying Orthodox Revelation edicts for distribution across the Valley. She described the edicts in detail, reciting several from memory, which made Kandri long for the weevil talk to resume. Then he realized that she was looking directly at him.

"I saw your *friend*," she said, with eyes full of scorn. "The doctor."

Kandri's hand froze halfway to his mouth. "Ariqina?" he said, trying and failing to sound casual. "Where was that?"

"At the temple. She came rushing through the gate just as the Father and I were stepping out to visit the town council. He went back in after her. I was surprised, because he's got a busy night ahead."

"How's that?" said Lantor Hinjuman, gnawing a parsnip.

"I don't know, Papa," said Nyreti. "Some sort of ceremony, maybe, but it's all a big secret. He even had some younger priests up from Ashfield to help him cover the windows in the sacristy."

Kandri moved his spoon from bowl to mouth, bowl to mouth, like one of his father's mechanical toys. So it was happening after all. Confession, abasement, dabs of holy oil. And maybe a little grope for the kindly Father? There was more than one kind of bribe, wasn't there?

You should prevent it, coward. You're her man. If you don't protect her, who will?

His premonition came again: something awful was brewing, something Ari should not have to face alone. But if she was going through with the cleansing, it meant that she wished to marry him after all. How could he dare to interfere?

He looked up and saw Mektu watching him across the table. Kandri's hand shook; soup splattered his thighs.

છ

After the meal, he stepped out into the street. The air in the house was stifling, but it felt little better out there.

Go to her.

Don't go. Trust her, do as she asked.

Go to her!

Keep away, don't push, you could lose her forever.

He was pacing, swearing, looking down at his feet. He walked right into his father's chest.

"It's that bad, is it?" said the Old Man.

"Yes," said Kandri, "but I don't feel like talking about it."

"If you tell me, I'll try to help you."

"Oh, horseshit."

He was almost as shocked by his words as the Old Man himself, but he pressed on. "Help me, Papa? Tell the truth. You'd just sneer. You'd explain what I should have done, what *you* would have done. But I know all about your approach. I lived it, up there on the mountain."

His father was despicably composed.

"I couldn't bring your mother down here, Kandri. Things were complicated. I wish I could make you understand."

Kandri laughed in his face.

"You had two women at the same time, and you got them both with child. You left us up there so no one would know. It's not complicated, Papa; it's cruel."

"You don't have the whole story."

"I don't want another story. Do you know how cold it was in winter? Do you know what we ate? People died up there, Papa. She died. And all of a sudden, you want to help?"

His father shrugged. "Open up to someone else, then. Keeping all that steam inside can't feel good."

He started to turn away. Kandri grabbed his arm and held tight.

"This matters to me, Papa. More than anything ever has."

"I can tell," said his father.

"And that's why I won't talk to you. When have you ever trusted me with what matters to *you*? I used to ask, remember? And you'd tell me to get lost."

Lantor Hinjuman closed his eyes. He raised his hand, felt for Kandri's own where it gripped his arm. Their fingers interlaced. For the first time in his life, Kandri knew he'd struck the target. The war in the Old Man's heart was as plain to see as the stubble on his chin. Would he speak? Would he give the trust he was asking for?

His father opened his eyes, and the answer was written there: *No, not yet.* He was almost in tears—they both were—but somehow, he conjured his old, wolfish smile.

"I'd be a true prick, wouldn't I," he said, "not to respect a man for keeping secrets?"

"Yes," said Kandri, "you would."

That night Kandri slept in the courtyard with the dogs. He could not face another grilling by Mektu, he told himself. But there was another reason. From the yard he could slip away without alerting his brother.

It was easy to imagine: clawing over the temple wall, blundering into the sanctuary, smacking old Marz away from Ariqina, leading her out by the hand. But lead her where, save into disgrace and the loss of her clinic, her dream?

He lay there with a dog for a pillow, watching the stars wheel overhead.

He must have slept, for in the dead of the night, he thought he woke to the squeak of the front gate, and footsteps fading on the cobbles. But in fact his sleep was only half-broken, and though he struggled, he was soon once more in its embrace.

Just before dawn he snapped fully awake. Mektu was seated beside him, eyes open, legs crossed, hands folded in his lap. His stillness unnerving. Kandri felt certain he had been there a long time, staring fixedly at nothing, at the ghosts only he could see.

☙

The next morning a rumor began to creep through the villages: Dr. Ariqina Nawhal had disappeared.

The Hinjuman boys were the first to raise the alarm, but the town was slow to heed them. Most patients found their way to the clinic, but Ariqina had never been known to turn away a summons to the bedside of one too ill to travel, even if that meant tramping for hours along the black and rutted roads. Like as not, she was in Stone Gate or Ashfield, or some farther village, and would find her way home before sunset.

There was reason to doubt such a notion: Ariqina had a day shift at the clinic and had neglected to call for a replacement. She might have forgotten, but it would have been the first time in her short career.

Of course, she had been seen the night before in the company of Father Marz. It was commonly supposed that she had gone to him to discuss some crisis of the spirit; young women often did. Marz himself reported that she had left the temple at half past ten of the evening. Not a soul had seen her since.

Ariqina's office was locked. The duty nurse thought little of it until one of the patients remarked that he had heard soft voices—one of them Dr. Nawhal's—coming from the office well after midnight. The voices had sounded friendly, even playful: a strange occurrence, but not an alarming one. The nurse pondered this information another quarter hour before locating the spare key.

The office was in disarray. An empty Cotton Whiskey bottle stood on Ariqina's desk. Beside it was a letter announcing her resignation as Founding Director, followed by several pages of precise case histories for her patients, recommendation for their care and detailed accounts of the clinic's finances (they would find, in days ahead, that every last *gham* tallied: whatever Dr. Nawhal had been up to, theft had played no part).

Her writing was very neat. But the page itself was blotched with water— or whiskey—and below her name, she had added a hasty scrawl:

Her den-mates drive her from the cave that was her own:
Let them beware; she may return a panther, fully grown.

The passage rang a bell, but no one could quite place it until Nyreti Hinjuman revealed that it was part of the *War Choral*, her brother Mektu's favorite book ("He can't find time for scripture, but he can recite that profane verse in his sleep, the Gods save my family, they live like beasts I tell you, not one of them walks in the light"). Mektu confirmed that he knew the passage, and also that he had lent his copy of the *Choral* to Ariqina not long before. But when asked why she might have closed her letter with the words, he grew wary and said no more.

With the discovery of the letter and the empty bottle, the brothers' fear caught like wildfire, and the Upper Sataapre mobilized. Every farmhand left his labor; every shop closed. Patients had to be restrained from walking out of the clinic, and a few could not be. A solid thousand volunteers descended on Blind Stream, where the constables did their best to organize them into search teams. Uncle Chindilan rode for Wolf Kill to seek the army's help.

The mystery grew more troubling the longer one considered it. Ariqina was not given to drink. Her aunt and elder cousins were all the family she had. More to the point, she was universally loved. The clinic had changed lives, and brought fame and better fortunes to Blind Stream. So had Ariqina's famished pursuit of her medical degree. Few Valley youth had ever achieved such a level of scholarship. None who did so had remained, serving the needy in the place of their birth. Why would she abandon them, and where could she possibly go?

Despite the letter, most people doubted that she had gone very far. No horses were missing. No stagecoach was scheduled to pass through the Upper Sataapre by night. She was lost, that was it: she had gone for a walk before bedtime and gotten lost. Anyone could, in the deep clefts and wooded hillsides surrounding Blind Stream.

The town had some deadly hazards, too. There was an eroded cliff walk, and a stone quarry with several open pits. There was a boulder field where snakes were common, though most who were bitten managed to drag themselves into town. And of course, there was the spot that gave Blind Stream its name: a sinkhole in a distant meadow, though its shape was less hole than winding incision. Narrow enough for a man to step across, it was so overhung with grass that one could be within a yard and not know that it was there—save for the gurgling of the stream twenty feet below.

These morbid possibilities were all swiftly eliminated. The search parties walked in long dragnets under the fierce afternoon sun. Ariqina's name echoed through the hills.

Kandri and Mektu were madly suspicious of each other. Whenever their paths crossed, a mutual interrogation began. Had Kandri *truly* not seen her after the wedding? And why had Mektu suddenly appeared at Kandri's side in the courtyard? Was it he who had opened the gate a few hours earlier, his footsteps Kandri had heard walking away?

Kandri clung to the hope that Ari was somewhere nearby. She was in turmoil. They had made love with an abandon that had frightened her, and though he spilled his seed upon her thigh or stomach, there was the always the risk of an accident, wasn't there? Little accidents were all over the Valley. Some of them lived in the orphanage down the road.

She had been spied on, denounced to Father Marz. She had been forced to consider the insult of his cleansing ceremony. And Kandri, who had not even summoned the courage to say *I love you*, had suddenly begged for her hand. It was all too much. Ari had felt smothered, and so she had indulged in a dream of escape, penned a letter to make it real. She wouldn't get too far, though. Good sense would return to her soon, if it hadn't already. *Go back*, it would whisper. *Your people need you. Kandri needs you. And you love him; you said it to his face.*

But other thoughts, like furtive assassins, slipped through his defenses as the day wore on. If she had fled—if she was leaving him for some other life—Kandri knew she would make for Kasralys. *That* was her true dream, after the clinic: she longed for no other place. That foreign doctor was to blame: she had come spewing passions, conjuring visions of a better Urrath, painting the sky with rainbows. Ariqina had never been the same.

A beautiful secret, Kandri. Her work could change the world.

But nearly three years had passed since Dr. Tsireem's visit. Why now? What would make Ariqina drop everything and flee? Certainly not the bribe money, nor the prospect of a few humiliating hours with Father Marz.

Unless it was . . . more than humiliation.

Kandri, searching north of the village in a dense wood, stopped in his tracks. "Ang's cunt," he said.

"Brother! The Gods forgive you!" cried Nyreti, the nearest searcher on his left.

Kandri turned and started walking along the line, limbs shaking with rage. Mektu was nine or ten positions downhill. He started running. He called out for Mektu and eventually heard his brother's reply.

They met in a clearing; Mektu's face glistened with sweat. "I heard the gate close last night," said Kandri without preamble. "I know you went out. Just tell me what happened. You saw her, didn't you?"

His brother hesitated, then turned away with a shake of his head. "Stop fucking around," he said. "Get back on the line. You'll throw us all off."

"What did you do to her, you shit?"

Mektu whirled. For several seconds, he could do nothing but gape. "You think . . . you honestly believe I could—"

"I believe you lied about something."

They were circling each other. "So what if I saw her?" said Mektu. "You sick fuck. I'd rather be stabbed dead than hurt Ariqina."

"Where was she?"

"At the clinic. I didn't say anything because it was private. Kandri, how could you imagine such a thing?" Mektu gives him an imploring look. "You know me better than anyone. Don't you?"

That, of course, was precisely the question. Kandri wondered if he would ever truly have an answer. But no, damn it to hell: he did not, could not believe that Mektu had done Ari violence.

But if it wasn't you . . .

Kandri turned back toward the village. He heard Mektu calling behind him. The soft forest floor, a quicksand of leaves. He broke into a run.

More than humiliation. More than just an old man's lascivious lurches, a palsied hand grazing a breast.

There were soldiers on the road to Blind Stream: Chindilan's call had been answered. Kandri ran straight by them, ignoring their shouts as he had ignored his brother's, passing the turnoff to his own house, the primary school, the empty market, racing along the path beside the aqueduct, into Sed Hemon. At the bamboo grove, he turned right and climbed to the temple.

He had some younger priests up from Ashfield, helping him . . .

The gates stood open. There were old women on the temple steps, laying out offerings of fruit and flowers to the Gods. Kandri bounded up the steps three at a time.

The cries of the women reached the sanctuary, where those too frail or too important to join the search had gathered to pray. Father Marz, a wiry, hollow-cheeked old man in voluptuous black linen, moved among them.

He saw Kandri coming. Judged his face and intentions. He dropped the silver prayer bowl and bolted for his life.

"Don't run," bellowed Kandri. "I need some fucking moral correction."

"Help, help!" the old priest shouted. "Hinjuman's boy has gone mad!"

In the rear of the transept, an iron gate let onto the stairs to the choir loft. Marz was fumbling with the lock as Kandri closed on him. At the last possible moment, he wrenched the gate open, squeezed through and slammed it behind him. There was an inner bolt, but as he tried to drive it home, Kandri grabbed his hand and pulled his forearm through the bars. Marz squealed and clawed at him. Kandri twisted his arm.

"You old horny bastard! What did you do to her?"

"Stop! Stop! Anus of a swine!"

They were still at it when the constables appeared. Kandri surrendered, but they beat him anyway, with truncheons and canes. He looked past them. The pain a dull and distant thing. Somewhere in this building, Ariqina had chosen to break with the Valley, to prune the branch back to the trunk, to abandon him.

He was dragged to Blind Stream's tiny jail, between the alderman's office and the dog pound. One bench, one bucket. The floor white with bird shit. The other two cells were occupied by a simpleton prone to pleasuring himself in schoolyards and a shaggy mute convicted years before of murdering his father with a spade.

కు

Midnight.

Mektu retires to the bedchamber in the farmhouse, still complaining about the medicine, and Talupéké leads the others back to Oppuk's Mill. The road is deserted; Kandri breathes a little easier. They hurry downhill, barely speaking, until they reach the spur path into the ravine. It is darker within; only a little moonlight glimmers on the trickling stream.

"Be silent, now," says Talupéké, "and don't hold it against them if you're roughed up a bit."

"Roughed up?" says Chindilan. "What the hell do you mean? Are they going to beat us?"

"Only if you deserve it," says Talupéké.

The path hugs the ravine's north bank; ahead loom the mill and the crumbling silos. As they proceed, the ravine grows wider, the hills receding to either side. Eventually, they emerge into a long, flat field, and Kandri sees that the farm complex is larger than he thought. In addition to the mill and silos, half a dozen barns, warehouses, and meager homes are scattered about the field. All of them look careworn; some are clearly abandoned. Kandri finds himself wondering how many homes, how many dreams, ended with the river's demise.

"You're early, Tal."

Everyone but Talupéké jumps. The voice is like velvet, and it comes from the center of the stream. Kandri looks down and sees a rock come to life: a head raised, a pair of arms unfolding from around bent knees, a figure rising in one smooth motion. Not a rock, but a man balanced upon one, perfectly at ease. His face in shadow, a black cloak hiding one arm.

"Were you seen?" he asks.

"By a toad or two, maybe," says Talupéké. "You know who these people are?"

"I can guess, *hmm*," says the man, his voice stranger with each utterance, "but guesswork is not for us, is it, Tal? Not for those who live hunted lives."

"I couldn't agree more," says Kandri.

The man pivots to face him. "You will get further if you don't speak out of turn, Chiloto. A piece of friendly advice, that is. And here's another: don't walk any closer to the mill."

"Why not?"

"Any number of reasons. You might find it a disappointment: a few tired donkeys, an old man who grinds corn. Or you might find yourself wriggling on the end of a pike, *hmm*? Hard to tell, hard to tell."

Talupéké sighs. "Mansari," she says, "you haven't changed a bit."

He leaps, a sudden blur, and alights soundlessly before them. Kandri can see his face now, and gives another start. Is he looking at a man or a woman? The purring voice is that of a man, albeit a strange one. The face is sleek, with dark eyes that taper at the corners, small ears, hair cropped short enough for the Prophet's army. The body is compact and slightly curvaceous. Disoriented, Kandri watches him (him?) drop to one knee and lift Talupéké's hand. Rather than kiss it, he rubs his temple along her wrist: a strangely sensual gesture.

"I've missed you, Tal."

Talupéké frees her hand. "My sergeant's dead," she says.

"Stilts informed me," says the other, gazing up at her. "I *hmm*, grieve with you, my dear. Your sergeant had the soul of a prince."

"We'll avenge him," says Talupéké. "The general will see to that. I'll ask his permission to lead the reprisal raid. Has he picked a target yet?"

Mansari hesitates, then slowly rises to his feet. "We had better go inside," he says.

He leads them, hips swaying (*Man, woman, both?* Kandri wonders again) across the field and behind one of the larger barns. The structure is decrepit, listing, the wall planks rotted out along the ground. Pausing by a window, Mansari gives a low trill with his tongue. From somewhere within comes an answering trill. The man proceeds to a small door and swings it wide.

With some apprehension, they follow the stranger and Talupéké into the dark. The barn smells of urine and hay. Soft nicker of horses, a few tittering hens. Dimly, Kandri perceives another man in the darkness. He approaches Mansari, exchanges a few whispered words.

"Talupéké, what are we doing in a barn?" demands Eshett. "Is your General here or not?"

A match flares up with a serpent's hiss: Mansari is lighting a candle. "Step back a little, *hmm*," he says. The second man crosses to a stall door and frees the latch. Inside, Kandri dimly perceives the shape of an enormous draft horse. The animal snorts and stomps as he leads it from the stall.

"Slowly, girl, that's the way," murmurs the second man. The horse is laboring, pulling at two heavy ropes. Kandri follows them with his eyes: they pass through pulleys suspended from the ceiling, descend again into the stall where the horse had stood, and end in great iron hooks, from which a great block of stone now dangles, shedding dust and hay as it rises. Beneath it, a dark hole gapes in the floor of the stall.

"Quickly, now," says Mansari, plunging in with his trembling candle. Within the hole a staircase is concealed. "Go!" says the man beside the horse. "Don't make her stand here bearing this weight!"

In something of a chaos, they shuffle down the dark, steep stairs. Kandri, at the rear, has barely ducked his head underground when the man starts to urge the horse backward, and the great stone lowers into place. *Boom.* He gropes for a wall, stumbles against Eshett, furious with his racing heart. *Don't make a fool of yourself, Kandri. Talupéké's on your side; this isn't a trap.*

But it is a tunnel, narrow and roughhewn from the earth. Mansari's candle is already bobbing away. They follow, single file, for a hundred paces or more. Chill air, clammy walls. A roof so low, they have to stoop.

Eventually, the bedrock walls give way to brick. A few steps farther, Mansari leads them out into a much larger room, low-roofed like the tunnel but too large for the candle's meager light to reach the walls. Kandri strains his eyes: is that motion in the darkness? A shoulder? A faint glint of steel?

Mansari blows the candle out. And in the sudden darkness, feet approach from every direction at once.

Kandri lunges for Eshett, pulls her close. He draws his machete, holding her tight in the crook of his left arm, brandishing the blade. There is a stab of lamplight, followed at once by other lights from every side. Dazzled, Kandri glimpses brutal faces, hard hands, lowered spears. They are surrounded by some twenty men.

"Steady, Kandri!" says Chindilan beside him. "We're here to talk, remember?"

"I understood that you were, *hmm*, here to beg," says Mansari.

Their weapons are confiscated. The men are gruff and thorough but not overtly hostile. The room is plain stone, like a large prison cell, and now Kandri sees that the last, brick section of the tunnel projects well into the chamber—allowing, he realizes, for newcomers to be surrounded as soon as they emerge.

"About face, gentlefolk," says one of the warriors.

Kandri turns and sees that Mansari is standing by a sturdy door opposite the tunnel. It opens a crack, and Mansari exchanges whispers with someone just inside. Then he looks over his shoulder, puts a finger to his lips, and beckons. The door swings wide, the guards step back. One by one, the travelers slip through the door.

The chamber beyond reeks of smoke, liquor, bad breath, unwashed skin. It is very crowded. There is a round table, above which three iron lamps dangle, hissing. Around the table, a dozen men and women sit in high-backed chairs, their shadows flung behind them like capes. About them cluster another sixty or seventy figures, seated on crates and stools, or leaning with folded arms against the walls. The whole group is arguing, passionately but without shouting, as though they fear to be overheard.

Heads turn to study the newcomers. Their eyes—wary, wounded, sizing up the travelers with unflinching directness—leave no doubt in Kandri's mind. These are soldiers; they have seen blood. Their abundant weaponry an unneeded confirmation. *Tebassa's fighters*, Kandri thinks.

The debate does not pause.

"Friendship?" someone is saying. "Did I hear correctly? Would you truly waste our time with that word?"

The speaker is a large man with a dark purple birthmark, vaguely insect-shaped, upon his forehead. He stands behind one of the high-backed chairs, training his small, bright eyes on one warrior after another.

"What friends have we?" he demands. "What friends has the Lutaral ever had? Oh, we have tactical partnerships—for a week, a fighting season, a year or two at the most. But friends? Not a one. Friends do not forget you, or begin to slander and conspire against you, the moment they feel that they can live without your aid."

"It required friendship to overthrow the Kasraj," says a woman standing against the far wall, her muscular arms crossed over her chest. "The western clans fought as one then, Spider. And we handed the Emperor his head."

"Legends, sister," says another woman—much older, with deep-set eyes and a thick mane of silver hair—seated at the table near the speaker. "Who can say why the Empire fell? You also hear that their cattle starved. That a volcano opened its jaws in the north, and cinders rained from the sky for five years, and not a blade of grass would grow."

"What does it matter?" asks the man with the birthmark. "The world is different now. The sea is gone; the Kasrajis are gone. The Imperial wolf has been replaced by lesser jackals, but they rend us still. We need territory and a hard-fisted battle plan, not hazy dreams of an Urrath united. We must—"

"Talupéké!" says someone, barely repressing a shout.

The girl has entered last of the travelers, and her appearance provokes a flurry of gasps. She herself is silent, aware of some breach of protocol, but as she moves through the crowd, her whole body becomes radiant with feeling as scores of comrades reach for her, squeeze her shoulders, touch her hands. Some faces light with joy. A lesser number, with aversion or scorn. The man with the spider mark looks pointedly away.

"As I was saying—"

"Just a moment, Captain."

The voice, deep and gravely, carves a space of silence in the room.

"One of our own has just come back to us. Welcome, Sister Talupéké. It warmed my heart when they told me you still lived."

Tebassa, of course. From where he is standing Kandri cannot see him for the attendants crowding about his chair. But Talupéké can. She turns to face his chair, draws herself straight as a poleaxe, raises both fists to her forehead in a crisp salute.

"General—"

Her voice catches. Kandri and Chindilan exchange a look. This girl, who hurls knives and climbs towers, who fights like the devil incarnate, is afraid. Elated, perhaps even overjoyed—but afraid. Of displeasing Tebassa? Of something he might ask? Of accounting for herself since the loss of her unit?

"You've made some new friends," rasps the general. "Most peculiar friends, even by our standards. Take some wine, sister. We'll talk presently, and decide what to do with these mongrels. Now carry on, Captain—but briefly, man. This isn't dinner theater."

The laughter is too keen: these warriors like to flatter their general. As the captain with the birthmark resumes his address, Mansari crooks a finger, leads them toward an empty stretch of wall.

Kandri endures the warriors' merciless scrutiny. Who can blame them? Survival in war means grasping every possible threat, and their appraisal is no worse than what seasoned warriors show recruits on their first day of service to the Prophet.

But that reflection does not sit well with Kandri, somehow.

He claims his bit of wall—and turning, sees Tebassa at once. The man is large and haggard, with a broad brown face that is deeply scored rather than wrinkled: a face like an eroded cliff. Gray beard full and unruly, eyes full of wickedness and mirth. No hat, black or otherwise, but on his left forearm is a scar like a long purple centipede, trailing from the wrist into the sleeve he has rolled to the elbow. The arm, immensely strong, rests on the table. The hand is large and brutal, like a thing of hide.

With his other hand the general is jotting with a quill pen in a ledger book. The instrument looks absurdly flimsy in his grip, but the words flow smoothly. Eight or nine men crowd around Tebassa's chair. Stilts, the eldest by far, is pointing at a line in the ledger book and whispering in the general's ear. Tebassa nods. His cunning eyes flick upward.

"Thank you, Captain, that will do. Mr. Demaroc, you've paid our northern friends a visit, I believe. What have the Shôl to say for themselves?"

A tall soldier with narrow cheeks pushes his way to the table. "Little to nothing, my general," he says. "Their ranks have been decimated. They have a few men yet in the Shirisan Hills, but not enough to be of service to our cause."

"They were never of service to our cause," says the general, "but in the past, they could be counted on to fight for their own. You can't mean they're abandoning the southwest corridor?"

"Not officially, general: the flag of the Scarlet Kingdom still flies on the summit of Mount Inutuk. And the men there expect a relief force sooner or later. But *later* may prove too late. The Shôl have lost their other strongholds in this country already, and half their leaders are in chains. The relief force may find no one to relieve."

"And the provisions we bargained for?" demands the general. "Black rice and barley, and thirty cattle on the hoof? My men are peculiar, Demaroc: they like to eat."

The warriors laugh again. Discreetly, Kandri's eyes travel the room. In fact, not everyone is a warrior: at the table are two well-heeled men (fine cloaks, jeweled fingers) he pegs as merchants; a small fellow in horn-rimmed spectacles behind a heap of books and scroll cases; and a youth of eighteen or nineteen, regal of bearing, in a fine blue high-collared shirt with buttons of gleaming pearl. The youth's skin is dark olive, his hair glossy black. His hands, folded together on the table, have the cleanest nails Kandri has ever seen. His face is composed, but his eyes betray a certain anxiety.

Kandri is bewildered by the debate. The general is apparently reviewing the whole tactical situation of the Lutaral, but the names fly too quickly: are they discussing clans, roads, factions, militia, mountains? He cannot say, and yet he feels a throb of hope in his chest. A glance at Chindilan earns him a nod: his uncle feels it too. This is a war council. It is a good sign that they have been allowed to be here at all.

The council is a long one, however. For twenty or thirty minutes, the men speak of nothing but food. Another quarter-hour is devoted to speculations on the length of the winter, and when the first killing heat of spring will descend. Tebassa, even when silent, remains firmly in control. To some he is ravenously attentive; to others, mildly disdainful, scribbling in his ledger or muttering with Stilts as they speak.

At length, talk moves to the Prophet and whether or not she is likely to advance on the Lutaral in the near future. Kandri and Chindilan exchange looks. The Lutaral?

"She has the men for such an assault," says the man with the birthmark. "But she has marched them too far, stretched herself too thin. Fighting on three fronts, pouring her legions up and down the Mileya like so much sand through an hourglass, exhausting them: these are a brute's tactics, are they not?"

Many look surprised at this remark. The silver-haired woman at the table eyes him scornfully. "Your brute has taken four hundred miles of territory back from the Važeks, Spider," she says.

"But can she keep it?" says one of the bejeweled merchants. "Can the old dog swallow that much meat?"

"No," says Spider. "It will be torn from her jaws. Remember, brothers and sisters: the Kasraj never looked stronger than in its final years. This much I will grant, however: that the Prophet caught the Važeks with their breeches down—"

"Who can blame them?" interjects someone. "Who'd ever heard of *organized* Chilotos before she came along?"

"Let alone a Chiloto army," Spider continues. "But the Važeks aren't fighting bare-assed any longer. They have retaken the lowlands, and with it the breadbasket of their kingdom."

"And that is nothing," says the youth in the high-collared shirt, "compared to their alliance with the Shôl."

"Correction, my lord," says Stilts, bowing slightly to the youth. "They have an armistice, not a formal alliance."

"What matter the word?" says Spider. "Važeks and Shôl are no longer killing each other. Both will have men to spare for killing Chilotos."

"All the same, you underestimate the Prophet," the older woman insists.

The man's upper lip curls in amusement. "Far be it from me to doubt a grandmother," he says.

Someone hisses. The general, raising his eyes from his ledger book, studies Spider wordlessly. The old woman is unmoved. She gathers her thick silver hair in her hands and ties it at the back.

A look of great unease comes over Spider. He turns to the woman and bows. "Forgive me, elder sister. I referred to the Prophet only; not for all the world would I disparage you."

"Not twice, you wouldn't," says the woman.

"Captain," says the general, "finish your thought."

Spider nods. "It is merely this, sir: that the Prophet is no soldier. The great countries of the north are led by warrior-kings, men of iron and intellect, men trained in the oldest martial traditions of Urrath. But who leads this sloppy thing, this boneless mass called the Army of Revelation? I'll say it plainly: a bitch. A ferocious bitch, but a failing one, with rotten teeth and addled dreams of Godhood. A stumbling old seer with a pet baboon, and her eleven precious sons."

"Ten," says Talupéké, and the room goes silent.

All eyes turn to the girl. She looks back at them, standing her ground. Spider at last has no choice but to acknowledge her presence. His glance is cold.

"Ten?" he says.

"Or maybe nine," says Talupéké. "One of them was stabbed. I don't know if he lived."

Silence. For a moment, the chamber feels like what it is: a basement. Then the general begins to laugh.

"It's true," he tells the astonished crowd. "The Thirdborn, the maniac Ojulan, is dead. Chopped to pieces while savaging a child. And Garatajik, the scholar-son: he was ambushed and stabbed by an accomplice of the first killer. His soldiers found him at death's door. The news reached me just yesterday, and our sister Talupéké has confirmed it."

A soft explosion follows his words. No one shouts, but every face changes, every throat makes a sound of astonishment. Stilts and several others wave their arms and hiss, "Order! Order, damn it all. You're not in nursery school!"

"But who were these people who managed to strike the Sons of Heaven?" asks the youth in the high-collared shirt.

"Who indeed?" says Tebassa. "Master assassins, no doubt. They infiltrated the Prophet's army some years ago, and fled like the wind after their deeds. That is all I can tell you. Pray for these men of courage, if you're the praying kind."

Kandri sits frozen, not daring to glance at his friends. *He's keeping us a secret. He doesn't trust his men entirely. How could he, if there's really a traitor in the ranks?*

Tebassa's pen stabs up at Spider.

"Captain Sorfik. You dismiss the Prophet, known to her people as the Enlightened One and the Mother of All Chilotos, as a fool. I reject your verdict. I would sooner call him a fool who attributes twenty-five years of bloody conquest to mere ferocity. Her enemies are no longer fighting each other, true enough. But their armistice—and the word matters, Spider; words *always* matter—is a reflection of their fear of that woman. It is a well-grounded fear. She has stretched her forces thin, but they will stretch further yet, and with every mile clawed back from the Važeks she enlarges her pool of conscripts. More telling, though, is her gift for turning conscripts into believers, into worshippers who kill and die at her whim. In this, she is the master of her age. Yes, I would call him a fool who predicts the decline of the Prophet."

Spider stares fixedly at the table. He looks like a man who has taken a mule kick to the chest.

"I would call him a fool," says the general again, "except that by such measure, all Urrath is populated by fools. To this very day, the Važeks are waiting for her collapse—depending on it, even. As for the Shôl and the Lañatu, and the other great clans: they have simply no idea. The Prophet is a volcano, and thus far, she has belched only a little fire. If she should erupt, no one, absolutely no one, will be prepared."

The youth in the high-collared shirt gestures at Kandri and Chindilan. "What of these newcomers, general? For I would swear they too are Chilotos."

"Even Chilotos may be enemies of the Prophet, my lord," says Tebassa.

"Did they bring you the news of the assassinations? Are they collaborators of yours?"

"You will forgive me, Prince Nirabha, if I observe that my council's guest list is none of your affair. In fact, it serves no one's interests for me to answer such questions—not even yours, or your city's. What's that you're saying?"

A soldier is whispering to Stilts, who bends in turn to speak into Tebassa's ear. "Good!" says the general. "Let them enter. I should like to see the proof."

A door on Kandri's left is unbolted and swung wide. Four huge, filthy soldiers pass into the room and stand in a cluster. They reek of sweat and horses; mud and grime rain from their clothes. They draw themselves up and salute the general, and Tebassa answers in kind.

"Riders," he says, "you're back, and your faces make plain that you've succeeded. Am I right?"

"You are, my general," rasps one of the men. "We rode one horse to its death, and Rifalan's was failing—we left him in the care of the monks at Sigra Cross. But we did the job"—he lifts a canvas sack uncertainly, eyes swiveling around the room—"exactly to order, sir."

"Show us, then."

The sack is tied with rope. The man's soiled fingers tear at the knot; then the sack yawns open to a buzzing of flies. The man reaches inside and withdraws two severed heads, dangling from his fist by their hair.

Kandri is afraid he will disgrace himself by vomiting. A man's head and a woman's. Their eyes are open and their lips puckered. Gore is clotted thick below their chins.

Kandri catches his uncle's eye. *What the fuck are we doing here?*

"Mr. Dimas?" says the general.

A man approaches the table, grimacing. He is small and plump, with sweaty cheeks and pouting, babyish lips. Eshett turns to Kandri and whispers, "That's him! That's the owner of the caravan, the one we spoke to this morning."

The man presses a kerchief to his mouth as he studies the heads.

"These two were their leaders," he says. "The ones who robbed me. I didn't know you planned to kill them."

"They would not yield, general," says the man holding the heads.

"Perhaps they expected to be turned over to the Ursad," says Stilts. "I wouldn't yield either, if I had that on my mind. I've seen how he punishes theft."

"What about the gold I paid them?" says the man with the kerchief. "Was that recovered?"

"You recall the terms perfectly well, Mr. Dimas," says Tebassa. "We keep the gold, and you keep your reputation as a man not to be trifled with." He leans forward on his elbows. "You are not, I trust, having second thoughts?"

"Not on my life, sir," says the caravan owner, with a gesture of appeasement. "It is merely that I could prove the extent of my gratitude by doubling what your men have taken off these scoundrels, if I had funds left for the trading journey to Shefet Ang."

"And I could give my troops a month of roast duck and royal consorts, if I could seize the Važek throne," says Tebassa. "No, Mr. Dimas, I will not part with our winnings, and I cannot spare the men you wish to hire as a desert guard."

"But General, what am I to do?"

"I should think the choices fairly obvious. Secure such men as you can and brave the crossing, or sell your camels and wait the season out." Tebassa looks away from the caravan owner. "Riders, well done. Go to your rest; you can report in full on the morrow. Now, then, about the Lo'ac Brigades—"

The four riders depart with their grizzly trophies, and Mr. Dimas, stunned, returns to his chair. Kandri, hardly less unsettled, glances at Chindilan. The message in the smith's eyes is unmistakable. *No one's safe with this man.*

Talupéké's head is bowed; there is a heaviness in her shoulders. Behind her mask of callousness, the girl is worried for their sakes. Dawn is surely near. Will their plight even be discussed? Maybe the general is toying with them. Maybe he will grill them for information and then cast them out on the road.

His head jerks up. Once more, the chamber has fallen silent. Black Hat Tebassa is looking at him fixedly.

"This one's gone wool gathering," he says. "You didn't even hear my question, did you boy? Well, what about you then, blacksmith? What would you do with the killers of the Prophet's sons?"

"What, sir, myself?" sputters Chindilan.

"That is what I meant by *you*. How would you respond, if they appeared at your door seeking refuge? Asking you to hide them, or help them escape?"

"I would have to ponder that question, general."

"Bollocks. Answer me. If the winds of Urrath blew these two men, whoever they might be, to your doorstep, would you help them?"

"Yes," says Chindilan, "I suppose I would."

"Even if one of them was an unhinged clown?"

"Yes."

"Even if you had a family to protect?"

Chindilan squares his shoulders. "Who's to say I haven't?"

"I say it," says Tebassa. "I say you're a washed-up Sulonji bush walker who's just dragged himself across the Stolen Sea. You may have had family, but you've abandoned them, or let someone take them from you."

"Who in Jekka's hell do you think you are?"

"The last chance of a fat old ironmonger," says the general, "so watch your mouth, and answer the fucking question. Would you help them, if to do so put your family at risk?"

Eshett's hand is on Chindilan's shoulder. The smith crosses his huge arms. For the third time, but now almost spitting the word, he says yes.

"By the Gods." Tebassa smiles without warmth. "We have a saint among us, boys. We should file by and kiss his ring. But then, saints get themselves killed all the time. As for protecting their family, that's not something a saint cares to think about."

His face twists with sudden irritation. He pushes the chair back from the table and lifts his arms. The men behind him retreat a few steps—all save Mansari and the warrior to his left, who bend down swiftly to either side of the general. Tebassa puts his arms over their shoulders, and the men lift him from the chair.

Kandri tries not to stare. The General's legs dangle limp beneath his powerful torso. His large brown feet are bare, and as the soldiers carry him, they drag and scrape along the floor.

Black Hat Tebassa is paralyzed.

His men bring him abreast of the travelers. Talupéké stands rigid, eyes locked on the General's face. Her mouth works. Tebassa grunts at his men, who pause.

"Blackworms," he says. "Didn't you wonder how I escaped the slaughter at the Megrev? Our dead were left where they fell. The walls of the gorge were so steep that the Prophet's men could not extract the corpses. To be sure that none were still alive, they poured blackworms on us from above. Ten feet from me, a man was feigning death, but when the worms struck him, he could not bear it, he snatched at them, and the Chilotos shot him full of arrows. When my turn came, I lay still, and the vermin buried themselves in my flesh. What do you think of your general now, Talupéké? Can he carry on the fight, do you think?"

The girl is visibly trembling. She opens her mouth to speak, but no sound comes.

"I can move my right foot, since yesterday. That is something. And I can feel the prick of a pin on both heels. The doctors tell me I shall never walk again. I tell them my plans require it."

His eyes move to Kandri. "Do you know that cluster of stars men call the Scythe?"

Kandri nods. "I know it, sir."

"Then get yourselves to the Hermit tomorrow night before the Scythe drops below the horizon. That is about six minutes to midnight, this time of year. If you're late, don't bother to come at all." He turns to Talupéké. "You must take your leave of them now, girl—unless you wish to quit my service?"

"No!" hisses Talupéké. "General, I—no."

Her voice is tight with alarm. Tebassa's eyes soften a bit. Taking a deep breath, he frees his arm from around Mansari and reaches—lunges, really—for her shoulder.

"I am glad," he says, as she catches his weight. "You're irreplaceable, you know. Mr. Stilts, Sister Talupéké needs a uniform. As for you"—his eyes rake Kandri, Chindilan, and Eshett—"give thanks to Ang that your paths crossed this little one's for a time."

He flings his arm around Mansari again, and the three figures move toward the door.

༄

The council dissolves; the warriors rise and leave one unit at a time. "Wait here a bit," Stilts tells Kandri's company. "You're going with me, and I'm last out the door tonight."

"The doctor," says Kandri. "My brother—"

"All in good time, boy."

"Stilts," says Talupéké, still visibly shaken, "where are the rest of us?"

The Naduman looks at her over his spectacles.

"The main force," says Talupéké. "I thought they'd be here tonight. I thought you were bringing everyone to the city."

Stilts takes Talupéké's hand, guides it gently to the back of a chair.

"We did," he murmurs. "You're looking at them. But keep silent, for Ang's sake. There's guests among us yet."

For the second time in five minutes, Talupéké is rigid with shock. "All of you, back over there," says Stilts with an impatient gesture. He rushes to intercept the merchants, who are drifting toward the door, whispering and frowning. Chindilan looks at Kandri, wide-eyed.

"How does Tebassa *travel?*" he whispers. "Do they drag him around like a sack of meal?"

Kandri shakes his head, dumbfounded. The questions run deeper than that. How does Tebassa keep their loyalty when he can't even stand up from the table, let alone lead any more of his famous raids?

Stilts takes gracious leave of each merchant by name. He seems to be having three conversations at once, all in soothing patter. "Concerned? Gentlemen, of course he's concerned! Your security is our security. Who knows this better than the general?"

"He certainly knows who butters his bread," grumbles one of the merchants.

Stilts assumes a look of elaborate injury. "Dear sir, is that fair? Go home; we're all exhausted. And think of how well you sleep knowing who guarantees the safety of the Smoke Road. Your trade routes are safe today and will be safe tomorrow, and what is that not worth? Friends help one another— sometimes with arms, sometimes with gold and provisions. It's that simple. Go in peace."

He pivots away from them, his smile gone faster than a flung shoe. His eyes sweep the chamber, settling at last on the youth in the fine blue shirt, the one the general had addressed as a prince. The Naduman approaches his chair and makes a formal bow. The youth sweeps his fine black hair back over his shoulders and rises with dignity. Stilts conducts him to the door, nodding at the man's quiet words.

". . . a disaster not just for my people, Mr. Stilts, but for all Urrath, and even the world beyond. That is the heart of my missive. And I would know that General Tebassa has received it, before I leave empty-handed."

Once more, Stilts affects a wounded look. "Empty-handed? Come now, my lord. The general has expressed his deep commitment to your cause. But these campaigns take time."

"There is less time than anyone imagines, I fear."

"Then no time at all for mistakes, Prince Nirabha. Charge in like a bull and be slaughtered like a bull, and what good will that do your city? But a fox will watch and learn, and move in silence, and strike unseen when the moment comes. We must be foxes, my lord. Surely, you can see that for yourself."

The young prince gives him a long final look. "The sartaphs of the north," he says, "do not mount bull's heads on their walls. But I have heard they carpet the floors of their bedchambers in pelts."

Stilts smiles, but Kandri does not hear his reply, for at that moment, Talupéké touches his arm.

She has banished every trace of shock from her expression. She stands with a dozen soldiers, ready to depart. "Kandri," she says, and he realizes that she has never before spoken his name.

He feels a startling ache. The girl is only doing as she promised she would, as Eshett will do when they reach her village, as everyone does in time. All the same, he would like to hold and protect her. Ridiculous sentiment. Which of them has done the most protecting?

"The Gods keep you safe," he says. "Where are you going, do you know?"

"Where they send us," says Talupéké. "The south, maybe. Plenty of fighting down there."

"We'd have died without you," says Kandri.

Talupéké nods in agreement. From the doorway, a soldier calls her name. Again, Kandri feels the urge to embrace her. As if sensing the impulse, she pivots away from him, one side of her face smiling scornfully.

"Keep Mektu alive. He's . . . unusual."

"He is that," says Kandri.

"Like some kind of rare bird. And he loves you, so—"

She breaks off. Chindilan has stepped near her. The smith's face is frozen in a hard expression, but his eyes are moist. Talupéké fidgets, her smile still more forced, her gaze anywhere but on him.

"Old goat," she mutters.

Chindilan starts to twist a ring on his finger. Talupéké sees what he is doing and mutters, *Fuck*. Chindilan grits his teeth and pulls, and the ring pops into his hand.

"Blade steel," he says, holding it out to her, "from my grandfather's forge in South Molonj. He made it for me from a piece of *his* grandfather's sword, and that weapon came from Imperial times. He was a clever man, my grandfather. He said I'd know when to pass this ring along. Even if . . . I never had a child of my own."

Talupéké flings her gaze at the door.

"Will you wear it?" says Chindilan. "Ang's tears, can you not even *look* at it?"

The girl is straining against invisible ropes. She snatches the ring, lets it lie there on her open palm. "More weight," she says, "that's just what I need."

"Wear it," says Chindilan.

A shrug, a snort. She puts the ring in her pocket, starts to turn away again. Chindilan catches her hands. They turn to fists, rock-hard, unyielding. So it is these he kisses goodbye.

ॐ

The door by which they exit leads to a second tunnel, far longer than the first. Stilts, with a three-warrior escort, guides them with the stump of a candle, which a draft blows out near the tunnel's end. Then a ladder, a small trapdoor. When they surface at last, it is through the floor of a grain silo, quite hidden from the road.

Dawn is breaking: scores of *tuhu* birds sizzle in the underbrush, feeding on ants; a woodpecker rattles a cardamom tree. In the east, beams of gold are spilling over the dark mass of the Arig Hills. They pass swiftly through the well-tended farmyard, over a field jagged with the snapped bones of last year's corn. The path winds into a second arm of the ravine. Although he looks twice the brothers' age, Stilts is agile, moving quickly through the stones and clumps of pincushion grass. After a hundred yards, he beckons to one of his men.

"These farmers kept the dog inside. They did everything we asked. Send them a ham—a decent one, not some rancid leftover. And tie a Gods-damned bow around it this time, will you?"

"A bow, sir. Yes, sir."

"It's the little touches, boy." Stilts turns to the travelers. "Well, you heard the general. He's arranged something for you, but you'll have to get your-selves as far as the hills before the Scythe drops below the horizon. You're *certain* you know the Scythe?"

"Everyone knows the Scythe," says Eshett. And that is true: the zigzag constellation is one of the brightest in the Urrathi night.

"Remember what he told you: it's gone before midnight this time of year. By the Gods, don't push your luck! He promised you'd find nothing if you came late, and the general damned well means what he says."

"We won't be late," says Kandri, "but you'd better tell us where this her-mit lives."

Stilts smiles. "Don't worry, she's a hard one to miss."

He leads them on, and after several minutes, they find a low spot in the ravine. They scramble up the embankment and force their way through tall grass. Before them stretches the wide Lutaral plain. Half a mile to the south rises the city wall, black and enormous, but Stilts points east to the Arig Hills.

"Look there—four round hills like babies' buttocks, see? And to their right, a gap, and then a taller hill standing alone. That's the Hermit. Don't climb it, for the love of Ang! Round it to the east, until you come upon a little wall of fieldstones. One of us will meet you there."

"The Hermit's just a rendezvous point?"

"Precisely."

"More skulking and sneaking," says Chindilan. "Tell me something: are you a company of men or rats?"

"We're rats, when necessary," says Stilts. "Rats are good at staying alive."

"Mr. Stilts," says Kandri, "what's waiting for us out there?"

The older man's lips compress to a line. He looks at them a moment, then turns his face away.

A moment later, faint sounds reach their ears. Kandri turns and sees Mektu scrambling up the side of the ravine. At the bottom stands a young woman in a plain desert *kanut*; she gives Stilts a silent nod and turns away.

Kandri scrambles down the slope to meet his brother. Mektu is sweaty, disheveled, as though he too has been awake all night. He smiles at Kandri, misses a step, winces. But the smile never leaves his face.

Kandri tries to take his arm, but Mektu waves him off. "I'm just fine—stop making a fuss! But listen, brother, something's not right. I think we've stayed too long."

"It won't be much longer," says Kandri.

"Not much longer is too long."

His fixed smile is disconcerting. Kandri thinks of how he smiled in Eternity Camp, breaking the news about the Spring Offensive. *You're with me, aren't you?* Kandri had felt heartless, turning on his heel, leaving the question unanswered. But what choice did he have? What answer could he have given but no?

"Lean on me, you're hurting."

"Forget it, Kan."

They emerge from the ravine, and Eshett pounces, lifting Mektu's shirt. The wound is angrier than ever. "You should have let Kandri help you," she snaps.

Mektu glares at her. Then he breaks into a little dance, shuffling in his army boots, clapping his hands above his head and singing.

I've known sorrow and pain and nights in the rain,
But I've loved my share of ladies—

Stilts waves desperately for silence, grinning despite himself. Eshett does not grin. "More than your fucking share," she says.

Mektu stops as suddenly as he began; the little caper has exhausted him.

"Nephew," says Chindilan, "that wound is bad."

Mektu is shocked—not by the diagnosis, but by the smith's concession, at long last, of the bond they share. "It's bad," he says. "Yes, Uncle, it's bad.

But I have this feeling, you see. We should run. We should stop asking any-one to help us, and run. As for this"—he touches his side, twitches sharp-ly—"I'm going to lance the fucker and be done with it."

"Spoken like a peasant," says Kandri. "'Cut it open, bleed it clean.' Gods, Mek, don't you remember *anything* from—"

"Ariqina's clinic?" says Mektu. "Oh, yes, I remember. You can be sure I do."

Kandri tenses. His brother has a gleam in his eye; he is going to say something vile, something vicious, and they will have it out right here in front of Stilts and his men—

Eshett places a hand on Mektu's cheek. She leans close, eyeball to eye-ball. "Don't touch your wound," she says. "Promise me. Let the doctors take care of you."

Kandri turns away, fighting for calm. Her gentleness, his uncle's gesture: these unsettle him more than Mektu's provocation. They are frightened for his brother, too frightened for the usual scolding.

"Where's this doctor, Mr. Stilts?" he demands.

"Relax, boy, we're on our way." Stilts rests a hand on Chindilan's shoulder. "You and Eshett must go back to the farmhouse; our sister down there will show you to the road. Pull your things together, and pay Yehita-Chen. Be generous: she's a loyal supporter, but she still needs to live." He gestures at Kandri and Mektu. "These two should be along by midday if all goes well. If it doesn't, you'll need to go to town and buy provisions for four."

"What sort of provisions, exactly?" asks Chindilan.

Stilts narrows his eyes. "Water," he says. "As much as you can carry, and new faska of bison or camel skin. Dry food, better headscarves. Bone meal, black limes, dates, and figs."

Desert provisions, thinks Kandri. *Why not just come out and say it?*

"Set out well before sunset," says Stilts. "You'll need three hours to reach the Hermit by foot, and one more to round it in the dark." He gestures to the brothers. "Come along, you two."

The travelers look at one another. Orange light in their eyes, blue flies buzzing their faces. Chindilan scratches one bulky shoulder. "'Til midday, boys," he says gruffly.

Kandri nods. "'Til midday, Uncle."

Eshett looks at each brother in turn. She frowns, as though biting back some impulse, then gives Mektu's hand an awkward squeeze. "Do as he tells you," she says, "and come back healed." She turns away, and Mektu's hand rises a little of its own accord, reaching after her.

ॐ

Although the northern gate is closer, Stilts takes them around the wall once more to the east. "You've yet to pass through the Dawn Gate," he said seriously. "That's a bit of good luck you don't want to spurn. Not where you're going."

In the morning sun, the red-orange stone is even more beautiful, glowing with an inner fire. The guards are many, however, and as the three men approach, they rise and step forward, lowering their spears. Kandri nudges Mektu to keep his eyes downcast. *We're in your hands, Stilts. Ang's tears, I hope you know what you're doing.*

But as it happens, the Naduman does nothing but smile. As soon as the guards catch his eye, they raise their spears and step backward. No one speaks. The brothers hesitate, but the older man pulls them on. Breathless with relief, they pass through the iron gates, under the glowing stone.

Kandri stops. A chill is passing over him, from his spine to the tips of his fingers. It is not the chill of fear, but it is deeply strange and unsettling. Mektu's eyes have gone wide. Stilts looks from brother to brother.

"You feel it, then," he says.

"I—yes. What is it?" The chill energy has not left him yet. Stilts turns them by the elbows, making them look back out through the Dawn Gate. Between the market tents, Kandri sees the sun rising over the plain, and a flock of egrets lifting, and the black, jagged line of the Arigs. His heart races. He is breathless, overcome by the immensity of what is out there, the infinite distances, the world he has never seen. And suddenly, he is eager for it all.

"The Gate's blessing," says Stilts. "Everyone feels it the first time, if they're still young enough, that is. I guess you're young enough."

"And this is why you brought us here?" Kandri asks.

"I brought you here to save your brother from septic agony," says Stilts, "and because my general so ordered." He glances meaningfully at the guards, still carefully ignoring them. "You'll be paying sixty-eight true gold for *that* little service, by the way. Let's be off."

They follow him into the city. Kandri is thinking of Tebassa's ledger book. *How deep in his debt are we sliding? How many ways will he collect?*

Mab Makkutin remains in shadow; the sun has yet to clear the wall. Few lamps, dark doorways. Nothing stirs in the alleys between the white clay homes.

"Mr. Stilts?" says Mektu. "Why do they call you that? Were you in the circus as well?"

"Hmph," says the older man. "Someone's been talking."

"Not true," says Mektu. "But you know the girl, our crazy girl, and with a name like yours—"

"I worked for the circus," says Stilts. "Quite a few of us did. Mansari walked the tightrope; he was our balance boy. Spider climbed like his namesake—walls, poles, stacked barrels, towers of chairs. He and Talupéké's sergeant performed as a team; she learned from both of them. And her grandmother Kereqa made it all happen. She was our founder, manager, bookkeeper, mistress of ceremonies. And her knife work was flawless; she's never been equaled, although Tal herself might get there one day. We called her *Tappu*, the pole at the center of the tent. But enough reminiscing, by damn. That life ended a long time ago."

"At least you *had* a life," says Mektu. "Kandri and I have never gone anywhere. We've never done a fucking thing. How could we, when nothing happens in the Valley? You don't know; it's just horrible. People get so bored, they fuck donkeys. They throw strange things in the fireplace, hoping they'll explode. Go on, tell us more. What did you do in the circus?"

Stilts gives him a sideways glance. "I took care of the freaks," he says.

They follow the main avenue for several blocks, then veer into a side street. Now at last there are signs of life: men and women unlocking their storefronts, fanning coals under blackened tea kettles, chalking their doors with prayer symbols for a day's prosperity.

"Mr. Stilts," murmurs Kandri, "why didn't Black Hat tell his men who we were?"

"That's for him to explain, if he wishes."

"He hasn't decided whether to help us, has he?" asks Mektu.

Stilts gives him an ambiguous smile. "You'll have to judge for yourself, I'm afraid."

"Maybe *he's* the one who's afraid," says Kandri.

Almost imperceptibly, the Naduman slows his step. He does not look at Kandri, but his voice is distinctly colder.

"Let me tell you something, boy. After the killing at the Megrev Defile, when the enemy tired of pouring blackworms on our dying troops and marched off, General Tebassa slid down the side of that gorge and crossed a stream and clawed up the opposite slope. He found a stand of trees. He got a fire started, somehow. Then he stripped the gold brocade from his scabbard and heated one end of the wire in the flames. He lay on his stomach and drove that wire into the worm-holes in the small of his back."

"*Jeshar!*"

"Over and over," says Stilts, "until he'd burned out all the worms and shriveled their eggs. When he was finished, his legs would not move, but if he hadn't, those creatures would have burrowed all the way to his guts, devoured him, left him hollow as a gourd.

"Shall I tell you the rest? He was found two days later by the Jathra folk of the Megrev. He'd dragged himself to the outskirts of their village, through six miles of mountains, with just his arms. So spare me your thoughts about the general's courage. Is that clear?"

Kandri nods; he can think of no retort. In his mind's eye he sees the two severed heads. *Exactly to order, sir.* A man like that would kill them too, without a moment's hesitation—kill them, or deliver them to death. And yet Tebassa seems truly fond of Talupéké. And he had arranged for this doctor, as well.

The streets narrow. They pass a soup kitchen (browning onions, that heavenly smell), a temple (incense, frangipani, sage), an alley full of ragpickers, still asleep. Mektu is pressing his hand to his side.

Piles on the devil's ass! Kandri thinks. Why wouldn't Tebassa just explain his intentions? Why not just say, *I mean to help you escape?*

Because he means to do nothing of the kind, says the voice of fear in Kandri's head. But in that case, why bring them to the war council at all?

Of course, one of them was not.

The thought leaves Kandri cold. Talupéké had spoken to the general about Mektu, and Tebassa had barred him specifically. Had he chosen a different fate for Mektu?

"This doctor," says Stilts, shattering his morbid thoughts, "may insist on examining your eyes. If he does—well, there's nothing to be done except to get out of town quickly when you're finished. Don't try to bribe him; you can't. And don't lie if he asks you about the Prophet. In fact, don't lie at all—except on one point."

The brothers look at him quizzically.

"It's a simple matter," says the Naduman. "The doctor only treats patients he finds interesting—everyone else can go to hell. So we had to make your brother sound interesting. And there's just one certain way to do that. We told him Mektu was a survivor of the Throat Rust."

"The Throat Rust!" cries Mektu. "What, you mean the Plague?"

"The World Plague, exactly. You had it last year, and recovered. That's all we said to him—all we needed to say. You can fill in the rest as you like, but for the love of Ang, keep your story straight. This man's used to fakers. If you contradict yourself, he'll toss you out with your pants down."

"But I didn't have the Plague!" says Mektu.

Stilts chuckles. "Sure you did."

"What kind of doctor are we talking about?" says Kandri. "My brother's flesh is rotting. He needs a wound treated, not some disease he never had."

"You want him treated? Then stop jabbering and do as I say. We've had years to learn how these cuckoos think. Of course, they may not believe you. We'd like to scar your neck, as though you'd been clawing at yourself, trying to breathe. But you need at least a week for that. The bruises have to heal."

Scar his neck. Kandri has a sinking feeling about the whole excursion. And Mektu is no different: behind Stilts' back, he motions with his eyes. *Let's just run.*

Kandri shakes his head. They walk another fifty yards, then turn left at a corner. Before them is a curious alley, very long and straight between high and featureless walls. No people. No windows or balconies: just a small door at the alley's end, with a single torch beside it mounted in a sconce. "Excellent, no one's waiting outside," said Stilts. "We were wise to come early."

Their footfalls echo strangely; the alley is devoid of other sounds. Also oddly clean. Strangest of all, the door when they reach it is iron—solid, massive iron, like the door of a vault. Stilts steps up to the door and pulls a chain; faintly, they hear the ringing of a bell.

"This is a hospital?" says Kandri.

"Of course not," says Stilts.

A slit opens in the iron door, framing two eyes. They appear to belong to a young woman, but there is something curious about their color, or their shape.

"I've brought case number twenty-seven," says Stilts. "Also an escort, his brother."

The eyes swivel. "Turn around, twenty-seven. Chin high, if you please."

A woman's voice. An accent like nothing Kandri has ever heard. The brothers glance at one another and slowly turn in a circle.

"Just the patient," snaps the voice. Kandri steps back. This woman is used to being obeyed.

"Your throat is unblemished and symmetrical," she declares. "You haven't had the Throat Rust, twenty-seven."

"You're wrong, I have," says Mektu calmly. "I lay in bed from the first to the twenty-fourth day of autumn. I couldn't speak for twenty days or chew food for sixteen. I lost twenty pounds. I ate papaya gruel and coconut water and goat's milk when I could get it. The papaya burned my throat, so for four days I drank straight from the coconuts. For the last three days, I slept propped against the wall. My teeth hurt, my bowels were empty, I felt as though a hand were inserted there and squeezing. My tongue swelled like a—"

"Stop!" cries the woman. "You're lying. You're just making things up. Find a local doctor, or come back for our public clinic, three weeks from tomorrow."

"Three weeks?" says Kandri. "We'll be dead in three weeks!"

"We?"

"He. I said he. I meant he."

Stilts turns away to hide his look of despair.

"I really did have the Plague," says Mektu. "I thought you'd want specifics."

"Specifics, were they?" says the woman. "Go ahead then; I took notes. Repeat those specifics. I am listening."

"I lay in bed from the first to the twenty-fourth day of autumn. I couldn't speak for twenty days or chew food for sixteen . . ."

Mektu says it all again, smooth as a priest at morning prayer. Kandri does not catch a slip. When Mektu finishes, there is silence from behind the door. Stilts glances at Kandri, his eyes gone wide.

"Stand by for processing, twenty-seven," says the woman. The window slit bangs shut.

Gaping, Stilts leans close to Mektu. "I don't know what the fuck just happened. But you're in, somehow. Well done." He straightens, speaks normally. "This is as far as I go. As for our next meeting, you've been warned to be punctual: heed that advice." He lifts a hand in farewell. "The Gods' luck be with you, gentlemen."

Kandri, feeling a fool, takes Stilts' hand in both of his and squeezes it. He sputters, "You're close to Talupéké as well, aren't you?"

Stilts raises his eyebrows. "She's my sister's grandchild, if you care to know."

His face reveals no hint of encouragement. Kandri drops his hand. "Did you help her convince the general to aid us?" he asks.

"As you yourself observed," says Stilts, "what he is convinced of remains to be seen."

He starts to turn away, but once more Kandri stops him.

"Our names, Mr. Stilts. You said Talupéké didn't tell you. So how did you know to call us Hinjumans?"

The Naduman smiles, suddenly roguish. "You feared that name had reached the streets already, along with your deeds. Nothing of the kind. It's just that the two of you, standing there in the market, were like twin portraits of the man. Or competing portraits, maybe—one by a cold artist, an artist with a razor eye, the other by a wild exuberant. But in both of you I can see him plainly. I mean your father, that unbearable rascal. Ah, here's the nurse."

ॐ

The iron door flies open with a boom and a strange hiss of air. Kandri and Mektu shield their eyes: a dazzling light is pouring into the alley. So are guards—small men in spotless, sand-colored uniforms, closing the brothers instantly in a circle of gleaming spears. They pay no attention whatsoever to Stilts, who is already a good distance away. Kandri wants to shout after him—*You knew our father! Stop, talk to me!*—but the spears press close, and the Naduman is all but running. Bewildered, Kandri turns to face the chamber again.

There is the nurse, the owner of those eyes. Tall, elegant, impassive. Sky-blue uniform, and skin of a pale amber-yellow. The guards' skin is identical. "Welcome to the Xavasindran Medical Mission," says the nurse.

Xavasindrans. Of course. The best doctors in Urrath are not Urrathis. He has heard the claim a hundred times, but has never been close to one of these outlanders—has never glimpsed one, save for that single man in the crowd at Eternity Camp.

Don't gape, idiot. They're just another kind of people, just one more clan.

For the second time in a matter of hours, they are frisked and disarmed. Then the nurse waves them inside. "Quickly, twenty-seven. The door must not stand open."

The chamber is a stark, bright rectangle. There are two additional doors, one desk, five or six wooden chairs. A window behind the desk is covered with a fine metal grille, like chain mail nailed to a frame. What the hell can it be for? But even stranger are the lamps, which are innumerable and recessed into the ceiling—one every few inches, wall to wall. Their light is emerald-tinted and blinding. Kandri cannot look at them for long.

The door closes softly. There is a whirring sound, like a great beehive waking, and Kandri feels a sudden pressure in his ears. The guards take up position around the walls of the chamber. The nurse extends an exquisitely clean hand, drops something into Kandri's palm. It is a round plug of lead engraved with the number 27.

"Do not lose this coin," she says. "If you lose this coin, your weapons will not be returned."

Kandri finds he can only nod. The nurse looks them up and down.

"By your expressions," she says, "I infer that you have never visited a Mission before"—she glances at Mektu—"or never been admitted."

She slips into the chair behind the desk. She does not invite them to sit.

"Do you have a number too?" Mektu asks, already leering. The woman ignores his question but asks many of her own, jotting Mektu's answers in a notebook.

Kandri listens agog to his brother's effortless falsehoods. Very soon he is angry: unreasonably angry, for at this moment his brother is only saying what he must. No, his anger is for other moments, other lies, for the years of small performances.

You're a terrible actor, Kandri.

You've never understood, have you, Mek? I was never acting at all.

"Dr. Skarrys will attend you presently," says the nurse, without looking up. "The waiting chamber is to my left. You may proceed."

The chamber into which they pass is strangely chilly. There are four chairs, a second door, and a low table with an odd, globular sculpture: a mushroom, maybe, or a clot of worms. Dominating one wall is a large glass window. No daylight enters there; in fact, Kandri can see nothing beyond it but darkness.

With another hiss, the door shuts behind them. Mektu turns to Kandri, his face transformed. "We shouldn't have come here," he whispers. "They look like demons. This place is all wrong."

He is terrified. His behavior outside even more a performance than Kandri understood.

"Enough nonsense, Mek. Your flesh is rotting. And the Xavasindrans are from across the ocean; naturally, they don't look like us."

"Nothing is natural here," says Mektu. "The lamps, that noise in the walls. And the cold in this room, it's sorcery. Not even father could build this sort of thing."

"No, not even him."

"I don't want them touching me, Kan."

"Not even that nurse?"

He winks, desperate to lighten the mood. If Mektu panics they will be tossed out yet.

His brother glances at the door. "I don't know. She was beautiful. But what if they do something to me?"

"All they're going to do is ask you questions about the Plague. Now relax. This isn't sorcery. Chindilan said they had tools unlike anything in Urrath, and he heard it from the Old Man."

"Why don't they share it, then? If it's natural, why don't they show us how to make that sort of lamp?"

Kandri hesitates. The Quarantine? The fabled Xavasindran oath of non-interference?

"I can't explain that," he admits. "Princes play games with the world, and we're just the chips. Nobody explains things to the chips. It's wrong, but it doesn't matter today."

"I'm not a chip," says Mektu.

"You're sick, and they're going to heal you," says Kandri, "so don't piss the bastards off."

Mektu paces. Kandri tries one of the chairs but jumps startled to his feet again: it is like sinking into a cake. He leans against the wall across from the window. He tries to distract his brother with something pleasant. Tell me a joke, Mek. Give me that bit from the *War Choral* about the old king and his swine.

But Mektu just remarks that the pigs end up as sausages.

Kandri moves on to Eshett: "She's become a little fond of you, I think." Mektu's face brightens, but only for an instant. He says that Eshett has a husband in her village.

"A husband? Eshett is *married?*"

"Or a lover, anyway. She told me there's someone she's thinking about all the time."

Kandri shrugs. "That could be just about anyone. Her mother, or some favorite niece."

Mektu shakes his head. "I bought her pussy for a night and forgot about it."

"That doesn't help," Kandri agrees.

"She's no more fond of me than that nurse is." He stops his pacing, lifts his hands to his temples. "It's back," he says. "That feeling I had in the ravine that something horrible's coming. Let's just go, can't we, please? Before it's too late?"

"Don't start that again," says Kandri.

"They might take something while I'm cut open. They might take my balls."

"Good. You're not using them, anyway."

Mektu glares at him, says he isn't afraid. Kandri smiles with one side of his mouth. But when Mektu's own expression hardens, he knows he has made a mistake.

"I use them," says Mektu. "I'm not the one who buys time with a girl and then just sits there like a *lulee.*"

Kandri shuts his eyes. So Mektu knows about that.

"What's the problem?" asks Mektu. "You can't get it up? When you're finally alone with a woman, your candle melts, is that it?"

"No," says Kandri, "and shut your vulgar mouth."

"You should have told the girls to shut theirs," says Mektu. "Ah, but you did, didn't you? You probably even paid them: otherwise, the whole camp would have known. But they told me because they were worried. It's incredible: even the whores were worried about Kandri. You're the one people *always* worry about. And you have a go at *my* manhood."

"It wasn't about that, Mek. Calm down, for fuck's sake."

His brother's chest is heaving. Kandri cannot fathom what has set him off. *Unless—*

He looks Mektu in the eye. *Unless you really are in that kind of trouble. Pitfire, on top of everything else.*

Once again, Kandri's face has given him away. Mektu looks at him, sneering. "Don't worry about *me*," he says. "*I'm* just fine with women. And you know who could have told you that."

"Don't you dare."

"You should have asked her. 'Tell me, Ariqina, do you sleep with my brother?' Why didn't you just ask?"

Kandri feels a loathing settle deep in his limbs. This freak. This twisted little shit who's plagued his life for ten years. This mean-hearted, worthless, unwanted brother. Yes, they could just walk out—and go their separate ways. Kandri could ditch him at the first street corner, leave him to his lies, let his wound burst like a pressure cooker, let him rot, let him go.

His brother's face is defiant, but his jaw is trembling: he has gone too far.

"You want to leave?" says Kandri. "Take our chances in the city? Find some Mab Makkutin sawbones with ale on his breath?"

Mektu blinks at him. "You mean it?"

Kandri doesn't know if he means it, but he knows he must beat Mektu at his own game for once. He grabs his brother by the arm and starts to drag him toward the door.

"Come on," he snarls. "There's a rusty knife with your name on it."

"Get your hands off me," says Mektu.

"You're right," says Kandri, releasing him. "I'm doing this the hard way."

He is almost to the door. Mektu stands rooted to the spot. "Where are you going?" he says.

"On with my fucking life," says Kandri, gripping the doorknob.

"Brother," says Mektu. "I don't know what to do."

Kandri's looks over his shoulder. Mektu stares at him, beseeching. Never in his life has Kandri seen him so vulnerable, so crippled by doubt.

"Kandri," he says, "this place scares the shit out of me."

There is a blaze of light.

Kandri flinches; Mektu all but jumps out of his skin. It is the window, suddenly shining. Beyond it are eight seated figures, staring at them through the glass.

The brothers recoil, as though caught in some indecency. Four women, four men. All of them studying the two soldiers with a quiet intensity, like theater-goers waiting for the show. Most are amber-skinned like the nurse and the security guards, but one woman is blacker than Chindilan; and one man, to Kandri's slight disgust, is a pale gray with shades of pink, with veins clearly visible in his neck and forehead. All eight have notebooks in their laps.

Kandri, shaken to his senses, takes a few halting steps in their direction. "Is one of you the doctor?" he demands.

No answer. Kandri is not certain they can hear him. One of the men leans close to his neighbor and whispers, pointing at Mektu with a pencil. The man beside him nods.

Kandri feels a sudden revulsion for the figures. To be examined thus, with such indifference, the way a butcher might examine his hogs . . .

Gods of death. What if Mektu is right?

But look again: they are not all indifferent. One person in the back row—a short man with black, braided hair—seems positively anxious: fidgeting, frowning, glancing sidelong at the others. *What's wrong, what's happening?* Kandri asks him silently. But the man will not meet his eye.

The door near Mektu opens, and a smiling Xavasindran steps into the room. He is tall and graying at the temples; the effect is startling against his amber skin. He settles a pair of thick black spectacles upon his nose.

"Twenty-seven," he declares. It is neither question nor greeting. It is more formal than either: a labeling, perhaps.

"Yes, that's me," says Mektu. "I had the Plague last year. I lay in bed—"

"I am Dr. Skarrys, *Epidemia Omnic*. The Plague last year, and thoracic trauma earlier this month. An arrow. Very good. The Mission is glad to be of assistance in exchange for your interview. It is an equitable arrangement." He turns to Kandri. "You are the brother escort. Will you please participate?"

Kandri swallows. "Of course," he manages to say.

"Very good. Elder brother or younger?"

"Elder."

"By just three days," says Mektu under his breath.

There is a stirring among the figures behind the glass. Kandri starts, looks over his shoulder. *They can hear our every word!*

"Three days?" says Skarrys. "Your mother must have been exhausted. Were you tangled in the umbilicus?"

"Oh, no," says Mektu. "We were poor folk. We didn't use such things."

The doctor looks from brother to brother. "Let's sit down," he says.

The interview is strictly physical: age, diet, habits of exercise, hours of sleep. Most of the questions are for Mektu, and a good quarter of his answers are deranged. *I can go two days without pissing if I want. I decided to stop seeing the color red.* Kandri wants to kick him. The figures behind the window scribble furious notes.

After some forty minutes, Skarrys takes off his glasses and just stares. Kandri cannot decide if he is angry or defeated. Mektu, his mask of bravado very much in place, gazes back at him.

"You are a drug user, I think?" says Skarrys.

Mektu nods solemnly.

"Mek!" Kandri forces a laugh. "He's not serious, Doctor. That was years ago, and even then it was just *vaha-vipi*, joyflowers. You chew them. Some people make tea."

"Kids' stuff."

"Exactly."

"I imagine the Prophet put an end to that."

Silence. The eight behind the window look up from their notes. Skarrys has had a good look at their eyes.

"Doctor," says Kandri, "let me explain."

Skarrys stands, gives a curt little bow. "This interview is concluded," he says, and moves toward the door.

"Wait!" cries Kandri. He pulls up Mektu's shirt: the wound is bulging and hideously discolored. "We answered all your questions," he says. "You've got to help him, you promised! He's going to die!"

The doctor's hand is on the doorknob. "Do you know why we come to Urrath, Soldier of Revelation?" he asks quietly. "To fight death, that is why. Not to conquer the next clan. Not to seize territory or demand revenge. Make no mistake: we are soldiers too, and missions like this one are outposts in a war. In our years in Urrath, we have eliminated two terrible diseases, and driven a third almost to ground. But our true enemy, our mortal enemy— he still has the upper hand. I mean the Throat Rust, of course. The World Plague. Have you ever watched a man die of Plague?"

"I haven't," Kandri admits.

"Of course not," says Skarrys. "This continent is barely affected. Few Urrathis ever contract the World Plague, and those who do mostly recover on their own. Your resistance is almost supernatural. Only one in eight thousand Urrathis dies of Plague. But in the rest of the world? Have you any guess?" He slices the air with one hand. "Do not guess; I can stand no more chatter. The figure is one in seven."

Both brothers gape in horror. "Ang's sweet tears," says Kandri. "Why?"

"Why, why!" booms the doctor. "That is the question that consumes us. We are glad to treat your lesser diseases, your parasites, your foolishly neglected wounds. But our quest is for the secret of your immunity to the great butcher of mankind. Urrath has a treasure for the world, sir. But it is buried somewhere in this wilderness, buried in your pitiful disorder. We must dig for that treasure. Nothing else matters in the end."

"My brother matters."

Skarrys opens the door and stands aside. "I said the interview was over, not your visit. Wait here, brother escort. Twenty-seven, kindly follow me."

෭

They depart, the door closes, and the figures behind the window stand and rearrange their chairs. The new focus of their attention is the window on their left. Bright lamps have been lit behind it now, but from Kandri's angle, the glass is merely translucent. Dimly, he sees his brother and Skarrys entering the room, the doctor's gesture, Mektu unbuttoning his shirt. They stand thus for several minutes, the doctor bending closer to the wound. He can hear the faintest pulse of their voices. Then they move away from the window, and Kandri can see nothing at all.

But the watchers can see everything, clearly. They are, Kandri notices, all rather young. His own age or younger, probably—but who can be sure with faces like that? In any event, they have forgotten him. Whatever is happening to Mektu holds them transfixed.

Kandri begins to pace the room. *Trust them. Miracle workers. Just look at these lamps.* But that doctor was angry. *Yes, and who can blame the man? He's fighting the World Plague, and Mektu lied through his teeth.*

What about the general's odd remarks in that bunker, though? *He wasn't eager to help us; and Mektu seemed to worry him especially. Is he looking for a way to divide us? Could the Xavasindrans somehow be part of that plan?*

Kandri thinks suddenly of Chindilan's words in Eternity Camp. *There's nothing I can do for your brother. I've tried, Kandri. More than you know.*

And again, the chaser: a feeling that scalds him with shame. The knowledge that he, Kandri, would understand Tebassa's decision—for who in their right mind would consent to any journey with Mektu Hinjuman, the "unhinged clown"? Yes, he understands it. He could even forgive it, could he not?

Even, in some rotten wormhole of his heart, feel a certain gratitude?

But the general does not know his heart. No matter his brother's idiocies, the general must have assumed that Kandri would never abandon him, or take up with anyone who meant him harm. So what does a cold-blooded bastard like Tebassa do with that fact? Abandon them both, abandon all the travelers?

Or find a way to eliminate the clown?

A way Kandri will have no reason to connect with Tebassa himself? And if that is the plan, how fortunate, how perfect, that the clown is already in danger of death. But could Tebassa really have such sway with these foreigners? Could any doctor, foreign or Urrathi, be so depraved as to kill a patient for the convenience of a warlord?

Kandri freezes: music. Someone is playing a piano, a jaunty and rather cloying tune. It seems to be coming from the wall opposite the window.

He goes to the wall and touches it. The wooden planks vibrate on the low notes. A beer-hall musician in a surgery. What the fuck, what the fuck.

He sits down in a sponge-cake chair. His fears are running away with him. *You had to bring him here. You don't want some local jackass wielding that knife.*

Then, faint and distorted, he hears a voice shout, *No!*

"Mek?"

"*NO!*"

Kandri sprints to the door. Locked. Mektu is bellowing, *No no no get it away from me stop!* Kandri flies across the room to the door they entered by. Then stops short. A dozen guards wait in that chamber. Mektu cries out again. Kandri grips the doorknob and turns.

Locked.

He hurls himself against the door. He runs to the window and pounds with both fists. He begins to shout at them, to demand they release his brother, to threaten and curse. The watchers do not spare him a glance.

Mektu gives a wordless scream. Halfway through the rending cry, something muffles his voice—a hood, a mask, a pillow held down . . .

Kandri goes to the table, lifts the round sculpture, hurls it at the window with all his might.

The sculpture bursts in a thousand pieces. The window is not even scratched. He lifts a chair and swings it too, and only manages to crack its wooden leg. He is reduced to screams himself.

"What's happening? What the living fuck are you doing to him?"

He can see only one side of the watchers' faces. They lean forward, talking, gesturing, fascinated by the procedure. But one chair stands empty. The pudgy man with the braid has slipped away.

₧₧

Hours later, Kandri is slumped in the chair. No one has come. The watchers have drifted away; the room beyond the window is dark. His throat is raw from shouting. In his hands is a small brass plaque: the faceplate of the shattered sculpture. He stares at the neat Kasraji words.

THE HUMAN BRAIN

It might as well be his own brain, there in shards under the window. He is brain-sick, brain-weary, undone by a presentiment of death. Mektu's death. A thing he has wished for sometimes, may the Gods forgive him. A thing he will never recover from, if it should actually come to pass.

It was Mektu who showed him how to scale a palm tree, hugging the trunk with all four limbs, a rope loop joining the feet. Mektu who taught him to play the fiddle: a five-song repertoire, the same five as Mektu himself. Mektu with whom he built a still in the loft of a neighbor's barn, from bamboo and glass milk jugs and an old oil drum. Mektu who shared his guilt when the barn caught fire, and the next six months rebuilding it, nail by nail.

Mektu who carried him over the River Shev, his head cracked open, the Ghalsúnay arrows falling like rain.

The screams have long since ended. The piano, however, plays on, faint and tedious. The tune changes, but the musician never pauses for more than a breath or two. No one claps. No one speaks or even clears a throat. It is as if there is no human involved, as if the keys are being struck by some tireless machine.

And now—*Jeshar*, is it possible? Yes, it is. The man is playing, butchering, his and Ariqina's song. *Give me one last hour with my true love, and keep your cold Forever.* Kandri laughs: such a shameless kick in the gut. He leans back in the chair and pummels the wall.

"Play something else, you hear me? Play *anything* else!"

The tune does not falter. Kandri groans and covers his ears.

∾

For a few weeks that summer, the stories from Blind Stream became almost unbearably rich. First the young Dr. Ariqina vanishes. Then Kandri

Hinjuman assaults a priest. Certain townsfolk came to the prison, knocked on the wall, shouted his name. It was not done out of solidarity but merely to prove to themselves that it was really happening. When Kandri answered, they had few words of comfort for him, but many questions. He answered with questions of his own, all concerning Ariqina.

The gossips put two and two together. The boy had clearly lost his mind, and what but love could account for it? Father Marz broke his silence only to confirm that Ariqina had come to him with "a crisis of virtue" on the night of her disappearance; he made no mention of the cleansing ceremony. Surely, the youths were lovers, then—or fornicators, rather, brazenly defying the Prophet's chastity edicts.

But Ariqina had repented, and it was to her credit that she had laid her guilt before the Valley's elder priest. What form of atonement had Marz demanded? Some public humiliation? Whatever it was, the young doctor had balked, fled the Valley in shame. And Kandri had taken out his frustration on her confessor.

All this made a salacious kind of sense. But then came the oddest twist of all: Mektu Hinjuman's announcement that *he* and Ariqina had been secretly engaged.

It was more than an announcement, in fact: it was a performance. He wept out his heartbreak, rolled in the dust, cried to the Gods to bring her back unharmed and take his own life instead. His speech borrowed liberally from the *War Choral* and other poems. "Ariqina! The cold mists have taken you! Come back, return the sun! You're the blossom of the Valley, the woman of my destiny and dreams!"

That his brother was dreaming was plain enough. Mektu's public agonies only underscored his guilt in Kandri's eyes. He had spied on their lovemaking, and jealousy had driven him out of his mind. There was no other explanation. Who else but Mektu could have betrayed them to Father Marz?

The first time his brother came to see him in prison, Kandri had reached through the bars and taken a hopeless swing at his chin. But as the days wore on, a portion of Kandri's fury was transmuted into awe. Deluded or not, his brother was doing some good.

"We had no carnal relations," Mektu told the villagers, "but I will tell you the truth, people: it took all my strength to resist her advances. Ari was feverish. I reminded her of Our Prophet's teachings on the matter of lust, and she heeded me. She went to Father Marz for moral correction, and to confess."

You? asked a great many, bewildered. *Not your brother, not the one who jumped the priest?*

Mektu bowed his head. "Kandri loves her too, of course. We were rivals, and he never could accept that I'd won. He's gone just a little mad. And somehow my poor brother's decided that it was Father Marz who swayed her, convinced Ariqina to choose me. Don't blame Kandri. Love makes fools of us all. I'm sure the good Father has forgiven him already."

Why did she run off, then? asked the skeptics.

"Don't you see?" Mektu barked at them. "She *didn't* run. She has no reason to run. She's still out there—lost, hurt, caught in a wolf trap, pinned under a rock. We have to find her before it's too late."

This last claim, at least, he believed with all his heart, and his conviction persuaded more than a few. The search continued, and Mektu gave himself to it body and soul.

The wilder part of his fantasy—that Ariqina had been his fiancée rather than Kandri's lover—also had some good effects. It cleared the taint of promiscuity from Ariqina's name. It even won some sympathy for Kandri, would-be priest killer, as the law pondered his fate.

But the days wore on, and Ariqina was not found. The search parties dwindled, then suddenly ceased. Mektu went on alone. Some time on the eleventh day, he too went missing, but before a new search could begin, word came that he had walked all the way to the tavern at Wolf Kill and drunk himself into a stupor.

When he returned, his story appeared somewhat tarnished. Perhaps Ariqina had wanted to break off the engagement—if she had ever truly pledged herself to Mektu Hinjuman? Perhaps there was someone else altogether, in Nandipatar maybe? Or brigands, kidnappers? The lands around Blind Stream had been scoured. Wherever the truth lay, it grew hard to credit that Ariqina herself was lying in a ditch.

Kandri feared he really would go mad in that cell. Ari could not be dead. She had left the Valley the way she had entered his life—in pitch blackness, guarding her secrets, hiding her tears. He knew now that his love for her was beyond anything he would ever feel again, and that to lose it would be to pass through this world condemned to half measures, meaningless pursuits. He should have proposed months before. He should have stood watch outside the temple; he should have gone with her when she fled. He should be on the road with her that very minute. Even if she refused him. Even if she were bound for a place so strange and distant that it was hard to believe it could exist.

Physically, matters could have been worse. His discomfort seemed paltry compared to that of the dogs, who bayed and whimpered through the nights. Kandri at least had visitors. His mother came often, and so did all his siblings (save for Nyreti, who had not yet recovered from "Ang's cunt"). Several friends visited as well, with gifts of bread or sweets or lighted cheroots; matches, of course, were not allowed in the cell. Most wanted nothing to do with him, however. Kandri had assaulted a priest, a defender of the Prophet's word. Heartbroken or not, he could only be shunned.

His very first visitor, however, was Lantor Hinjuman. The Old Man was disheveled and exhausted: his part in the search had been a hard ride to Nandipatar, and a frantic survey of everyone who remembered the girl from six years before. Afterward, he rode straight to the jail, contemptuous of visiting hours, and simply blustered his way past the guards. He stared at his son with similar belligerence. For several minutes, he did not speak at all.

"Papa?" said Kandri at last.

"What did she tell you?"

Kandri stood up and walked to the bars. "Ari? Nothing. She didn't say a damned thing. What's the matter?"

"You're not lying, are you, Kandri? I won't forgive you if you lie about this."

"Lie?" shouted Kandri. "Go to hell, Papa. *I* haven't lied to anyone."

His father waited. Kandri threw up his hands, turned and kicked his cot, stormed back to his father and whispered, "She's obsessed with Kasralys City, and that plague doctor, what's her name, Tsireem—"

"Yes, of course," said the Old Man, "but did she say nothing else? Tell me the truth, I say. On your life, Kandri. On all our lives."

He was even more frightened than angry, but stranger than either was his odd look of guilt. "What's going on here, Papa?" hissed Kandri, seizing the bars. "Do *you* have something you should tell?"

The Old Man stood rigid. He raised a hand, trembling, and brought it near Kandri's own. "I have something I should never tell," he said, "and if you care about her, or your family, you'll never ask me about it again."

₧

Two weeks later, Kandri received a visit from Father Marz himself. The old man was escorted by a pair of younger priests and an army captain. He kept a good six feet from the bars.

"I've brought you this," said the army captain, passing Kandri a book. He had a rather kindly face.

"Thank you, sir. Do you know what's to become of me?"

The captain shook his head. Then one of the young priests spoke up sharply: "Father Marz wishes to know if you have anything to say to him, Kandri Hinjuman."

Any groveling pardon to beg, that is. Kandri looked the old priest in the eye. He could accuse the man right there, before that officer. But would it matter? Who was the more powerful, a young captain or a senior priest? And why did Kandri imagine that this captain would wish to help him at all?

They were busy men, impatient with his silence; if he did not speak quickly, they would be gone.

"Did you rape her, Father?"

It was a whisper, but it reached their ears. The younger priests all but burst with indignation. Marz restrained them with a gesture, his own eyes blazing. "*Jeshar*, is that what you think? What devil's mouthpiece whispered that in your ear?"

"His own sick fancy," said one of the younger priests. "Let us go. This one will not avail himself of your kindness."

333

"I thought you rather sane for a Hinjuman," said Marz. "Not mindful of Our Prophet's teachings, but then you started life on the barren mountain, with no priest at hand, and your birth-father rarely seen beneath your roof. His sins were not yours. And your brother Mektu's behavior, his disgraceful playacting, his ugly ideas of mirth. None of this I ever thought to hold against you. But then this disgrace—"

Greatly daring, he took one step toward Kandri. "My task," he said, "was to cleanse the girl, in keeping with our Prophet's law. Anyone who claims I did else but that is a liar and an enemy, a stooge of blackest hell."

"Beg the Father's pardon, wretch!" growled one of the priests.

"Nay, not my own," said Marz. "Let him beg the pardon of Ang Most High, in our holy Prophet's name."

With that, he tottered away, and the priests trailed after him. The army captain lingered a moment, considering Kandri almost wryly.

"What's to be done with me, sir?" Kandri.

"Get some rest," said the captain, starting away. "I think you're going to need it."

℣

The weeks that followed were the lowest Kandri had ever known. There was his suspicion of Mektu, who visited him often in the cell, but who chattered in such a tactless manner that Kandri often wished he would stay away. There was his fear for Ariqina: how could she possibly manage such a journey on her own? There was the ache of her loss, a shard of glass lodged in his lungs, stabbing him with every breath.

But worse than any of these was the lingering mystery. If Marz was telling the truth, and no one had harmed Ariqina, what had made her flee into the night?

Of course, his own fate too was waiting to be decided. Someone had heard the priest mutter, *Ten years for Lantor Hinjuman's brat*. Ten years! He would be an unimaginable *thirty* by the time he stepped out of that cage—if the lice had not devoured him, or killed him off with some disease.

The simpleton made animal noises. Goats, cows, roosters, especially at night. Sometimes, he rambled about friends Kandri suspected were imaginary. The old murderer just watched him, small eyes bright under a shock of greasy gray hair.

Ten years. Kandri dared not contemplate such a sentence. But what else did he have to think about? What else but Ari's fate, Mektu's guilty expression, their mother soaking her sarong with tears?

In desperation, he picked up the book from the army captain. It was called *The Five Atrocities,* and it described, in horrific detail, the crimes visited on the Chiloto people throughout history. There were far more than five. But the book began with an essay on the origins of the Chiloto clan, and that is where Kandri found himself spellbound.

It seemed his people were the first true kings of Urrath. They ruled the continent long before the slave-built empire of the Kasraj, before the still-earlier kingdom of Ut'xing the Conqueror, before even the ancient sartaphs, the builders of stone cities long since drowned in desert sands. But none of these were instructive. For the Chilotos (the book explained) had built a different kind of kingdom, one not of masters and servants but the natural fealty paid by a grateful continent. They had treated all peoples with justice, defended the weak against the strong, lifted the poor from their misery, built schools, consecrated temples. Under their stewardship, all clans had prospered. Few if any had seen a reason to resist, for it was clear that this arrangement was better than any feasible alternative. Some clans were born to grow wheat, or brew palm wine, or quarry stone. The Chilotos were born to rule other clans and help them forward into the Light of Ang. This might seem strange today, but in the beginning, everyone understood. The conquered peoples thanked the Gods for their rulers. On the fringes of the Empire, clans begged the monarchs to enter their lawless territories and plant the Chiloto flag.

Kandri's ancestors, the book continued, were also the most learned people of the ancient world. They had invented matches, windlasses, bore wells, cotton fabric, leavened bread, fiddles, oil paints, arithmetic, astrology, stoneware, steel. Princes from foreign lands came to learn the secrets of the

Chilotos (for the Plague would not appear for centuries) and apprenticed their sons to the clan's master craftsmen. The Chiloto, open-hearted, shared their knowledge gladly, with no thought of recompense.

But they learned to their sorrow that not all the world's clans were so benevolent.

☙

One day Mektu burst shouting into the jailhouse: "You're to be pardoned tomorrow! I heard them! Marz is willing to forget the whole thing!"

Kandri jumped up with his heart in his mouth, but Mektu had not come during visiting hours and was driven roughly away. Tomorrow came and went, and the next day, and the next. Dyakra Hinjuman told him to keep his chin up: "Lantor is negotiating. He's sure to cut some sort of deal."

Her words did not reassure him: the Old Man was the last person who should be pleading his case to Father Marz. The two men were enemies, and rivals of a sort: both were considered men of influence, but their beliefs and instincts could not have differed more.

"*Sepu*," said Kandri, resorting to the name she'd given herself the day they met, "would *you* talk to old Marz? Could you, please?"

His second mother was, without question, the gentlest soul he had ever known, a fact that made her response all the more startling. She looked away from him, gazed fixedly at the small, clouded window at the end of the hall. She hugged herself, washtub-rough hands enfolding knobby elbows. "If I must," she said, "but that should be the last thing we try. Your father is dramatic, yes—Mektu gets it from him. Still, Lantor can keep his cool with Father Marz. I manage as well, Ang knows. In the street, at the festivals . . ."

She rose, straightened her sarong, making to leave although she had arrived just minutes before.

"But leave me in a room alone with that man and only one of us will come out alive."

The next day Dyakra told him that Mektu had given up the search. He had gone instead to work at the clinic, but the nurses had sent him home because his compulsive spewing of mawkish poetry was upsetting the patients.

Kandri was far more curious about his father's secret, but somehow, he knew that he must respect the Old Man's admonition—if not forever, at least for a time. Nor did he dare ask his second mother about her hatred of the priest. She had walked out once already, and he looked forward to her visits more than he liked to admit. She also brought him bread, sometimes fresh from the oven, with a white knob of butter melting inside.

So, a safe topic of conversation. He told his mother that he really did love Ariqina. She nodded. "I know that. You always have. And I hate their sense of humor."

"Whose?" said Kandri, sitting up. "Are people making *jokes* about her?"

"Not people. The Gods. They make jokes of us all. Very cruel and senseless jokes."

"Well, there's nothing funny about it," said Kandri, confused. "She loved me too, Mother. Loves, I mean. All Mektu's talk about a secret engagement is just his craziness."

"Good!" she said brightly. "There's a bit of mercy, anyway."

"You and Papa don't like her much, do you?"

"Where in Ang's name did you get that idea?" asked his mother. "We love Ariqina. Both of us."

Kandri studied her a moment. She was smiling, but her eyes were moist, and she would not look at him directly. She was, he thought, more upset than the day they spoke about the priest.

"I hope you do," he said carefully, "because one day, I'm going to make her your daughter-in-law."

"Oh," she said, popping from the chair as if a spring had been released. "Oh, my. That's extraordinary. What a beautiful young man you are, Kandri. Goodbye!"

౮

Days became weeks. The negotiations had evidently failed. One of the guards began to demand half of everything Kandri's family brought him; when Kandri refused, the man reported that Kandri had lunged at him at mealtime, and in punishment he was denied all visitors for a month. The guard also confiscated all the books Kandri's family had brought to him to fill the empty hours—all save *The Five Atrocities*, which Kandri had by now read forward and backward.

His beard grew long. He paced the cell like an animal. When the month ended at last, his father brought seven-year-old Perch, his baby brother, to visiting hours. In the corridor, the same guard frisked Lantor Hinjuman, then crouched before the child, who was sucking his forefinger.

"Are you a good boy? Do you say your prayers each night? Or are you another lout like your brother in there? He smells bad, you know."

The boy took the finger from his mouth and poked him hard in the eye. Kandri and the Old Man broke into unfortunate laughter, Perch howled and put his head on the floor, the simpleton began to rub his genitals, and visiting hours were cancelled until the spring.

౮

On his eighty-first day of incarceration, the guard delivered half a sugar cake from Dyakra Hinjuman and a letter from Nyreti. His elder sister, who had never visited, informed him tersely that Cheema had won a maths competition, that the yellow hound had killed a neighbor's goose, that his father had made something explode in his workshop, and that Ang All-Merciful would *very certainly be sending you to hell.* Kandri wolfed down the cake, then turned the page over.

But in the meantime, it appears you shall go free.

Once more his heart leaped. Surely, this time the nightmare was ending. He waited until sundown; no one came. Through the long night that followed, he stared at the ceiling, sleepless, thinking of Ariqina and the city of Kasralys, wondering who would sell him a horse.

The next morning he sat against the bars, where he could see a slice of the corridor. He was so exhausted that he dozed, and when he woke, he felt a warm pressure against his shoulder. Mektu sat outside the cell, wide awake but slumped in almost the same posture, hands folded on his legs.

"Imagine," he said abruptly, "all of us out here going on with our lives, visiting you of course, but not able to change anything. Watching you rot in there for years, watching you get older, stiffer, like some animal forgotten in a cage."

"Thanks for cheering me up," said Kandri.

Mektu's eyes were distant. "It's all right, brother," he said. "I'm at peace with it now."

"You're at peace?" said Kandri. "Mek, just tell me what's going on. Nyreti says I'm to go free."

"Is that how she put it?"

Footsteps echoed in the corridor. Kandri pressed his face to the bars, saw the two men approaching, saw the deal they had struck as if it were written in the air.

"No, Mek," he whispered. "Hell, no. Get rid of them, please."

But Mektu just sat there, eyes sad and knowing. "Ten years is too long, Kan," he said.

The first man was their father. The second was the army captain who had lent him the book.

The choice was simple: enlistment for both brothers, and a clean record, all charges dropped. Or likely conscription for Mektu within the year—Valley youths were next on the army's list, the captain confided—and for Kandri, twelve years in jail.

"Twelve?"

The captain nodded. "Our discussions with Father Marz were not without incident."

The Old Man looked away. Kandri stared at his father's bald patch. Twelve years in this box. Twelve years of lice and hunger, frigid nights, howling dogs. Twelve years without Ariqina, without even the sensible hope that he could find her. There was no choice; he was caught like a rabbit in a snare. But . . . *Mektu?*

"Leave my brother out of this," he said to the captain. "I'll enlist. I'll do whatever you want. But not with him."

The Old Man shook his head. "The captain and I have been over this, Kandri. For days."

"Maybe you don't get along, need a break from each other?" says the captain. "Not to worry; we're used to that. We can assign you to different units."

"No!" cried Mektu.

"No," said Kandri, "that's not the point."

"What *is* the point, son? Mektu knows what he's getting into. Corporal Betali's letters made sure of that. He's healthy, he's quick, he's strong as a mountain lion."

"He's a dunce," said Kandri. "A dreamer; he loves this idiotic verse. You can't make a soldier out of someone like him."

Mektu's upper lip curled in rage. Before he could spit out a retort, the officer began to laugh.

"I've made soldiers of worse," he said.

Kandri looked at him helplessly. *No you haven't.*

"And volunteers get better appointments," said the captain, "You'll see less combat than the boys we drag kicking and screaming. When you sign, we'll hand your mother a nice little purse. And you, Kandri: when you return to the Valley one day, you'll ride in like a man, with full honors. Serve twelve years in here, and you'll crawl out pale and feeble, a washed-up bum no woman will look at, no mother speak of with pride. Is that the life for a man like you?"

Man, thought Kandri. He was not certain he merited the word.

"It was the best I could do, Kandri," said his father. "I'm sorry."

"Sorry?" said the captain, suddenly irate. "What is it with you Hinju-mans? The Prophet is offering you *much* more than a way out of prison." His eyes fixed on Kandri. "Did you read that book?"

Kandri took a deep breath. He nodded.

"Show me."

Kandri retrieved the book and tried to pass it through the bars. The captain shook his head. "Well thumbed, excellent. All I wanted to see." He leaned closer, holding Kandri with his gaze. "Her Radiance needs you, Hinjuman. The Važeks are still on our doorstep. What you read in that book is still happening to our people in the north. If we grow lazy, it will be happening here again by the moon's next quarter. Your sisters, your little brother, your second mother who loves you more than life itself—they will be *dead*. You understand me, son? Dead, or worse than that in the case of the girls, if men like you say no. And it won't end with our defeat. This is a war to save the Chiloto people, of course. But it's also a war for the salvation of Urrath.

"I won't lie. It will be rough. You and your brother will know sheer misery at times. But that's the way of the world, Hinjuman. Only the dead are free from pain. Those who hide from pain end up hiding from life, cowering behind the strong, until even their own kin have no use for them. They wither, like grass under a rock. They betray their own souls."

He looks the boys over again. "That's the key to all of this, my boys. The Prophet needs the strength of our arms, but she asks for something much greater. She asks us to give our souls. And in return, she makes our souls, like our bodies, stronger than all the pain in this world."

He spoke with such obvious sincerity that Kandri's scornful retorts died on his lips. Mektu looked at the captain, wide-eyed; the speech was new to him as well. Their father gazed at the grimy floor.

"Are you ready for a new life, Mr. Hinjuman?" asked the captain.

Kandri shook his head, but only slowly, as though he were struggling in a vat of glue. The captain smiled. He reached into his coat pocket and produced a key.

"The jailors entrusted me with this," he said, "and I trust you. Don't make me regret it. You're no runner, are you? Not a piss-yellow coward who would take this and flee?"

Once again, as if it were his only trick, Kandri shook his head.

"Good," said the captain, extending his hand through the bars. "I'll be here until the end of the week."

They left, his brother and father murmuring goodbyes. Kandri stood alone in the dim morning light, in one hand the book of atrocities, in the other the key to his cell.

ॐ

"Twenty-seven is finished! *Epulu besat!* Twenty-seven is complete!"

Kandri leaps from the chair. The voice is Dr. Skarrys's, bellowing from some adjacent room. Other voices answer, sharp and excitable, none of them in a language he understands.

Green light fills the room beyond the window. Half a dozen Xavasin-drans are dashing from one doorway to another, debating anxiously. One or two glance up at Kandri as though startled to find him still in the building. Elsewhere, doors slam and boots thump down corridors. Some kind of strident mechanical bell begins to ring. The piano player continues his performance, like a man deranged.

Click, whoosh: the door to the front room opens, and the nurse rushes in.

"Who the *hell* do you people think you are?" says Kandri. "I was locked in here like a dog."

The nurse has lost a good deal of her composure. "You must come with me now," she says.

"Where's my brother, damn you?"

"The procedure is concluded. Twenty-seven will be returned to you. Oh, hurry, brother escort, please."

"Returned to me? Alive or in a fucking box?"

She crosses to the far door, not glancing once at the wreckage of the room. Kandri follows, biting back another outburst. They enter a narrow hallway. The green lamps in the ceiling flicker. Two neatly uniformed sentries march by at an intersection, spears in hand.

At the hallway's end, she opens another door, seizes his elbow, pulls him swiftly through.

"Kandri!"

"Oh, Gods, Mek!"

342

Kandri rushes forward: Mektu is standing in the room's center, fully dressed, beaming. Dr. Skarrys is at his side, squinting at a thermometer. The brothers embrace. "Careful!" snaps the doctor. "Twenty-seven is not to stretch or twist for a week."

He is wearing a pale green smock. Alone of all the Xavasindrans, he seems untouched by panic, indifferent to the strident mechanical bell. High on his forehead is a strange brass eyepiece held with a strap. A drop of blood glistens on the lens.

"I'm healed, brother, look." Mektu raises his shirt, and Kandri finds himself almost in tears. The swelling is gone, the flesh already returning to a healthier color. Black stitches, fine as needlework, close both the entry and exit wounds. Ang is merciful. Tebassa has not betrayed them.

"Your brother is fortunate to be alive," says Skarrys. "The infection had spread downward, into the lining of the intestines." He glances irritably at Kandri. "Those are . . . tubes, if you like. Very important tubes."

The brothers exchange a look. "We've seen them, Doctor," says Kandri. "On the battlefield."

"They must be treated with the greatest care," says Skarrys, "and that is how I treated them, brother escort, despite your howls and yammers. My work was impeccable. If I had not intervened, he would have died within a week. If you please, nurse."

He moves to a washbasin, and the nurse, frantic, bustles to his side. Kandri starts to babble his thanks, but the doctor cuts him off.

"*Impeccable* does not mean *perfect*, you understand. When disease has intruded this far into a body, not even Xavasindran medicine can guarantee its total removal."

The nurse pours water over his hands, pats them dry with a towel. Kandri sees that her own hands are trembling.

"As a precaution," says the doctor, "I have left a benign resin inside the wound. The substance kills putrefaction but is quite harmless otherwise. Eventually, his body will dissolve the resin into the blood." He removes the eyepiece from his forehead, frowns at the spot of blood. "I expect no complications—provided you behave yourself, twenty-seven.

No hard labor, no horseplay or running or the like. That wound must not reopen."

The nurse tugs at his arm, speaks in a whisper that verges on a squeal. Skarrys responds with a noncommittal grunt.

"Doctor?" says Mektu.

"What is it, twenty-seven?"

"In school, they taught us that *every* Urrathi carries the Plague inside, like a seed. Is that true?"

"Nearly all, yes," says Skarrys. "It resides in the tissue of the lungs."

"Then are you risking your own lives, by coming here to fight it?"

"Not at all," says Skarrys, still bustling with his tools. "Among Urrathis, as I told you, roughly one soul in eight thousand is susceptible to the Plague. In the Outer World, there is a mirror phenomenon: one in eight thousand or so is immune. Only those rare few may apply to join the Xavasindrans. As you can observe, most of us belong to the same clan."

"A yellow-skinned clan?"

"Obviously. Kvinuks, we call ourselves."

"And do Kvinuks get the Plague caught in their lungs, like we do? Are you a danger to your own people when you return?"

Skarrys, struck by the question, turns to look at him at last.

"We are a danger," he says, "and for that reason, we too are quarantined. On an island in the middle of the sea. We remain there in small cottages, keeping apart even from each other. We test ourselves weekly, inhale astringents, cough into tubes. Gradually, our lungs eliminate the spore. When we pass five tests in sequence, we are declared Plague-free and may board the next ship for home."

"How long does this . . . process, keep you stuck there?" asks Kandri.

"Three years, normally, but in some cases, as many as twelve."

"Twelve *years*? You'd give twelve years of your life to fight the Plague?"

"If necessary."

"I hope you're paid well at least," says Kandri. "Are you, if you don't mind me asking?"

But Skarrys does mind, apparently. He turns his back on them again. "The clerk will return your weapons in the vestibule. Provided you have not lost your coin."

ॐ

Minutes later, they are standing in the same long, windowless alley where they took leave of Stilts. The iron door clangs shut behind them, and the warmth of late afternoon bathes their skin. Mab Makkutin. Even in this sterile alley, he can smell her cookfires, her rubbish and latrines. It is like returning to Urrath from some cold foreign netherworld.

A world they could destroy just by breathing on it. A world they'll never see.

Mektu straps his machete to his belt. "You should let me keep that," says Kandri. "You'll forget, and tear your stitches. And then Eshett will kill you."

Mektu shakes his head. "I won't forget. And I still want people to think I'm dangerous."

"You damn well are."

The brothers lock eyes, then burst out laughing, stupid with relief. Mektu has just stepped back from a cliff.

"Mek," says Kandri. "Those tools of theirs, those lights. What in Jekka's hell are they?"

"That cold," says Mektu, shaking his head.

"Exactly, the cold. Not even the old man could explain that. Are they magicians? They seem more like . . . tinkers, mechanics, I don't know what. Brother, can the whole Outer World be full of those people, those tools, while we're stuck here inside the Quarantine like pigs in a pen?"

Noises in the distance: a wash of shouts and bellows, a crash, the nicker of a horse. "I *really* think we should leave," says Mektu.

They rush down the alley. It is hours past noon. They will have no time for a proper rest at Yehita's farmhouse. Perhaps, thinks Kandri, they can at least wolf down a meal, stretch out for five minutes on the good woman's floor, watch the dog and the chickens, pretend for a moment that the world still makes sense.

The cries grow louder. "A fight's broken out," says Mektu. "Bit early for drunks, isn't it?"

"Mek," says Kandri, "what were *you* shouting for, when they took you away?"

Mektu's glance is confused. "I didn't shout," he says.

"The hell you didn't! '*No, please, take it away!*' You scared me out of my pants."

"Kandri," says Mektu, "I didn't shout. They gave me some kind of liquor, and it made me sleep. I never felt a thing."

Kandri stops in his tracks. A vague dread, like a scream from some locked and distant chamber, is stealing over him. The voice was Mektu's: of that he has no doubt. What is happening? Can his brother be lying again? He glances over his shoulder at the cold iron door. But the Medical Mission is sealed like a fortress. The Xavasindrans are finished with them.

At the mouth of the alley, something gleams on the cobbles. Kandri peers at the dark red puddle.

"*Jeshar*, that's fresh blood."

"Charming," says Mektu. "Turn right."

For three blocks they walk in silence. A boy sprints past them, a worried-looking dog at his heels. They see more blood: this time, a smeared handprint on a whitewashed door. All the while the distant shouts crash and echo, waves among rocks.

Kandri is impressed by his brother's calm. Perhaps the drug has not quite worn off? How useful to have a supply of that, something you could, every so often, slip into his tea—

Mektu jumps with great violence.

"*Harach,*" cries Kandri. "What's the matter? Stepped on a nail?"

"Oh, Gods," says Mektu.

"Your stitches? Your wound?"

"No, Gods, shit."

"Mektu—"

"We're dead, Kandri! Flaming shit!"

"Mektu, talk to me!"

"The man who was watching you, with the beard. We damned well *have* seen him before. He's the third Tirmassil, the one Atau left behind with the camel when we descended that ridge."

"No," says Kandri. "No way in hell. That man's beard—"

"Was black and white, like a skunk. He must have dyed it, Kan. It's him, think, you know it is."

"Oh, fuck." The mouth, the forehead. Mektu is right. And the man fled from the marketplace like wolves were at his heels. Or like a man about to earn the prize of a lifetime, if only he can run fast enough to claim it.

But run to whom?

"You never listen," says Mektu. "I *told* you, didn't I? We should have just gotten out of here."

They quicken their pace. Bells are ringing in some temple or tower, anxious and discordant. Kandri tries to reverse the steps that brought them to the Xavasindrans, but the task proves hopeless. They have entered the city in the gray light of dawn; now the day is ending and the shadows are long and black. The streets meander; all the smooth white walls look alike. There are people about, but they are wary and in haste: some running with armloads of vegetables, others dragging children by the hand. One man carries an old woman on his back, frail as a hatchling; another locks a chain around a gate. Quite a few people steal glances at the sky, as though wondering how long they have before the night closes in.

The shouts and cries grow nearer. Is this the tailors' district they passed in the morning? Kandri thinks so, but Mektu says they are still too far south. At last Kandri collars a street vendor pushing his cart of limes at a run, and demands directions to the Dawn Gate. The man waves frantically, rattles off lefts and rights. His headscarf trails a yard of muslin; a bruise discolors his cheek.

"What's all the brawling about?" Kandri demands.

"Brawling!" cries the man. "Is *that* what you'd call it?"

Before the brothers can answer, a high, murderous yowl echoes along the street. The vendor flees, abandoning his wares. Kandri, in a horror of recognition, grabs Mektu and pulls him down behind the cart. At that very instant, an enormous gray *sivkrin* appears at the corner. On its back rides a Rasanga.

The Prophet's commando holds a long spear, five feet of which are dark with gore. The big cat snarls again. Kandri hugs his brother ferociously, a hand clamped over his mouth. The cart is barely large enough to hide them both.

They do not breathe. Beyond the cart's edge, the long shadows of rider and mount stretch toward them. Kandri can almost feel them debating which way to turn. Then a second mounted shadow appears beside the first.

Mektu looks like a horse in a lightning storm, wild with fear. Kandri mashes their cheeks together, closing his eyes. *We can't beat them. We can't outrun them. If they come this, way we die. If you make a scene, we die.* But his brother is as still as marble, and the Rasanga pass on.

They get up. Kandri's limbs are shaking. "They're here for us, Mek," he says. "Someone's tipped them off."

"Atau's man," says Mektu. "Who else? Old Skunk-Beard must have sent word north, to the Seventh Legion. Or ridden there himself, like the wind. But how many can there be?"

An excellent question. The Seventh Legion is twelve thousand strong. But it is not a mounted legion, and no foot soldiers could have reached Mab Makkutin so swiftly.

Kandri looks at his brother. "They must have a special detachment. Riders, I mean."

"They have eighty-six horsemen," says Mektu.

"You're making that up."

"The hell I am. Eighty-six Shessel, and four Rasanga with sandcats. We had a cooking order last month. We smoked meat for the Seventh."

"All right. Ninety riders." Kandri blinks, dizzy with fear. "But they wouldn't send all ninety, would they? And even if they did, it's not enough to assault the city. So what the fuck are they up to?"

"Maybe they didn't come from the north," says Mektu. "Maybe they're what's left of the Wolfpack that chased us across the Stolen Sea."

"In which case, there's even fewer of them," says Kandri. But his words bring no comfort. They have killed men of that Wolfpack, with the help of Ornaq vultures. Those left alive have even more blood to avenge.

They move on, no longer seeking the avenue, clinging to the darker streets. Many others are doing the same: by the next block, they have joined a stream of frightened men and women rushing the Gods know where. The white homes give way to the taller, darker hulks of old warehouses and counting-houses, relics of the city of fisherfolk. By what he gleaned from the vendor's babble, Kandri thinks they must be close to the Dawn Gate. But is there any hope of exiting there? If even a dozen of the Prophet's forces have reached the city, surely every gate will be watched?

Atau! One man, one greedy coward. But his malice still clung to them, even after his death. And what if the black-bearded Tirmassil found an accomplice? Some common grafter, paid to dog their heels all the way to the old woman's farmhouse? Chindilan and Eshett and the girl might already be—

Shut up. Keep moving. Get your brother out of here alive.

There, dead ahead, is the wall at last. The Dawn Gate is just visible, a few blocks farther north; the bells they've been hearing are in the turrets to either side. The avenue is crowded and jostling, but the heart of the turmoil is at the gate itself.

When they reach the wall, Kandri sees that its inner face has been abandoned more fully to the ravages of time: vines sprouting everywhere, stones cracked and fallen, planks bridging gaps in the walkway under the parapet. But the sentries, armed and numerous, are on duty all the same. Kandri pulls his brother back into an alcove.

"We can't let *them* see us, either," he says. "They may be under attack, but that doesn't mean they won't hand us over. For all we know they're seeking us desperately."

"We still have to get through that gate," says Mektu.

True enough, but around the gate the crowd is roaring. They wait until the nearest sentry's back is turned, then dash for the next hiding place: the doorway of yet another grand, decrepit warehouse. From here the gate is hidden, but they can see most of the plaza before it. The crowd is hundreds strong. Townsfolk, mostly: young men with machetes and clubs, but at the vanguard stands a large detachment of sentries. To Kandri's surprise, they look rather formidable, with their ring mail and lowered spears. He cannot decide whether that is good news or bad.

Mektu taps his shoulder: the door behind them is unlocked. They slip unseen into the dark of the warehouse, drawing the door shut behind them. The building is abandoned, hollowed out, reeking of bird dung and mold. Although its shell is stone, the interior is all wood and has not fared well. The high, vaulted ceiling has mostly collapsed, affording dim views of a second story. Cries and bellows from the street echo weirdly around them.

"Useless," says Mektu. "They've bricked the windows over."

Kandri points through the gaping hole. "Not up there, they haven't. Find a staircase. I want to know what the hell's going on."

The staircase is a horror: the framing beams long since plundered, the treads rotting out. "No climbing for you," says Kandri. "Stay here. Watch the door for me."

"I'll be fine," says Mektu.

"Damn right you will. Watch the fucking door."

The staircase sags like a hammock as Kandri climbs—first gingerly, then in a wild scramble as he feels the structure yearning to give way. With a last sickening bounce, he gains the second story. But the floor here is equally terrifying, a crust around a gaping hole, the planks flexing and sinking like piano keys underfoot.

Hugging the wall, he makes his way to the building's north face and crawls the last few yards to the window. Carefully, a turtle from a shell, he lifts his head above the sash.

The Dawn Gate is closed. Under the great red arch, the doors of latticed iron have been swung into place and crossed with two beams of steel. The beams are clearly a latter-day addition to the defenses: they look strong if rather crude beside the majesty of the older structures. Two enormous locks secure them to the turrets flanking the Dawn Gate. A battering ram might rip them from the old stone, but nothing lesser would.

Hundreds of sentries and a like number of townsfolk cluster near the gate. Outside, Soldiers of Revelation are milling about on horseback. They are indeed Shessel, riders like those who accompanied Garatajik, and one of them holds aloft the standard of the Seventh Legion. It is true, then: these men have ridden from the Aricoro front in the north. The riders are shouting, gesticulating, demanding entrance. Some have nocked arrows to bows.

Among them Kandri sees but one Rasanga: a huge woman upon a caterwauling *sivkrin*. How did the others enter the city? Did they storm another gate, or fight their way in before these iron doors could be closed?

And why are so many people glancing up at the sky?

Kandri creeps to the east side of the building. Here, he can see a longer stretch of the wall. Yes, the inner side has been let go; in some places, the stone and masonry have collapsed in piles to the street, like shards of an eroding cliff. The sky above the wall is a dark, bruised orange. Already he can see a few early stars.

"Brother."

"*Harach!*" Kandri nearly jumps out of his skin. Mektu has climbed the stairs and crept to his elbow. "Damn your sneaky ass! I told you to wait!"

"Brother, quickly. Come and see."

Mektu leads him back to the windows overlooking the square. Down the long avenue, a second mob is approaching. Like the first, it is a mix of townsfolk and soldiers, but many of the latter are riding the lean, high-stepping horses of the Lutaral. And at the heart of the procession is a breathtaking creature: enormous, slate-gray, with ears like torn flags and a nose like a beheaded python.

"That's an elephant," says Mektu. "That's *Talupéké's* elephant! Vuceku, wasn't it?"

"Vuceku," says Kandri, nodding.

"That thing could kill a *sivkrin* with a toss of its head."

The animal is draped in finery and foil armor; its tusks are painted a brilliant aquamarine and capped with gold. Two handlers with iron goads sit astride its shoulders, and behind them, upon a crimson saddle, rides the Ursad of Mab Makkutin.

He has not gone to fat as Mektu imagined. On the contrary, he is large and imposing, with straight black locks, a neat spade of a beard, and a bright shield with a version of the old Imperial bull embossed at its center. Under his right arm is a simple spear, like those wielded by his guards.

The crowd at the gate falls back, making room for the city's master. The soldiers outside merely wait. As he reaches the center of the square, the Ursad lifts a hand. The procession stops, the bells fall silent, the shouting dies away. The Ursad gazes down at the soldiers of the Prophet. Then he reaches beneath his tunic and draws out a brass key. It is nearly as long as his forearm.

"I think you hope for this," he says, "but you shall not have it, animals. You stand at the gate of Mab Makkutin, and here just one man's word is law. We have been pleased to make common cause with your Prophet these several years. But today, you have marred that friendship, and we do not soon forget. I warn you now: withdraw!"

The crowd roars, shaking weapons above their heads. Outside the gate, the Soldiers of Revelation make no response at all. The Ursad waits, looking somewhat at a loss. Once more he raises his hand.

"To come thus, demanding, threatening?" he says. "To smuggle killers on hell-cats into our midst? To shed our blood, upon our very streets? Think well on what you do here, little instigators! Your Prophet will not reward you for squandering the love between us."

Once more the crowd erupts. Kandri winces, closing his eyes. *The love between us. Gods, man, you don't understand her at all.*

The roaring lasts. Suddenly, the lone Rasanga swings to the ground, tosses the *sivkrin's* lead to one of the riders, and walks up to the iron bars. When she turns her head, Kandri sees four livid, parallel scars at an angle across her cheek, like something a bear might inflict.

The warrior stands there, enduring the howls and heckles of the towns-folk, and even a few rocks that clang against the iron bars. At last the Ursad himself calls for silence, and the crowd obeys.

"The Enlightened One," says the Rasanga, "has not sent me here to bargain or to beg. The Twin Abominations must die. Unlock this gate; we will find them and be gone. Oppose us further, and it will not go well for you this night."

"I have two thousand soldiers, woman!" snaps the Ursad. "You will need something more than thirty horsemen and five braggarts on *sivkrin* to back up your threats."

"I do have something more," says the Rasanga. "And I do not threaten; I inform. Ursad, can you not sense prophecy at work? Look at the sky, listen to the murmur of your people. They proclaim what you yourself fear to admit. The Time of Madness approaches. Would you hasten it? Would you be the spark that sets this town ablaze?"

"Rubbish and lies," says the Ursad. "The fate of Mab Makkutin is her own. You will not frighten us with children's tales."

This time, there is far less cheering. Quite a number of the townsfolk make surreptitious blessing-gestures. The Ursad clears his throat. "What *exactly* do you want?" he says. "Speak plainly. We do not care for mysticism here."

"You will surrender the Abominations," says the Rasanga, "or you will not, and all the same they will be found. Which path do you choose?"

"Abominations," says the Ursad. "I tell you, we know not of what you speak. And we harbor no enemies of the Prophet in Mab Makkutin. That is a further insult."

"Open the gate," says the Rasanga. "Every moment you delay heaps more misery upon your people."

"Do you bear no scroll or letter from your Prophet, woman? I will entertain a missive if it bears her seal."

"No time," says the Rasanga. "Our orders came on wings. Open the gate, you nattering fool! This is the last time I shall—"

Her head snaps to the right. Someone has thrown a rock, which by ill luck has passed through the bars and struck her face, right on the cheek with the scars.

Cries of fury behind her: the cavalry urge their horses up to the gate. But the Rasanga lifts a hand to still them. A stripe of blood runs from cheek to collarbone, but she shows no sign of pain. In utter silence, she gazes at the Ursad and his guard. Then she turns and walks away.

The brothers look at each other, and for once, the understanding between them is perfect. "Let's get the hell out of here," says Kandri.

"Wish I'd thought of that."

"No point in checking the other gates," Kandri says, ignoring the jab. "We'll have to go over the wall." He looks sharply at Mektu. "Without climbing. Or mixing you up with a fight."

"Climb without climbing." Mektu gives a snort of despair.

"I didn't say *climb*, I said *go over*. We can do it if we get our hands on some rope. Tie you a loop to sit in, brace the rope on the parapet, lower you down."

"How do you plan to get me up there to begin with?"

"Where the hell would I have gotten a plan?"

"Kandri, what did you *do* for all those hours?" says Mektu. "Were you daydreaming, thinking about that nurse's ass?"

Movement below: the Prophet's soldiers are falling back. The townsfolk roar and jeer. For a moment, Kandri can see no one beyond the gate: only the well-trodden earth, and a yellow butterfly stitching back and forth between the bars as though flaunting its freedom.

The mob falls silent.

A small figure is approaching the gate from the outside. It is a child, a girl, so thin and slight that a stiff wind could almost bear her away. She might be eleven or twelve, stands no higher than a man's elbow. Her eyes are famished, her hair long and filthy. She wears a tattered gown that drags in the dust. Although ragged, the gown is lace-laden and frilled, the attire of a half-starved child bride.

But that is not what stops the crowd from breathing. Every bit of the girl—hands, face, lips, hair—is white. Not pale: white. The hard white of marble. The submarine white of a fish's belly. The cold, bright white of the moon.

Both men recoil, dropping below the window sash. Mektu grabs his brother's arm. *"What the living honest fuck is that?"*

Kandri forces himself to look again. The tiny girl has reached the gate. She pauses, gazing up at the ancient stone. All at once, Kandri feels what he felt in Eternity Camp, in the octagonal courtyard with the palanquin: a flood of guilt and terror closing over his head.

"The White Child," he says.

"Some kind of devil!" says Mektu. "It is, isn't it? Why would they bring it here?"

The girl lowers her chin, looks straight at the Ursad, and now Kandri sees that her eyeballs are not white but exactly the opposite: a solid, lustrous black. When she blinks, the blackness vanishes a moment under luminous eyelids. The effect is somehow obscene.

Turning sideways, the girl passes one arm through the bars. Then one leg. The squeeze is tight, but she manages, gown and all. Once through, she walks without hesitation toward the sentries.

Atop his elephant, the Ursad forces out a laugh. "What is this? So you have a freak of nature in your keeping? Do you think we are peasants, to frighten into submission? Hold that creature at spearpoint, men of the Guard."

But the Guard, it seems, is afflicted by the same terror Kandri feels. The man directly in the Child's path falters first, sidling backward against his comrades. Others follow suit, and then the whole crowd is parting, as if they cannot bear the scrutiny of those eyes. Many look ashamed of their cowardice, yet still they retreat. Horses begin to nicker and prance. Only the elephant is still.

The Ursad barks at his men. As though shaken from a dream, ten or twelve leap forward and point their spears at the girl. But once more, something breaks in them. Spears droop, and soldiers step backward, grimacing with fear and shame.

Now the girl stands before the elephant, looking absurdly small. That trunk could lift her like a weed; those painted tusks could break her every bone. Gazing at the Ursad, she lifts a stick-like arm, hand spread wide as though begging for alms.

"The key," shouts the Rasanga from the gate. "Surrender it, Ursad. There is no other way."

"Why do you stand there?" shouts the Ursad at his men. "Drive her off. If she resists, stake her body to the earth!"

The Child hisses at the Ursad. With a spastic motion, the captain of the Guard leans forward and jabs at the Child with his spear. The girl's only response is to lower her hand to the elephant's leg.

At her touch, a violent shudder passes through the animal. It throws its head back, lifts its trunk to heaven—

And dies. The front legs buckle; the men on its back are pitched like dice into the street. The animal topples forward, tusks scraping the cobbles, and falls with a leaden *boom* onto its side.

Absolute panic ensues. The Guard scatters; the townsfolk stampede. One of the elephant's handlers has been crushed under the creature's shoulder; the other is trampled by the mob. Two guards rush to lift the Ursad, bloodied and barely conscious, but when they see the Child approaching they simply drop him and flee. Kandri and Mektu kneel by the window, gasping and swearing. Mektu is the first to come to life.

"Get up! Move!"

Kandri lets his brother haul him to his feet. They edge around the broken floor. "Wait, wait!" hisses Kandri, astonished at himself.

"Like hell! Get your ass up!"

"Mek, this could be it. Our only chance."

"*Chance?*"

"She's going to take that key to the Rasanga. They're going to open the gate and charge in, searching for us. But they won't expect us to be right here, will they?"

"You said we had to go over the wall."

"Maybe not," says Kandri. "Maybe we can just . . . slip out."

He drags Mektu back to the window. The Ursad's body lies face down in the plaza beside his elephant. The White Child is pawing at his clothes.

"Your stitches," says Kandri. "You're not supposed to run."

"Well fuck that up and down!"

"Just be as careful as you can. Please, brother. I want you to live."

The Child has found the enormous key. She rises, holding it with both hands, and starts to walk toward the gate. The Rasanga stands waiting, stretching her hand through the bars. Behind her, the Shessels' stallions nicker and prance.

Six feet from the gate, the White Child stops walking. Her head lifts, searching; it is as if she has been startled by an odor, or a noise somewhere. The Rasanga calls out, but the girl ignores her. Extremely slowly, she turns around.

Her black eyes fix on the warehouse.

The key falls from her hand.

She tilts her head. Listening, fascinated. Her lips move as though she is sounding out words. Then she speaks, and the voice is the same little girl's voice Kandri heard from the palanquin in Eternity Camp. And that is bad enough, but what she says—

Gods of death, what she says.

It is just one word. Impossible, ludicrous, depraved. The brothers look at each other again, and once more Kandri sees his own feelings mirrored in Mektu's face: denial. A total incapacity to believe.

The Rasanga gropes for the key with her sword.

Then the Child starts to walk toward the warehouse, and horror takes them so completely that they cannot even gasp. They just run. The staircase cracking and shattering as they slide down its length. The door sticking horribly, the door stuck fast and every lower window bricked, tears of horror on Mektu's face, tears in Kandri's own eyes, *what the fuck, what in the Pits,* until they remember that the door swings outward, not in, and they fling it wide and burst into the street—

She is there, ten paces away. Her flesh aglow like white embers. She lifts both hands and smiles, and her mouth, like her eyes, is a black hole as she speaks the word again.

Kandri surrenders any thought but flight from this nightmare. He runs with his arm around Mektu, trying to steady him, expecting to smell the blood of a reopened wound, crying uncontrollably although he can't say why, do any wounds heal, is evil done ever truly erased, and what was it, Papa, what did you do, what sin that took root in the mind of this girl, this monster, to make her turn to us and speak your name?

ఴ

Perhaps it will end as it began, that night with Ojulan's corpse steaming at his feet: in darkness and panic, an unforeseen horror thrust upon him, a child's voice ringing in his ears. But then at least Mektu was unhurt, and Kandri knew a way out, and no search for them had started.

They are running in near-darkness now, Kandri supporting his brother. Avoiding crowds, avoiding lamplight, glancing over their shoulders for the creature that pursues them with calls of "*Lantor, Lantor,*" in that drawn-out singsong voice, as though summoning their father to a game. At times, they pull ahead, and the voice disappears. Then a wall or a locked gate stops them cold, and suddenly she is closing: that lambent, stick-thin, dead-eyed girl. From the left or the right, or directly behind. Never stopping, never blinking, reaching for them like a prize.

They pause for breath in an alcove. Each brother studies the other's face, searching for answers, reasons, some least thread to tug.

"She thinks one of us is Papa."

"I know. I know."

They keep the wall in sight, hoping against hope for an open gate. "Him and his fucking secrets," says Mektu. "I hate the Old Man."

"Don't say that."

"I hope he didn't fake his death. I hope it was real. How could he send us off into the army, knowing *that* was waiting for us, and not say a thing? You'd never do that, Kandri. No decent person would do that."

"Maybe he didn't know."

Mektu shoots him a disgusted look. "That creature knows his *first name*. She says it like he's her fucking sweetheart."

Kandri has no answer. Just weeks before, they had laughed about the Old Man's ways. But there was no laughter that first night in prison, when his father came to him alone. *Something I should never tell. And if you care about Ariqina, or your family, you'll never ask me again.*

So Kandri hadn't. Was he right to keep that silence? To give his trust once more, when the Old Man so clearly refused to do the same?

A flash of light. Sudden shouting. Kandri whirls and sees a red glow above the wall. The cries are from guards along the parapet, gazing down at the plain.

"Fun to be had out there as well," says Mektu.

"That's not the worst of it," says Kandri. "We're going to be left behind. The others must already be on their way to that hill."

"Uncle Chindilan won't abandon us."

"Uncle Chindilan's not in charge," says Kandri, "and he heard what Black Hat said about being late. He knows it won't do any good to wait for us at Yehita's house. No, he'll go straight to the Hermit and expect us to do the same."

"Black Hat doesn't much like us, does he?"

"Why should he?" says Kandri. "What have we done for him besides— oh, *Jeshar.*"

The White Child has rounded the corner.

Lantor. I see you.

They run. At least the Child does not run. If only they can reach the plains, put miles between them. Did she walk all the way from Eternity Camp, Kandri wonders? Straight over the Yskralem, leading the Rasanga, tracking the brothers like a hound on the scent? No, impossible. She had not even been aware of them at first. It was only when Kandri gazed at her, when his mind filled with the horror of what he was seeing, that she had sensed him, turned, and called their father's name.

Mektu stops dead.

"Do you see where we are?" he says. "The Xavasindrans' clinic, where we started. Look, that's the alley right there."

"Gods *damn,*" says Kandri, for his brother is right. "We're going to run out of wall. It turns a corner soon, back toward the cliffs."

"And she could trap us in that corner," says Mektu.

Another burst of red light. This time, Kandri sees it plainly: a shooting star, lovely, dazzling, with a bright tail of crimson. But the star does not wink out. It plummets, blazing still, at a sharp angle like a downward sword-stroke, and vanishes behind the wall. For an instant, the light flares brighter than ever, and the men on the ramparts let out a wail. Then the light goes out.

"I think it struck the earth," says Mektu.

"A shooting star can't strike the earth."

"Yes, it can. Read a book."

The thought comes in a flash: he will never read another book, never learn if Mektu is mad or well informed, never stargaze with Ariqina or show their children the night sky. No matter how long death walks at your elbow, the thought of it can still pounce and astonish. And that is how it will happen, finally. In the long storm of arrows, one at last knows your name.

Somewhere off to their right, a *sivkrin* growls. Ahead, another cat gives an answering cry. Two Rasanga, very close. And that, yes. That is the pounding of hooves.

"They've opened the Dawn Gate," says Mektu. "The whole force must be looking for us now."

Soldiers ahead, soldiers to their right, and behind them a girl who kills with a touch. They flee in the only direction remaining: straight to the foot of the wall.

There is no gate in sight. But not far to their left is another spot where the inner wall is crumbling. Or, rather, *has* crumbled, into a steep, leaning hill of rocks and masonry, almost as high as the outer façade.

They scurry closer. Two sentries pass overhead, bearing no light, picking their way along the broken parapet. Kandri sees no others sentries, but lamplight shines from the windows of a turret some five hundred yards to the south.

The rocks are massive; the pile has the look of a deathtrap. Kandri tugs at a great chunk of stone at shoulder height. It does not visibly yield, but his hand senses a looseness there, and gravel pelts his feet.

"Mek," he says, "can you climb this?"

He feels heartless, putting the question to his brother. But Mektu's thoughts have run in the same direction. "Watch me," he says, and begins to scramble like a goat.

"Be careful, damn it!"

At first, the going is simpler than he feared. But the higher they climb, the more the pile narrows, and the more unstable it becomes. They slow their ascent. Then slow further. Rocks grind and shift; gravel sluices like water around their feet.

"Gods," whispers Kandri, "this whole thing could come down."

Mektu says nothing. Kandri can sense his terror: this is a far greater danger than the rotten stair. The ground feels distant, but the parapet is still six feet above. He reaches up for the next handhold, and a stone the size of a bucket gives way. The whole pile trembles as it crashes to the street.

"Don't . . . move," whispers Kandri.

"I won't," says his brother.

They are two flies on a sleeper's lips. A very light sleeper. Kandri looks his brother in the eye.

"I'm going to pull myself up on the platform, then turn and lift you. By the armpits. You protect those stitches with your hands."

"All right."

Kandri reaches up to the walkway, probing for a handhold. Stones move underfoot, but not too many, or too large. If only Mek were like this more often. If only he would say, *All right*. Life would be sweeter, the struggle more bearable, his urge to kick the fool in the face would—

"Hinjuman!"

Kandri's head snaps around. Three Chiloto soldiers are scaling the rubble behind them. Awkwardly, gingerly, their horses abandoned in the street. "I told you!" crows the same voice. "It's them! The Abominations! Follow the White Child, I said—"

"Betali?" says Mektu. "That's you, isn't it?"

"Mek!" cries the second soldier. Kandri winces, but there are the grouse-wing ears to prove it. The man is Betali, his brother's best friend.

"They really did let you join the cavalry," says Mektu, his voice almost proud.

"Mek, Mek," says Betali, "you're a traitor. Oh, Mek. You have to die."

"Shut your mouth and watch your balance!" snaps the third soldier, an officer by the tone he takes. "And you, blood traitors: you know it's over, come down. There's no way off that wall."

"How could you do it?" says Betali. "How could you shed their holy blood?"

"I didn't mean to."

"You cut Lord Ojulan to pieces," says Betali. "And Lord Garatajik. You stuck a knife in his chest."

They are within ten feet. Debris cascades at their every movement, but somehow their confidence is unshaken.

"Betali," says Mektu, helpless. "You and I, we're—"

"No, fucker, no! I'm not your friend anymore, I can't be."

A catch in his voice. Kandri gropes along the platform overhead.

"If you reach the wall, the city guard will only kill you," says the officer. "Come down, and we'll slay you painlessly. I'll tell the army you fought us to the end."

"No, he won't!" shouts Betali suddenly. "They'll torture you. Stab yourselves, stab yourselves or jump! The things they're planning—"

"Betali," says Kandri, "is Garatajik dead?"

The soldiers lunge. With a groan, Kandri pulls himself onto the walkway, rolls, grabs his brother by the shirt. Rocks are sliding, Betali and the third soldier snatch at Mektu's feet, Mektu kicks and flails. Then the whole face of the slope peels away like a rind.

The horses bolt. The soldiers' cries are stillborn, dust choking them even before they are crushed, even before their bodies vanish from sight. Kandri, veins popping, heaves his brother onto the wall.

"He touched my foot, Kan."

"They're dead. Don't worry."

"He touched my foot."

Mektu sobs like a baby in his arms.

ଚ୦

The officer was right, of course: the wall is sixty feet high and perfectly sheer on its outer face. How in Ang's name are they to descend?

Kandri looks north to the Dawn Gate: twenty or more Shessel are stationed by the iron doors, which have indeed been opened. Atop the wall, still distant, a few lantern-bearing figures are moving their way. He cannot tell if they are the city's soldiers or the Prophet's. What difference will it make?

Night has fallen, but the plain is alive with light. Some of the shops and stalls of the Desert Market are on fire; the braver merchants are fighting the blaze. North of the city, one of the lookout towers is burning like a torch. And in the dark miles between the city and the Arig Hills, other fires are burning, crescent-shaped and low.

Brush fires. And a stiff wind to fan them. Kandri says a quick prayer for the people of the Lutaral, their winter crops, their homes. He pulls his brother up and leads him south.

Falling stars. Tears of the Gods. But who are they crying for? And who is to blame? Not us, that's impossible. What God could weep for Ojulan?

He looks south along the wall. No one between them and the next turret, but the windows of the latter are alight.

"That way," he says, gesturing. "If there's a way out of this mess, it's through that turret, somehow."

Mektu wipes his nose on his sleeve. Kandri puts an awkward hand on his back.

"I'm sorry. About Betali."

"You called him a fool."

"I'm still sorry."

Mektu shrugs off his hand. Of course, Betali *was* a fool. Only a fool would risk closeness to Mektu at Eternity Camp. *And what does that make you, Kandri Hinjuman?*

They walk. The platform is spongy with moss, leaves, underbrush. Also pitch black. After a few yards, Mektu bends and lifts something from the stone.

"What is it?"

"A lamp. Hold it up."

"It's broken, Mek. And we shouldn't light it, anyway."

"Did I ask you to light it? Just take it, can't you do that much?"

Kandri takes the dead lamp. They shuffle on, increasingly dazzled by the turret's windows.

"Is there a bell?" says Mektu.

"In the turret? I don't know; I can't see one. What the hell does it matter? Don't tell me you have some crackpot—"

"Why did it have to be him, Kandri? Do you think he volunteered?"

Figures move past the windows. Not many. Perhaps just three or four. Kandri has the beginnings of a hunch about Mektu's intentions, knows he wouldn't dare such a thing himself.

They are thirty feet from the turret when the door bursts open.

"Oil!" snaps Mektu. "How much do you have? We're in the dark here, and you're lighting the place up like a grog hall."

His outburst appears to stun the young sentry in the doorway, both hands on his lowered spear. "We just have the one lantern, same as ever," he says. "Who are you? Where's Aggathon?"

"Where's Aggathon!" Mektu quickens his pace. "He's dead, that's where. They sent him for oil, and he fell in the dark and broke his skull. Now they've sent us, and *we* almost fell. Here, take our lamp and give us yours."

"He fell? Per Aggathon is *dead*?"

"Sons of bitches!" Mektu has actually started crying again. "Don't pretend he was *your* friend! Did he wait all day to see *you* in the dinner line? Were *you* the only one who could make him smile?"

"Dinner line?"

"Please," Kandri hears himself say, "just give us the lamp."

Mektu is snarling, one hand covering his wound. Behind the sentry, Kandri has a brief glimpse of the tower chamber, and a thick rope passing through floor and ceiling. A bellpull.

Two more guards join the first. They cluster in the doorway, peering into the dark. They are large, awkward, crowding each other, their spearpoints bobbing up and down.

Younger than us, thinks Kandri.

"Be reasonable," says the first sentry. "We can't give you our only lamp—"

"Then fill ours, jackass, and hurry up," says Kandri. He holds out the lamp, but it is his brother who seizes it. Brazen, Mektu swats the spears aside and thrusts the lamp into the sentry's hands.

The sentry turns sidelong. Light from the doorway falls on the lamp. It is a relic, a joke: the mantle crushed, the oil pan split open like a fruit. Mektu roars with indignation. He snatches it back, turns it, hurls it from the wall.

"Piece of shit! Stupid bastards! Why doesn't anyone cooperate?"

He throws the sentry from the wall. Two fistfuls of shirt, a vicious movement, release. The boy's face is horribly plain for an instant; he cries out, gripping the spear as though it were anchored somewhere. Kandri wants to be sick, but Mektu has already caught the other spears beneath his arm and is drawing his machete, and Kandri dives into battle at his side.

One of the men manages to draw a dagger, but there is little contest. As Mektu grubbily slashes and stomps one man to death, Kandri lunges for the other, takes off the arm that reaches for the bellpull, cuts his throat on the upswing, stops the scream, and feels a twist in his brain, a spasm that almost brings him down atop the corpse. Then he is sick, copiously sick, why should he live if the cost of staying alive is this butchery of innocents, if they are the weeds between him and the future, the path he must clear to Ariqina.

Dr. Ariqina. The healer.

She will hate him if she ever learns what he's become.

Mektu, steaming with blood to the elbows, reaches for the bellpull and begins to raise it, length after length. Kandri sinks to the floor. He cannot weep. He doesn't have that in him, suddenly. But he cannot go on killing, either. Not for his brother's sake, or his own.

"Kandri," says Mektu, "we're saved. This thing must be eighty feet long."

The coils of rope spill around them. Over the trickling puddles, the sectioned limbs.

Mektu drags the end of the rope out the door. "It will reach the ground, Kan," he calls. "Stand up. This is it."

Kandri studies the face of the man he's just killed. Bulging eyes, wide open mouth. It comes again: that inner twisting, that pinch.

Be reasonable.

Mektu puts a hand on his shoulder. Reading him, as only Mektu ever could.

"Do you know why you have to get up?" he says.

Kandri shakes his head.

"Because Garatajik was good to us, Kandri. And he put a letter in your hands."

He looks up: Mektu, this monster, his kin. But the truth of the monster's words cleaves down through Kandri's despair. He stands. He lifts his brother's shirt and sees that the stitches are intact. There is blood on Mektu's stomach, but none of it is his own.

Well, then: survival.

They wind the rope three times about a solid-looking section of parapet. "Now just tie a loop for me to stand in," says Mektu, "No length to spare, unless you want me dangling by the arms."

Kandri does not want him dangling by the arms. But lowering him is not easy: the rope binds and snags, and leaps when Kandri stops straining against it. Time and again, he must hurl himself with all his might against his brother's free fall, then relax one muscle at a time, waiting for the next jarring yank.

He leans into the effort, over the inner wall and the city. *Goodbye, Mab Makkutin. Never will be too—*

"No. Oh no."

The White Child is standing beside a corpse—beside the body of the sentry Mektu hurled from the wall. She bends and pokes at the shattered skull. Intrigued, she studies her fingers: scarlet on chalk. Then she looks up at Kandri with those dead black eyes. Kandri imagines, with instant horror, that she wears another's face. A familiar face, but whose?

Lantor. You would not help me escape.

Her lips do not seem to move, and yet he hears her. And suddenly, the sky is full of shooting stars. They scatter and flash like scarlet minnows; they skip and go dark and blaze again; they trickle earthward like rain on glass. For an instant, he is aware of nothing but their beauty, a heaven strange and infinite and open.

The Night of Blood. When the Gods weep tears of fire.

Distant shouts. Men with torches are running south along the wall, straight toward him. His brother is shouting too: can the word be *Horse*?

The rope goes slack: Mektu has reached the ground, or released the rope in any case. Kandri glances into the city once more. The White Child is smiling at him.

I'll find you.

An arrow sings past his ear: the men on the wall are closing. Kandri ties a clumsy timber-hitch in the rope, tests the knot. One shaving of the moon has risen above the Arig Hills. There, backlit, is the Hermit, where the General's men will be waiting. And there is Mektu, running east, arms flailing like a madman. Abandoning him.

Kandri tests the knot. Another arrow closer than the first. He steps backward off the wall.

It is not hard to catch up with Mektu, but it is very hard not to turn him by the shoulder, drive a fist into his teeth. *Ditch me now, will you? After everything? After what we've done today?*

He is reaching for that shoulder when Mektu hears him and turns. "What the fuck took you so long? There's a horse, help me catch it! Scared to death, poor thing, it must have bolted—"

Kandri hears the animal, snorting and stamping. They follow the sound into a stand of wiry trees, and there it is, a dark, skinny mare, hauling at reins snagged in the underbrush. Terrified, not wounded. And the stab in his chest is sharper than any other that evening, for it is hope again, that crazed persistent suitor, that tease who cannot break with him, or stay.

❧

The mare has no saddle. Also no wish to remain anywhere near Mab Makkutin. The trouble is not catching the lean animal or even riding her, with one arm clamped around Mektu's belly and the other gripping both reins. The problem is her fear. Once the reins are free, she runs like a mad thing, and it is all Kandri can do to guide her out of the advancing brush fires.

The next hours pass in a bewildering dream. A level mile they race over in silence, a blazing silo, a pair of jackals licking their lips. Three enormous shooting stars raking the heavens, the last unmistakably striking the northeast plain in a burst of fire, and a shockwave he feels through the body of the horse. A crowd of farmers joining hands around a temple in flames, singing a prayer-song. A ghoul tugging a corpse from the ground with hands and teeth.

Another soundless mile. Then hoofbeats, many hoofbeats, and a storm of riders engulfs them, charging west toward Mab Makkutin, sixty or seventy warriors flowing indifferent around them as though their horse were a stump. The light is too dim to see them clearly, but then a last red star streaks overhead, and Kandri sees a dozen faces he recalls from Tebassa's bunker, and with them Talupéké, mounted behind a stranger, a glazed ferocity in her smile.

No one looks at the brothers. The host is gone, and what are they to do but keep riding? They keep riding. There is no pursuit. The hill called the Hermit rears up, and the mare, not calm but exhausted at least, bears them quickly around its southern flank.

Kandri too is bone weary: they have been awake for some thirty hours, and he cannot keep his thoughts from the morbid question of when, if ever, they will again know a night of untroubled sleep. But there ahead, just as Stilts promised, is the rock wall. They halt the mare, and almost at once, the sound of other hooves reach their ears. Down from the shadowy hillside come five riders, their clothes and horses so dark that at first, Kandri can perceive no more than their eyes. At their lead is a small, broad-shouldered figure in a tight-fitting leather jerkin.

"The man in the hat sends his greetings," he says without preamble.

"We're not too late, then?" says Kandri.

"You are quite late," says the rider, "but three hours ago, our orders changed. If the moon had climbed another finger, we were to ride out and seek you."

"Seek us?" says Mektu. "I didn't think your boss particularly cared whether we showed up or not."

"If he did not care, would he have helped you to begin with? Come, shift over: that poor animal of yours is weak with fear." At the man's gesture, a spare horse is brought alongside their own, and rough hands help them slide from one animal to the other. "Now follow," says the first rider, "but make no sound."

The path is long and circuitous, winding deep into the smooth-sided hills. They climb steadily, and the wind grows strong and cold. Once, they halt in a patch of moonlight. From a hilltop above comes a faint cry, like the echo of a curlew's call. One of the riders cups his hands to his mouth and gives an answering cry, and the journey resumes.

Kandri is nodding over the saddle horn, Mektu is snoring on his shoulder. As his eyes grow heavier, the despised sound infiltrates his dreams, mutating into the bellow of a camel, until he is certain the spiteful creature has begun to gnaw at his shirt. He tries to pull away, but another camel has locked its jaws on his leg. Their obtuse lowing surrounds him; perhaps they will gnaw him to death.

"Wake up, Chiloto."

The horse has stopped; their escort has disappeared. In their place stands Mansari, Tebassa's oddly feline warrior, shaking Kandri by the leg.

"Dismount," he says. "You're to be welcomed, earnestly this time, despite that cloud of, *hmm*, misfortune that clings to you."

Kandri can still hear the camels—and now, fully awake, he detects their oddly agreeable, scalded-milk stench. His brother, already dismounted, is leaning against the horse like a drunkard. Kandri swings a leg over the mare's rump and slides to the ground, and is startled to find himself on sand. He pulls Mektu upright.

"You bleeding?"

"No. Stop asking me that."

Mansari smiles thinly. "You are most certainly brothers," he says.

They are in a narrow canyon with a floor of soft sand. The vertical walls are smooth and undercut, as though by some vanished river. But human hands have shaped this place as well: carved into the cliffs are five or six levels of galleries, revealed in the dark outlines of pillars and porticos, windows and stairs. The openings throb faintly with firelight.

Here at ground level, however, is the largest opening by far: a rough cave mouth, ten feet high and many hundreds wide, like the maw of some primitive whale. A line of guards stands at this threshold. Behind them, in the vast interior, Kandri dimly perceives a throng. It is not an army: there are children and frail elders, a few dogs, many camels. Some of the people are asleep, wrapped in blankets or crowded onto rugs, but most are awake, murmuring, busy with inscrutable tasks. Deep inside the cavern, a few small ground fires burn.

"Are these people your prisoners?" asks Kandri.

"Idiotic question," says Mansari. "This is the Cavern of the Owls, and a holy place. The hill clans have always sheltered here in times of war and disaster. Tonight, they are sheltering from the celestial fires—and from your, *hmm*, comrades."

"Former comrades," says Mektu.

"Have the Prophet's forces come this far, right into the hills?" asks Kandri.

"Not as far as we know," says Mansari. "But one can see their handiwork from many a hilltop. The fearless New Orthodox cavalry, crossing blades with goatherds, laying siege to barns."

"Why are you guarding the cave mouth, then?"

"Try thinking; it is a beneficial habit in a soldier," says Mansari. "This Cavern is far from the Lutaral plain and little known to outsiders, but it is not impregnable."

"So you don't trust these hill people."

"No clan is without its, *hmm*, deviants," says Mansari. "Some wretches in the Lutaral have even embraced your Prophet's cause. We can take no chances tonight."

And someone betrayed your general, Kandri thinks.

"This is a box canyon, isn't it?" says Mektu, squinting at the darkness. "Just one way in or out?"

"Climbers and mountain goats might find another way."

"Mansari," says Kandri, "what about our friends? The Parthan woman, and the smith—"

"Turn around, Kan," says Mektu.

Chindilan and Eshett are standing just beyond the line of guards. The smith is bickering, pointing at the brothers, demanding to be let through. One of the guards looks at Mansari, who nods. A spear rises, opening a path, and their uncle barrels toward them. He does not shout, for the hush upon the crowd is somehow law, but there is no disguising his relief.

"You mad lost dogs! We were going out of our *minds*. What in Ang's name happened to you?"

Not waiting for an answer, he throws a burly arm around each brother's neck and pulls them close. Eshett, coming up behind him, crosses her arms over her chest and says nothing. But then she catches Kandri's eye and holds him there, a moth on a pin, wondering if she is going to laugh or break down in tears. But this is Eshett; she does neither. Her gaze slides to Mektu, and Kandri wonders if his brother still has a chance.

"You've bathed," he says to Chindilan.

"I have," says his uncle. "And someone's going to trim this wild hedge of a beard, thank the Gods. You're supposed to walk *out* of the desert looking like a crazed holy man, not go in that way."

"Very witty, very droll," says Mansari. "Come, the general is waiting."

So he can ride, somehow, thinks Kandri.

Within the cave, animals outnumber people: there are donkeys, mules, goats with soft satin ears. And camels. Two or three hundred camels, filling the low space with their brays and snorts and snuffles, their flatulence and flies. Some are asleep beside their handlers, necks and chins flat on the ground. Others stand with great loads strapped atop them like peddlers' bundles, seemingly ready to depart.

A boy appears with a torch. Mansari takes it and chucks him under the chin by way of thanks. The people grow quiet as they pass, their dark eyes staring: Kandri and Mektu are a terrible sight. Most of the huddled figures are small and sun-wrinkled, dressed in *kanuts* or the plain tunics and sarongs of the Lutaral. But a few are clearly wealthy, resembling in their attire the seated guests in Tebassa's bunker.

Kandri blinks. It is more than a resemblance: there, in a cloud of blue smoke from the water pipe he is smoking, is the very merchant who complained to Stilts about the general's priorities. And there is the mysterious Prince Nirabha, not alone this time but attended by some dozen guards, all of them slender and olive-skinned like the young monarch. The prince is seated in some manner of canvas chair, studying a book by the light of a small oil lamp. The lamp in turn dangles from a kind of shepherd's stick at his elbow, thrust deep into the sand. Goats and dogs trot about him; moths swarm to the lamp; peasant children watch him, dumbstruck. The prince takes no notice; he reads.

And there, finally, is Dimas, the caravan owner: the short, plump man who had identified the severed heads, the man who had told Eshett to come back with thirty soldiers.

"What's Dimas's business here?"

"Profit," says Mansari, "if he can convince Mr. Ifimar, the caravan master, to port his wares across the desert. That's Ifimar on his right."

Dimas looks even smaller beside his companion: a tall, sinewy man dressed in *kanut* and headscarf, dark jewels on his fingers, massive broadsword on his belt. He turns, and Kandri sees his profile. Long face, thin eyebrows like wires stitched to his forehead. Ifimar and his employer are inspecting a row of camels jostling at a water trough. The beasts drink with abandon, noisy as drainpipes in a storm. Ifimar feels their stomachs, groins, ankles, utterly absorbed in his task.

"Caravan owners rarely brave the desert," says Mansari. "They hire masters to take that risk, but when the profits are tallied, they still claim the, *hmm*, lion's share. Ifimar's fees are twice that of other masters, but that is the privilege of excellence. He is one of the finest masters ever to work the Ravenous Lands."

Kandri starts. "You mean the caravan might be setting off after all, without the thirty guards Dimas wanted?"

"It might," says Mansari, "if he opens his purse a little wider, and Ifimar agrees."

"Then we have to speak with them! Uncle, Eshett, have you—"

Eshett shakes her head. "Dimas said he was through with discussing men he never met. Kandri's right, Mr. Mansari: we must go to them, right now."

"What you *must* do, Parthan woman, is greet your host and benefactor. Don't worry about the caravan: no one leaves this place without the general's blessing. Come along."

The cave stretches deep into the hill. They pass doorways, side chambers, stairs. Mektu begins to chatter at Eshett ("A nurse was flirting with me, I tried not to notice"). Kandri and Chindilan bring up the rear.

They turn left into a straight, breeze-swept passage. Kandri grips his uncle's arm. "I'm going to ask you something," he says, "and I won't take kindly to evasion."

Chindilan is startled. "*Harach*, boy, that's a hell of a way to pose a question. Can't you just—"

"What is the White Child?"

His uncle misses a step.

"You know, don't you?" says Kandri. "You've known this whole fucking time."

"No, no, I don't. It's not what you think."

"Forget what I think. Talk to me."

"Kandri, the general's up to something." Chindilan's voice is very low.

"Evasion."

"The hell it is." Chindilan slows his pace, letting the others vanish around a curve. "Listen to me: in that mill, Tebassa barely spoke to us. Tonight, he's been shouting for you every fifteen minutes: *The brothers! Why haven't they arrived, what's keeping those Chiloto fools?* I don't know what his game is, but he's itching to have you and Mektu under his thumb. We need to think fast, Kandri. We need to know what to say to him."

"How about the truth?" says Kandri. "A little more truth from everyone—that couldn't hurt."

"Couldn't it?"

"Have you seen that creature, Uncle? It . . . *smelled* us, from blocks away. It picked out the building where we'd hidden ourselves and made right for us, as if it could see through walls."

"Kandri," says Chindilan. "you're upset and exhausted, I realize that. But shut up about the Child! The Prophet collects freaks: so what? We have bigger problems."

"Her face was familiar. Why is that, Uncle?"

"Because you're upset."

Kandri spins his uncle brutally around. "You're fucking right I'm upset. That thing killed with a touch. *And it called us by Papa's name.*"

Horror in his uncle's face. He clutches at Kandri, mouth working, and Kandri realizes the smith has been fighting panic from his first word.

"Don't blame Lantor," he whispers.

"Blame him for what?" says Kandri. "Did he *make* that thing, somehow?"

"No, no. Fucking hell."

"You'd better just explain."

But as they round the curve, they find the others stopped and waiting. Mansari watches the stragglers keenly, and suddenly, Kandri knows his uncle is right: they must not speak of the Child now, must not provide Tebassa's men with any new reasons for fear or mistrust. Not until the general shows his hand.

"If your little conference is, *hmm*, concluded?" says Mansari.

Behind him stands a pair of swordsmen. Spiked to the wall between the guards is something dark and shaggy: a sheepskin. At a nod from Mansari, one of the men lifts it like a curtain, revealing a small door-shaped hole. Within are warmth and firelight, and many soldiers, and dim, smoke-thickened air.

"After you," says Mansari.

The chamber is large but does not feel so, crowded as it is with Tebassa's men. A rough circle, it has other entrances scattered about the perimeter, and a great fire in a hearth at the center; the smoke vanishes above through a funnel-like hole. Many of the warriors from Oppuk's Mill are here. Stilts is holding a basket of oranges, tossing them to the waiting men and women with quick snaps of his wrist. A woman wags a finger at a small brown dog. Spider, the bald captain with the birthmark, is arm-wrestling a larger man, and winning. Observing the match from a seat near the fire is the general himself.

He sees them, beckons them near. Spider too looks up, and his opponent takes the opportunity to slam his hand down in triumph. Tebassa laughs; therefore, everyone laughs. Kandri senses a difference in the way the soldiers look at them. At Oppuk's Mill, there had been suspicion and little else; now there is excitement, an eagerness almost breaking out into smiles.

But there is still uncertainty, a waiting to see more. *He's told them we're good news,* thinks Kandri, *but he hasn't told them why.*

"No sign of girl trouble," says Mektu. "I mean, Trouble Girl. I wonder if she's—"

"Talupéké can take care of herself," says Eshett, with a quick glance at Chindilan.

They thread a path to the general. He beams at them, and his hands keep beckoning: *Closer, closer.* When Kandri is less than an arm's reach away, Tebassa pulls him down and kisses his forehead. He does the same to Mektu.

"You're alive. That's *very* good. We have a great deal to discuss after you shed those blood-blotters you're wearing, and wash the stench away. I mean to take good care of you, boys; you won't be sorry you've joined us. Send the wine back this way, whoever's hogging it."

Now all the men are smiling. Kandri forces himself to do the same, but he cannot force himself to believe in this charade. Tebassa's kiss has put him in mind of a farmer kissing a prize pumpkin before it is weighed at a fair.

Someone thrusts a wineskin at him; he takes a long, thirsty pull. "That's the way," says Tebassa. "Corporal, tell the women to feed these gentlemen— after your first errand, of course."

A young soldier salutes, vanishes. Kandri passes the skin to Mektu, then bows low. "General Tebassa," he says. "The Xavasindrans saved my brother's life. We thank you with all our hearts."

The general's smile does not change. "Your thanks should begin with Talupéké and with Master Stilts. She's the reason I spoke to you in the first place. And he's the one who swore that you were who you claimed to be—Hinjumans, that is."

"He knew our father, sir," says Kandri.

"We all do," says Tebassa.

"You *know* him?"

"The last time I checked, Lantor Hinjuman was very much alive."

Kandri turns and embraces Mektu. Chindilan, with a rumbling laugh, throws his arms around them both. Hope is one thing; news is another. Tears well in Kandri's eyes.

"I knew it, I knew it!" burbles Mektu. "You can't kill our Papa, can you, brother? Can you?"

Kandri releases him, grinning, wiping his eyes. "Do you know where he is, General Tebassa?"

"We know," says the general, "and we have just sent him word that you're among us—although the missive may be long in reaching him. Go and rest awhile, though: I must see to various matters now that you are safely arrived." He looks them up and down, then adds, "I have urged him to join us. No doubt he will be eager to see his sons."

Mektu, forgetting himself, squeezes the uncapped wine skin, spraying Chindilan below the belt. Tebassa roars with laughter at the smith's embarrassment. "Go! Mr. Stilts, rid me of these brave buffoons! The high chamber, I think, and some privacy for Mistress Eshett. Food will follow, along with such comforts as we can provide. Be gone now, Chilotos. I will send for you presently."

Stilts claps a hand on Kandri's arm: the interview has ended. The older man takes a torch from another's hand, and the travelers follow him out through another sheepskin-cloaked doorway. They stand now on a kind of landing at the foot of a narrow stair. "The general means it, you know," says

Stilts as he begins to climb. "You're to meet again in two hours, and privately. Be careful, now: some of these stairs are broken."

"The hell with the stairs," says Mektu. "Where's our father, Mr. Stilts?"

But Stilts, to no one's surprise, dodges the question with a hazy promise: the general will reveal everything in time.

"What about sleep?" says Eshett. "Are we ever to be left alone, to sleep?"

Stilts just chuckles. His torch knocks along the ceiling, black and glistening with untold ages of soot.

The staircase meanders upward through the stone, like a worm wriggling toward daylight. They pass other landings, where corridors branch off into the darkness, some sealed behind iron gates, others simply vanishing into the dark. They climb higher and higher. Kandri thinks of the rooms and balconies he had glimpsed on their arrival: surely, they have passed the highest of these already? Which means they are bound for some secret place, without windows on the canyon. A place never meant for common folk.

At last the staircase ends. Before them another corridor opens, wide and straight and lit by several torches. A chill breeze travels it, tossing sand about their feet. Eshett hugs herself, and Mektu puts his arm over her shoulder. Further along the passage, more sheepskins are pegged to the stone, cloaking further openings. From one, a gleam of firelight escapes, from another a whiff of steam.

Stilts leads them down the passage. "You've nothing to fear tonight," he says. "Our forces are mainly here in the north galleries, but we're watching every approach to the Cavern. The general has shown you rare favor, by the way: these were his own quarters in the past. Tonight, men begged for the honor of carrying him up those steps, but he wouldn't hear of it. 'I'll curl up with you, lads,' he told them, 'one more dog in the den.'"

"Do you mean we're to be left alone up here?" asks Mektu.

"Officers will bed down in the side chambers," says Stilts., "and there are servants about, of course. Good hill-clan people, from families well known to us. I selected them myself."

The passage ends in a dramatic archway engraved with odd images: horses, camels, wriggling serpents, radiant suns. Actual curtains, not skins, have been mounted on the stone there, and when Stilts parts them, a sumptuous chamber is revealed. Like everything they have seen, it is carved from the living rock. There is no furniture at all. But here again, a generous fire is blazing, this time in a hearth emitting a low moan, wind on the distant chimney. The floor, swept clean of sand, is strewn with rugs and pillows. There is a samovar on a stand by the fire, a rich smell of brysorwood, a small pyramid of folded clothes.

Slender hands part the curtains on the far wall, and a young woman appears, dressed humbly like the peasants below. She is carrying a wide brass dish upon which something smolders: incense, perhaps. She jumps at the sight of them, then shyly lowers her eyes and advances into the room. Stilts walks forward and takes the dish; the woman bows and flees.

"So much room," says Eshett. Her eyes seek out Kandri, and for the second time that evening, he feels the sharpness of her look. Not a coincidence. *What is it you need to tell me, Eshett?*

"There's a bath chamber," Stilts is saying, "just off the passage; you saw the steam. And if you follow the girl through that doorway, Mistress Eshett, you'll find an alcove when you can sleep apart from these hairy beasts. Your clothes will be in there already."

"But we bought clothes," says Eshett. "Dry food as well, and faska. Everything you told us to buy."

"Did you?" Stilts looks mildly chagrined. "Well, it seems the general is in a lavish mood. Enjoy it while it lasts."

"Where's that girl gone, by the way?" asks Chindilan.

"To fetch your dinner, I expect."

"I meant Talupéké," says the smith.

He speaks with a casual air any fool could see through. Kandri and Mektu exchange a look. They have not mentioned their glimpse of her riding west over the plain.

Stilts studies Chindilan for a moment before he answers. "My niece," he says at last, "is following her heart's desire, and taking revenge for the slaughter at the Megrev Defile. Few of your Prophet's cavalry will make it back to legion headquarters. The word *Megrev* will be written on the foreheads of the slain."

"It's quite a party, this Night of Blood," says Mektu.

"Keep that flippant tongue in your mouth," says the Naduman. "This is no party; it's a reckoning. Whether you believe in the *Darsunuk* or not hardly matters. The clans of the Lutaral have seen one invasion after another, one bloody tyrant after another. They march in and take what they like—cattle, grain, children, hope. If they've exploded with anger and frustration, the only wonder is that it took so long. The brush has been piling up for decades, for generations. The spark had to come."

His vehemence catches them all off-guard, as perhaps it does Stilts himself. With a vaguely apologetic grimace, he starts to fish in his pocket. "Here's a trinket. Don't let me catch you praying to it, though."

He flips a coin in Mektu's direction, but it is Kandri who snaps it from the air. The coin is large and bright, newly minted silver. On one side is the image of the Palace of Radiance. On the other, the Prophet herself—or rather the Prophet as she was nearly fifty years before, and as she likes still to be portrayed. The young visionary, not yet a mother, soon to launch a war.

"The future Empress of Urrath," says Stilts dryly. "Well, I'll be off. A good meal's coming, but for the love of Ang, go and bathe while the water's hot: you boys look like cannibals. And lads—" He raises a warning finger. "Don't go exploring. The exits are guarded, but the Cavern's immense, and something of a maze. Stick to these chambers until you're sent for again. Do I make myself clear?"

"As a bell," says Chindilan. "Don't worry. I'll keep them in line."

"Do that," says Stilts. He pulls the curtains shut behind him, and his footfalls echo down the hall.

Kandri turns on his uncle. "Keep us in line," he says. "Still counting on that, are you?"

The others look at him, speechless. "Don't talk to him that way," says Eshett at last. "He's your elder, no matter what he's done."

"What's he done?" says Mektu.

Kandri flips his brother the coin. Mektu holds it up to the torchlight, reverses it—and freezes.

"Oh."

"Mektu?" says Eshett.

Mektu hides his face in his elbow. The coin falls, landing soundless on the rug between them. It winks, the silver contours of a young woman's face in profile, slender cheeks, dimpled chin, deep enormous eye.

"That's her," says Kandri.

The smith looks slightly crazed. "Of course," he says. "It's the Prophet, the Prophet in her youth."

From Mektu's chest, a barely audible moan.

"Do you mind telling me," says Kandri, "why she has the face of the White Child?"

Mektu jerks like a snapped bowstring, turning from them, careening for the doorway. Eshett rushes after him. She tells him not to be a coward.

"This isn't cowardice, this is intelligence," he shouts. "Don't tell him, Uncle. Don't say another fucking word."

Eshett steps into the doorway, blocking his escape. "You need to hear this, whatever it is," she says. "Maybe he should have told you a long time ago, but all the same you need to hear it. You can't stay ignorant forever."

"Hell if I can't," says Mektu. He lunges past her and through the curtains. Eshett follows, calling his name. Kandri rounds on his uncle again.

"We have two hours," he says. "If you want to *keep me in line*, you'll tell me everything. I'm liable to get very far out of line if you put me off again."

"I don't *know* everything," says Chindilan. "I can't explain where she found the Child, or how it was made. If it was made."

"Stop telling me what you don't know."

"Shouldn't you bathe first? They've heated water, by damn, and you smell like the back of a butcher's shop."

"Uncle."

"Right." The smith makes a gesture of surrender. He rubs his face, big hands trembling. Then he jabs a finger at the samovar.

"Is there tea in that fucking thing?"

ଔ

They were children, all of them. A pack of boys, the eldest barely sixteen, the youngest, Lantor Hinjuman, a gangly nine. He was the mascot, the tag-along. Bright, foolish, everybody's darling. Educated, too: his father was the headmaster of the Secular School in Ashfield. Well fed on rice and milk and mutton. Barefoot half the year.

Of course, the Chilotos remained a subject clan and had to yield a quarter of all they grew or built or earned to the Važeks. They were expected to embrace the obscene idea of a single God, and to kneel if the regional governor should pass. But the conquerors' presence in the Sataapre Valley never amounted to constant, day-to-day control. They were simply too few. They seized Nandipatar and slaughtered its ruling families, billeted soldiers at Green Pass and Bittermoon, now and then staged an execution. But the great purges happened elsewhere. The Valley, never known for courage or resistance, coughed up treasure without much prompting, and so escaped the worst.

Lantor Hinjuman knew about Važek atrocities, which had claimed some of his distant kin. He had also heard of the Quarantine and the Plague. Yet he was happy in those early years. The summers were warm, the winters bearable. His father indulged his love of tools and tinkering, let him dismantle an accordion and his mother's wind-up music box, and called him "a whip crack" when both devices, reassembled, sounded better than before. They were well off. They had livestock and windows that sealed. They had cords of dry firewood, a cask of wine in the basement, an icebox filled each year with a thick slab cut from Moti Lake. Lantor's good fortune embarrassed him. He wondered if anyone else in Blind Stream had half so many things.

Then his father met a Lañatu woman of exceptional beauty and ran off with her to the south, and overnight, they were poor. They gave up meat, sold the cow and horses and even the barn that had housed them. Lantor's elder brother and sister quit school and took jobs in Nandipatar, sending home any money they could save. Lantor's mother worked like a fiend, sewing clothes, buying finished leather and fashioning it into bridles and belts, hawking her creations door to door, from Sed Hemon to Ashfield and beyond. Some days, Lantor imagined that all that labor was for him, the youngest, the darling, the one who earned no money. How could they help but despise him?

That same spring, Lantor's pack of friends was abruptly decimated. One boy was killed by fever, another in a fall. Two others, cousins to Lantor, were snatched up by Važeks and marched away to the Loro Canyon, where they died in one of many attempts to repair the Imperial bridge.

Hunger, fever, death: it was all mere happenstance. ("But what compares to happenstance," says Chindilan, "in the shaping of our lives?") Nine-year-old Lantor was crushed and frightened. He had many evenings alone while his mother dragged her wares about the countryside. He needed someone. He fell in with older boys.

They were nothing like his former friends. They called themselves the Strays. They made him walk a little behind, cuffed his head if he spoke up or laughed too loudly, especially in front of girls. But they were also fond of him. He cut capers, did impressions of adults. He made them laugh. And young though he was, Lantor Hinjuman could be counted on to notice things: a shortcut, a spot in the river where the fish were plentiful, an unfriendly glance.

Their leader's name was Samidya. He was a tall boy with a long, flat brow and shoulders that rounded forward, as though he were pulling a cart. At sixteen, he was already a thief, a small-time counterfeiter, and a peddler of his father's dubious moonshine. He did not boast of these pursuits; in fact, he rarely spoke of them at all. This had the effect of making them all the more alluring. Samidya was careful. He inducted the boys only gradually into his secrets, his petty crimes. But a day came when Lantor, licking his fingers after his share of a stolen lamb pie, looked around at the older boys and thought, *Pitfire, you're just a gang of crooks.*

And these crooks were all he had.

That night Samidya told them something startling. He had a girlfriend—or as he called her, "a lick." Lantor did not understand why Samidya spoke of her in this vulgar way, nor exactly what a girlfriend was. He did understand that they were valuable, something to be coveted, something likely to be stolen when your back was turned. "Who is she?" someone asked.

Samidya explained that she was the oldest girl in the New Life Orphanage. "She's not even a Chiloto. She's fair-skinned, like a Jút. She's a nasty piece of work, but she gets away with it because she's built. Just you remember that she's mine, though. Don't look at her. Find your own."

"How are we to do that?" said Lantor, dejected, for Samidya would leave them now, and once again the circle would collapse. Girlfriends had this curious power: they made boys forget friends, husbands walk out on wives.

Samidya made as if to cuff Lantor as usual. But the hand froze in midair. He looked at the younger boy, but he was not really looking; his eyes were distant and fascinated. Then he blinked and gave them all a cunning smile.

Two nights later, very late, Lantor awoke to the sound of pebbles striking his window. Down in the street stood one of the older boys, all but dancing with impatience. Lantor lifted the sash. "Get your clothes on," the boy called softly. "Samidya has a job for you. Five gham."

Five gham! Lantor dressed in the darkness, praying his mother would not wake. The gang's leader had summoned him at night before—to climb a drain spout, to slip under a fence—but this time would be different. Samidya had never paid anyone for their services.

"Five gham?" he repeated when he stood beside the boy.

"Six," said the boy, mistaking Lantor's wonder for hesitation. "Make it six. I don't care. Two now, and four more when it's over. If you do your job."

"Who's paying me? You or Sam?"

The boy dug in his pocket, slapped two dull coins into Lantor's hand. "I'm paying. But Samidya said it had to be you. No one but Hinjuman, he said."

Without further explanation, he led Lantor at a run down the Sed Hemon road. Lantor was thrilled. He couldn't guess the nature of the job, but he was almost certain of their destination. Ten minutes later, he was proven correct when they turned up the path to the New Life Orphanage.

The institution was already some eighty years old. It consisted of a square, squat building, too large for its thirty girls and five keepers, and a miasmic garden that had gone years without a pruning. A high stone wall surrounded both. In the daytime, the girls were allowed into the garden, but the wild exuberance of the plant life kept them confined to an ever-shrinking circle of grass. Their mistresses, aging women from an austere sect known as the Sisters of Ang, were abstracted and poorly paid. They kept order by keeping a tight grip on the keys, and an even tighter one on the girls' imaginations.

("They were pitiless, those Sisters," says Chindilan. "They told the girls who'd come there as infants that they'd been saved from shipwrecks, rubbish tips, cannibals. That they'd be treated as fallen women—beaten, raped—if they set foot outside the wall before they were twenty.")

Until then, the orphans prayed and studied and washed their colorless frocks out with rainwater. And made pillows. Thousands of pillows. Day and night, winter and summer, plucking geese, ducks, greenfowl, babblers. Lantor had seen the dead birds arrive by the cartload and emerge naked, bound for Valley butcher shops. But he had never seen a New Life girl. How had Samidya managed to smuggle one out?

As it happened, he had not: fear was too powerful a gatekeeper. But Samidya had at least discovered a gate—or rather, a door. It was hidden by a bamboo thicket, and locked of course. But Samidya had both tools and talent, and the girl inside had been whispering to him for days. *I want food. I want candy. Bring me candy and you can do what you like.*

("You have to wonder, by the Gods," says Chindilan, "what sort of Urrath we'd be living in today, if one girl had not wanted sugar, one petty thief not known his locks.")

The door opened into an abandoned potting shed, built into a far corner of the wall. That night, when Lantor and the older boy arrived, Samidya was already inside. He opened the door some eight inches (as far as the bamboo allowed) and snapped at them, "Get *in* here. What took you so long?"

In the putrid shed, he lit a candle. He barely glanced at Lantor. His hand was extended to the older boy.

"Where's the other fifty?"

The boy produced a handful of coins, each one thicker and heavier than the two he had given Lantor. Samidya counted them, nodded, and poked the other boy in the chest.

"If she tells me you went too far—"

"I won't, Sam, I promise!"

"Ten minutes," said Samidya. "Don't leave nothing on that porch, you hear me? Not a fucking fingernail." Suddenly, he grinned, and clapped the other boy on the cheek. "Go on, enjoy it."

The boy vanished into the weedy garden. Only then did Samidya look down at Lantor. He was still grinning.

"Fahetri and I are going to make a pile," he says. "This is just the beginning. There's three more up there."

"Three more what?"

"Girls, Hinjuman. Three more old enough for tricks. They haven't agreed yet, but they will, once they see what Fahetri's bringing in. Until then, she'll do. You can see her titties for five gham, touch 'em for fifteen."

"What does a hundred get you?"

Samidya hugged Lantor's head to his chest. "Things you're too young to know about," he whispered, like a teasing uncle. "That's why you're perfect."

He extinguished the candle, peeked out through the door, and led Lantor back into the street. When he turned to face Lantor again, he held a small loop of iron chain. At the bottom of the loop dangled a key.

"Fahetri swiped this from the old bats," he said. "The lock's oiled now and working like new. This is what we'll do, Hinjuman. I'll send the key to you with somebody on the night you have a job. You slip out and come here and let the customer into the garden. Then you watch and wait. Nobody much on the Sed Hemon road after midnight, and hardly anybody likely to take interest in this dump. But people get nosy, don't they? Sometimes they come looking for trouble."

"I don't," said Lantor.

"'Course not. You're the door guard, Hinjuman. You're a part of the team. You give a whistle if anyone starts up the path. The customer will clear out quick. Shut the door and lock it behind him, and scamper off yourself into the bush. Nothing else. It's an important job, Hinjuman. You'll be paid every time." He handed over the key, along with a piece of chalk. "Make a doodle on the wall."

"Why?"

"Because that's your cover. You're doodling, you're playing a prank. An older lout like me gets seen here, there's no way to explain it. But you, you're practically in diapers. No one could think ill of you, could they, now? You've probably never even had a stiffy."

"A what?"

"You see? A stiffy's what a lick can give you."

"I don't understand, Sam," said Lantor.

But Lantor learned on the job. Samidya left him in the doorway, and he looked in just in time to see a girl somewhat older than Samidya emerging from the orphanage, with a finger to her lips. The boy from his gang dropped his pants right in front of the girl and hoisted her frock. So that was a stiffy. And that . . . oh, that. It wasn't worth a hundred *gham*, but the boy looked as though he would have paid any price. The girl just looked absent, as though she had taken refuge in some chamber deep in her body, from which the boy was trying in vain to dig her out. Less than five minutes later, she twisted away from him and hurried back into the building, and the boy stumbled dazed and bedraggled to the potting shed. Lantor was so stunned by his transformation—sweaty, glassy-eyed, one hand in his pants—that he forgot to ask for his four remaining *gham*. It was the only night he made such a mistake.

And there were many nights: up to four a week, when the news began to spread. For Lantor, the job had a changeless rhythm. The key, slipped into his pocket by one of the boys in the gang. The time, a whisper in his ear. The scramble along the deserted road, the impatient customer loitering in the shadow of the wall. Lantor's hand extended: six in advance. The ecstasy of earning, of not asking his mother for coin.

A second girl began to alternate with Fahetri, and then a third. Sometimes, they fought with the men—silent blows, voiceless curses, a weird pantomime of lust and rage. The three girls were nearing twenty and saving money toward the day of their freedom, or so Samidya claimed.

Lantor rarely saw Samidya at the orphanage: the real money changed hands elsewhere, long before the trysts. If the gang leader appeared at all, it was in the manner of a surprise inspection, a quick nod to Lantor, a proprietary squint at the figures on the porch.

("But this makes no sense," blurts Kandri. "All that thumping, all that sex? How did they get away with it, night after night?" "Don't you see?" says Chindilan. "They *didn't* get away with it. They weren't fooling anyone. That was part of the sham.")

The Sisters had tried for fifty percent but settled for a third. It was filthy money, but what else to do with these destitute creatures? Did they have prospects, did they have suitors? Were they ready for life? The Sisters sighed and cursed the coldness of the world, and put the money in their pockets. The hush everyone maintained in the garden was out of consideration for the youngest girls.

(These last words, Chindilan speaks as though they have putrefied: *Consideration. For the youngest girls.*)

There are couriers for every vice. In short order, the news spread by dark whispers across the whole of the Valley, and even beyond. It was a glad and generous exchange, a brotherhood of predators. Men appeared who wanted "licks" far younger than eighteen, and in time, such orphans were persuaded to oblige. But even they were not so young as the girl who crept through the weeds one night to speak with Lantor Hinjuman.

She was fourteen at the most. Thin and frail, with eyes that belonged to some small tree creature, eyes so large they made the rest of her face seem an afterthought. She rose up from a dark corner of the potting shed and touched his arm.

Lantor nearly screamed. "Who are you? Get out of here, go back to bed!"

"I'm not one of them. I'm not a whore. I won't do that."

"Good for you," said Lantor, meaning it, "but get away from me, I can't talk, it's not allowed, Samidya will—"

"Let me out."

"What?"

"I have to leave this place. No one will hurt me out in the world—those stories are lies. I know that. It's here where I'll get hurt."

"You're a fool. Samidya will come after you."

"I'll hide from him," she said, "and from something much worse than him. I know this for certain. A God told me, in my sleep."

"Back inside, back inside!" Frightened now (for he had never seen madness before), Lantor shooed her with both hands.

The girl stood her ground. Their eyes met, and Lantor saw her intention at the last possible moment, and jumped. He was outside with his back to the rock-hard bamboo and his foot against the door before she reached it, flung herself against it, pushed with all her might. But she was a slight fourteen, and the door opened outward. Lantor had the advantage and would not be moved.

The girl pleaded. Lantor tried not to hear. After a time, he realized that the girl was sobbing—and then she fled into the garden, for the customer's time was up.

"Who in Ang's hairy armpit was *that*?" the man demanded when Lantor let him out into the street.

"Nobody," said Lantor, turning the key in the lock. He had never, of course, been more wrong.

This was in the seventh week of Samidya's enterprise. The girl came back the next night and tried again. "Something awful is going to happen," she said. "I have to get out of here. I'm supposed to be running by now."

"Running where? Running from what?" asked Lantor.

"From my fate," said the girl. "There's still time to escape it. The God told me that, too. But I don't have much longer. Something's coming. Let me out."

She kept a good six feet from Lantor Hinjuman, almost out of the potting shed, but he stood ready to slam the door all the same. "I don't believe you," he said. "You'll tell me anything to get your way. Anything you imagine will scare me."

"*I'm* scared," said the girl. "The customer, the one who's inside now? He saw me this time. And he looked at me funny."

Lantor forced out a laugh. "Stay inside if you don't want them to look. Anyway, it doesn't matter. He didn't come here for you."

She was right, however: the client, a youth from Sharp's Corner with crooked shoulders and a slight, hopping limp, did look strangely at the girl as he passed through the courtyard. When he was gone, Lantor glanced in through the door a final time: the girl was standing in the moonlight, appalled.

On the next occasion, her face was like stone. She stood as close as she dared and said he could feel her up. Or have her. Anything he wanted, if only he'd let her go.

Lantor was blindsided. "I'm too young," he said, for it was what Samidya had told him. "And so are you. Don't say such things."

At once, the life returned to her big eyes. She was relieved—and suddenly, very pretty.

"I can't let you go," he said. "Not ever. Samidya would cut off my ears. You'll have to escape some other way."

"I've looked for other ways," she said. "There are bars on the windows, padlocks on the doors. This place is a jail."

Lantor looked out at the road.

"Come with me," said the girl. "I'm allowed to have a friend. I'll take you where you're supposed to go."

His lips felt dead, his teeth all wrong in his mouth. "We're not friends," he told her, "and I don't want to go anywhere. I belong right here in the Valley."

"Are you sure?" asked the girl, and then the customer, drunk and finished with his girl, swatted her aside and lurched into the shed.

The next morning Lantor walked the four miles to Samidya's house and told him he didn't want the job. The older boy slouched in the doorway, looking him up and down. "What's the matter?" he said. "Someone treating you bad? One of the customers, maybe? One of the girls?"

"No," said Lantor.

"How about seven gham a night? I was going to give you a raise anyway, soon."

Lantor shook his head. "I just don't want it anymore."

"The thing is, I trust you, Hinjuman. You make a good dog—a good watchdog, I mean. Better if you stick around until I find a replacement."

"No, Sam, I won't go there again. I—resign."

"Resign? Resign?" Samidya grabbed him by the shoulder. He said that Lantor's mother would be told that her darling boy was a pimp's assistant. "And so will everyone in your life. Your teachers, your brother and sister. Your worthless Papa, if he ever comes back. They'll know you took money from men who screw little girls. Your whole family will be disgraced, Lantor. Other women won't let your mother scrub their floors. They won't even speak to her, the mother of a pimp. You want that, do you?"

Lantor stared at his feet. He did not want that. Two nights later, he was back at the New Life Orphanage.

I won't look at her face, he reasoned. For he could not be strong enough to deny her again, if he saw those pleading eyes. But of course, he had to open the door for the customer—a large stranger in a mud-spattered cloak who smelled vaguely of horses—and he was supposed to keep an eye on the man as well as the road.

He compromised: he held the door open an inch. When the girl drew near, he saw a ribbon of cheek. "Who gave you that bruise?" he whispered.

"Fahetri," said the girl. She brought the dark welt close to the gap. Then she shifted, and he saw her mouth, her thin nose, one probing eye.

Someone's going to kill me, Lantor thought.

"What's your name?" she asked.

"Lantor."

It didn't matter if she knew. It didn't matter *what* he said to her. She was going nowhere for six years. "What's yours, then?"

"Tamahín," she said. "It's a Kasraji name. I'm not pure Chiloto. But in the future, everyone will think so."

"Did your God tell you that?"

She nodded seriously. He was shaking like a leaf.

"Lantor," she said, "you have to make up your mind."

"I know," he whispered. "I will."

"Not eventually," she said. "You have to decide right now. Because if you don't let me out now, it will be too late."

Her conviction shattered what was left of his poise. What if she did talk to Gods? What if he was fighting more than a crazy girl? She slipped a hand through the crack and he shoved hard, a warning. The hand snapped back.

"No tears," he said, for she was crying again. "It won't work. I'm not listening."

"The man on the porch," she said. "The man with Fahetri right now. He stared at me on the way in, Lantor. He told me, told me with his look."

"Never mind," Lantor heard himself say.

"*Never mind?* Are you crazy? Are you just like the rest of them, the same kind of beast?"

"That gimp from Sharp's Corner stared at you too," he said, "but so what? They're just looking. They want older girls. That's what they paid for, isn't it?"

"Let me go, Lantor."

He was going to obey her. He was falling into a pit. The girl knelt down, said she believed in him, that she knew he was different, that his kindness could change the world. He took his hands from the door. *Go ahead*, he thought, *just push*. She didn't notice. She was sobbing, repeating his name. He closed his eyes, shut out her voice with the first thing he thought of: a prayer.

"Ang All-Merciful, protector of multitudes, nearest in our need . . ."

The door smashed open. Lantor was crushed against the bamboo. The man in the mud-spattered cloak stepped out with the girl under his arm. She was not screaming, only groaning for breath; he had dealt her a blow to the stomach. With his free hand he lifted Lantor clear of the ground.

"You didn't see me take her," he snarled. "I left alone, like anybody. That's the *only fucking thing* you saw."

He slammed Lantor's head against the wall, then flung him aside. Bleeding and all but senseless, Lantor watched him toss the girl over his shoulder and start down the path. The man paused only once, when another figure stepped from the shadows. It was the crooked-shouldered youth from Sharp's Corner, his hand extended, a nervous smile on his face. The man flung a handful of coins at him, contemptuous. From farther down the path, near the Sed Hemon road, came another man's voice (*Hurry the hell up, will you?*) and the stamp of horses eager to run.

ಙ

"And you know what followed," says Chindilan, squatting on his heels by the fire. "Or at least a version of it. They were flesh traders—Tirmassil, if you like. They didn't need to buy pussy from a hayseed pimp like Samidya. They wanted young girls to sell—especially girls with huge, dark eyes. And they found one, thanks to a young kid named Marz."

"No."

"He took shelter in divinity school, the phony bastard, when he saw what he had done. Of course, it was too late by then. And Lantor—he's been making amends all his life. Traveling to war-torn lands, snatching up orphaned kids before the Tirmassil arrive, finding homes for them all. But it's never enough, is it? There's one kid he can't go back and save."

Chindilan pokes at the fire with a stick. "I met him three years later, and we've been best friends ever since. I don't believe he's told another soul, except Dyakra, of course." The smith looks at Kandri, desolate. "It's consumed his life."

"He was *nine*," says Kandri.

"Try telling the Old Man that. I have, for damned near fifty years."

"What did they do with the girl?"

Chindilan sighs. "Don't go stupid on me now, Kandri. They had a buyer already. A man who paid in diamonds for big-eyed girls. The fact that he was a cave-dwelling, Važek-slaughtering Chiloto warlord didn't matter one bit."

Kandri stands clutching his ridiculous teacup. He cannot speak. Like his father half a century ago, he feels himself falling, head over heels, into a lightless pit.

"Warlord?" he croaks at last.

"*The* warlord," says Chindilan. "Bitruk Uslor, who made his base at Hunger Cliff. Who added that girl to his stable of wives, and sired four sons on her." Chindilan raises his fingers, counting. "Jihalkra. Ojulan. Garatajik.

Etarel. I don't know where this White Child came from—whether she created it, or called it up from hell. I don't know how she came by her gifts. But that girl was our Prophet, Kandri. And the vision that came to her a few years later? The rising of the Chiloto, Heaven's Path, and the War of Revelation? I suppose that was the fate she was trying to avoid."

ᛡ

The water is only lukewarm, but while he is soaking, a youth from the hill clans appears with a great clay vessel held by tongs. It is glowing at the base. Kandri stands, numb and naked; the youth empties it into the copper bathing tub. Kandri sits. Now the water is too hot, burning really, but the pain is a distant thing. The dried blood lifts from his forearms in translucent flakes.

He scrubs himself. There is a feast laid out in the main chamber that he could not make himself touch. He is soaking in the blood of the tower watchmen; he is drowning in the blood of the world. Like his father, those three guards were told to stand and wait for trouble to find them. Three weeds, cut down by all-powerful happenstance, the great mower of mankind.

No, Kandri. Cut down by your brother and you.

The youth is also waiting, peering anxiously at Kandri's face. "Thank you," says Kandri. "Go away now. I don't want anything else."

"Dethen sara nanasin, ko."

Kandri cannot even identify the language. "Kasraji?" he tries.

The youth shakes his head. No Imperial Common. Maybe it never penetrated these hills. Kandri puts his hands together, palm to palm, hoping his thanks will at least be understood. The youth hesitates, then bows and slips away.

As he lifts the curtain, Kandri sees Mektu in his own bath, twenty feet away. His head is thrown back as though his neck is broken. He is sound asleep.

The Prophet's name is Tamahín.

Or was. Kandri has never heard so much as a whispered rumor that she possessed an earthly name.

A Kasraji name. The Mother of All Chilotos is only part Chiloto. We worship a mongrel. And without her, we'd still be in chains.

Kandri slides down, plunging his head below the surface. Too hot. Stay down anyway. Burn out your eyes.

Endless war. Misery, horror, theft, poisoned fields, burning villages, burning houses, screams of children within. A liberation become a march of hate and slaughter, a fever dream of eleven sons on eleven thrones, all Urrath bowing before one family, before one twisted, unstoppable lie.

That was what his father was carrying: the blame for *all of it*. Because he'd been afraid to open a door.

Egotist! How can you cling to that? You were a child, Papa. No child can be held to the standards of a man.

He rises. Next to the tub stands Eshett, wrapped in a white sarong.

He sits up so quickly that water sloshes onto the floor.

"What's the matter?" he demands, covering himself.

"Nothing's the matter. Hush."

She is freshly bathed; steam rises from her skin. Something about her face has changed, as though some force has taken hold and reimagined it, the knowing eyes, the wet locks plastered against her cheeks.

"That servant," she said. "He was trying to tell you that we're expected below. In ten minutes. You and your uncle talked a long fucking time."

"Ten minutes?"

Eshett shrugs. "Forget I told you. If they want you on time, they should send someone who can speak your language."

She steps closer, until she is alongside his knees. Through the wet muslin he can see all of her, save the breasts concealed by one arm. He tries to avert his eyes. Succeeds in averting one of them, momentarily. Why hasn't he looked at her before? This desert woman. This Parthan who held him in a tunnel beneath a grave.

"Eshett, my brother is in love with you."

"It doesn't matter," she says. "In a few days, I'll rejoin my clan. I'm a sand rat, and he'll never be. It doesn't matter what we feel."

"And me—I love—there's this woman—"

"Don't say it, don't say her name again. You think I don't know?"

"Where's my uncle?"

All at once she is exasperated. "Somewhere else! *Echim baruk*, can't you ever stop talking? I am clean. Hurry up."

He lifts a hand from the water, reaches for her, grazes her hip through the sarong.

"You don't understand," he pleads, withdrawing the hand. "What Uncle told me was too terrible. There's no way."

She puts a hand under his chin.

"You're afraid that you're a bad man," she says. "Stop thinking that. It's not true." Her fingers rise, trembling, teasing his lips. "When I go, I'll never see you again. I want *anga* with you, sweet *anga*, that's all."

"I'm sorry," he says, turning away.

"So I disgust you, maybe."

"What?"

"You have ideas about Parthans, our bad habits, our smell."

"Eshett, Eshett, no."

"Why don't you say it? I'm still dirty, in your eyes. Once a whore, always—"

He puts his lips to her sex, clumsy, the muslin between them thinner than smoke. He no longer knows anything, the world is broken, his arm is tight around her hips, her body shudders, her dark curls wet his face. Maybe he's crying. There are yards of this white stuff. Her hands strong on the back of his neck, she leans into him and whispers his name and no he's not crying, except with gladness maybe, Eshett, beautiful Eshett, and then the muslin parts and her leg hooks over his shoulder and his tongue finds the way.

෨

When they return to the general's council, it is as if no time has passed at all. The whole company is present, the fire bright, the wine making the rounds. Chindilan is brooding. Mektu, his hair still wet, looks sleepy and disoriented; Kandri is disoriented for very different reasons. Only Eshett is perfectly herself.

Tebassa, who warned them to reach the Cavern on time or not at all, makes no mention of their lateness. He asks if their new clothes fit, if the food is to their liking. They answer yes without hesitation. All of them, even Kandri, have just wolfed down beef and yams and bread and apples, squatting in a circle, eating with both hands.

"And the baths?" asks the general.

Kandri swallows. Chindilan's mouth works, as if he were chewing a lemon.

"The baths were perfect," says Eshett.

"You've treated us like princes, general," says Mektu.

"Better," says Tebassa. "Our young Prince Nirabha is out there with the camels and dogs."

The room explodes with nervous laughter. Suddenly, Mektu drops to one knee, crosses the knee with his forearm, and bows his head until eyebrows meet wrist. Kandri and Chindilan glance at each other and quickly mimic the gesture, as they know they must. It is an old and formal salute.

Tebassa looks very pleased. "Rise, rise," he says, and they do. The whole room is beaming, none more so than the general himself. "I grant favors only to the deserving," he says. "And tell me: who is more deserving than the killers of the Prophet's sons?"

Silence, quick as a candle snuffed. The general twists around to look at his men.

"You heard me. These are the assassins who struck Eternity Camp. No cheering, now; there are civilians nearby. We don't want the whole of the Arig Hills to know who we've added to our company."

Kandri feels the prickling of hairs along his arms. *Our company.* He knows at once that he must speak, must shatter Tebassa's implication before it can harden into fact.

"We haven't joined your company," he blurts.

"You've not had the chance until now," says Tebassa.

"But General, we can't. And we never asked to. We have our own plans."

Sharp looks from the soldiers. Chindilan clamps his big hand on Kandri's shoulder. *Slow down.* The general shows no surprise, but his smile has faded.

"What do you suppose we're discussing, here, Mr. Hinjuman? A social club? A farmer's cooperative? No doubt there are some houses where a man may come begging and pounding on the door, and then hesitate when the door is thrown open, but this house is not among them. We are the Unified *Survival* Forces. As long as you're willing to aid that survival, you're our brothers, and we'll move heaven and earth for you."

"We need your aid, General," says Chindilan, "but we need it to make good our escape. From the very start, we've known what we had to do: reach the Great Desert and vanish from the Prophet's sight. We're almost there. All we need is your good word to that Mr. Ifimar."

"My good word," says the general. "Is that so slight a thing?"

"You know we can't remain in the Lutaral," says Kandri. "There's no safety for us here."

"One can live without safety," says the general. "Some of us have done so all our lives. A true soldier dwells on other things. Honor, to start with—and, as my grandfather used to say, honor to end with, and honor at every point in between. Make that your focus, Corporal Hinjuman, and let safety take care of itself. You will learn once you've been among us awhile."

Kandri feels a stab of cold in his chest. Here it is: the doctor's bill. The cost of keeping Mektu alive.

"But they're *not* soldiers," says Eshett, looking hard at the general. "Not good ones, anyway. They're bunglers, idiots. They'd be useless to you."

"They take knives to the Prophet's children," says Tebassa. "The ones she claims the Gods themselves have chosen to be her ministers, when she rules over Urrath—and you call them bunglers? That is fanciful, I must say. Now *be still.*"

He straightens, and Kandri has the impression that he would like very much to rise from his chair. In the room's perfect silence, he looks from face to face. At last his eyes settle on Eshett again.

"You, Parthan woman, can go your own way with our blessing. Seek your people, resume your life. But for you three"—his gaze swivels to the men—"I suggest you pause and reflect. You are still not so very far from home. One day we will emerge victorious, not just in the Lutaral but in all these western lands, and men like you will return to the Sataapre Valley as liberators. But cut the cord, and who knows what you will become? Drifters, faithless men. Vassals of some country so strange to you that your hearts will only sleep there, and your days be dross. If you even live to see such a place."

"You're trying to scare us, General Tebassa," says Kandri.

"It is your plight that should scare you," says Tebassa. "The choice you face is stark. Join the Survival Forces and have a family. Embrace our code, our dangers, our loves. You may find lifelong mates among us. You will certainly find satisfaction for your natural wants. But above all, you will find honor. We are true men and women. We do not fuss and fiddle about and tell half-lies for the sake of convenience. We live and die by our word. And we fight for the restoration of a just rule in our corner of Urrath. It is a fight Lantor Hinjuman understood, when he sat beside me in this room."

The thought flashes instantly through Kandri's mind: *But he didn't join you, did he?*

"General, sir, where *is* he?" Mektu pleads.

"Join us," continues Tebassa, as though he has not heard the question, "or strike out alone into a hostile world: no other way for you exists. I know the dream you have followed thus far. I know there is a certain face that teases your hearts: a girl's face, and a sweet voice to go with it. But that girl is no more, lads. She left you cold in the Sataapre. She has either perished or found another love, and built another life in which you play no part."

Mektu is trembling a little. Kandri, abashed and furious, looks at Chindilan and Eshett, but their wide eyes protest their innocence. Who told this old monster about Ariqina, then? Talupéké? What had Chindilan shared with her on that hilltop in the Stolen Sea?

"I've struck the mark, haven't I?" says Tebassa, for once without a hint of a smile. "An exquisite lover, was she? Hands made to touch you, a voice to cut your heart, the closest thing to perfection in this world? Don't be ashamed, lads: you're hardly alone. Look at the faces around you. Everyone's perfect love is lost. Fortunately, imperfect love comes at need, and with care and dedication grows into something fine, if unimagined. Wait and see."

He makes a flicking gesture with two fingers and a thumb. "Or don't wait," he says. "Keep running from life, and good luck to you. But do not base your choice on an illusion."

"An illusion, General?" says Kandri.

"Lad," says Tebassa, "all the miles and wounds and visions and noble suffering a soul can endure will not restore her to your arms."

He sits back, crossing his arms. His perfect seriousness, the disappearance of any teasing or derision, somehow unsettles Kandri immensely. The whole room waits in silence: clearly the travelers are to tender their decision here and now.

Kandri turns to the others and sees the same terrible anxiety he feels. Pledge themselves to Tebassa? Ridiculous. Not this side of hell. And yet, whispers a second part of himself, it would be an answer of sorts, a refuge. To become soldiers again, once more a part of a whole—and this time, a whole small enough for the mind to grasp, small enough that everyone would soon learn your name. To be executing another's decisions, to lose this exhausting burden of choice.

And with it, Ariqina.

Kandri pinches shut his eyes. All rubbish, manipulation, a steaming pile of goat shit. Black Hat Tebassa cannot protect them from the Prophet. He can't even protect himself, the old fool.

Don't lie to yourself, Kandri. Tebassa's no fool. Even a wise man's luck runs out eventually. Look at Garatajik.

Ah, Garatajik. Who else is going to see that his letter reaches Dr. Tsireem? And suppose I agree that Tebassa's intelligent. That doesn't mean he's not a conceited old prick. How dare he talk of abandoning love? What does he know of our bond, mine and Ariqina's? Whatever made her run off wasn't lack of love for me.

But you've just been with Eshett. What does that say about your bond?

Kandri will not answer that question. He wants to be with her again, tonight, as soon as possible. *Then persuade her to stay with you.* No, no, no. Imagine the madness that would erupt in your brother. He'd never forgive you. Not after Ari chose you as well.

Hundreds of eyes on them. Tight, calm smiles. *The general always gets his way. So think once more, Kandri: what if it is the best way? What other allies have you found since you crawled under that fence at Eternity Camp? And isn't he already working to put you in touch with your father?*

More to the point, wouldn't you be dead already without Tebassa's help? How is dead the better choice than alive and delayed?

Kandri shakes himself. He knows all about delay.

There is nothing for it. They must refuse; they must go to the outer cavern and buy passage with that caravan, help Eshett reach her village, brave the desert and all it contains. And yes, find their way to Kasralys, and to Ariqina. Sometimes, the fate you see is a good one, not a horror. Sometimes, you shouldn't try to escape.

To his immense relief, he sees the same resolve in his brother's face. Silently, Mektu mouths, *We should leave.* Kandri has to smile: it is what his brother has been telling him for months.

Eshett meets his eye and nods, places a hand on her chest. *I'm with you.* Kandri smiles at her, loving her, grateful beyond words. How had Tebassa's offer even made him hesitate? The absurdity, the sheer lunacy of the idea—

Chindilan. He is staring at the entrance. Talupéké has slipped into the room.

She is winded, gasping, her riding clothes soaked through with sweat. Mouth sarcastic, eyes imploring. Holding herself as still as possible and holding the smith like a bird cupped in a hand.

Eshett, fearful, touches Chindilan on the arm. The smith shrugs her off with a twitch. Then he draws a deep breath and turns away from Talupéké. "Time we were leaving," he whispers in Chilot.

℣

Their decision causes an uproar. Growls give way swiftly to hisses, muttered oaths. Tebassa sits quietly, bemused. Stilts, with a worried look in his old eyes, attempts once more to change their mind, but he and everyone else know the struggle is over.

"We're not ungrateful, General," says Chindilan. "Your generosity means a great deal to us."

"Not so very much, it appears."

"You're wrong there, sir. We *aren't* faithless men. In fact, we're trying to keep a promise—"

"To whom?"

Chindilan works his hands, looking suddenly miserable. He cannot possibly mention Garatajik. "Another benefactor," he says lamely.

"And where is this mysterious person?"

Kandri leaps to answer: "Kasralys City, General."

"Kasralys," says the general. "How in Ang's wildest dreams do you propose to get there?"

"As part of that caravan, of course," says Kandri, "at least until we reach the far shores of the desert. Then we can take our leave and finish the journey alone."

"The caravan is out of the question," says Tebassa.

"Why is that, General?" asks Chindilan.

"Because it departed hours ago, with my consent."

Now it is the travelers who cry out in shock and rage. A deception, a trick. The general gives a casual signal, and his soldiers rush to lay hands on the four. Kandri lashes out, but he is immobilized before he can land a single blow. The others fare no better. In seconds, the three men are subdued, and Eshett is forced into a chair, her hands held firmly behind her. Kandri looks hard at the general.

"Honor?" he says.

Mansari turns with a whipcrack motion, striking him in the jaw. Kandri does not cry out or avert his eyes from the general. A taste of blood on his tongue. Mansari wears rings.

"Honor is for brethren," says Tebassa. "I am bound by many promises to my soldiers, none to you."

"My friends made no promises either," says Eshett.

"Nor does a man swimming alongside a boat and begging for rescue," says Stilts, a few paces behind the general. "Once aboard, though, he's got to abide by the skipper's rules."

"Or be returned to the, *hmm*, elements," adds Mansari.

"Release them," says the general. "If they misbehave again, cut them to pieces."

The soldiers step away from the travelers. The nearest dozen draw their blades.

"General Black Hat?" says Mektu. "I'd like to explain something. Eshett is telling the truth. We aren't what we seem."

"Obviously not," says the general, "for you seem to be a witless ape with too much spittle in your mouth, and yet you hacked a path of death from Eternity Camp to my door. And when do you choose to arrive? Why, at the start of a true *Darsunuk,* a Time of Madness, plain as any storybook. Right down to the Gods' flaming tears."

Mektu gives him a lopsided smile. "There's a lot more madness about than you realize, General."

"Trust me, boy, I've seen every sort in Urrath."

"Not my sort."

The other travelers flinch, gazing at Mektu like a trio of murderers. *Stop!* Kandri howls at him silently. *Don't say another fucking word!*

Tebassa leans forward, eyes keen as a raptor's.

"We're not special," says Mektu, "but all these things that we've done, that have happened to us—it's more than bad luck. When you struggle in a net, you just get more tangled."

"You're about to prove that point again."

"Things went wrong from the start," says Mektu. "Kandri attacked the priest because his girl disappeared—I mean *my* girl, she's mine—and the town elders put him in jail, and the priest said eleven years. But then our captain went to the Old Man and made an offer, two for one, he said—"

"Two Sons of Heaven?"

"No, two recruits," says Mektu. "The Prophet had nothing to do with it, really. Sometimes, her priests act alone. Father Marz, for example. Girls went to him for destiny services, to pray for rich husbands, not to be groped under their frocks."

"That's enough," says Tebassa.

"He hated our family," says Mektu, "and he took it out on me, in my boyhood, before Kandri and I ever met. That's where it all started, sir." Mektu lifts a trembling hand to his temples. "And now it's back, you see. It's happening again."

Oh, Gods of Death.

Mektu is about to speak of the yatra. And that could be fatal: some of the fiercest warriors Kandri has ever known are afraid of the soul-thieves. And even if Tebassa does not believe in the wicked spirits, what if his men do? What if this ruthless general knows full well the danger of yatra-terror in the ranks?

A number of warriors already look suspicious: Mansari is studying Mektu with narrowed eyes. Panicked, Kandri leans close to his brother's ear. "Shut the fuck up," he whispers in Chilot.

"No, I'll keep talking," says Mektu aloud. "I'll speak my mind while it's still mine to speak. General Tebassa, the main thing is—"

Kandri, scalded by shame, pokes his brother right in his wound.

Mektu howls. He turns, grabs Kandri by the throat, but when Kandri makes no move to protect himself, his brother hesitates, one fist raised to strike.

For a moment, no one knows quite what is happening. Then the man called Spider rises to his feet. "General," he says, "may I speak bluntly, sir?"

Tebassa sighs. "Why not, Captain? Perhaps you can elevate these proceedings."

Spider bows. "I have served you twenty years, General. In that time, you have always shunned those whose presence would make us a target, unless they be committed body and soul to our cause." He gestures at the travelers. "These four deserve nothing. They spurn our offer of brotherhood. And if they have truly killed the sons of the great Chiloto bitch, they are marked men—marked like no one we have ever harbored. They wish to go? Let them. But with no further assistance, save our boots to their backsides."

There are murmurs of agreement: a great many, in fact. Kandri glances at Chindilan's face, sees concern there to match his own. The ground is shifting again.

"I wish you no harm, Chilotos," Spider continues. "Beyond all doubt, you are marvelous killers—prodigies, even, to have struck as you did."

"Not true," says Eshett.

"But you are not *our* killers," says Spider, "and we have already rewarded you handsomely. Our sister Yehita-Chen sheltered you. Our influence opened the Xavasindrans' door and saved one of you from death."

"My acting talents opened that door," says Mektu.

Chindilan, his breaking point reached at last, leans over and cuffs the side of Mektu's head.

"Ouch!" cries Mektu. "What's that for? What did I say?"

"You are the strangest men," says Tebassa.

"Strange or simple, they have no right to ask more of us, General," says Spider.

The affirmative voices are louder now. A second figure rises: the woman soldier from Oppuk's Mill, the one with the immensely strong arms.

"General Tebassa," she says, "Spider is right: assassins bring death to those who shelter them. We fight the Prophet already, Ang knows, but we are not first among her enemies. If they remain with us, that will change. Even aiding them further could lead that madwoman to seek revenge. Look what the mere *rumor* of their presence has done to Mab Makkutin."

"And their eyes are stained," puts in another. "They'll be spotted anywhere we go."

"They will be our doom," says Spider. "Let us be rid of them, General, while there is still time. Drive them off."

Nearly all the soldiers cry out in assent. Only those nearest the general—Stilts, Mansari, the old woman who had clashed with Spider—begin to argue to the contrary. "Drive them off?" says Stilts. "You might as well stab them dead and be done with it. Have you no hearts?"

The uproar is passionate. But after several minutes, a quiet laugh bubbles up through the mayhem: Tebassa's laugh. When the soldiers perceive it, they fall silent at once. Tebassa wipes his eyes.

"Ah, Spider," he says, "you have read the situation perfectly, but the lesson you draw from it is backwards. You think I've brought them here out of mercy, out of gratitude? Come, am I not your Black Hat?"

"You don't even *wear* a hat," says Mektu.

"Interrupt me again, slobbering ape," says Tebassa, still smiling, "and by the Gods, I'll take that poker from the fire and burn the tongue from your mouth, and your manhood from between your legs."

Mektu hides his face in his elbow.

"Survival is for the cleverest," says the general. "not just the strongest or most skilled with a knife. Yes, these men have spurned our friendship. They may live to regret that choice. But we shall keep them in our pocket nonetheless. Survival means wasting no tools." He twists again in his chair. "And what sort of tool are they, pray? Can't one of you tell me?"

Eyes flash around the room. The fire crackles. Kandri glances again at Mansari, sees the corners of his lips slowly curl into a smile.

"A dog whistle," he says.

Tebassa nods. "An *irresistible* dog whistle, lads. An enchanted whistle. The kind that could send the Prophet anywhere we like. Look, says Sister Jiat, at what the mere rumor of their presence has done. Look, indeed. You there, Kandri. Tell us how the Ursad of Mab Makkutin fares tonight."

Kandri's nails bite into his palms. "The Ursad is dead," he says.

Now the cries are amazed and joyful. The soldiers look at one another almost in disbelief, as though a great burden had suddenly been lifted from their hearts.

"The brothers Hinjuman spend fifteen hours in that town," says Tebassa, "and bring an end to twenty years of rule by that backstabbing Ursad. What do you suppose the Prophet will do when she learns that they have been glimpsed in Sendu? When rumor has them breaking bread with the younger sartaph? We can kindle that rumor easily enough. It might not even be necessary to take the fools there."

One of the soldiers laughs aloud. "Ang's tears, General, the great whore will go *mad!*"

"And when the legions of Sendu lie eviscerated, and still the brothers are not found?"

Smiles all around the chamber. "Another rumor?" says Jiat.

"You have it, sister. Let the Prophet hear that they have slipped north through her fingers: say, into the embrace of the Važeks. With a little taunting and needling, she will follow the blood-scent north and abandon Sendu."

"To us," says Spider.

"To us," agrees Tebassa, "as it should be. Can't you see what we have here, brothers and sisters? The Hinjumans are priceless. They will clear mountains from our path."

Looks of hope and wonder: the bulk of Tebassa's soldiers are convinced. Weapons are raised in unison. Suddenly, the whole room is chanting.

"Black Hat! Black Hat!"

We're tools, thinks Kandri. *Nothing else. He planned this from the start.*

And yet there are doubters in the chamber. Stilts is not smiling. Nor is Mansari, whose gaze has not left Mektu.

Chindilan is wild-eyed. "General," he says, "if you'd only—"

"Cut the face of the next one who speaks uninvited," says Tebassa. "Better yet, cut the other two. Don't touch the Parthan woman, however. She is blameless—as far as we know."

As he speaks, his gaze lifts to the back of the chamber. To Talupéké. The girl's back is to the wall and her expression is stricken. With guilt? With pity? She must have answered all of Tebassa's questions. Did she ask any of her own?

"We have taken the liberty of removing your effects from the high chambers," says Tebassa. "There is a padlocked cell in the warren behind me; that will do for you, I think. And I'll have to ask you to return those clothes. You have others, I trust?"

The travelers say nothing. Kandri takes care not to glance at Stilts. *You know about the clothes we purchased. You haven't reported our every word. That's interesting.*

"Our guests are less talkative, suddenly," says the general. "No matter. Bring it all to me."

A path opens, and the travelers' mud-stiffened backpacks are arranged before the general. Men open the buckles, tear at the rawhide knots. Kandri's breath grows short. *You vile fucker. You're going to—*

"Rope," says Tebassa, tugging the dusty coil from Mektu's pack. "Empty faska. Sealed faska. A melted candle, that's a fool thing to carry. Salt plums. Sugared dates. A copper cookpot. Someone's idea of a hat."

As he names each item, Tebassa sends it flying into the crowd. His men, taking the cue, begin to rend the clothes, stomp on the breakables, gnaw the leathery food.

"Underclothes—great Gods, burn them! No, don't, actually: we'd send the whole cavern running from the smell."

High hilarity grips the chamber. Mektu feeds it by his fury, seething and bucking in the soldiers' grasp but not daring to speak. Kandri shares his rage, though he manages to deny the warriors the pleasure of seeing it. Chindilan just looks lost. He is searching the chamber with his eyes—for Talupéké, Kandri thinks. But the girl has disappeared.

The mattoglin, thinks Kandri suddenly. *He'll take that too, unless he leaves Eshett's pack alone.*

Tebassa has moved on to Kandri's belongings. "Fish meal. Tooth powder—there's someone who means to survive. A fine field telescope; hold onto that for me, Stilts. And see here: they're not paupers after all."

Tebassa holds up the purse of coins from Garatajik. Kandri's heart, if possible, sinks even lower.

"Good and heavy," says the general. He hands the purse to Stilts. "We'll hold that in trust, to pay for their food and water and other expenses. You can start by subtracting the cost of that bribe you paid to get them past the gate at Mab Makkutin. Well, now, what's this?"

Kandri's eyes snap up. *Oh no. You bastard. Don't fucking touch it. No.*

Tebassa is holding the stiff leather envelope containing Garatajik's letter to Dr. Tsireem, Ariqina's hero, the great physician of Kasralys. Kandri hurls himself at the general, to no avail. The men just grip him tighter, laughing. Tebassa notes his distress with amusement as an aide saws through the rawhide stitching.

No, no no! Kandri has never in his life felt so impotent. He cannot even speak. The aide pulls the envelope apart.

Within is a second envelope, of heavy linen with a curious sheen. "Waxed," says the general, "against moisture and"—he sniffs—"I thought so: infused with sulfur, against the nibbling of insects or mice. Someone was *very* keen on this letter's survival. What do you say, brothers, sisters? I confess my curiosity's aroused."

"Open it! Open it!"

The soldiers are having the time of their lives. Tebassa nods: *If you insist.* He tears open the letter, flattens the pages on his knee.

Chindilan makes a strangled sound. Eyes bulging, chest heaving like a draft horse, he manages to drag the six men holding him a yard closer to the general. Mansari slips casually between them, looking the smith up and down. Kandri recalls the words his uncle reported, Garatajik's words. *That letter must reach Dr. Tsireem. If I could trade my life for its certain delivery, I should do so at once.*

Chindilan heaves again—and at the same time, Mansari moves in a blur. A slash with one foot at Chindilan's ankle, an elbow thrust into his neck. The smith's face spasms with pain as he crashes to the floor.

"You will have to forego the, *hmm*, beard trim," purrs Mansari.

"Dear me," says the general, holding the letter above the fray. Turning it to catch the torchlight, he reads in a loud, mock-formal voice.

"*To My Cherished Senior Colleague, Mistress of Medicine and Science, Dr. Tsireem Fessjamu, May All Benevolent Powers Rain Down Gladness Upon You.*"

Shouts and jeers at the formal language. Tebassa glances at the travelers like a schoolteacher making sure he has his pupils' attention.

"*I beg you to forgive this most irregular of letters, but I find that two couriers unforeseen and indeed undesirable*'—You brothers, I presume?—'*are departing the Mileya even now in great haste*' —there's an understatement—'*with your city as their ultimate goal. Therefore, without the least elaboration*' —Good sir, you elaborate amply—'*I beg leave to inform you that I have solved our algebraic enigma. I do not jest. Read on, doctor, but be seated, for what you hold in your hand is nothing less than . . .*'"

Tebassa's voice dies. His lips freeze in mid-utterance. He raises his eyes to his warriors but does not appear to see them.

Silence falls; the entire room holds its breath as the old warrior tries to master himself. He gestures, the beginning of an order, but his hand shakes, and the words do not come. He looks down at the letter again, as though waiting for it to disappear. When it does not, the hand that holds it rises, ever so slowly, and presses the linen to his chest.

"Their belongings," he whispers. "Replace them . . . repack them. The gold as well. And bring . . ." He waves, fumbling. "Cat gut. A needle. Mr. Stilts, you'll seal this letter in my presence. The rest of you, the company—"

He focuses on them at last, but his gaze has no command, and almost no recognition.

"Dismissed," he says.

VI. A LIFE WORTH LIVING

The lover you forsake in dreams becomes a wolf at daybreak:
run softly, leave no trace,
pass light-footed through the years.

Or else lie down with the wolf, let her find you.
One drop of blood will suffice.

ANONYMOUS, SHÔL

FROM *TWELVE CENTURIES OF WAR*

EDITED BY THEREL AGATHAR

"A cure," says Mektu. "A cure for the Throat Rust, the Plague."

"Apparently," says Kandri.

"A cure."

"Make him stop, *hmm*, saying that," growls Mansari.

"A cure for the fucking *World Plague*, Kan. You were carrying *that* around in an envelope and never bothered to tell me?"

"He didn't know himself," says Eshett.

"How do *you* know he didn't?" snaps Mektu, "and why are you always taking his side?"

"Because we're secret lovers." She meets his gaze, yielding nothing. *Gods*, thinks Kandri, *Mek's not the only one who can bluff.*

The council chamber is all but deserted; only the travelers, Stilts, and Mansari remain. The fire is snapping and gnawing through a last armful of cedar. Stilts is winding a bandage around Chindilan's ankle. Mansari is trimming his beard.

"I told Kandri not to mention that letter," says Chindilan. "And I'd do it again in a heartbeat. What you do when you open your mouth is as hard to ignore as what a skunk does when it lifts its tail."

"That's not fair."

"It's fucking charitable!" snaps Chindilan. Then he sighs, and grips Mektu's shoulder. "Knowing would have just made you feel worse. You'd just stabbed Lord Garatajik."

Kandri slides the calfskin pouch, newly resealed, safely down into the depths of his pack.

"We should be celebrating," says Eshett. "Shouldn't we?"

"It would be unlike you to squander a chance to bicker like, *hmm*, imbeciles," says Mansari.

"Shut up and trim me," says Chindilan.

"We should *all* be celebrating," says Stilts. "This is an earthquake. We may live to see the end of Quarantine, the transformation of the world. Unless Garatajik is a liar."

"We can't even read the damned thing properly," says Mektu, for the fifth or sixth time. "Why would he *do* such a thing? Why would he deliberately make it unreadable?"

The letter, as they all learned when Tebassa let them approach, switches languages after the first page, from Kasraji to some entirely different tongue, and only returns to Imperial Common in the final paragraph, exhorting Dr. Tsireem to *act with courage, but trust in very few, for our foe has a million eyes.* Between the opening paragraph and these closing words are four mystifying pages. Not even the characters are familiar.

"He must have chosen a language known to Dr. Tsireem," says Kandri. "He wanted to keep the cure a secret from everyone but her."

"What for?" says Mektu." Why didn't he scream it from the rooftops? Or at the very least take the cure to the Xavasindrans?"

"Lack of time?" says Stilts.

"No, not that," says Chindilan. "He didn't even try to contact anyone, at least in the five weeks I served him. Maybe he was only certain of what he'd found in those last days. He was acting oddly then—almost as if he were drunk. This in a man who never touches the bottle."

"But why *only* tell Dr. Tsireem?" Mektu insists. "Why not a hundred letters?" He stands straight, cups his hands to his mouth. "'SEE HERE, WORLD: THIS AND ONLY THIS WILL PROTECT YOU FROM THE WORLD PLAGUE! PASS IT ON, PASS IT ON!"

"Money?" says Eshett.

"Very likely," says Stilts. "The Plague kills one in seven outlanders, doesn't it? They must want a cure more than all the silver, gold, and diamonds in this world put together."

"You think he planned to *sell* the cure?" Chindilan shakes his head. "Garata-jik was no mercenary. A quiet life and enough money for books is all he ever wanted. Or wants, if the man's still breathing. He'd never have muddied his hands with power and influence if his mother hadn't threatened the world."

"What did he intend to fight her with, *hmm?*" says Mansari. "Not books, I think."

"Your general ordered you to give me a haircut," snaps Chindilan. "Obey him, will you, and then clear out? We're doing fine without your wit."

Stilts chuckles. "Let go of that bone, smith. You forced Mansari's hand— or his foot, if you like. You're terribly dangerous men, and not even a child is permitted to approach the general in a threatening way. During the council, Mansari was assigned the guardianship of the general's person. If he hadn't struck you, he'd be breaking his oath."

Mansari gestures with the scissors. "And if I had wished to break that ankle rather than bruise it—"

"Enough," says Stilts. "We've no cause to taunt them any longer."

Mansari makes an extravagant bow. "Forgive me, master ironmonger, I beseech you. And now listen. Your bags are repacked, your stocks of food and water replenished, your absurd boots have been replaced with fine desert sandals, your, *hmm,* curious notion of survival gear has been supplemented. Even your beards have been tamed." He steps back, considering Chindilan's face. "Done. You are hardly ready for the desert, but you are as ready as forty minutes can make you.

"And now we must be off. The night is passing, and the caravan will increase its speed at first light. We must catch it tomorrow or risk losing it altogether." He turns to Stilts. "The high road, is it?"

"The high road," says Stilts with a nod. To the travelers, he adds, "There's a way into the desert that skips along the top of the Arig Hills. It's a marvel-ous shortcut, as long as your guide knows his business. In this case, he does, for that guide is me." He smiles. "Mansari will come along as well, to the high peak of Alibat S'Ang. I shall see you all the way to the caravan. And I'm authorized to speak for the general. Mr. Ifimar will take you on, I guarantee it."

Kandri feels a burst of affection for the Naduman. But there is still so much he does not understand. "Why did Tebassa change his mind, Stilts? What did that letter mean to him? It shocked everyone, of course. But with him, it might as well have brought the mountain down."

"That it did," says Mansari.

"We'll speak of that later, on the trail perhaps," says Stilts. "Mansari is right. We must go."

"I will take them to the general's chamber," says Mansari. "He will wish to say some last word before—"

Stilts touches his elbow, shakes his head. Mansari lowers his eyebrows in a frown.

They make final adjustments to their clothing, their packs. "Another march," grumbles Mektu, bending to tighten a sandal. "I'll be glad when we're on camelback at last."

"That day will only come if you are sick or wounded," says Mansari. "The camels carry provisions, water, trade goods. Sometimes a pregnant woman, or a royal guest of the caravan. Not lazy, *hmm*, tagalongs. You will cross the desert on foot, like any common man."

"That's not much of a joke." Mektu stares at him.

"It is no joke at all. You will walk."

"Fuck a monkey!" says Mektu. "My legs still ache from the Stolen Sea." He looks at the others as if hoping for deliverance. "Thank the Gods I slept in that bathtub. It was heaven. Did *you* sleep at all, Eshett?"

She shoulders her backpack. Her elbow, no doubt accidentally, grazes Kandri's cheek.

"I closed my eyes," she says.

&

Once more up the winding staircase. Stilts, again the torchbearer, moves with surprising energy, as though an old mode of being, an expedition mode, has suddenly been dusted off and returned to service. They pass straight through the high chambers, where no sign of their brief visit remains save for Kandri's teacup, forgotten on a windowsill. Beyond the servants' entrance are several further rooms, all deserted now, and then another long passage, broken repeatedly by lesser staircases. They climb half a dozen of these and turn at several junctions. Then Stilts slows. He and Mansari raise their left hands to the wall, fingers trailing over the stone. Stilts is mumbling, and Kandri realizes that he is counting his steps.

"Thirty-six from the corner," he says at last.

"Your steps are short, old man."

"We'll see about that. With me, now—"

He counts aloud, and on three, both men slam their shoulders against the wall. There is a soft, deep *click*, and a door-shaped block of stone swings back into darkness. A puff of cold wind vexes the torch. Stilts looks at his companion, smiling.

"Smugness does not, *hmmmm*, become you," says Mansari.

Beyond this strange doorway is a small, chilly room containing nothing but the dead remains of a fire and a small stack of logs. In the opposite wall is an archway, the source of the wind. Kandri sniffs: clean mountain air. They have reached the cavern's end.

The stone door is well over a foot thick and mounted on an axel secreted in the wall. He helps Mansari swing it back into place, and marvels at how completely it vanishes: by torchlight, he cannot even make out the crack. "How do you open it from this side?" he asks.

"You do not," says Mansari. "I will be returning to the Cavern by another path."

He turns, glancing sharply at Stilts. The Naduman is bent double, studying the floor. His free hand moves over the stone.

"Someone's been here, see? And not so long ago—a day or two at the most. What's your guess? Boots or sandals?"

"How can I guess *now*?" snaps Mansari. "Give me the torch, you lumbering, *hmm, hmm*—you lumberer. Stand aside."

Mansari, it appears, has some expertise with tracks. But after a meticulous examination of the floor, he sits back on his heels in defeat. He wags a finger at Stilts. "Ruined, obliterated. Why didn't you speak up, if you saw tracks?"

"I *didn't* see them 'til we'd all stomped in like elephants." He grimaces. "We can hope it was a goatherd getting out of the wind. But keep your voices low, and your eyes open. And I don't mean just for enemies. They'll be cliffs and cracks and slippery places along this trail, and we're going to have to do without torchlight, I'm afraid."

He snuffs the torch in the dead fire's ashes and leads them out through the arch.

A great cloak of stars drapes the sky. They are on the spine of an enormous, barren hill, very nearly a mountain. The night is cold and still. On both sides, the ground falls sharply, decaying into cliffs on one side, rising in crags and boulders on the other. All about them are the Arigs, range upon range of black, heaving stone. A narrow path winds away along the ridge top.

The way is treacherous. The path climbs and plummets, and the stones feel loose underfoot. Chindilan shuffles, cursing under his breath. Kandri walks close behind him, ready to pounce if he should stumble but not wanting to embarrass him by taking his arm.

Suddenly, Eshett grips his elbow. She is far more frightened than Chindilan: heights, of course. Her touch wakes his whole body to the memory of the bath chamber. He cannot steady them both. He should tell Eshett to lean on Mektu, but he does not.

Only Mansari walks with perfect ease. Kandri recalls his first glimpse of the man, the fluid leap he made in the darkness, landing at Talupéké's side.

Then Stilts freezes. His hand flies to his mattoglin, and the others draw their weapons in turn. Kandri, knowing he cannot possibly stand alongside the others on the narrow trail, nocks an arrow to his bow. Mansari crouches low, one hand on the ground, the other gripping a curved knife, tip downward like a giant fang.

"Who walks there?" hisses Stilts.

"Only me, commander," says a man's voice from above them. Kandri looks up to see a dark form squatting on a boulder, black against the stars.

"Spider—good!" says the Naduman. "Come down, let's have your report."

"Captain Sorfik, here?" Mansari is flabbergasted. "Did you know of this, Stilts? When was this man dispatched, and by whom?"

Stilts gives him an all-in-good-time gesture. Spider, meanwhile, turns and shimmies down the rock face, almost without effort, like a man descending a ladder. When he reaches the trail, he is barely winded. *Talupéké's teacher*, Kandri recalls. By the starlight, he can just perceive the blue birthmark on the man's forehead.

"The path ahead is clear," says Spider. "I've run it twice, all the way to Alibat S'Ang. Not so much as a lost goat bleating in these hills."

"That ought to make me feel better," says Stilts, "but it doesn't, somehow. You drop behind us, but not too far behind. Stay close enough to shout a warning, if it comes to that."

"A warning?" says Chindilan. "Who in Jekka's hell do you think is behind us?"

"No one," says Stilts, "and if I'm wrong? Hill people. They're out before dawn, setting nets for birds, snaring rabbits. We must have scattered *them* like rabbits when we passed. Still, you can't be too fucking careful. There are brigands in the hills, and ghouls. And worse things crawl out of the desert once in a while."

"Yes," says Spider. "Just look at what Talupéké dredged up from the Stolen Sea. How she loves her surprises, that girl."

He nods to the travelers, a mocking gesture. Stilts looks him up and down. "You're a good man, Sorfik," he says. "I won't pull rank on you for talking down a fellow soldier. But if you go on speaking ill of my niece, I will shame you. By kicking your ass."

Spider lifts his chin. "She is a danger to the company. I will feel shame the day I betray it, and not before."

Stilts sighs. "Loyalty's a great virtue, Captain. And wisdom's another. Now fall back, but stay close on our heels."

There is a hint of mockery in Spider's salute. *What happened between him and Talupéké?* Kandri wonders, watching him vanish down the trail. *How did he come to despise her?*

Stilts is moving forward again. Kandri watches Mansari hurry to catch up with the older man. He murmurs something: a harsh question or demand, but Kandri catches nothing save for Spider's name. The Naduman's answer does not satisfy: Mansari only shake his head. The men's voices begin to rise.

"It was not your decision to make, Stilts."

"Someone had to act, didn't they? The man was comatose."

"The general overcame his, *hmm*, discomfort, enough to issue various orders. But not this order. What excuse do you have?"

"Excuse? That I'm his loving servant, that's my fucking excuse."

"I do not wish to report you."

"Go ahead and report me. I'll take the punishment. This is the World Plague we're talking about."

Mansari says nothing, and they walk on in silence. Heat lightning sizzles; the forlorn voices of the owls ring from crag to crag. The path levels off, and the footing improves. Looking back over his shoulder, Kandri sees a few faint glimmers up and down the cliff wall: fires still burning in the Cavern.

"Will you answer the question now?" says Chindilan. "Why did that letter affect the general so? He acted like a man whose life has just passed before his eyes."

The Naduman heaves a sigh. "I'll answer. It's not much of a story, though. You know that we're immune to the World Plague, we Urrathis, save for an unlucky few."

"One in eight thousand, according to the Xavasindrans," says Kandri.

Stilts shrugs. "Perhaps that's accurate; I don't really know. What I do know is that the vulnerability tends to run in families. Tell me, have you ever watched someone die of plague?"

"I have," says Chindilan. "and it's a horrible sight."

"First a cough that won't abate," says Mansari. "Then a burning, as the cough irritates the throat. Finally, the rust itself, which grows inward, closing the windpipe. Nothing can be done about the rust, *hmm*. It cannot be removed without tearing the patient apart."

"The poor souls can't speak, can't swallow," says Stilts. "In the end, they're breathing through straws, narrower and narrower. When the straw closes, they die.

"One in eight thousand: good odds, you might say. But again, the risk runs in families." Stilts' eyes are downcast. "When Tebassa was sixteen, the Plague carried off his mother and her four other children—all his brothers and sisters—in a matter of days."

Kandri almost stumbles. Eshett's sharp breath beside him is almost a sob.

"*Jeshar*," says Chindilan. "No fucking wonder."

"His father became insane," says Stilts. "He declared that the boy's survival proved he was illegitimate, that his dead wife had taken a lover. He started drinking, and then moved on to wax and graverobber's snuff. He died of the latter within a year."

"It was not only memories that pained the general tonight," says Mansari. "It was that he'd made sport of you, and that letter. Perhaps he came close to tossing it to the company to mutilate. Or into the fire."

"But he didn't, did he?" says Mektu. "And now he's making amends. He's a good man, your general."

"I doubt you truly believe that after tonight."

"I believe it," Mektu insists. "You and Stilts serve him, don't you? That's reason enough."

"*Hmm.*" For once, Mansari sounds pleased.

"We have a last climb ahead," says Stilts. "Be careful. The morning fog can wet the stones."

He sets off at a brisk pace, and soon they are ascending, mounting the shoulder of the highest hill yet. The rocks are indeed slippery, but Stilts keeps them to the center of the path. When it divides, he does not hesitate; when hazards loom, he warns them in advance.

But five or six times, he pauses and gestures for silence, facing back the way they have come. Kandri listens but hears only the owls' forlorn voices, far below them now. After each pause, Stilts frowns and shakes his head, then quickly resumes the climb.

The wind rises, but their exertion keeps them warm. Kandri finds his thoughts awash with all that he has learned that night. His father and the Prophet. The treachery of Father Marz. Tebassa's heartbreak. And a cure—a cure for the World Plague! A miracle, entrusted to his care.

And that's not the only miracle. He permits himself a smile in the darkness, remembering Eshett's kiss. Once again, she has taken his arm.

Horror and beauty, a broken general and a girl's sweet love. Has he betrayed his brother? Or Ariqina, the love of his life? He is not certain, and yet if he is honest with himself (if not now, when?) he feels no regret. *Touch is a sacrament, not a sin.* Ari herself had had said that, naked with him and entangled, on their last night by the streamside. *I'll never apologize for it, not to anyone. Because I'll never do this unless I'm in love.*

Hardly Eshett's philosophy, was it? Eshett, who wondered why he could possibly hesitate: after all, she was clean. But rather than guilt or confusion, Kandri merely feels humbled by joy. *These women.* Great hearts, brilliant minds. Their honesty equal, if opposite. And he the lucky bastard who is somehow, in a death-drunk world, a Night of Blood without certainty of daybreak, allowed to love them both.

He and Ari had had just three minutes together, maybe four, after they both grew still by the streamside. He brushed her nipples with his eyelids. She turned the copper ring on his thumb.

Kandri looks east, where perfect darkness has given way to a pale eggwash of light. He thinks: *Of course the dawn will break. And we're running that way, running straight at the sun. And not just to save our skins.* It is a great comfort, to think of themselves not as killers but couriers, bearing the words of Garatajik, a good man sprung from the Prophet's womb.

And even the Prophet had come from innocence. From the darkness of the orphanage, a prison called New Life. From the weakness of a nine-year-old Lantor Hinjuman, and the greed of Father Marz. From the rage of a childhood betrayed.

No, Kandri thinks, he won't give in to regret. He won't drown in the beauty or the blood. He will be a survivor, like the general; a healer, like

Ariqina Nawhal. And someday, when he is much older (but not yet too old), he will be like Uncle Chindilan, a guardian—or like Stilts here, a guide. That is a life worth living, isn't it? Most certainly, it is.

The ground levels off: they are near the summit at last. The path divides several more times, braided through boulders. Then, dead ahead, a last, enormous outcropping looms over them, a stone crown on the hill.

Stilts comes to a halt. Once more, he looks back down the trail. His face is in shadow, but something in his demeanor conveys a great intensity of feeling. Kandri is unsettled. Stilts is not lost in memory, not dreaming of things far away. He is (Kandri is certain, somehow) concentrating furiously on the moment at hand.

"What is it?" he whispers.

Stilts blinks at him. "I was thinking about the Quarantine," he says. "Do you know, the moment the general broke the seal on that letter, all these years of struggle changed? The fight we've waged for our own little corner of the world, for the Lutaral: that can't go on as before. We're like ants fighting on a leaf, but there's a tree as well, isn't there? And we can't pretend we're not a part of it."

"Is that what the general says?" asks Kandri.

Stilts shakes his head. "That's what I say."

He beckons the others close. "Listen carefully. Spider should have given us an all-clear whistle. He has not. That means we may have company after all, coming up from behind."

"What sort of company?" asks Chindilan.

"How should I know?" says Stilts. "We can speculate later on. Just keep close to me now, and don't make a sound."

Mektu takes this as his cue to make a sound. "Mr. Stilts, is that a staircase?" He is points at a gap in the looming rock.

"*Quiet!*" hisses Stilts. "Yes, a staircase, you impossible fool. This is Alibat S'Ang, highest point in the Arig Hills. Mansari is to turn back here, and I'm to lead you down the eastern slopes into the sand. But we'll all climb that staircase first."

"What, up to the Chalice of the Sun?" hisses Mansari. "Whatever for? If there are enemies about, they could trap us up there like flies in a bottle."

"We need to locate the caravan, brother," says Stilts. "There's more than one desert track, and if we don't spot them at daybreak, we might just lose them in the glare. Besides, there *is* another way down, and you should use it too. If we want to lose whoever's dogging our heels—"

"*May* be dogging them."

"—we'll have no better chance. No chance at all, as a matter of fact."

"Another way down from the Chalice? What, *hmm*, lunacy. There is none."

"You see?" says Stilts. "You don't know about it, and with luck, neither do they. Come along."

The staircase is barely two feet wide, a meandering slash through solid rock. The steps are tall and irregular; Kandri cannot see the end of them. Up they climb, higher and higher. Kandri feels light-headed, watching the starry ribbon of sky above them grow nearer.

"Shame we're in such a hurry," murmurs Stilts. "In all Urrath, there's no lovelier place to watch the sunrise than Alibat S'Ang."

Finally, the staircase ends. One by one, they step up onto a huge, square, windswept slab of stone. Wide as a castle courtyard. Featureless, unrailed. Blackness surrounds them; no other peak stands so high.

Kandri feels exposed and weightless, as if the wind might hurl him from the peak. The stars envelop the earth, zenith to horizon, as though etched in a dome of crystal. Beneath him, the land spreads like a black banquet, even as dawn kindles in the east.

A strange unease creeps over him. Something is down there, vast and hungry, where the night is bleeding away.

"The desert," says Mansari softly. "The Land That Eats Men. Crossing it will be a mighty test. I wish you faith and good fortune, Chiloto. You will remember me, I hope."

"You've certainly made an impression," says Kandri.

Mansari actually laughs, a weird nasal sound. "As have you and your, *hmm*, dear brother." He starts forward, then pauses, as if weighing his next words. At last he glances back at Kandri, resolved.

"Your father went to the desert as well," he says. "Nearly three years ago, it was. Look for him at the Font of Lupriz, if you should go that way."

Kandri does not dare to speak. He wants to grip this strange man by the arms, shake out the rest of what he knows. "Please tell me," he whispers at last.

"What is there to tell?" says Mansari. "He too sought the general's aid. I never saw the man in the flesh, but I gather he was quite the, *hmm*, salesman."

"What was he . . . selling?"

Mansari's eyebrows lift. "Victory over the Prophet. What else?" He starts forward again. "Now, then, Mr. Stilts: about this second way down—"

The light grows by the minute. From the north end of the terrace, Stilts beckons to them with some urgency. Mansari glides toward him. Kandri and the others trail in his wake.

Mist is curling around the edge of the north cliff. Stilts, slow and deliberate now, walks right up to the precipice. Gingerly, he leans over the edge, peering down into billowing whiteness. Kandri bites his lips. The man looks small and vulnerable, with the wind whipping his traveling cloak, revealing pale, thin ankles and a scar below the knee. He is smiling slightly—but Kandri is certain the look is forced. The cliff's edge is eroded, strewn with gravel. What the hell can he be looking for?

"Mind your balance," Stilts calls over the wind.

"I trust you are not warning *me*," says Mansari.

While the others hesitate, Mansari walks to the cliff's edge with a nonchalance that is almost arrogant. Kandri draws a sharp breath but resists the urge to call out. *Tightrope walker. Circus freak.* Still, he finds himself annoyed with Mansari, who shows not the least patience with the older man's unease.

Stilts creeps closer, pointing at something far below their feet. Mansari leans back into him, sighting down his arm. For an instant, they look like dancers holding a difficult pose. Then Mansari shakes his head, frowning, and Stilts pushes him from the cliff.

"I wasn't, no," he says.

ಚಿ

The sound of impact is a long time in coming: the cliff must be taller than Kandri thought. But at last he hears it, a flat thud like a sack of grain slapped down on a barn floor.

"Right, who's next?" says Stilts.

Kandri does not think: someone or something thinks for him. He whips his bow from his back and snatches an arrow from the quiver and trains it on Stilts and draws. The Naduman watches him, impassive. He takes one careful step away from the cliff.

Eshett gasps. Beside her, Chindilan's expression is horrorstruck—but he is no longer facing Stilts. Bow held steady, Kandri looks over his shoulder.

Rasanga.

They are closing already, stealthy as cats. Two women and two men. All four enormous, their eyes blazing with satisfaction, with hate. The men have bows of their own, drawn and pointed at the brothers' chests.

"We'll take that letter now," says Stilts.

As always, the commandos are led by a woman. Kandri knows her at a glance, by the long straight scars on her cheek like the mark of a bear. She is the one who confronted the Ursad at the city gate, the one who brought the White Child. A mattoglin twitches in her hand.

"Surrender," she says quietly. "The chase is ended. My archers cannot miss."

"Neither can I," says Kandri.

"If you kill me," says Stilts, "my sisters here will draw out your Parthan whore's suffering for a year. Or a decade."

His sisters. Ang's tears, the man's a believer.

"The Parthan whore," says Eshett, looking steadily at the archers, "will throw herself over the cliff. And you'll still be dead."

Chindilan sighs expansively and rubs his face. He looks, suddenly, unafraid, merely angry and exhausted.

"Matter of fucking fact—"

His big arms sweep outward, catching Mektu and Eshett in a violent embrace. With three long steps he hauls them right to the cliff's edge. They stand there, conjoined, a few paces from Stilts.

"You'll take no prisoners back to Eternity Camp," says the smith. "Corpses, maybe. But corpses feel no pain."

"Very good, Mr. Chindilan," say Stilts. "You've discovered the second way down I spoke of. The only way. But shift a little to your left."

"Shut your dog's anus of a mouth," says Chindilan. "Kandri, if that bastard moves a finger—"

"He dies," says Kandri. "That's a promise, Mr. Stilts."

"Naduman," says the Rasanga with the bear-claw scars. "Which one of them carries this letter of cure?"

"The one who just promised to shoot me," says Stilts. "It's in the pack he's wearing, along with some suicide pills I expect he's wishing he'd thought to distribute. But the letter is a fake, holy sister. An attempt to divide us by casting doubt on Lord Garatajik. They're clever, these four. They chose Garatajik because he's a scholar and a pilgrim, and has walked in far-off lands. As if either fact could turn a Son of Heaven into a traitor."

"Lord Garatajik speaks for himself," says Bear Claw.

Even now, with death staring him in the face, some part of Kandri registers the word. *Speaks. Garatajik is alive.*

"Kandri," says Stilts, "you must step off the cliff. Do it now, while you can."

"Shut the fuck up!"

"If they take hold of you—"

"Be silent, Naduman," growls Bear Claw. "The Prophet wants them alive."

"And you have never understood these two," says Stilts. "First you mistook them for killers in the service of your enemies. Now you mistake them for cowards, afraid to jump. You have a problem on your hands."

"What problem, *harach*?" says the second archer, with a twitch of his eye. "If they choose to jump, that is the will of heaven."

"Not the devil?" says Stilts. "These are the Twin Abominations. Surely they answer to him?"

"The old one's tongue is free today," growls the second woman, turning a knife in her hands. "I can change that, mistress."

Bear Claw studies them in silence. As when she stood at the gate of Mab Makkutin, facing a mob hungry for her death, there is nothing in her expression but confidence and purpose.

"Kandri," says Stilts, almost pleading. "Jump."

Deep in Kandri's mind, a voice is howling: torture, misery, defeat. He pushes that voice aside with all his strength. *They want us above all things. But they also want the letter. To clear Garatajik's name, or condemn him. Use it, threaten to destroy it, pull it out of your pack.*

Impossible. As impossible as fighting your way past these monsters. Even if their arrows somehow missed.

Bear Claw walks over to the first archer, rock solid behind his bow, and pulls something free of his belt. A coil of rope, light and strong. She reaches into his quiver and removes a second arrow and ties the rope to the base of the shaft. Tests the knot. Then whispers in his ear.

The archer, blindingly fast, relaxes his bow just long enough to drop his own arrow and aim again with the arrow tied to the rope.

Bear Claw looks directly at Kandri. "The Naduman is right," she says. "You're no fool. You can see what will happen if you do not relent. The arrowhead is barbed. Our brother will shoot your brother in the shoulder, and the rope will detain him long enough for us to take him in hand. Then the agony will start. But who can say how long it will endure?"

Mektu's eyes are downcast. The howl in Kandri's chest will not much longer be silenced.

"The blackworms will not be the worst of it," says Bear Claw. "The Prophet's interrogators have rooms full of wasps. Rooms of heat, rooms of drowning, rooms like iron jaws that slowly close. He will be starved, then offered a meal of human fingers. He will be given drugs to induce madness. Although the latter will not be needed very long. And then there is the Child—the White Child, that is. She will feast on his soul. Already her mouth waters for it. You may kill yourself, but your brother will live on in pain beyond all description."

Kandri's mind is bleeding. *No way out, no way out.* Tell Mek to jump before they shoot him. Once he's airborne the rest of us can follow. End it now—brother, uncle, lover, you yourself, in a last splatter of limbs.

Or shoot Mek yourself, Kandri. That would do it. Shoot your brother, in the heart.

"No."

All eyes snap to Mektu, standing there crooked by the cliff.

"No," says Mektu again, "that is not what is going to happen here. You Rasanga, you are going to ride away and tell the Prophet that you could not find us. That we were not in Mab Makkutin after all. That the trail has gone cold."

Stilts chuckles. The Rasanga gape. But they do not speak the lines Mektu needs them to speak, so he plays the part himself, cocking his head to one side, and offering a fair, almost excellent, impression of Bear Claw's voice.

"Ride away? Are you a lunatic as well as an assassin?"

Mektu answers the question in his own voice: "I don't believe I am."

And again, as Bear Claw: *"Ride away. Lie to Her Radiance? Why would we do that, you maggot in the offal of hell?"*

His own voice: "Because I'm not a maggot. And I'm not Mektu Hinju-man, either. Do you know what I am? I think you do. I think you're beginning to see."

No one breathes. Mektu's eyelids droop a little. He gives the Rasanga a sly little smile.

Liquid fire fills Kandri's temples. He screams, so loud that birds lift from the rocks beyond the terrace. His vision reddens. But somehow, he keeps the arrow trained on Stilts.

Mektu's eyes roll back in his head.

"You will go now," he says.

The pain in Kandri's head ebbs almost as swiftly as it came, but the horror only deepens. Mektu's voice is not his own—not even a distorted version of his own. Chindilan snatches his hand from Mektu's shoulder, appalled.

"You will go, because you love your Prophet, honored Dreamers. And I do not love her, nor any creature of blood and bone and awkward flesh."

An unearthly voice, reedy and sharp, like wind sighing beneath a door.

"You know me by my deeds," says Mektu. "I am the thief of souls. I came among you quietly. A petitioner. I joined you at the Feast of the Boar. I paid homage to your Enlightened One, but she spared me no thought, no simple courtesy. It is hard to cross all the wastes of Urrath only to be turned aside.

"I departed, honored Dreamers, but I left my calling-card. That was my right, you will allow. I took the Brothers Hinjuman as my instruments. I led them to Lord Ojulan, and they bid him goodbye on my behalf."

"Playacting!" snarls Bear Claw. "You take us for children! A mummer's jape will not save you, we will—"

Another cry of pain. It is Stilts, this time, bending double, hands on knees. His face is clenched and his eyes squeezed shut.

What the fuck is happening? Kandri is as lost as his enemies. His brother makes a mewling sound, like a cat.

"The Naduman is in league with them," says the archer with the tethered arrow. "Let us shoot him first, mistress. He is mocking us, mocking Her Radiance."

Stilts waves his hands at them desperately. He sucks in a great breath as though surfacing from a dive. But before he can exhale, a new spasm of pain wracks his body.

His knees buckle. He sways toward the precipice, making no move to save himself.

Soundless, he rolls over the cliff.

I've gone mad, thinks Kandri. *The whole world has gone mad*. But madness does not stop him from swinging the bow to point at Bear Claw.

"The Emperors of old loved me better," says the thing that is not Mektu. "They knew what some forget in latter days: that only courtesy divides us from the beasts. Withdraw, noble Rasanga. These brothers shall be my conveyance across the sands."

"Mistress, it is the yatra!" says the second archer. "Let me kill it! Give the word!"

"If you kill this body, I will seek another," says the thing, "Yours, perhaps. If you are strong enough. If the vessel does not . . . burst."

"Yatra!" says Bear Claw. "Do not threaten us. You know nothing of the Rasanga if you think we bow to fear."

"All the world knows your courage," says the voice. "No, you do not fear to die. But have a care, have a care. Is there not one death that would frighten you? Is there not one whose passing would extinguish the sun?"

"Shoot him," says the Rasanga with the knife.

"She would not receive me," says Mektu, "though I came with gifts and compliments, and a message from the pilgrims of the Void. What could I do, great warriors? I went away, but I left my gift, so carefully chosen, a thing made just for her. It is a shawl of darkness, and she wears it yet."

"Creature—"

Mektu's body jerks. His arms snap up, his posture straightens. "Guard?" he shouts, in an entirely new voice, a woman's, reedy and thin. "Why don't you answer me? Jihalkra, are you there?"

Sheer horror on the Rasangas' faces. The voice is unmistakable. Even Kandri feels a chill.

"Guards!" shrieks Mektu. "What has happened to the daylight? Where are my sons? There is a weight upon me, get it off."

His lips curl. He looks at his arms with astonishment, with disgust. He claws at his shoulders. He screams.

"*Get it off! Get it off me!*"

He falls writhing on the stone. His nails tear at his collar. Spittle flies from his mouth.

"All a lie," says Bear Claw, but her voice is hollow. She cannot tear her eyes from the man before her. Mektu's nails are bloody, and his lips. He has bitten his tongue.

"It will kill her, kill the Prophet!" cries the archer with the tethered arrow. He turns a wild, almost mutinous glance on his commander. And Kandri, his mind clear as glass, closes one eye and shoots the archer through the throat.

He has sealed his own death, of course. The second archer whirls and fires at him and cannot possibly miss. His last thoughts are wordless flashes, lightning of the mind. The sweetness of moments, naked with Ariqina, with Eshett, the joining spasm and the snuggling afterwards, joys of home, greyback geese over Blind Stream, wolf pups on Candle Mountain, the Old Man's grin, Dyakra's singing voice, Ari's eyes on you believing in you loving what she alone could see, your spark, that sacrament, the Well of Fire calling you to drink—

The arrow misses.

The archer's hands grope for the sky. Fifty feet back from the cliff, an old woman with silver hair rises from a throwing stance. Beside her stand three soldiers, among them Talupéké. And the archer: he has been skewered by a spear.

"Kandri, Gods!" bellows Chindilan.

Then the blades and the madness. Bear Claw flies at Kandri and nearly kills him before he can drop the bow and draw his machete. It is his uncle who saves him, by hurling his axe. The Rasanga flexes backward, an impossible contortion; the axe just grazes her chin. Kandri has the machete now, but he is not remotely her equal. Blindingly fast, she drives him back toward the cliff—parrying, flailing, one step ahead of death. No hope (the blades crash, his arm is wrenched), no balance (she could take three of him), he can't breathe, can't sustain this, he will not see the final blow.

Bear Claw screams. A knife juts from her shoulder, buried to the hilt. Without reaching for it, she shifts the mattoglin to her left hand. But now Kandri has recovered. He jumps away from the cliff and strikes, a killing overhead slash. He sees her eye, the calculation, the astonishing response. Once again, she twists aside just in time.

But she has forgotten the knife. The machete strikes the hilt, gouging open the wound. Kandri whirls away from her counterattack and then whirls again, she is *still* driving him, still the better fighter, with one arm limp and gushing like a spring. He parries. He leaps and feints, never letting her close on him, never landing a blow.

Don't stumble. Don't give her one fucking inch.

"You will die, Abomination. You and your brother. On Rasanga steel."

Is she even human? Where can she be hiding so much blood?

"The White Child will find you. The Dagger of Remorse will bleed you dry. The Prophet's justice is as certain as the sun."

In the warrior's eyes Kandri no longer sees hatred. Only wonder, and a curious need to be heard.

"All Urrath will be her kingdom. Her feet walk Heaven's Path."

When she falls, he hears her teeth crack on the terrace. And recognizes the knife.

ॐ

"The last Rasanga?"

Talupéké turns to look at him, draws a finger across her throat. "She didn't fight half as well as her mistress, but she was still a beast: it took all of us to bring her down. Kandri, I saw your brother. What the fuck was he—"

"Not yet, Tal," he begs.

The girl is shaking and twitchy; freckles of blood are drying on her cheeks. "Tell me this, at least," she says, "How did these bastards know you were here?"

Kandri shuts his eyes, but there is no way to erase what he has seen. Stilts, their friend, her uncle. Calling Mansari to the cliff's edge. Pointing down into the mist.

"I couldn't say," he tells her. It is not altogether a lie.

Chindilan draws near. Talupéké gives him a long, steady look. She hides her right hand, but Kandri has seen it already: his uncle's bright steel ring.

"Talupéké," says the smith, "what in Ang's name are you doing here? How did you know?"

"I didn't," she says. "It was the general; he had a hunch. Ever since the Megrev, we've known that the traitor in our ranks served the Prophet—and then you appear, the worst enemies the Prophet's ever seen. The traitor wouldn't dare let you escape. So the general kept five or six pairs of eyes on you at every minute. That's why you were put in the high chambers, you know: because every room has a spy-hole." She glances from Kandri to Eshett and back again. "*Every* room," she repeats.

433

Chindilan's eyebrows climb.

"No one tried anything in the cavern," says Talupéké. "So that left the path through these hills. But hours after you left he woke up shouting orders. He'd guessed the real situation: that the Prophet had been tipped off *much* earlier, and had forces waiting for you on the path. That's why we're here."

"I wish he'd sent more fighters from the start," says Kandri.

"What if one of them had turned out to be the traitor?" says Talupéké. "You'd have been too easy to kill, in the darkness on that trail. A knife in the ribcage, a wire around the throat. No, the general only dared to send his best, the ones he'd trust with his own life. Where are they, anyway? Where are Mansari and Stilts?"

The men look at each other. Kandri doesn't intend to say a word. Fuck the truth. It can wait. But the scalding doubt in his own mind: what is he to do with that? He had given Stilts more than his trust. He had started to love the man. What could have turned the general's closest aide into a creature of the Prophet?

And is that truly what he was? That madness, that unblinking zeal he had seen in the eyes of so many fanatics: was there even a glimmer of it in Stilts?

Kandri clears his throat. This girl knows them; she can read their looks and silences. In another heartbeat she will grasp it all.

"We lost them," Kandri hears himself say. "I'm sorry. We lost them in the dark."

"So you climbed up here and got cornered. That was bright." She wipes the sweat from her chin. "Well, fuck, we go on without them. General's orders. My unit will bring you to the caravan and travel on with you from there."

"You will? All the way?" Chindilan face is a door flung open to the sun.

"All the way to Kasralys," says Talupéké. "I'm to see that letter delivered to the doctor's hand. If we find the others, Stilts will join us. Mansari will go back."

Kandri glances sidelong at his uncle. "Back to the Cavern, you mean?"

Talupéké shakes her head. "The Cavern's lost," she says. "The Prophet's men attacked an hour after you left. They must have marched all night, from the battlefields up north. They were ragged, but there was no end to them. And they knew just where to find us. Someone led them to the Cavern's mouth."

She bends over and spits. "One day," she says, "I'm going to cut the head off that son of a whore."

"Did the general escape?" asks Chindilan.

Talupéké straightens, glaring at him. "He will," she says. "This isn't the way he's meant to die."

Her voice is sharp, defensive. She looks at each of them in turn.

"He sat there, watching me pack for the desert," she says. "I've never seen him look so old. I've never seen him look old at all. When I finished, he called me over. 'All my life, I've prayed for things to change,' he said. 'For this damned war to shift in our favor, for power to flow into our hands. I want children like you to have something you can nourish. Something more than what I've given you, these armfuls of smoke. Tonight, Ang forgive me, I failed to notice that the change I prayed for was beginning. And why? Because I am not the chosen instrument. Because I will be an afterthought, when the stories are told. Go quickly. Find them before the Prophet does. They may be all the legacy we have.' Then he kissed me, and pointed at the door. And I'll never see him again."

"You don't know that," says Kandri.

Talupéké is trembling. "I wanted to talk. I wanted to give him some fucking promise, but I just stood there, the God was interfering, the God wouldn't let me speak."

Chindilan puts his hands on her shoulders. She flinches, baring her teeth.

"Tebassa knows," says the smith. "Why else would he trust you with those words?"

"You're a foolish old man," says Talupéké, in tears.

Kandri turns away from them. He walks back across the terrace, past the splayed bodies of the Rasanga, to the northern edge from which Stilts and

Mansari fell. It is still very windy. He has to argue with his feet before they bear him to the edge.

The morning mist has fallen by a hundred feet. He stares down into the drifting whiteness, probing for some glimpse of the land below.

Who were you, Stilts?

Pale ghosts at the foot the precipice: boulders or treetops. He cannot tell.

What made you betray us? And what in Jekka's hell made you fall?

A sea of cotton, churning. Then suddenly, a moment's clarity: yes, those are cedar trees below. And something caught in their branches. Something rippling, voluminous, like the sail of a ship.

The wind gusts; Kandri lurches back from the cliff. When he creeps forward again, the mists have closed.

Thoughtful, he crosses the terrace again, this time to the western edge, which none of them have yet approached. The sun is warm against his back.

He knows he is too far to see the Coastal Range. But surely he will see Mab Makkutin and the rim of the Stolen Sea. And if he can glimpse the Yskralem, then he can imagine its farther shore, and the villages of the Mileya on the road to Eternity Camp. From there, home is in reach, as Mektu tried to tell him. A day's ride on a fast horse.

But when he reaches the cliff, he knows that something is wrong. The Lutaral plain is still in shadow, but the colors are wrong. A gray-black stain, punctuated by countless, tiny points of light, engulfs the land between the hills and Mab Makkutin. For a few seconds, Kandri thinks with horror that he is looking at the ashes of a single, cataclysmic fire. But no, that's not it. Like the mist, the stain is churning. The points of light move to and fro.

Lamps. Torches.

Men.

It is the Seventh Legion. Not a detachment, not a brigade. Everyone. There is no other force of such size in western Urrath. They press to the very edge of the Yskralem; they surround Mab Makkutin; they break against the feet of the Arig Hills. The Prophet has abandoned the northeast front, marched them here through the night, driven them like animals.

She has lost her favorite son . . .

He turns and looks at the survivors. Eshett is kneeling beside his brother; she has lifted his hand to her cheek. Mektu is lying flat on his back. Eyes open, drinking in the dawn.

. . . and her wrath is beyond description.

Well, then, why describe it? Why mention it at all?

He walks back across the terrace. Eshett rises and meets him a few paces from Mektu.

"That woman," she says, glancing at the silver-haired warrior with the spear. "The one Spider argued with at Oppuk's Mill. Do you know who she is?"

"Talupéké's grandmother?"

Eshett nods. "Kereqa. Stilts' older sister. The founder of the circus, the one who put a roof over Tebassa's head when the plague took his family. She's twelve years older than the general."

"Jeshar," says Kandri. "Some people only rest in the grave."

"If then," says Eshett.

Kandri looks at her sharply, waiting for her to explain the remark. He feels an odd chill. Somewhere deep in his mind, a girl's plaintive voice is calling his father's name.

Eshett extends her hand, offering him something wrapped in a scarf. He puts his hand on the object but does not take it from her. It is the mattoglin, Ojulan's priceless blade.

"You need this more than I do," she says.

Kandri shakes his head. "We're rich enough," he says. "Keep it. Find a good buyer, someday when it's safe."

"Someday." She turns to the east. "Your uncle spotted the caravan, with your scope. It's not too far ahead. The old woman thinks we can catch it by midday."

"And three days later you'll be gone."

Eshett reaches for him, then checks herself, touching him only with her eyes. Kandri meets her gaze, and for some reason they both smile.

He crosses to Mektu and bends down.

"Anything broken?"

Mektu shakes his head.

"Still got a tongue in that mouth?"

Mektu nods.

"That's too bad."

The remark earns him a ghastly grin. Kandri holds out his hand, and after a few blinks, Mektu takes it and rises, stretching.

Kandri steps back and lifts his hands above his head. He gives three loud claps, and the others fall silent. Facing Mektu, he bows as low as he can.

"Congratulations, brother, on the performance of a lifetime."

There is laughter. Immoderate laughter. Even Kandri is laughing, his back turned firmly to the Seventh Legion, clear morning light in his eyes. *What's wrong with us, are we crazy?* he thinks. *Death all around us, and we can't stop with the jokes.*

"It *was* a performance, wasn't it?" asks Chindilan.

Silence again. Kandri glances at the edge of the cliff, thinking of Stilts' cry.

Mektu turns to face the smith. "Uncle," he says, "will you step over here?"

Chindilan frowns. He sidles a little closer. Mektu points at his own ear.

"Have a look, will you? Anybody in there who doesn't belong?"

The smith cuffs the back of his head. Then he guffaws and embraces Mektu and kisses both his bloody cheeks. The whole party is roaring. "My nephew is a genius!" shouts Chindilan, one arm tight around his shoulders.

Kandri hugs him next. Weak from mirth and violence, the brothers hold each other, swaying like dancers. Or like boxers in a clinch.

"You haven't answered the question," says Kandri.

Mektu's look says he's aware of that.

"Come on," says Eshett, "we have a caravan to catch."

The Fire Sacraments *continues in Book Two*, Sidewinders.

ACKNOWLEDGMENTS

Getting a novel written is a solitary business, but the burden of that solitude is shared. A part of the writer is, by necessity, out of reach. When I return to earth, I catch glimpses of what this means for family and friends, and can only tell them, at every opportunity, that I'm grateful for their caring and their faith.

The making of *Master Assassins* has been an epic in itself, replete with storms, curses, death marches, alliances broken and renewed. There were no villains but many heroes. If not for the latter, this book (and its author) might still be out on the desert highways, shambling towards a hallucinatory coast.

Pat Rothfuss, singular paladin, read the book in a moment of darkness and happened to like it, and his support since then has made all the difference. Earlier, when the book was still a tangle of thorns and impulses, readers gave me priceless feedback: these included my parents, Jan and John Redick; as well as James Heflin, Mira Bartók, Adam Shannon, Stephen Klink, Judi Kolenda, Bruce Hemmer, Ed Zavada, Mark Roessler, Jedediah Berry, Emily Houk, Jon Redick, and Christy Crutchfield.

I'm grateful beyond words for the talents and energies of my editor, Cory Allyn; my agent, Matt Bialer, and artists Lauren Saint-Onge and Thomas Rey. My thanks as well to Gillian Redfearn and Tricia Narwani, for their kindness and wisdom. John Jarrold, Simon Spanton, and the late David Hartwell also contributed to the emergence of this book, and have my sincere thanks.

I wrote much of *Master Assassins* in a house in Bogor, Indonesia: *terimah kasih banyak* to Ibu Amah, who fed me; Pak Hasim who built the table where I worked and the lattices that kept out the screeching night toads; and my *compañera*, Kiran Asher, who took me there, and who has walked beside me through twenty-five years of love and joy. *Gracias, mi sol.*

Robert V.S. Redick grew up in Iowa and Virginia; his father worked in nuclear non-proliferation and his mother as an electron microscopist. He is the author of the critically acclaimed epic fantasy series *The Chathrand Voyage Quartet*, which begins with *The Red Wolf Conspiracy* and concludes with *The Night of the Swarm*. The books have been published in five languages and nominated for several major awards; *Locus* magazine calls the Quartet "one of the most distinctive and appealing epic fantasies of the last decade." Robert holds an MFA from the Program for Writers at Warren Wilson College and an MA in Tropical Conservation and Development from the University of Florida.

Robert's twin passions have always been storytelling and internationalism; previous employers include the antipoverty group Oxfam, Hampshire College, and the Center for International Forestry Research. He has lived and worked in Indonesia, Argentina, Colombia, and the United Kingdom, and traveled extensively in Latin America, Asia, and Europe. Raised in Iowa and Virginia, he now lives in Western Massachusetts.